Rose

Rose
a novel

Ruth Bass

GADD & COMPANY PUBLISHERS, INC.
A Division of The North River Press

The characters and events in this book are fictitious. Any similarity to real persons, living or dead, is coincidental and not intended by the author.

Copyright © 2010 Ruth Bass
All rights reserved. Except in the case of a review which may contain brief passages, no part of this book may be reproduced in any form or by any electronic or mechanical means, including information storage and retrieval systems, without permission in writing from the publisher.

Gadd & Company Publishers, Inc.
A Division of The North River Press Publishing Corporation
79 Boice Road
Egremont, MA 01230
(413) 528-8895
Visit our website at www.gaddbooks.com

Printed in the United States of America
ISBN: 978-0-88427-908-2

Gadd & Company is committed to preserving ancient forests and natural resources. We elected to print this title on 30% postconsumer recycled paper, processed chlorine-free. As a result, we have saved:

7 Trees (40' tall and 6-8" diameter)
2 Million BTUs of Total Energy
669 Pounds of Greenhouse Gases
3,224 Gallons of Wastewater
196 Pounds of Solid Waste

Gadd & Company made this paper choice because our printer, Thomson-Shore, Inc., is a member of Green Press Initiative, a nonprofit program dedicated to supporting authors, publishers, and suppliers in their efforts to reduce their use of fiber obtained from endangered forests.

For more information, visit www.greenpressinitiative.org

Environmental impact estimates were made using the Environmental Defense Paper Calculator. For more information visit: www.edf.org/papercalculator

With much love to Milt,
who opened so many doors for me

About the Author

As a newspaper reporter and columnist, Ruth Bass has been telling the stories of real people for a long time. A descendant of generations of New Englanders, she has also listened all her life to people like the characters in *Sarah's Daughter* and *Rose*.

A resident of the Berkshires in Massachusetts, she has won many awards for writing and editing, and was recently inducted into the New England Press Association's Hall of Fame. She is a graduate of Bates College and of Columbia Graduate School of Journalism, and has been an elected town official. In 2009, she received an honorary doctorate of humane letters from Westfield State College. She and her husband, novelist Milton Bass, have three adult children.

She writes a weekly newspaper column on everything from politics to puppies, is author of eight cookbooks, and in her spare time turns to gardening, reading, knitting, photography, travel, tennis, and golf.

CONTENTS

	Prologue	1
1.	Social Bidding	4
2.	A Suitable Suitor	20
3.	Chaperones Again	28
4.	A Special Delivery	36
5.	A Day of Rest?	45
6.	Girl Talk	64
7.	Rubies and Cows	75
8.	A New Tutor	84
9.	The Clock of Grief	104
10.	Kissing and Telling	120
11.	A Different Kind of Tutor	138
12.	Spring Cleaning	151
13.	Filling the Spaces	172
14.	Intentions	189
15.	Backsliding	207
16.	Barleycorn Wins	218
17.	In Sickness and In Health	235

18.	Calf Comfort	258
19.	Starting Over	270
20.	By the Sea	282
21.	Smiles and Tears	300
22.	Learning and Letters	317
23.	A Fine Seam	331
24.	Lonely and Not So	340
25.	First Day of School	352
26.	A Sneaky Killer	365
27.	Ups and Downs	379
28.	Heart to Heart	389
29.	Of Cakes and Stars	400
30.	Looking for Answers	409
31.	Cows and Conversation	420
32.	Joining the Links	435
33.	Good Things in Threes	444
34.	Making a New List	456
35.	Confronting Demons	467
36.	Ever After	475

Rose

PROLOGUE

Wearing her beaver-fur coat and her warmest boots, Hattie Munson set out in her buggy for a quick ride in the crisp winter air. While most of her neighbors disliked the February cold, she thought Eastborough was at its best in winter, when snow covered the shabby lawns, and the dirt roads were frozen solid instead of muddy. She flicked her whip lightly on her horse's back, and the buggy rolled quickly along the main street of the village.

Always alert for something new to gossip about, Hattie noticed that Henry Goodnow was offering snow shovels at a lower price at the general store. Probably business was off, she reckoned. Or maybe Rose Hibbard, who seemed to have a sharp eye for storekeeping, was telling him to get rid of them before spring came.

Hattie had figured Rose all wrong. First, she had thought Rose would die after she ran off and was found near-frozen by her mother's grave. Then she told any number of people that a girl like that would come to some bad end. But Rose had turned her hand at the store with great ability, was apparently keeping up with her schoolwork, and had wisely decided her little sister couldn't live at home any longer.

It was Hattie's way to find fault rather than give

Rose

praise, but she had to admit that Rose needed to protect herself and her little sister from their father. Silas Hibbard had taken to the drink after his wife was killed and didn't seem to have his wits about him when it came to preying women. No young girls, Hattie told herself, should have to put up with that woman from the hotel, the one they called Miss Jennie.

It was dead wrong, though, to leave young Charles with Silas. Hattie had no solutions to offer, but she was happy to tell anyone she met that a thirteen-year-old boy was too full of mischief to be pretty much on his own. Someday he would burn the barn down, she predicted. Or get himself killed doing farm work beyond his years. Still, no one could expect the teacher to take in Charles, too. Even Hattie had to admit it was generous of Miss Harty to make a place for Rose in her house. She figured that wouldn't last much longer. The teacher had no experience in the upbringing of a girl on the threshold of womanhood, and there would be hell to pay sooner or later.

Hattie liked to say hell in her head, but she wouldn't dream of saying it aloud. It was tempting sometimes to consider uttering that word, or one like it, in front of that righteous fool, Calvin Lockhead. She would not miss Sunday morning services for the world because she wanted to see who was there and what they were wearing, but she fretted through his fiery sermons every week, sitting rigidly in her pew.

These people had their failings, but they appealed to her. For one thing, even though she asked questions about everyone and everything, they minded their own business and never pried into her past. She knew they had to envy her the beaver-fur coat. Certainly none of them could afford one. Come to think of it, they took their disinterest too far on occasion. While they were carefully minding their own business, the Hibbard children were facing great danger with their father in his cups half the time and morose the rest. He must feel quite guilty about the woodpile crushing his sweet wife.

Tonight she would see them all at the box social. She wondered who would bid on the fancy feast she had prepared for the occasion. She turned the horse, flicked the little whip again, and headed home into the wind.

CHAPTER ONE
Social Bidding

Rose grinned as she tied one of her hair ribbons to the handle of the basket. Newton would know, she told herself. He would have to know. He sat behind her every day at school with those ribbons right in front of him. Even if boys didn't look at things like hair and bows, they'd have to see something that was practically dangling on their desk. As for Newton in particular, his eyes were riveted on the back of her head, or so he said. Well, she hoped so. This was box social night, and she wanted Newton to bid on the supper she had made. Then they would find a corner somewhere in Town Hall to share it. The very thought sent a tingle down her spine, the same feeling she sometimes had when he poked her back with a pencil at school.

Social Bidding

She frowned suddenly, wondering if her father would be there and whether he would speak to her. Was it only last year that her mother had wrapped her food in a red bandana and tied it to a stick, hobo style? Everyone had been very taken with that idea, and Father had to go as high as five dollars to get it. It must have cost him all the egg money, Rose thought. But her mother had been pleased. Rose's face softened as she remembered the smile on her mother's face, all the tiredness gone, when Silas Hibbard had insisted on paying top dollar to eat with his wife.

"After all these years," she had said to Rose, as she stood and went forward to meet him. "After all these years."

Tears as hot as boiling jelly suddenly burned Rose's eyes. There should have been a lot more years, she thought. A lot more. Instead her mother was ice-cold in the cemetery, and she was living in the teacher's house, at least for now, and Father was drinking whiskey at lunch with Miss Graves, that woman from the hotel. She hated them both sometimes. It was hard to believe God could put someone like Miss Graves in her mother's place. Perhaps Miss Graves would get herself killed, too, she thought, and then shivered at the very idea of having that idea. A tear spilled out of each eye, and Rose wiped her cheeks with her sleeve and told herself to stop thinking about all that.

She'd be meeting her best friends, Emily and Alice, at the social, and if Emily caught sight of the bow, she might tell Newton, Rose thought. She would cover the whole thing with a tea towel to make sure Emily didn't see. This was a secret, at least for a short time. Sometimes it was hard to keep a secret. Secrets had a way of just slipping past your teeth and lips as if they were on wheels covered with lard. She just hoped she had figured a way to let Newton Barnes guess it was hers. And she didn't want Emily to spoil it by telling him how to bid.

She had made fried chicken, rolling the legs and breasts (ooh, she wasn't supposed to use that word, not ladylike, but perhaps chickens didn't think that way) in a little flour and then frying them with as little fat as possible in the cast-iron spider. She had tucked in two thick slices of Hannah's Oatmeal Bread, wondering who in the world Hannah might be as she followed the recipe in Miss Harty's notebook. She remembered her mother occasionally saying, on very humid August days, that it was hotter than Hannah, and she didn't know what that meant either. Get back to the task, she told herself sternly. This is no time for the mind to go wandering around. The question of overheated Hannah would have to wait.

She didn't want to pack knives, so she slathered both pieces of bread with butter and put the buttered sides together. She added two slices of cake, placing them on top so they wouldn't crumble. She smiled again as she thought how busy all the kitchens in town were right now, each girl and woman packing a supper for two for the Valentine's Day social. She hoped her little sister Abby was doing a basket at Aunt Nell's house—she

Social Bidding

worried that Aunt would say Abby was too little, but Rose knew Abby would love putting a feast together.

Rose added a string of paper hearts to her basket, stood back to admire how it looked, and then dropped the clean tea towel over it. Feeling a little anxious about her father and Newton and the possibility that some stranger—or that rude Peter Granger—might buy her basket, she started to bite the nail on her index finger and then remembered Miss Harty chiding her, not just for making a mess of her fingernails, which were already pretty shabby, but for how she looked, just turned fifteen, with a finger in her mouth. She needed to keep busy. She checked to make sure the fire was dying out in the black wood stove and then turned her mind to the question of what to wear.

Maybe the almost new red skirt. That would go with Valentine's Day, and she had a nice white shirtwaist and Sarah's black knitted shawl. She still hadn't gotten her brain to think "Mother." That hurt so much that she always referred to her mother as Sarah, telling herself that a person who was dead could not care about a thing like that. Sarah would chide her for being wasteful, she decided, so every now and then she asked her brother to bring her something from Sarah's chest of drawers, and she found it was actually comforting to be wrapped in one of her mother's scarves.

Miss Harty had asked if she could have some of the chicken Rose had prepared, so Rose figured the teacher must be hoping someone would sup with her. She'd never heard anyone call her an old maid, and Miss

Harty had said something one time about still having her chances, whatever that meant. But no one seemed to come calling. If Miss Harty really wanted to attract a special person, Rose thought grumpily, she should have made her own chicken or cold roast, instead of taking for granted that Rose would make enough for two suppers. Ungrateful you, she reminded herself, given how the teacher had taken her into her house. Besides, she is very pretty, and someone must have noticed that, and perhaps even kissed her.

The very idea of kissing made Rose's stomach twist around, but in a pleasant way. Newton had kissed her, and after a bit of panic she had found that she quite liked it. It certainly was nothing like the quick pecks Grandmother Emma planted on your cheek. If they had supper together tonight, would he insist on seeing her home and maybe kiss her again? Rose hoped so, even though the kisses made her want to just get as close to him as skirts and petticoats allowed. She wondered if that was all right, or if it was a bad thing. Someday she'd have Emily ask her mother.

Get back to the tasks at hand, she told herself again. Take your bath. Brush your hair. Get dressed. At least, here, she could look forward to taking a bath. For the first time in her life, Rose didn't have to fold her long legs into a small metal tub in the middle of the kitchen, and she didn't have to save the water for the next person, either. Miss Harty's bathtub was in her bathroom, and even though the galvanized metal cooled the water quickly, it was what Rose considered a real luxury. Miss

Social Bidding

Harty had cautioned her not to use too much water, so it wasn't like the soakings the ancient Romans indulged in, but it was private.

Her little brother Charles would have no such privacy, not that he prized it much. He'd be taking his bath in the kitchen at Father's house. She knew Father hadn't put in a real tub yet, nor a flushing toilet. They used the privy, which didn't smell much in the winter but was so cold that she had always put off going at all. Her mother had chided her about that, telling her that she would get all bound up if she didn't go regular, but she hadn't always heeded that advice. She did worry about Charles being there without her to see to him, but everyone said he was all right. Charles said so, too. Still, he would say that, no matter what.

Most of the time she liked that he was there. In his funny, brotherly way, he kept her up on what was going on. If Miss Graves came to lunch, he told Rose about all the crumbs he found around her plate and how she didn't put her napkin back in the ring. He said the oatmeal Father made in the morning was so lumpy that he'd taken over the job. One lump per bowl, he said, no more, no less. The chickens remained dusty and annoying, and the cat, which often sat in his lap and purred while he did schoolwork by the stove after supper, often cried at other times. She would like to have the cat, Sarah's cat, but she couldn't see her way clear to ask Miss Harty to take in a cat as well as a girl, so she hadn't brought it up.

By the time Rose was scrubbed and dressed, Miss

Rose

Harty had come home, checked the fire, packed her supper into a blueberry pail wrapped in pink and white checked gingham and was ready to head for Town Hall with Rose, who at the last minute had tied her hair with a ribbon that matched the one on her basket. As they set off, Rose thought how odd it was to sometimes think of this teacher as a friend instead of the rather strict woman who made the Granger boys behave and taught everyone to write beautiful capital letters in rows across lined paper. She did wonder how old the teacher was. Could she be twenty-five? She must be more. She'd been here for years. Anyway, she was, at least in this town, pretty much past the marrying age so she couldn't really be Rose's friend. Still she seemed like one, Rose thought, as real as Emily and Alice, even if she didn't make her own chicken.

Just inside the door of the Town Hall, the two friends were waiting. She tried to hide her basket at her side, but the sharp-eyed Emily—why couldn't she miss something, just once in a while—lifted the tea towel and giggled when she saw the ribbon that matched the one in Rose's hair.

"Hold your tongue," Rose said sharply, and Emily's smile faded.

"I won't tell," she promised. "I won't."

Rose and the teacher tucked their containers under the clean sheet that covered the long table by the stage, and Rose went off with Emily and Alice to wait for the bidding. She couldn't believe how many people had come. She saw Mr. Hawks, who owned a soda fountain and store a couple of towns away; and Mrs. Munson, who seemed to watch everyone all the time and then gossip about whatever she thought she saw or heard. She glimpsed her father off in a corner with Mr. Chandler and some other men. She didn't see Miss Graves anywhere, but suddenly she saw the back of Newton's head and felt her face getting warm. He would recognize the ribbons, he would have to. She didn't even sit behind him, was almost never behind him, in fact, and she knew what his head looked like, front and back.

"He's here, Rose, he's here. Stop looking around the room as if you were the sheriff on a manhunt," Alice said.

"She may not be sheriff, but she is on a manhunt," Emily said, giggling again.

"Stop it, you two," Rose said, a bit sharp again, and saw Mrs. Munson turn around to look at them. "I already saw him," she admitted in a whisper, to her friends' great satisfaction.

Emily and Alice saw Mrs. Munson watching and quickly turned their backs to her. They had all decided that she not only listened and looked but could read lips, too. No need, Rose thought, to give her anything to talk about at the store or in the parish hall. The girls moved away and found three seats facing the stage.

Mr. Goodnow would be the auctioneer tonight, and he was getting ready. He's as precise about this as he is about his store, Rose noticed, as Mr. Goodnow carefully placed a gavel on the small table and put a tumbler of water next to it.

Rose

"He'll be needing that water when he gets going," Alice said. "He really shouts, and don't you love all that dum-diddy-dum-dee-dee-dum-do that he puts in the middle just before he whacks the gavel and sells the supper?"

"It's not a good idea to be right up front," Emily said. "Sometimes when he really gets going, he spits."

"Oh, Emily," Rose said. "He is so good to me at the store."

"Which," Emily said, "has nothing to do with spitting at the Town Hall," and then she and Alice dissolved into laughter while Rose shook her head, wondering if all her responsibilities had made her old and crotchety in spite of her best efforts. Just then, Mrs. Munson lowered herself into a chair in the front row, Emily and Alice's elbows poked Rose, and her giggle joined theirs. Mr. Goodnow then pounded for order and lifted a pretty box out from under the big cloth. "Who will have this," he asked, "this exquisite box with food to match inside?"

A few bids were made, Mr. Goodnow sniffed the box and said he detected an aroma of chocolate in there, and after some of his dee-dee-dum-dums, the first box went for thirty-three cents to Mr. Hawks. The whole audience groaned as Mrs. Hawks stood up and went to join her husband.

"She must have told him which one it was," Alice whispered. "Oh, oh, there's mine, but I didn't give any hints to anyone," she added, as Mr. Goodnow began the bidding. In a few seconds, a new boy in school named

Ethan had won the chance to share supper with Alice. It cost him fifty cents, and Rose was surprised to see that Alice looked a little flustered as she left them to join Ethan.

The bidding went on, and suddenly Peter Granger had outbid everyone for Emily's basket, a man they didn't know had bid three dollars for Miss Harty's, and Uncle Jason had watched in dismay as the Reverend Lockhead went off with Aunt Nell. Rose was still worrying about her own contribution when she heard Newton Barnes' voice rising above the others. Thirty cents, he said, then forty-five. But several others were bidding against him, and the price kept going up. Newton was at one dollar, and Rose had to put her hand over her mouth to keep from shouting that he should stop right there.

"Going, going, gone," Mr. Goodnow intoned, and Newton had a beribboned basket for a dollar-twenty-five, the highest price of the evening so far, except for the teacher's pail. Just as she realized her perfect plan had failed, Rose recognized the ribbon and saw Abby scampering up front to find Newton, her face so full of pleasure that Rose could not be angry. Minutes later, Charles shouted a dollar-fifteen when Rose's basket was held up, and after allowing only a brief pause, Mr. Goodnow pronounced it sold.

"I never get to see you enough," Charles said, joining Rose with the basket in hand. "And the second I saw that ribbon, I knew it had to be yours. Been a long time since we broke bread together."

Rose had to laugh. Her younger brother and sister

Rose

were so excited that she couldn't be upset about the failure of her grand plan. She and Charles headed for the stairs by the stage, one of the best places to sit, and just as they perched, she saw that Newton was leading Abby in that direction, too.

"Thought I had that hair decoration in hand," Newton said cheerfully. "Certainly seen it often enough when your well-combed head provides me with shelter from the teacher's steely looks. But at least I picked the right family. May we join you?"

Without waiting for an answer, Newton sat down on the stair next to Rose and settled Abby on his other side.

"I'm hungry as a horse," he said, "so I hope a lot of goodies are packed in that basket.

"Hungry as a horse?" Abby chortled. "I didn't bring grain. Or does bread count?"

The little group ate quietly for a few minutes, each of them watching the others in the room. Rose spotted Miss Harty, sitting in a corner with the man she now thought might have been the one at the square dance last fall. But she didn't think he danced much with the teacher that night. Then she remembered that Peter Granger was the high bidder for Emily's supper. She began to worry. Would Peter Granger behave in the loud way he did in school? Brash, she thought. That's the word that fits Peter Granger. He's not really bad, he's just brash.

"Where is Emily sitting?" she asked. "Peter Granger bid for her supper and I can't see them anywhere."

Newton's hand came up as if he were going to pat her knee in reassurance, then stopped in midair.

"They're over near the door," he said, putting his hand and arm in motion again by pointing toward the far side of the room. "Over there."

Rose wished that hand had dropped, then was glad it hadn't. If he'd touched her, she would have turned red, and Charles and Abby would have noticed and made comments. Once in a while those two showed a little discretion, but most of the time they just blurted out whatever was in their heads.

"I see them," Abby said, her mouth half full of bread. "Emily is unpacking food and she doesn't look happy."

"She must think Peter looks like the big bad wolf and will eat the food, the basket, and probably even Emily," Charles said, laughing. "Except for Uncle Jason, they're the funniest pair in the room."

"I can't see Uncle, either," Rose said, sitting up a little straighter. "And he's never funny, so what's making you grin like something from Lewis Carroll? Has he gone down the rabbit hole?"

"Well," Charles said, always loving a good story enough to make it last longer than it should, "I don't know much about rabbit holes, but you did see the reverend going off with Aunt Nell, right? And that left Uncle on his own, his stomach growling with hunger and perhaps a bit annoyed at having the minister steal his wife and..."

"Stop it, Charles, just stop it," Rose interrupted. "Where is Uncle?"

"Now that I have your attention," Charles began, but gave in when Rose poked him with her elbow. "He's with Mrs. Munson, and I will bet tomorrow's eggs that he's talking even less than usual."

"And what would a boy like you know about a person like Mrs. Munson?" Newton wanted to know, leaning forward to see what kind of food was still in Rose's basket.

"She gathers up stories as handily as you pick up drops under an apple tree, and she grinds them up and passes them on, sometimes quite different from the original harvest," Charles said, adding quickly, "and get your eyes off the food I bought, Newton. I gather stories, too, but I just pass them on exactly the way they happened."

"If she listened at keyholes and from behind bushes the way you do, Charles, she would have enough fodder to feed people for a week," Rose said, remembering the times Charles had listened in on Father's conversations with Uncle Jason and with Miss Harty. "Not that your slinking around hasn't been very, very helpful at various times in the past."

Charles smiled up at her, then bent to serious eating from Rose's basket, and she forgave him once again for wrecking her careful plan with the hair ribbons. How could she be so selfish? It was no doubt the best meal he'd had in a week, maybe longer. She munched on a piece of chicken herself and scanned the room once again, this time looking for her father. And there he was, squatting on his heels by Aunt Nell and the minister,

Social Bidding

who must have invited him to join them. Was he still grieving so much over the loss of Sarah that he couldn't bid on a supper? Or had he used up all the money in the new sugar bowl on drinking and card playing at the hotel? Mrs. Munson might be the only person in the room who knew the answer to her questions, and she reckoned she wouldn't ask her.

She felt Newton shift his weight on the stair next to her and then his leg was touching hers, and even through all the fabric of her skirt and petticoat and unmentionable undergarments, she could feel how close he was and knew her face was turning pink. What on earth was she ever going to do about the way her face behaved, she wondered. It wasn't just Newton's leg that did it. She felt pink even when she had to stand and recite in school.

Blushing was what people called it, and sometimes grownups seemed to think it was cute. Crushing, she called it. Or blood rushing. Flushing was what she'd like to do with it, but she guessed it wasn't as simple as that.

"Rose?" Charles said, a bit crossly. "Can you hear me? Are you still with us, or has your head gone off somewhere? I'd like a piece of cake now, please."

"Sorry," Rose said, lifting the two pieces of cake out of the basket. "It's called a daffodil cake because it has a blob of yellow in the center of each slice."

"Very pretty," Charles muttered, as he took a large bite.

"How did you get that yellow in there?" Abby wanted to know.

"Me to know and you to find out," Rose told her, still a little miffed that Newton had picked the wrong hair ribbons.

"She injected it with a needle from Dr. Potter's office," Newton offered.

"Yuck," Charles said, pausing before his next bite of cake. "Oh, you're just trying to get me to stop eating it and leave some for you," he added, recovering quickly and shoving the rest of the piece into his mouth. "I reckon you'll have to be stopping at Miss Harty's house if you want a taste of this cake," he mumbled with his mouth half full.

Rose looked down at her cake and beyond the cake to her shoes, her size nine shoes. Was everything going to send her into a swivet today? Nothing would be nicer than to have Newton come calling at Miss Harty's, but Charles was a rascal for suggesting it. And she ought to be scolding him for being greedy and for eating the cake that way. He was spilling crumbs all over the place.

You are not his mother, she reminded herself. Right now, you are not even seeing to him. But it was her fault, wasn't it, that he had lumpy oatmeal? She was the one who had moved out and left him there, a mere twelve-year-old, with an often grouchy father who talked very little and drank much too much.

Newton nudged her. "If you are not going to eat your cake, I'll do it for you," he said.

Rose handed it over, wiped her hands on a napkin, scooped up Charles' crumbs off the stairs and immediately considered whether she was turning into a real housewife. She might as well pile her hair into a bun on the back of her head and spear it in place with one of those tortoiseshell hairpins Sarah had used. Instead of walking to the river with Alice and Emily, she'd have to put her mind to spring cleaning, getting rid of the crust of winter all through the house, blacking the stove and doing up the parlor curtains. If she went back to her father's house, she'd have to do all those things, and she knew her mouth would soon set in that straight line her mother's had always been in by evening.

She frowned, and Newton bent his head down to look up into her face, his own a little troubled. Had her frown made a noise? She thought frowns were soundless—oh, now she knew. Her back had gone as stiff as an ironing board when she frowned, and he'd felt that. She flashed him a reassuring smile and decided she'd leave his crumbs and Abby's right where they were. Let one of the town housewives sweep them up when the social was over.

CHAPTER TWO
A Suitable Suitor

Miss Harty looked over at the little group on the stairs and started to smile. They certainly were sticking together, those three motherless children, and that sweet Newton had made himself quite at home in the little group. Her smile widened when she thought about Newton bidding for what he thought was Rose's basket, and indeed it had those familiar hair ribbons on it—but no hearts. She'd seen Abby's excitement about sharing with Newton, who had bowed and smiled as she came toward him. He hadn't bargained for this partner, but he was taking it well. In all her years of teaching, she had rarely encountered a boy with a brain and heart like his.

Still, she hoped he wasn't going to sweep Rose off her feet and marry her within the next couple of years. She had watched him carefully after he rescued Rose from nearly freezing to death in the cemetery and had been amazed at how he transferred his farm knowledge into saving her life, and she could see that Rose's life meant something special to him.

If Rose had been living at home, her father would never have allowed Newton to visit her while she recovered. But there was nothing wrong with a sick child having an almost daily visit from a friend, she had told herself. So Newton came, spending fifteen or twenty minutes a day at Rose's bedside, and Ruthann Harty breathed not a word of the visits to anyone.

Perfectly harmless, she told herself. She was the chaperone, and she left the room for only forty seconds at a time, coming and going with such irregularity that she knew he was being a perfect gentleman, despite his obvious feelings for Rose. Still, she was quite sure he had sneaked in a kiss or two during some of those visits. It hadn't crossed her mind at first and she had nearly panicked the time she came into the room and found Rose's face very flushed. The fever must have returned, she'd thought. But it was just Rose's fair skin reacting to something Newton had said or done as he left.

"Hello?" said a voice next to her. "Calling Ruthann, where are you?"

"I am so sorry," she said, turning to the tall man who had purchased her supper box. "I was watching a group of my students across the way there."

"I know," he said. "Who are they?"

"The pretty one in the center of things is Rose, the girl who has been living with me since she left her father's house. The younger boy is her brother Charles, and the little girl is her nine-year-old sister Abby, who now lives with their Aunt Nell. So they are all living in separate houses because of problems with their father, and tonight they have gotten together."

"So, who's the fourth?"

"Newton Barnes. He's the one who found Rose half-frozen at her mother's grave in the town cemetery and lugged her like a sack of potatoes for a half mile or more to my kitchen, where he proceeded to instruct us all on how to get that poor child warm again."

Ruthann Harty started to laugh, and her supper mate looked puzzled. "It doesn't sound like it was very funny," he said.

"Well, it was not amusing at all at the time," Ruthann said. "But looking back, it makes me laugh to remember Newton telling us what to do and explaining, just as straight-faced and worried as he could be, that he had saved the life of a calf that way. None of us thought of Rose as a calf, but Newton turned out to be quite right, and when the doctor came and found us snuggled up beside Rose on the floor, bathing her frostbitten fingers with cool water, he congratulated the lad on his quick thinking. She is my very favorite pupil, and now, a friend as well. If I dared, I would just hug her every morning."

"If I dared," Joshua Chittenden remarked, "I would just hug you right now."

"Now that," Ruthann said, giving him a wide smile, "would undoubtedly end my employment here before the next train whistles. But it would be great fodder for Mrs. Munson."

Joshua knew all about Mrs. Munson's love of a new piece of gossip. "The real question is," he persisted, "would it be fun for you?"

"Oh, I warrant it would," Ruthann said, "but I will not double dare you as if I were some flirt on the playground."

As a compromise, he circled her waist with his arm, figuring not even Mrs. Munson could see that, squeezed quickly and then let go. It would not do to embarrass the teacher in front of a crowd that included all sorts of people who expected she would never behave in what they considered an unseemly fashion.

Warmth ran in both directions along her spine as his arm tightened. She had finally admitted to herself that it pleased her mightily that this tall, quite handsome man chose to come such a distance to see her. She wondered if he was becoming a genuine suitor. She hadn't had one in several years now. She glanced across the room at Mrs. Munson, who was so busy chattering with two older women that she had seen nothing. Her eyes then flew to Dr. Potter, and she was startled to discover that he was looking right at her and Joshua. He saw it, she thought. He would never have missed it. He sees just about everything, and he's single and nice, and he only comes to my house when a girl is near death in the guest room. She hadn't thought of setting her cap for him, whatever that meant, but it was certainly a possibility, and one close at hand.

"Calling Ruthann," came the voice beside her once again.

"I'm sorry," she apologized. "Rose is always saying her head comes unhitched sometimes and just goes off somewhere, and now it's happening to me."

Joshua's calloused hand reached for the back of her neck and turned her head ever so slightly. "It's as firm as the carved pineapple on a bedpost," he said, "but I would take it kindly if you'd look at me and not at that middle-aged man with his napkin tucked under his chin."

"He's not middle-aged," Ruthann answered much too quickly. "He's Rose's doctor, and some pineapples on bedposts can be unscrewed," she added, hoping she wasn't getting red in the face the way her young friend always did.

"Hmmm, not the high quality ones," Joshua said. "And why on earth was that pretty girl at her mother's grave in the midst of winter anyway?"

"After her mother's death," the teacher began, "Rose was working her fingers to the very bone feeding and clothing that family while trying to keep up with her schoolwork. She wants to be a teacher, and her father had announced that she would have to leave school come spring and take care of the family day in and day out. At the same time, he was at the drink and cavorting with a woman from the hotel, so Rose decided her little sister couldn't grow up in that house. She moved her out and went to discuss her troubles at her mother's grave, fell asleep from sheer exhaustion, and nearly froze to death."

"Judas Priest," Joshua exclaimed, shrinking back a little as several heads turned in his direction. He immediately turned his attention on the food basket again and noticed that the little group on the stage steps had started to move. Rose was on her feet, heading toward the table where Aunt Nell was supping with the minister and trying to be polite to her brother-in-law.

"Rose thinks she has to say hello to her father, and she knows it's safe here," Ruthann said, forgetting all about the doctor for the moment. She watched as Abby excused herself from Newton and skipped along after Rose, who bent down to speak to the little girl.

"Nicely done," Rose said as they walked across the room.

"Thank you," Abby said. "Aunt Nell is pretty fussy about manners, just like Mother was. But she's very nice, Rose," she added quickly. "It's just that I want to live with you every single day, not with them, and not with Father, either."

"Aside from finding someone's unused henhouse, it's hard to imagine how we could manage that," Rose said. "I'd like to be under the same roof you are under, but not if it involves my perching all night on a flimsy roost made from an ash sapling."

"Oh, Rose," Abby said, starting to giggle and then choking a little as she said, "but we will be in our own beds under one roof some day soon, won't we? There's not room for us all at Aunt Nell's, and she says there's no way on earth or in heaven that she'll let her sister's children go back to Silas Hibbard."

"You sound just like her, Abby," Rose said. "Does she talk like that often?"

"Uncle Jason always tells her to get off her white horse and stop galloping about," Abby said. "I don't know what that means."

"Knights in shining armor," Rose answered. "She's talking about the knights who dashed about on beautiful white horses doing good deeds and rescuing damsels in distress. They wore suits made of metal to protect them against enemies, and they fought with swords."

"It's a good thing they had horses," Abby said. "They'd never be able to walk to school or the store in a metal suit. Does she mean we are damsels in distress? I don't think I'm old enough to be a damsel."

"You are just old enough to be a very funny little girl," Rose said laughing. "We rescued ourselves from our distress, and now we have to figure out where we go from here. But it's nothing to really worry about. We all have good places to live," she added, hoping she sounded more optimistic than she felt. She wasn't sure about Charles. Father was so angry at times, and she would hate it if Charles had fear hanging over his dear head all the time.

He seemed all right, but she had better get over there of a morning now and then, stir up some lump-free oatmeal and make sure the sheets on his bed were reasonably fresh. She hoped they'd been changed at least a few times since she had left the house, but come to think of it, she had rarely noticed any wash hung out to dry there. She didn't know if Father even knew how to launder clothes, and she was now thinking that she had never given Charles any instruction on that chore. Besides, doing the wash took so much time, starting with heating water on the stove. She hoped Father was getting around to putting in a hot water heater.

CHAPTER THREE
Chaperones Again

Newton swung the now empty basket as he and Rose walked quickly toward Miss Harty's house, staying in the middle of the road so they would not slip in the icy ruts made by wagon wheels. Their feet crunched, and Rose noticed that her breath and Newton's, visible in the night air, were alternating. She caught hers for a fraction of a second—how large would a fraction like that be, she wondered—and started to breathe in time with him, hoping he wouldn't notice her foolishness.

"So here we are," he said after a minute or two, "exhaling together as if we were side by side in a church choir."

Rose laughed. "I thought maybe you wouldn't see that," she said.

"I am fairly certain that I notice just about everything about you," he said, taking her mittened hand in his. "You must remember that I recognized the hair ribbons, and I consider that an achievement for a male person."

"Charles achieved the very same thing," Rose reminded him.

"Charles is both a pleasure to me and a thorn in my side," Newton answered. "He knows far too much for a boy of twelve or thirteen or whatever he is."

"Twelve, nearly thirteen," Rose said.

Newton stopped and guided Rose toward the edge of the road where the bare branches of an elm cast spidery shadows on the snow. "Why," he said with a bit of a grumble, "are we wasting our time talking about ribbons and Charles? This is no time for talking, this tiny slice of moon time when we are alone, not a chaperone in sight."

He turned Rose toward him and lifted her chin. She felt the basket against her back as he pulled her very close and kissed her. She had been thinking about this moment for hours and wondered if it was the same for him. Then she stopped thinking and kissed him back, her arms threaded between his arms and his coat, her whole body pressed against him.

It's like hugging a blanket, she thought, with all these winter things on—not nearly as nice as an indoor kiss, the kind that still scared her a little because she always wished they would go on for hours so she could just stay there, feeling his warmth join hers. The fewer layers, the better, she thought, still kissing him and deciding her mind had become quite wicked. Perhaps that was why she had seen Miss Graves' skirt on Father's bedroom floor on that awful day. Well, no, she corrected herself, Father and Miss Graves had been up to something far more complicated than sharing warmth. It was time she accepted that, even if she didn't like it.

Rose

"You've gone off," Newton said, pulling away. "I am still at this kissing thing, and your lips are limping along like a duck with a sore foot."

"Sorry," Rose said, pulling her arms back and putting her hands on his cheeks. "My brain swam off for a bit, but I'm back." And this time she started the kiss, which was interrupted almost immediately by Charles' voice, taunting them with a loud, "Aha!"

"Told you he was a thorn," Newton mumbled, his mouth still on hers. Rose pulled away, hurried back to the middle of the road and walked on, waiting for neither of them, furious with Charles for coming along just then and furious that she'd been caught spooning. Charles would tease her unmercifully, and it would be hateful, more like forks than spoons. Why did they call it spooning anyway? Spoons were for getting soup or oatmeal from bowl to mouth, usually at table—a far cry from hugging and kissing, as far as she could see. Then the boys caught up with her, one on either side, and they were silent. She waited for Charles to start riding her about having a beau, but all he said was, "I saw Abby back to Aunt Nell's. She had a very nice time, Newton. I hope you did, too, Rose."

"Of course I did," she said, "until you came sneaking up on me. Now skedaddle on home and give your elders a few peaceful moments."

"Peaceful doesn't seem like the right word, especially from a word person like you," Charles said, quickly moving out of reach of Rose's raised hand. "But I'm gone, out of sight and no looking back." And true to his word, he

Chaperones Again

disappeared into the darkness of the road ahead.

"Thorns," Rose remarked, "are rarely so obliging," hoping they were going to pick up where they had left off. But Newton only pecked her on the cheek and continued along the road. At Miss Harty's house they saw the stranger's horse and buggy in the driveway, and as they went up the porch steps they discovered that they weren't the evening's only kissing couple. Miss Harty and her supper mate were standing in her parlor, a single silhouette against the lamplight, their lips joined.

About to open the door, Rose gasped and stood still. "Hush," Newton said, turning her around and pulling her close to him again. "You can't watch. That will turn you into Charles." And before she could answer, he kissed her so hard that she thought she might stop breathing entirely. Perhaps Miss Harty and the stranger would keep on kissing, and she could do this for another hour. But Newton let her go and then rapped sharply on the door.

In a minute or so, her hands pushing back loose strands of hair, Miss Harty opened the door, invited them in and said she wanted them to meet her friend, Joshua Chittenden. "He's a farmer up past Ripton," she said, "a dairy farmer and a breeder."

"I've heard a good deal about both of you tonight," Joshua said, shaking Newton's hand and nodding to Rose. "Ruthann and I were just considering what to do about that air outside."

"Air?" Rose asked, thinking what she had glimpsed in the parlor had little to do with the night air.

31

"The wind's shifted," Joshua said. "It feels like a storm's coming, and I don't want to get caught in that before I get home. I'm figuring on sleeping in that small haymow in Ruthann's barn and setting out at first light."

Newton frowned. "Excuse me, sir, I don't mean to be impertinent, but that seems like a poor idea to me."

"How so?"

"Well, Miss Harty here is the teacher, and the town is mighty fussy about its teachers, and you could put a stain on her reputation by sleeping out there," Newton said and then paused. "You see, sir, you would not be chaperoned, and this town puts a lot of stock in chaperoning, especially with you being a stranger and all."

Rose began to smile, thinking about the first time she had heard Newton on the subject of chaperones, and Miss Harty laughed out loud. "I've been trying to tell Mr. Chittenden that very thing, Newton," Miss Harty said, "but I must not have put it plainly enough. You, however, have been very clear. But it's also true that he should not travel tonight, and the hotel doesn't rent rooms at this time of year."

"You would be more than welcome to bunk at our house, Mr. Chittenden, and you'd be part of my mother's news after church tomorrow, or at the store on Monday, so the whole town will know exactly where you slept."

This boy, Ruthann Harty thought, never ceases to startle me with what's in his head. He wants to shield Rose from everything bad, and now he's worried that a man in the haymow will make my reputation as tarnished as that silver necklace Miss Graves wears. Rose may be too young to have him come calling—and too innocent—but she will come to no harm from this one.

"It's a good plan, Joshua," she said aloud. "Perhaps we should all have a cup of tea before you make your way to the Barnes' house. Is there room for his horse there, Newton?"

It was as if they were old friends, not newly met or teacher and pupils, Rose thought, as the foursome made their way to the kitchen. She lit the kerosene lamp on the table, added a stick to the wood stove, and put the blue and white enamel kettle over the fire, while Newton reached for Miss Harty's better teacups, which were on the top shelf of the cupboard.

"What kind of cattle are you breeding, sir?" Newton asked, as he pulled out a chair for Miss Harty.

"First, you'd better call me Joshua, even if you have to go on addressing Ruthann as Miss Harty, because no one ever calls me sir. Second, I'm raising about eighty-nine percent Jerseys because they give the creamiest milk, and people in these parts like their top milk so thick that it can be whipped if a woman has enough patience, and forearm strength to match. I milk a few head, but I'm more interested in the science side: which cows and which bulls ought to mate to create the ultimate Jersey milker."

"Jerseys. I don't know much about Jerseys," Newton said.

"They come in from England or from their original home, the Island of Jersey," Joshua said. "Hence the name. I started with a few from Jersey and have a few from Canada now and I'm looking to get one or two from a place up in Vermont that seems to be on the same track I'm taking. Compared to some of the cattle we have around here they are quite beautiful, much more delicate in build, and usually the color of summer fawns, but with black noses, and no spots. Now and then an all-black shows up, but I don't have any of those."

Rose, who likened the teakettle boil to a conversation, heard the water begin to chatter. She poured hot water into the stoneware teapot, added tea leaves from the little metal canister and set the pot on the back of the stove to steep. In a few minutes, she poured tea all around, barely looking at the cups but not spilling a drop. She kept glancing sideways at Newton's face, which had a whole new light, a look she had never seen before. Because of cows, she wondered, because of cows?

"I'd like to see them, sir, uh, Joshua, if you'd be of a mind to let me visit your place one day," Newton was saying eagerly.

"Anytime, young man, anytime. Nothing I like better than showing off those ladies up there. But we'd better turn our attention to these ladies here for the time being, or we'll be seeing the wrong side of the front door."

A bit later, after Newton and Joshua had left, Rose lit a candle to light her way on the stairs, said good night, and went to her room. Ruthann Harty went to the front window and watched as the boy and the man walked toward Joshua's buggy, Newton as tall as the older man. Thank the good Lord, or whoever was in charge of such things—Cupid perhaps?—that Rose had come along when she did. Now she had time to think about Joshua's question, although she didn't think it would take any deep pondering.

"Will you marry me?" he had said, taking her face in his hands and then kissing her for what seemed like a whole minute. And she was about to give an impulsive answer, a joyous yes, when the rap on the door made them both jump. How long, she wondered, had those children been out there? Long enough for Newton to worry himself about what the town would say if Joshua slept in the barn. She took off her apron, smoothed her skirt with her hands and then laughed aloud. She would say yes, even though it would take her away from the school and the children she loved, even knowing she would turn into a farmer's wife. She wondered if Rose would think that unthinkable. Rose had run away from a farm, a farming father, a farm kitchen. Rose wanted to be a teacher. Ruthann Harty frowned, thinking about Newton Barnes' excitement over Joshua's cows.

She brushed Rose and Newton's future aside, remembering the warmth of Joshua Chittenden's hands on her face. With a small smile on her face, Ruthann turned down the wicks on the kerosene lamps until the flames died, then made her way to the stairs in darkness.

CHAPTER FOUR
A Special Delivery

Rose slipped into the pew next to Uncle Jason at church, her head so full of last night's doings at the box social that she was afraid she had little space for whatever the Reverend Lockhead had to say. Sitting between her uncle and aunt, Abby leaned forward to smile at Rose, and Uncle Jason gave her a little pat on the arm. Rose could not locate her father and Charles anywhere up front, and she knew better than to turn her head in church. Her mother had been dead set against that kind of behavior.

Dead set against. Now that was a terrible expression. Sarah had been set against and dead, down there at the woodpile that fell over and killed her It was no better to turn it around, make it into dead and set against. That's almost what she had been at the cemetery that day when she went to talk to her mother. She set herself against Sarah's gravestone, and she was nearly dead, apparently, when Newton found her and carried her to the teacher's house.

The Reverend Lockhead had come to call when she was still feeling quite poorly, but she remembered his stern look and his saying, "You have to face life, Rose, not deny it. It is a sin to give up when you get the idea that it's too hard. The Lord watches over you and every being, right down to the smallest sparrow." She remembered the tiny bubble of spit that rolled onto his lower lip and quivered there while he spoke. She had wondered why he didn't lick it up, or dab at his lip with his linen handkerchief. She had seen him use the handkerchief and was grateful that she didn't have to iron such. It was so easy to burn linen when the iron was hot from the stove top; and hard to get it smooth if the iron wasn't nearly red-hot and the linen evenly damp.

As for the sparrow, she knew the Lord didn't have his eye on the chickadee that had smacked Miss Harty's kitchen window and dropped to the ground, instantly dead. Didn't have his eye on Sarah when the woodpile crushed her. Didn't stop her father from kicking Sarah's cat.

Maybe the Lord was distracted sometimes, just as she was. She brought her mind back to the church service and stood with the rest to sing "Onward Christian Soldiers," one of the new hymns with a marching tempo that made her feet want to tap as if she were at a square dance or a parade. Just then she caught a glimpse of Miss Harty's head, right next to Mr. Chittenden's, in the fourth or fifth row.

Oh my, she thought, Newton will think Miss Harty is tossing her reputation into the fire, although it made no sense that she should be hurt by having Mr. Chittenden sleep in her barn. Surely he would be the uncomfortable one, and possibly chilled as well. But if it was a problem, Newton's mother would have to be quick with her chatter, or Miss Harty apparently would be tarnished. He did say "tarnished," didn't he? And then she nearly choked, trying not to giggle. Mrs. Munson was right behind the teacher and her beau, the pheasant feather on her hat bobbing up and down, and beside Mrs. Munson was Newton, her Newton. Was he really her Newton? The idea gave her the shivers, the same odd feeling she'd had when he said last night that he noticed everything about her. She hoped that didn't include the shoes she had failed to shine. She still couldn't see Father or Charles, and she felt her worry bug starting to rouse after a snooze that had lasted several days, almost a record for her.

The minister was finishing his long prayer, but she heard little of it. It would be Emily's mother singing the solo while the collection plate was passed, and she let the notes fall over her head like pleasant raindrops, still not absorbing any words. When the sermon started, she tried to listen because he was talking once again about temperance and the meetings that would be held in tents on the town square as soon as warm weather arrived.

"These are not just for those who have been tempted by the drink," he counseled, "but for those who want to avoid temptation and for those who suffer because their loved ones have fallen into the abyss. Those who have sinned in other ways may also want to attend and try to cleanse their minds," he said, his voice rising enough to bring Rose's own mind back into the fold. He hinted that important guests would honor the town by attending the meetings.

Father won't go, Rose thought. He just won't. He didn't go to the one meeting in January, and he will tell himself that he can manage on his own, that he doesn't need a flock of women and a minister telling him what to drink and what not to drink. He promised he would turn a corner in his life, but he'll figure he can draw his own map. Rose wished she had a map for what would happen next. She wanted to be a teacher. She had dreamed about having a classroom of her own since she was three. But then there was Newton. He seemed fearful of her being a teacher, worried that she was going to run off somewhere. Had she been so focused on what she wanted that she hadn't even asked if he had a dream? They would have to bundle up warmly and make their way to her rock for some serious talk. She would like sitting on the rock—her rock—with him again. At least she could do that bit of mapping.

Lost in thought, Rose didn't realize everyone was standing for the closing hymn and benediction until her uncle put his hand under her elbow. She stood hastily, flicking her hand down the back of her long skirt to make sure it was smooth, and then joined in with the line, "casting down their golden crowns around the glassy sea." Too heavy, she thought. Golden crowns would shatter a glassy sea. But what turned it to glass? Glasses held water, but water wasn't glass. Really, she told herself, your head is surely unfastened now.

Outside the church, the congregation dispersed

slowly. She saw Newton's mother greeting Mrs. Munson and knew she'd get in something about where Mr. Chittenden had slept last night. But she still didn't see Charles or Father among the women's bobbing hats and the men's caps. Alice said she had a lovely time at the box social, and Emily said Peter Granger had been very nice about her box supper but she hoped never to spend time with him again because even on Saturday night he didn't smell very good.

"And how did Ethan smell, Alice?" Rose asked.

"Just as nice as Newton," Alice retorted quickly.

"Splendid, Alice," Emily cried. "You sounded just like me when you said that."

"Never mind all this," Rose interrupted. "Has either of you seen Charles—or Father?"

Both looked around, shaking their heads, and turned back to Rose. "We could go by your old house and see if they're up and about," Alice suggested, seeing the look creeping across her friend's face.

"Or we could ask Newton to do it," Emily said, thinking it was possible they could end up in a bad situation with Mr. Hibbard. To her mind, he was unpleasant at best, and at worst, quite terrifying.

"Do what?" said a voice behind them. "What do I have to do now, I who have said my prayers next to Mrs. Munson today and who saved Miss Harty from being tarred yesterday, if not feathered, and rescued Miss Rose from certain death?"

"Stop it," the three girls said, almost in unison.

"Just stop right there," Emily said, "stop being a beast

and tell us if you will go by the Hibbard house and see what kept Charles and Mr. Hibbard from church."

Newton frowned. Everyone went to church on Sunday morning. Not everyone was religious, he knew, but they went anyway. Of course he would stop at the Hibbard place, but he wasn't having a good feeling about it. In spite of himself, he was a little afraid of Silas Hibbard. If he strikes me, do I hit him back or just act respectful, he wondered. Then he glanced at Rose's face and nodded.

"I'll come along." Rose said. He started to say no but stopped when he saw that she was truly worried. "And we are coming, too," Alice said.

"Then why do I have to go?" Newton asked.

"In case they have both fallen into a well and can't get out," Emily answered quickly.

"We don't have a well," Rose said. "Wait just another minute while I tell Aunt Nell that I'll be along for dinner later."

As they neared Rose's house, they heard a cow blatting, the sounds harsh in the silence of Sunday. No one answered at the house, so they hurried to the barn, slipping a bit on patches of ice in the roughly shoveled path, the girls holding up their long skirts. They rounded the corner just as Charles emerged, jacketless, his bare hands covered with blood, and the left sleeve of his Sunday-go-to-meeting shirt rolled up but stained with brown and reddish-brown spots.

The scream that came from all three girls stopped as if cut with a knife when Charles began to laugh.

"We delivered a calf," he said. "We delivered a calf that couldn't get out, so we got her out, and she is fine and dandy, and Father says the cow will be all right in a day or two, and the calf wants to eat, but the cow is still lying down."

"Can I take a look?" Newton asked.

"Enter, sir," Charles said, bowing and sweeping his hand toward the barn door. "She is receiving. I trust you will leave a card?"

"Charles," Rose began, but her voice choked, and all she could do was throw her arms around him.

"Oh, Rose," Charles said, struggling to get free. "You saw we wasn't in church, and you figured I was dead, or at the very least mortally wounded, didn't you?"

"Weren't," Rose said automatically. "Weren't in church."

"And I was here being the hero of the day. You see," Charles went on in some excitement, "the calf's right leg was bent back at the knee, and the two front hooves have to lead the way out of the cow, but one of them was a knee instead of a hoof, and Father's hand was too big to get in there, so I had to do it, and I had to use my left hand because my right hand was on the wrong side."

"You put your hand in there?" Emily asked, looking a little sick. "Don't ever touch me again."

"He was saving a life, Emily," Alice said, keeping her eyes away from Charles' stained shirt and bloody hands. "The calf would have died, and maybe the mother, too."

"He's loathsome," Emily insisted.

A Special Delivery

Just then Silas Hibbard emerged from the barn, his dark eyebrows shooting to his hairline when he saw the group facing Charles. "To what do we owe the honor of this visit, Rose? You haven't graced us with your presence in weeks."

"We—I—we were worried when you weren't in church," Rose said, trying not to stammer. "We came along to see that things were all right here."

"Right as can be," her father boomed at her, "no thanks to you and thanks to Charles. The calf is yours, Charles, to raise and take care of and sell or keep, whatever you've a mind to do with her."

"Thank you, sir," Charles said so quietly that the others almost couldn't hear him. But he looked as pleased as if he had just eaten a dish of strawberry ice cream and beckoned Newton to follow him into the barn.

"Leave that shirt here," Rose called after him. "I'll need to get at those stains as soon as possible." She nodded to her father and turned away, walking up the hill toward the house with Emily on one side and Alice on the other.

Silas Hibbard watched the three girls and sighed. He'd had no need to ask Rose sarcastic questions, but the words had just slipped out. If Sarah had been there, she would have frowned at the very idea that he should say "no thanks to you" to his daughter when the birthing of the calf had nothing to do with her.

He wondered if she would ever come back, if he could ever persuade her. He had to admit that she looked happy and well, that staying with the teacher was agreeing with her. But he missed her. Not just because she ironed shirts and made breakfast and dinner and cleaned the chamber pots. He admitted to himself that he surely missed all those things, but he also missed just having her there. She wasn't Sarah, but Sarah had taught her well, and Rose had picked up the reins when she had to. He should stop drinking; stay as sober as he was right now. Rose would like that.

He wondered if he actually could give up his hard cider and the occasional whiskey. Drowning your sorrows, they called it. And he knew he was doing just that, except the sadness kept bobbing to the surface again, not drowned at all. He should have piped in the water for Sarah, should have found her an icebox. She had never complained about those things, but he knew she had wanted them, and he wasn't certain in his mind why he had resisted her so. Too stubborn for his own good, and now she was gone, her smile was gone, her sweet smell in the bed beside him, her way of doing small things to make him comfortable.

Still, he didn't have a mind to go to the Reverend Lockhead's tent meetings and stand up in front of everyone in town. Silas Hibbard figured that amounted to making a damn fool of yourself. But, he thought, in some ways I reckon I've already done that. He sighed again, walked toward the barn, and slid the wooden door on its rusty rollers. Time to see to that calf.

CHAPTER FIVE
A Day of Rest?

Sundays were the quietest days of the week in the village of Eastborough. A hearty dinner followed church, and then many folks nodded off for a few minutes before they changed out of their Sunday best. And while the regular barn chores could not be ignored, other work waited until dawn on Monday. Neighbors sometimes dropped in; families might take a buggy ride; older people welcomed a son or niece who might stop by for an hour of visiting. The devout as well as those who went to church more out of custom than belief agreed that this, as the Bible said, was a day of rest. Or more rest than not.

But for the Hibbards, this Sunday was busier than usual. They were scattered all around the village, even for the big meal of the day. After going back to Miss Harty's to give her the news about the calf, Rose returned to her family home and found that Charles, following instructions, had left his bloodstained shirt for her. Next to it was a large dirty sock with a sizable hole in the toe. She took that along, figuring it must belong to her father. She'd be obliged to wash and darn that, too. She hurried the half mile or so to Aunt Nell and Uncle Jason's house to have Sunday dinner with Abby and to get started on making Charles' shirt like new, or almost new. How gangly he looked these days, she thought, not thin really but as if his legs and arms were attached loosely. Gangly. She liked that word.

Soon after she arrived, the shirt was soaking in a pail of cold water. "Slosh it around every few minutes," Nell said, "and change the water when it's rusty."

Three times during dinner, Rose excused herself to take care of the shirt. Sort of like cleaning up those cloths she had to wear during her menstruation. She hated those. But after the third rinsing, she saw that the stains on the shirt were nearly gone, and she reported to her aunt that it would be saved.

"Now settle into your dinner, child," Nell said. "You're eating like a chickadee, and you need more nourishment with all the things you crowd into a day."

"My life is easy now, Aunt," Rose said, and hoped she didn't sound impertinent. "At Miss Harty's, I do only half the work I did at home. Sometimes it makes me feel as guilty as those sinners the Reverend Lockhead

A Day of Rest?

is always talking about. If I'd just faced up to things, maybe I could have stayed put and taken care of Abby and Charles and Father."

"Child alive," Uncle Jason almost shouted from his side of the table. "We nearly lost you during that time. You were overworked, overwhelmed, and grieving— enough to send a rock-steady adult running to hide in the broom closet. We are the guilty ones for not taking more notice."

Rose felt the color rising in her cheeks, but she knew she should finish, now that she had begun. "I'm worried about Charles," she said. "I told you about Father giving him the calf, and I know how exciting it was for him to help with the cow, but he was talking faster than an auctioneer, and Charles doesn't usually talk that way. The only time I remember him going on and on like that was when he had to help kill a chicken, and he ended up being sick to his stomach. He was babbling today like a brook in spring, so I think he's having a hard time there, even if he jokes about lumps in the oatmeal."

"Quite a long speech from you," Uncle Jason said, nodding. "And we'll have to see to Charles. But you know you can't go back there because not much has changed. You moved out because you had acquired the eyes of a grown woman, and your mind drew a picture of the future that you didn't like."

"And that your mother wouldn't have liked either, Rose," Aunt Nell chimed in.

"I didn't like getting up in the morning, Rose," Abby

said in a small voice. "And now I just jump out of bed and get ready for the day."

Both Nell and Jason looked at the nine-year-old with approval. She had just banged the nail on the head, and they were each thinking the argument ought to be over. And it was.

"Oh, Abby, I'm so sorry you were ever afraid or worried," Rose said. "And if you are happy now, then moving you here was exactly the right thing to do. But do you think Charles is all right?"

"Of course not," Abby said, but she grinned as she spoke. "He wants you to cook for him, sew on his buttons, and tell him what to do next so Father won't growl at him. And then he would tell you why he doesn't need to do whatever you wanted, and he can't tell Father that." She giggled and added, "I think if you made him a box of food once in a while, like what he had at the social, he'd be fine. He did throw up after killing the chicken, but he ate her anyway, once we had cooked away her meanness."

"Perhaps, Rose," Jason interrupted, "you could sneak in there in the morning now and then and make some oatmeal that's only as lumpy as it's supposed to be. You could take a look around and see if you think things are orderly." Then he changed the subject abruptly, asking whether Miss Harty was home alone that day.

"She is getting lessons ready," Rose said. "And she likes to be alone sometimes, just as I do."

Indeed, Miss Harty was having Sunday dinner alone

A Day of Rest?

and wasn't minding it a bit. She had rummaged in the icebox, pulled out the Dutch cheese, and was eating a mound of it on a slice of the oatmeal bread Rose had made. She had opened the oven door, taken off her shoes, and was resting her feet on the edge of the stove. The kitchen was cozy and warm, and she was reading her already somewhat worn copy of *The Adventures of Tom Sawyer,* anticipating the happy ending to the funeral scene where everyone was wearing black and thinking Tom was dead.

As the clergyman extolled the virtues of Joe Harper, Huck Finn and Tom, who had become quite heroic after everyone thought they were dead and gone forever, she took a sip of her tea and started thinking that she really must try to find some virtues in Peter Granger. Whenever she had to deal with that awkward boy, she felt as if she were plunging into a wild rose bush. He would soon be out for the spring and summer, but she was quite certain he was pretty smart under his prickly exterior. He had certainly managed her class well that one time she put him in charge. Perhaps that was the secret, she thought. She would put him in charge of ringing the bell and assigning others to bring in wood, instead of his doing it. She went back to the story, looking forward to the return of the supposedly dead boys and the congregation's astonished welcome, and trying to think how best to get her older students interested in this wonderful tale.

Despite the intriguing situation in the book, she was

having trouble keeping her mind on it. She kept thinking about Joshua Chittenden and that kiss in the parlor and the sound of his voice as he asked her to marry him. That was when Rose and Newton had arrived, and she had never answered the question. Certainly she hadn't answered it in church, although she was sure her face was as crimson as Rose's when he strode down the aisle and took a seat next to her. The space at the end of the pew was not quite large enough for his big frame, and his left leg was on her skirt before she could gather it up.

Now he was on his way back to his precious cows, and she hadn't an idea under the heavens when he would pass through town again. She'd lived among farmers for much of her twenty-nine years, and she knew those Jerseys might be fierce competitors for a man's attention. She hoped she wouldn't have to play second fiddle to a cow.

While she brooded, Charles was sharing Sunday dinner with his father and Miss Jennie Graves, who had put her best effort into serving a johnnycake and baked beans. She had actually bought the beans from the cook at the hotel, but she did not tell the boy and the man about that. And she was an old hand at johnnycake, a staple at her mother's table. Dessert would be baked apples, cored and sprinkled with brown sugar and cinnamon. She had fetched those from the Hibbards' barrel in the root cellar. They were Snow apples, which were her favorite and had kept nicely. She cooked them right along with the johnnycake, taking care not to make the oven too hot by overfeeding the fire.

She saw that Charles had set the table for three but had left Sarah Hibbard's place empty. That boy wasn't about to let her take his mother's place in any way, not even on a chair, and sure as shooting, he'd soon be talking about always having chicken for Sunday dinner.

When Charles and Silas took their places, she scooped beans onto their plates and passed the johnnycake and butter.

"I like cornbread," Charles said, "or do you call it johnnycake?"

Surprised, Miss Graves nodded that she did call it that, already grateful that he hadn't brought up the past. But her hopes soon flew out the window.

"We always used to have chicken for Sunday dinner," Charles said. "Even after Mother died, Rose would make it. She called it fricassee, and we had dumplings with it, all soaked in gravy."

"That will do, Charles," Silas Hibbard said. "Children should be seen and not heard."

"Unless they're sticking their hands into a blatting cow," Charles muttered.

Silas slammed his hand on the table, making the forks jump as if they were coming alive. "You will not speak back to me, young man," he said, "or we will repair to the woodshed for a special lesson."

"Sorry, sir," Charles said, looking quite unrepentant. "I meant no offense."

Remembering his thoughts earlier in the morning, Silas grunted and said no more. He did not want this boy to pack up and leave, and he knew it was entirely possible that Charles was as independent a thinker as his older sister. On the other hand, Charles had done a right good job that morning with the calf, and he was faithful about his chores. Sarah had taught him well when it came to taking responsibility. Silas pushed the last of his beans onto his fork with his knife and followed that mouthful with a bite of the johnnycake.

"Not bad, Miss Jennie," he said. "Not bad."

She gave a small sigh of relief and wondered if it were possible this difficult family might get a little easier. She and Rose would never be friends, she knew. That girl had eyes that went through your brain as if it were cheesecloth, and Jennie Graves was sure Rose would never willingly set a place for her. She did take to Silas, though, and even if things weren't entirely friendly, it was nicer than being all by yourself in an attic room at an old hotel.

Her face lit up when she heard Silas say, "I'll be taking the buggy out this afternoon, Charles. Think you can manage the harnessing for that?"

"You wanted Dolly, Father?"

"That's best," Silas said, picking up his dessert plate and bringing it to the kitchen where the boy was washing up the dishes.

"I can manage, sir," Charles replied, drying his hands on the roller towel, then taking his jacket from its hook and heading for the back door. He sat on the narrow bench by the door to exchange his Sunday shoes for his barn boots and then tiptoed back to see if he could hear anything interesting. Charles had long ago discovered that a tad of listening at doors or under windows often turned up worthwhile tidbits.

"Nice meal, Jennie," he heard his father say. "I reckon you have a way with that hotel cook and his beans."

"You always find me out, Silas," Miss Graves answered. Charles pressed his ear against the door, figuring he had at least another minute to spare. He could harness the horse right quickly, and he had high hopes of hearing something he could pass on to Rose. Or maybe not, he thought, if it was a story that would upset her. Rose worried about the least little things, and he wouldn't be the one to set her off if he could help it.

"I am going to find you out right now," Charles heard his father say. A silence followed, then Charles heard a squeal that nearly made him laugh. The sound had to have come from Miss Jennie, but all he could think of was the noise baby pigs made as they pushed each other aside to latch onto one of their mother's nipples. He decided it was high time he got a move on, and he crept quietly down the stairs, skipping the next to last because it always creaked.

In the kitchen, Miss Graves pulled away from Silas's embrace, sniffed, and turned to pick up her shawl from the back of the kitchen rocking chair. "I'm thinking what you need to find would be a plan for the future, Mr. Hibbard, if you are going to carry on like this."

Silas pulled the door open without answering and beckoned for her to go through. At the cellar door, he indicated she should wait, and he headed for the barn to see how Charles was getting on with harnessing Dolly. Within minutes, finding that Charles had done well, he pulled up in the buggy, gave Miss Graves a hand up, and spread the heavy buffalo blanket over her knees and his.

Coming up the path from the barn, Charles watched them leave with some relief. He could now do the dishes in peace, even if it was women's work, and then he would go back to the barn to check on his very own calf, which was already nursing quite nicely. After that, he hoped he could spend the afternoon in his attic bedroom with his wooden blocks. If one of his buildings came out well, he would try to draw it, but he found it wasn't easy to draw things that had four sides and a roof. He wondered if people who designed buildings just made separate drawings for each side and another one for the top. He wished he had some sizable sheets of paper.

While he sloshed plates in and out of the soapy water, he thought about where he would put the windows and doors in his next building. He looked up at the solid wall in front of him, covered in a plain wainscoting. Was he the only person in the world who thought the sink should face a window, not a boring wall? He thought wainscoting was a strange word and then smiled, thinking that his brain had at least a piece of Rose in it. His mind wandered to the squeal he had heard. Next time he saw the first star, he would wish Miss Graves would not come to meals and sit there trying to reach his father's foot with hers. Mother had never done that. Sunday dinners made him more homesick for Rose and his mother than anything else in the week.

A Day of Rest?

While Charles was feeling a little sorry for himself, the family buggy was bumping along the winter-rutted road through the center of town. Silas held the reins loosely in one hand, feeling for Jennie's hand under the blanket with the other. But when he squeezed her fingers in his, her hand felt as limp as cooked spinach. Without moving his head, he looked sideways at her face, which was completely still and unsmiling.

"Jennie," he began, and stopped. "Jennie," he began again, "I have no notion of what tomorrow will bring, never mind next Wednesday or on May fifteenth or next December. I enjoy your company, but I am dealing with only the day that is in front of me when I get out of bed in the morning. And I reckon I don't always deal with even that very well."

"My company? My company? Enjoy? Land sakes, Silas Hibbard, it's a good deal more than my company that you've been enjoying. You have been carrying on as if you never saw a woman before."

"I grieve for Sarah still, Jennie. You need to understand that."

"Hard to believe, Silas, when you are 'enjoying my company.' Hard to believe."

Silas fell silent again, his eyes on the up-and-down motion of the horse's head, and both of his hands now holding the reins. They were outside of the village, with Dolly trotting nicely and Silas keeping the buggy wheels in the ruts others had made in the dirt road. The trees still carried a layer of snow, and the air was crisp. It was a good day for cutting down trees, he thought, wishing he was out in the woods at that very minute, working a crosscut saw with another man pulling the other end.

He breathed in the cold, feeling it all the way to his stomach. When he exhaled, his breath turned into a cloud of vapor that matched what was coming from the horse's mouth and Jennie's. Still, spring was coming, the sun was higher in the sky every day, and the Chandlers had already tapped their maple trees. As soon as the mercury went above freezing, the sap would run, and he'd be giving Ben Chandler a hand with boiling it down to syrup. It would be a promising day when steam started rising from the sugarhouse again.

They reached a wide part of the road and he pulled up, carefully guided the horse into a turn, and started back toward the village. From the corner of his eye, Silas saw a flutter of surprise cross Jennie's face, and then her stony look dropped like a curtain. When he came to the hotel, Silas reined Dolly in, left the reins loose on her back and jumped down. By the time he reached the other side of the buggy, however, Miss Jennie had reached the ground without help and was picking up her skirt to walk over the snow. Without bidding him any kind of farewell, she stalked toward the long porch of the hotel.

Silas sighed, hoisted himself onto the seat again, and set off for home. When he reached his place, Dolly started to turn in, but he yanked the reins and kept her on the road. He had a mind to speak with Jason about the turn the afternoon had taken. He hankered to share a mug of Jason's hard cider with him, but he resolved

A Day of Rest?

not to give in to that urge. It was time, Silas thought, to sober up. It was the drink that had put him in this fix with Miss Jennie, wasn't it? Well, he couldn't blame it all on the drink. He was lonely and worried, and she had reached out to comfort him, and a man finds it hard to resist such temptations, especially when a low-necked dress was part of the picture. But it was the drink that put things on the present track, and he hadn't even half an idea how to slow down the train. Sober, he might have just looked and not touched.

He wondered if Rose would still be at Nell and Jason's. He wondered if she had found the sock and whether she would mend it or stuff it into the fire. He couldn't think what had possessed him to add his holey sock to Charles' bloodstained shirt, but she had taken both, so maybe it would be all right. He wanted Rose to do for him, wanted her to think she should, even if it was just darning a sock. You are a fool, Silas, he told himself. You want her to want to do something for you. You want her to still have feelings for you, even though you hardly deserve it.

He pulled the buggy into the Harris' yard and tied Dolly's reins to the post by the back door. He took the blanket he and Miss Jennie had been using and threw it over her back so she wouldn't be cold standing in the wind. He sniffed the air once, then again. It was cold, no question, but with a hint of softness that predicted a new season birthing. Today's calf was just the beginning of spring. Sarah's favorite season of the four, he remembered, and not a bad time to turn over a new leaf while the trees were thinking about pushing theirs out into the world.

Silas rapped on the paneled back door of his brother-in-law's house and took off his boots when he heard Nell's steps coming toward him. When she saw Silas, she glanced over her shoulder to see where Rose and Abby were and then greeted him properly and invited him in. Still in his stiff-collared shirt from church, Jason came up behind her, pumped Silas's hand, and muttered something about it being too long between visits.

"Not been much worth visiting with," Silas said, glad of their welcome and aware it wasn't quite wholehearted. "Hope I'm not bothering."

"Oh, no," Nell said, a touch of lemon in her voice. "Rose has just finished getting Charles' shirt as white as new, and she's taking a look at a huge hole in a sock. I reckon that wasn't Charles' sock, Silas, but for some reason, it hitched a ride on the bloody shirt. Rose won't be fixing it today, however. She's too worried about taking out stitches with her nose if she sews of a Sunday."

"Hard to figure how much and how many ways we miss that girl, Nell," Silas said. "Her grandmother told her anyone who sewed on Sunday would be assigned the heavenly chore of taking out the stitches with her nose, and she's shied away from that task on the Lord's Day ever since. I'll just say hello, and then I'd like to bend your ear awhile, Jason, if I may. I reckon you knew whose sock it was, Nell."

Nell said something that sounded like "humph," and

looked toward Jason for some indication of how things would go from here.

"We'll walk down to the henhouse so I can show you my new bantams," Jason said in an even tone. "They are spectacular."

"Bantams?" Silas asked. "When did you get into fancy chickens?"

"Not long ago," Jason answered. "I like looking at them. These are originally from China, and they're good layers. They also are regular mother hens, whether it's their own chicks or someone else's. The full name is Bantam Cochin, but they're also called Pekin. I reckon that's a Chinese word. They come in as many colors as Joseph's coat, but mine are white as snow in the hayfield."

Abby had appeared in the doorway from Nell's parlor and was going up and down on her toes, anxious to say something but afraid to interrupt.

"What is it, child?" Jason asked, thinking she looked as if she were half jumping jack.

"They are very soft, Father," Abby said. "I like to hold them. Uncle Jason, can I go too?"

"Not this time, Abby. I gather we have business to discuss," Jason said before Silas could answer. By this time, Rose had heard her father's voice, so she came in from the parlor and nodded to him while Jason was still talking.

"Hello, Rose," Silas said. "You are looking well."

"Thank you, Father. I am very well, as I was this

morning. Please tell Charles that I will return his shirt as soon as I have time to iron it for him, and I will mend your sock after I launder it."

Her tone, not exactly insolent but with a hint of rebellion in it, created a silence that lasted for what seemed a very long time, and then Nell flapped her apron at the two men as if they were chickens and said, "So get along with you, then, and come back when you're ready for a cup of tea."

"Give us a little time to suck an egg, if that appeals," Jason said. "I do appreciate a raw egg now and then, although it's a bit of a trick."

Once inside the warmth of the chicken house, while Silas was admiring the new chickens, Jason reached under one of the hens and pulled out a warm egg. Silas watched as his brother-in-law poked at each end of the egg with the small awl on his prized Holley pocketknife and then carefully sucked the egg out of its shell. He swallowed and licked his lips.

"Your turn?" he asked.

But Silas declined. "Never really took a liking to that practice," he said. "Druther have my egg fried in butter or boiled awhile. Don't even like the cooked ones if they run all over the plate. But my mother is a great one for taking a raw egg now and then, says it's a tonic for what ails her."

Jason chuckled. "So if Charles gets tired of Rose telling him how to do things, he can call up the old expression and just tell her to 'go teach your grandmother to suck eggs.'"

A Day of Rest?

"Mebbe so," Silas said, but he didn't smile. "Judas Priest, Jason, I didn't come here to see the pretty chickens, although I can see why you admire them. I came because I'm a desperate man. I need to turn myself around, and I can't get a grip on the left rein or the right and don't know which one I want anyway. I do know that I need to get sober and stay sober. I need to get my family back under my roof. And somehow, I need to move Miss Jennie out of my life. The trouble is, I want it all to happen today, and that makes me just another weak fool who has tangled things up worse than a cat in a knitting basket."

Jason put his hand on Silas's shoulder and squeezed hard. "Appears you've made a right good start just now, Silas. You are sober today, so I reckon you made your way through a Saturday night without a drink, so you are seeing things clearly, first time since Sarah's funeral. I don't know as I can give advice on any of those things, but I can see the order of things. First, the drink. Second, Miss Graves. Third, and mebbe this will come naturally or very hard, I don't know, the return of your family. Are you doing all right by Charles?"

"We get along," Silas said. "He's a good lad, taught well by Sarah and then by Rose. I reckon Rose told you about his helping get the new calf out this morning. Pitched right in, without a care about the slime and blood. Without him, I might have lost cow and calf. But I think he's too much alone. He doesn't say a whole lot to me except for the necessities. I don't want to lose ground with him." He paused, and when he spoke again, his voice was hoarse. "I don't want to lose him, too."

"I better think on all this," Jason said. "You are working on being sober, and I'll see what I can figure about Miss Graves. Nell might have an idea, if you don't mind my speaking to her about it."

"Not a-tall," Silas said. "She'll be more than pleased to help on that front, I'll wager."

Jason laughed. "Miss Jennie has been a thorn for Nell, Silas. No question about that. But she won't help because she begrudges you your lady friend. She'll help because she wants your family to get back together, if things are right. I reckon you know we're not talking about finishing all this up in a fortnight. Nell will be watching you like a hawk over a chicken yard, you know."

"However long it takes," Silas said, heaving a sigh. "And whatever it takes. I believe my ears have opened up again."

"You'll come in for a spell?" Jason asked as the two men left the chicken house and started up the short slope toward the house.

"No, I reckon Nell and Rose have seen quite enough of me for one day, Jason. I'll be getting on home to see what Charles is up to. He spends a lot of time looking after that new calf, but it has crossed my mind today that I've little idea of what else he does with his time."

"Rose says he makes buildings with his blocks in his room," Jason answered. "Serious buildings. And then draws them. You may have a budding architect there instead of a dairyman." He glanced at Silas and gripped his brother-in-law's shoulder for just a second. "Mebbe you'd join Nell and me for the Grange meeting this week?"

"My welcome there..." Silas began, but Jason interrupted.

"Your welcome there will be all right. It may have shaky moments, but they will pass."

"I'll think on it," Silas said and headed out to his horse and buggy.

CHAPTER SIX
Girl Talk

It wasn't really warm enough to be sitting on a rock, even a rock in the sun, but Rose and Newton had made their way to her favorite place in the woods and were busy telling each other that early March sun made it warm enough for a Saturday afternoon outing. They had seen each other only in school since the box social and the birth of the calf, and even then, he just looked at her back, and she tried not to think about him looking at her back. He was such a distraction from history and arithmetic.

"I want to know what your dream is," Rose said, almost as soon as they sat down.

"Dream?" Newton asked. "I dream different things, different nights. I've already told you, often as not, I dream of you running away from me, and even though I know I can run faster than you can, I never catch up. The only good part," he added mischievously, "is that sometimes you pick up your skirts and I get a glimpse of your ankles."

"Not that dream," Rose said. "That's a nightmare, and it's improper for you to be looking at a lady's ankles. Running away only matters if you are awake. And I haven't run away again, so that's a foolish nightmare. I figure on being a teacher and having a schoolroom all my own, and I've been so wrapped up in my life that I haven't even thought about your dream. You must have one." She looked at him expectantly and was surprised to see that his face was glowing like a lamp with a clean chimney.

"What," she said, "what, what, what?"

"Listen, my child, and you shall hear," Newton teased, knowing that Rose could recite Longfellow poems until the cows came home.

"Of the sudden death of Newton Barnes," she quickly parodied, "on the fifteenth of March in eighty-eight."

"You are being a beast," Newton said, "and as the only man in sight, I reckon I shall have to tame you." She struggled as he pulled her toward him, then gave in so suddenly that he toppled backward, taking Rose with him.

"Some taming," she said, but her laugh was choked off when he pulled her head down and kissed her on the mouth, then on both cheeks, then poked his nose past her scarf and kissed her neck. Rose thought that if she died right then, it would be all right, unless it was wrong for her to be lying on a rock in the woods kissing a boy. She still wasn't quite sure about that and didn't know who to ask. But she reckoned no one went to hell for feeling this good, not even in the Reverend

Lockhead's world. She sighed, pushed herself away, and when Newton tried to stop her, she said, "I'm all tamed. Tell me about your dream."

"Jerseys," he said, sitting up. "The world's best Jerseys."

Cows, Rose thought, he's talking about cows. To her, they had always seemed like the dumbest four-legged creatures around, not moving when you wanted them to move, moving when you didn't want them to, and mooing all the time, not a musical sound at all. Still, not as bad as the kwa-kwa-kwa sound of chickens.

"I don't have a full picture of your dream yet," she said, trying not to be sidetracked by the annoying noise of hens.

He took her hand, removed her mitten and put her bare hand and his into his pocket. "I want a farm of my own like Joshua Chittenden's, and I want to raise Jerseys that are even better than his, and his are on the way to being exceptional," he said. "I want to go to Canada to get two straight from the Isle of Jersey, and Joshua allowed as how I could start at any time if my father permitted me a little barn space."

Rose was almost speechless, but she managed to say, "You went home with him? Did you stay overnight? And where is the Isle of Jersey?"

"I stayed over. And my dream lost its blurry edges and became quite real," Newton said. He squeezed her hand, which was very warm in his pocket. "You can't even imagine what his place is like, the cows so beautiful, every one with a name on her stanchion, the barn so much cleaner than ours, the locust fence posts marching in a straight line along the pasture. And tools—he must have every tool there is, Rose. He has a horse-drawn mower, and he has this special treadmill where a horse walks and creates power to thresh the grain quicker."

"I never thought of a cow as beautiful, but I like fence posts, especially if they're lined up nicely," Rose said. "And I love the idea of cows having names. Tell me one." She jumped as Newton's head flew back and a roar of laughter came from his mouth.

"You still take me by surprise," he said, still laughing. "One of the cows is called Thankful, apparently a Puritan girl. And Miss Harty is going to hand me a hangman's noose, loop first, if we stay here much longer."

"Dead twice in one day," Rose said, removing her hand from his and swinging her feet off the rock. "It's what happens to people who go about without chaperones. You didn't say, by the way, where this Jersey place is. Not New Jersey, I suppose."

"Near England," Newton said.

"So they have to travel by boat, these cows?" Rose asked in astonishment. She was accustomed to farmers walking their cows down the road from barn to pasture or leading one that had been sold. But she'd never thought of a cow on a boat.

"Indeed," Newton said, pushing away thoughts of Chittenden's farm. "And we really must get a move on." Sure enough, the curtain on Miss Harty's front window shimmered a bit as they approached, so they knew she had been looking for them. At the front door, Newton was so close behind her that Rose felt the now-familiar tingle again, but the feeling vanished as if cut by a butcher knife when Miss Harty opened the door and asked where in the world they had been.

"To my rock, Ma'am," Rose said, knowing that Miss Harty had been there with Alice the day Rose had gone to the cemetery to talk to her mother. "We tried out the March sun." And then, seeing the teacher's frown, she quickly added, "And we behaved as if we had a congregation of chaperones around us."

"Almost," Newton added, thinking he wouldn't have much liked that kiss if pews of people had been lined up behind him.

That made the teacher laugh. Then she held up a folded sheet of paper and said Newton had a letter from Mr. Chittenden and was he of a mind to read it in the kitchen or take it home. Rose, anxious to know what was in the letter, even though she knew it was none of her business, realized that Newton's letter had no envelope, so it must have come along with one for Miss Harty. Perhaps Joshua Chittenden really was sweet on her.

"I have not presumed to read it, Newton," Miss Harty said in her most schoolmarmish tone, leading the way to the kitchen table.

They pulled out chairs, and Newton unfolded the single sheet, and Rose watched as his eyes flew down the page; saw him start to smile. "It's an invitation," he said excitedly, "an invitation to spend a fortnight at Joshua's farm, helping him out and learning more about his Jersey cows. And he has also written my father to ask if he will allow me to go."

Newton looked up, his pleased expression fading. "It's getting on toward the busy time for us," he said. "Another week of school, then knocking down our winter manure pile and fixing fences will be added to my chores." He sighed. "That pile is so high now that we have to roll the wheelbarrow up a plank to get to the top."

"No need to borrow trouble, Newton," the teacher said. "See what your father has to say."

Rose could not imagine why anyone would borrow trouble. Better to borrow happiness, since trouble seemed to barge in naturally without anyone looking for extra. Then she realized what the invitation meant. It would put Newton on a path to his dream. She knew his father only by sight. They had nodded to each other when she was working at Mr. Goodnow's store, and he looked pleasant, not fierce and unsmiling like hers. Without thinking about Miss Harty being right there, she jumped up and grabbed Newton's arm with both hands, pumping it up and down.

"It's your dream," she cried. "It's your dream coming into the real world, like a chick cracking through the eggshell and starting a new part of its life." She let go when she saw Newton's eyes slide toward the teacher and back to her, but she didn't stop talking. "He will let you go, he will. Miss Harty will help. Please?" she asked, turning to the teacher.

"I can't pressure a farmer who is facing a mountain of manure, broken barbed wire and spring planting," Miss

Harty said, "but Mr. Barnes is likely to consider this carefully. He tends to be a fair man."

"I'd better get on home and see what he has to say," Newton said. "I reckon it's better if he doesn't think on it for too long before we talk about it." He rose, nodded to Miss Harty, and bent quickly to give Rose a kiss on the cheek. "I will let you know what the verdict is," and he was gone.

Rose felt her face flush. She couldn't believe Newton had just dropped that kiss on her right in front of the teacher. What was he thinking? What would the teacher think? She looked up and found Miss Harty watching her, a small smile on her face.

"You two are very close, aren't you, Rose," Ruthann Harty said. "I have no idea what you know about boys and girls and kissing, but I think it's time we had a talk about these things. Unless your mother already did all that."

"She only told me about menstruation," Rose said, her face feeling even hotter. "I know mothers carry babies in their bellies, if that's what you are getting at. It's the same as cows and cats and horses. People must mate too, I reckon."

"Do you want to talk about these things, Rose, or shall I mind my own business? Perhaps you'd rather go to Aunt Nell. I happen to think a girl your age should know about these things, but your aunt could feel otherwise. Some people believe girls have no need to know anything until the night before the wedding, and some don't figure on ever talking about it."

Girl Talk

"I only talk to Aunt Nell about darning socks and my mother and why cakes sometimes come out with a volcano crater in the middle," Rose said, her eyes on a small knot in the wooden tabletop. "I have been wondering about some things, whether they were sinful or not, and I didn't want to ask Emily."

"Sinful?" Miss Harty exclaimed, looking startled. She hitched her chair closer to Rose, smoothed her hair, and took a deep breath. "Perhaps," she went on more gently, "you trust me enough to tell me about those things so we can judge whether they are sinful or not. You are right not to ask Emily because she may not have proper answers for you, and I would suggest you not talk to the Reverend Lockhead about such questions of sin."

"Oh, I couldn't," Rose said, tracing the knot on the table with her index finger and still not looking up. "His words are full of g-o-d."

"God?" asked Ruthann.

"Gloom or doom," Rose said.

The teacher started to laugh. "He is pretty gloomy and doomy," she said. "I'll grant you that. So let's get at these wonderings of yours, shall we?"

"Kissing," Rose said, finally looking up. "Not like that kiss just now, which I know was out of place, but real kissing. When Newton kisses me on the mouth for a long time, I just want to get as close to him as I can get and stay there, kissing him back and tingling all over. Is it wrong?"

"Kissing, Rose, is lovely," Miss Harty said. "I think you caught me and Joshua kissing the other night in the

71

parlor. Is that the kind of kissing you mean?"

"Yes," Rose said softly, back to watching the knot in the tabletop.

"The problem is, Rose, that humans have both brains and bodies. Your brain may say that you will kiss Newton on the mouth with your lips pressed together, and your body will be craving more."

"He kissed me on the neck today," Rose whispered. "Was that part of the more?"

"Possibly. But your mouths also might open, and when your tongues touch, it's a whole new experience. It's more passionate, and it's hard to go back to simple, sweet kisses. You may feel all tingly as you put it, and you may like that feeling, but Newton's body will be responding in a much greater way, and you will have to be the one to pull away and say no."

"Say no to what?" Rose asked.

"Say no to kissing over and over for, say, a half hour or more, say no to lying down next to him, on a rock or a bed or the grass, say no to letting him touch you, say no to taking off any of your clothing, say no to serious lovemaking."

"He does touch me," Rose said.

"Where?" the teacher asked, frowning and immediately wondering if she had gone too far.

"On the face, the arms, the shoulders," Rose answered, feeling as guilty as if she'd been caught taking coins from Miss Harty's jewelry case. "Around the waist," she added.

"Nothing wrong, or sinful if you want to put it that

way, about any of that, Rose. I meant more private places on your body, places that might make tingles into earthquakes."

"Oh, no," Rose said. "Newton would never do that. I wouldn't want that."

"What I am trying to tell you in my perhaps awkward way—this is an awkward topic, you understand—is that while girls are expected to say no, boys sometimes rush on. Some say boys can't stop, but I am of the school that thinks they can, they must and they will, if they respect the girl they are with. The fact is that once you have kissed, you won't go back to just holding hands. Once you have hugged, you won't want to stand apart and peck at each other like a hen looking for an ort of grain in the henhouse litter."

"I must be too young for this," Rose said suddenly.

"Perhaps," Miss Harty said. "But Newton isn't. He's seventeen, nearly eighteen, he does a man's work at his father's place, and he seems quite enamored of you. He is also one of the nicest boys I've ever had in a classroom, and I think you might even bring yourself to tell him about our conversation if the need arises."

"He wouldn't stay in the kitchen that day you sent him with my schoolwork," Rose remembered suddenly. "He said we didn't have a chaperone, and his mother told him never to be alone with a lady without a chaperone. I thought it was very funny, but I grabbed a wrap and stepped outside with him because he looked like a deer about to run."

"There you are," Miss Harty said, laughing out loud

this time. "I must say he seems a trifle obsessed with chaperones, but he's well brought up. But you are the one who says no."

"I think Newton can say no, too," Rose said. "I think he should."

"It seems he's not like every other boy or man," Miss Harty said, "so perhaps you're right."

"Thank you, Miss Harty," Rose said. "I reckon if you have no other chores for me that I'd better get at that wood stove. It could use some polishing, and the ashes are so deep that it's hard to keep the coals alive."

Following Rose's need to get away from the boy-girl subject, Miss Harty answered quickly, "If you take out ashes, Rose, remember to carry them out-of-doors. The tiniest hot coal can live a long time, festering under the surface like a carbuncle until it gets a chance to erupt."

"Yes, Miss Harty," Rose said. "I'm not of a mind to burn the house down. But I wish you hadn't said carbuncle. It's an ugly word for an ugly thing, and now it's in my mind."

"And, by the way, Rose, why does a cake sometimes have a crater in the center?" Without waiting for an answer, Ruthann Harty patted Rose's arm and said she would be in her room, catching up on her mending. As she left the kitchen, she heard Rose shaking the grate in the stove and getting ready to take out the extra ashes.

CHAPTER SEVEN
Rubies and Cows

A fortnight later, Rose was at Emily's for Saturday night baked beans, and Ruthann was once again thinking about a meal for one and realizing she had become pleasantly accustomed to having Rose's company across the kitchen table. She wondered if Rose would tell Emily about the kissing talk. There was a girl who would relish hearing it all but who had probably not ever kissed a boy. Certainly not Peter Granger, although the teacher had noticed that he was often looking at Emily in school these days. And that she wasn't looking back.

The sun was about gone, but the days were getting steadily longer, and Ruthann liked that. Pretty soon little spears of her narcissus would poke their sharp tips through mats of fallen leaves, but she'd leave them be until she was as certain as a body could be that the snow was done with. She'd wait even longer before clearing the winter mess away from the phlox and lily of the valley. It was hard not to just dash into the garden on April Fool's Day and clean it up, but that would leave tender shoots unprotected from spring frosts. It had taken her longer to learn garden patience than classroom patience, but she felt she had now mastered both.

She was losing patience, however, with Joshua Chittenden. It had been two weeks—no, three—since she had seen him, and she had received the one letter but no more. He had written a proper thank you for the box social supper, which made her feel a little guilty, since she hadn't made the chicken. He reported that his water pipes were frozen when he reached home the day after the social, and he wrote about the arrival of a new calf. Ruthann's excitement about the missive was on a downhill slide until she turned the page over and saw the last line: "You warm my heart, Ruthann, as nothing and no one else has ever done." He signed the letter quite formally: "Faithfully yours, Joshua Chittenden, Esq."

Esquire, indeed. She knew he had a law degree and was certain her father would be unable to comprehend why an educated lawyer had decided on Jerseys instead of court cases. Still, what came right before the stiff ending was more than she had expected. She didn't know how many times she had reread the letter, but now she was thinking she should have received another telling her when he would like to visit again. The question of marriage, after all, had not been answered by her, although she had practiced various ways, including "yes" and "of course" and "I would like to marry you and you need to ask my father." Sometimes she had even practiced in front of the looking glass to see what her various answers looked like. "Yes" automatically came with a smile. "I will" looked more doleful. When she tried a curtsey and a "yes, sir," she decided she looked plain silly. Some days she felt let down and convinced herself that he really wasn't interested in courting her at all and that she was no longer heating up his heart. Then she would be forced to remind herself that she had failed to answer his letter.

A knock on the back door interrupted her mental wanderings, and before she could get there, the knob turned and Joshua Chittenden stepped in. "Surprise!" he said, as he leaned down to unlace and remove his heavy boots. "Ready for a buggy ride at sunset, or can you give me a bite first?"

Discarding the idea that her brain had conjured him up, Ruthann did not hesitate. She all but ran to him, giving him barely enough time to spread his arms and take her in. "I'll give you a bite," she said, nibbling at his neck. And then she turned her face up for a kiss.

"Worth the trip," Joshua said when she pulled away. "Even without food." His hands slipped down her back, pulling her even closer. "Just tell me one thing. Are people about to knock on the front door or come barreling down the stairs, or are we the only ones in the house?"

"Just us," Ruthann said and kissed him again. This man stirred her, too, in a way she had never felt before, and while she often lay awake at night thinking about turning thirty, he made her feel as giddy as an eighteen-year-old.

"Ah," he said, "no chaperones." But instead of holding her, he gently pushed her away, took her hand, and led her to a kitchen chair. He took off his coat and hung it on a hook by the door, then pulled up another chair, facing her. He took both her hands in his and stared at her for several seconds. Their knees were touching, through his thick pants and her petticoats, and it occurred to Ruthann that she had never given enough consideration to the nature of knees. It was a good thing he had seated her or she might have melted into a heap.

"When you ask questions in school, Ruthann, do the children give answers?"

"Of course," she said puzzled. "If they know them. And sometimes when they don't."

"Last time I was here, I asked you a question. Then your friend Rose arrived, and there was no time for an answer. Even the next day, when we met at church, you gave me no answer. I have not had a decent night's sleep since, so the horse brought me here today to settle me down. Do you remember the question?"

"Yes," Ruthann Harty said in a very small voice. " I remember it well."

"Do you have a correct answer, Miss Harty?"

"I think so," she said.

"Then, land alive, Miss Teacher, recite it so I can either stay or go!" he exclaimed.

"Yes," she said. "Oh, yes. Definitely yes," forgetting all her practiced answers and wondering if he was going to leap into the air. He did seem quite set up about it all.

Instead, he just grinned, reached his arms around her, and without getting up, lifted her from her chair to his lap, the light wool fabric of her dress all but covering his pant legs. "You have made me the happiest man this side of Boston," he crowed, "or maybe even the other side, too. But I haven't asked your father for your hand, you know."

"Never mind the hand," Ruthann said in a saucy tone, suddenly feeling less anxious and more confident. "Just consider the lips." And he did.

A few minutes later, Joshua reached into his shirt pocket and pulled out a small box. He opened it, took out a ring with a small ruby set inside six small pinkish-gold prongs, and reached for her left hand.

"I will need a hand, even without parental permission," he said. "Along with whatever other body parts you are willing to share," he added with a hint of mischief in his voice. He put the ring on her finger and added, "It's your birthstone, and I liked it, and all my diamond money is in Jerseys right now."

She laughed. "I think it's beautiful, although it's a mite troubling to place lower than a herd of cows. As for my father, he no doubt will be pleased to be rid of me, since I'm sure he's already concluded I'm to be the maiden lady of the family. He's a far piece from here, so you might just write to him. He doesn't have to know we've put the cart before the horse. She paused and added, "But even if no one is going to appear from the upper regions, we are not sharing any more body parts."

"Sorry," Joshua said. "I was involved in the metaphor."

"Is that what they call it these days?" the teacher asked. "I think it's time to take that buggy ride."

"Food," Joshua said. "First a little food for a famished suitor."

Ruthann quickly cut thick slices of bread, fetched three slices of cold roast from the pantry, and set the plate on the table, along with a jar of her homemade pepper relish, the butter dish, forks, knives, and two plates. She provided a fresh napkin for Joshua, took her own out of its silver ring, and sat to enjoy a supper with someone across the table from her, someone so special she could hardly keep her mind on her food and wasn't at all sure her stomach would welcome it.

His eyebrows went up, but he didn't say anything when she gave a small laugh as she cleared the table. She was thinking about his metaphor. With her back to him, she spread the fingers of her left hand below the edge of the sink so he would not see, and admired the ring. They might indeed get back to metaphors, in time. Or perhaps sooner.

Outdoor clothes on, they went out to the yard where Joshua's horse was waiting and clambered onto the buggy seat. He flicked the reins, and they set off, cozy under a heavy quilt he produced from under the seat.

"Should have warmed this in the house," he muttered, "but I was in a hurry to knock on your door. It's been a long time. Can we get married soon?"

"I want to finish the school year," she said, even

though she would have liked to say, "Would tomorrow do?"

"Of course you do, Ruthann. And I reckon you'll miss that classroom in the fall, but they won't let you go back, will they?"

"Married women cannot teach in this state," Ruthann said. "It's hard to know what the thinking behind that law might be, but there it is."

"Not so hard. They don't want teachers up there with their bellies swelling by the month and children asking questions and the teacher having to explain about having babies."

"Not everyone who gets married has a baby right away," Ruthann protested.

"But you're not against the idea, are you?" Joshua said, taking the reins in one hand and putting his other arm around her.

"Of having a child? Of course not. Or even several," Ruthann said. "But it is foolishness. All these farm children know where babies come from, even if they don't know the details. They would hardly be embarrassed by having a teacher grow a baby in the classroom."

"It's the details that interest me most," Joshua said, laughing. "But when you said yes, you were saying yes to giving up teaching, becoming a farmer's wife and getting your hands all calloused and rough?"

"All but the hands," Ruthann said. "I'll be slathering them with potions of the best sort to avoid cracks, redness, calluses, blisters, and other unsightly problems."

Joshua stopped the buggy, put one foot on the reins

and pulled her close. "I do love you, Ruthann, your mind and your heart and your body, the smart and the funny and the niceness of you. And you are grand to just look at, with the setting sun making your face glow. But this isn't the time for just window shopping." With that, he pulled off his gloves, held her face and kissed her for what seemed a long time, starting with a tenderness that almost made her dizzy and building to an intensity that she felt all the way to her toes. When his lips parted and his tongue touched her lips, she drew back for only a second, then returned to him, meeting his tongue with hers, then making a circle of his lips with her tongue, carefully not entering his mouth and not letting him enter hers.

She heard him give a little moan, and she quickly buried her face in the scarf he wore around his neck. Rose, Rose, Rose, she repeated to herself. Hadn't she only a few days ago given Rose all that sage advice about saying no? Then she felt his mouth on her neck where he had worried her scarf out of the way and reached warm skin, and they clung to each other that way for several minutes.

"Know all about birds and bees, boys and girls," she heard him mumble. "Never hurt a one of them."

"None of them is here," Ruthann said. "I am not bird, bee, boy nor girl, nor am I afraid you'll hurt me. But my inner voice says it's time to move along, and Lettie's been stamping her feet and tossing her head for several minutes, so she thinks so, too."

"I cannot fight two females at once," Joshua said. He

kissed her lightly on the cheek, picked up the reins, and clicked his tongue at the horse. As the buggy started to move, he said, "What about August? It's after the first hay crop is in and before we need to cut the rowan."

"There I am again," Ruthann laughed, feeling as if her feet had just thudded to the ground. "Wedged between one field of hay and the next. But yes, August is fine. If my father says you may have my hand."

"I'm going to ask him for all of you. A hand is of little use without the rest."

"Use, use? You are not supposed to be using me. You are supposed to be marrying me. I have never been used and don't propose to be now," Ruthann said, her tone suddenly quite serious.

"It's going to be a trial, I can see, being married to the schoolmarm and forever getting my vocabulary right," Joshua sighed. "I should have taken rhetoric at Dartmouth instead of constitutional law. I won't use you. I'd rather you be Abigail and I'll be John, and we'll be partners, not king and subject."

"I will give you my hand on that," Ruthann said. "But I'll want you at home a whole sight more than John Adams was."

CHAPTER EIGHT
A New Tutor

The sun must at least be rubbing her eyes by now, Rose thought as she slipped out the door of Miss Harty's house early one Monday, but she'd better rise and get about the business of melting the last bits of snow. Rose had decided long ago that the sun must be female because it was females who made things warm. And besides, everyone always talked about the man in the moon, so the sun should be a woman, and even if the men never say so, much of the day revolves around women. She guessed Reverend Lockhead would not agree with that. He was always talking about men and their responsibilities, and he certainly referred to God as He. Religion appeared to be a male world, but Rose knew all too well that home was a female world. Hadn't her own fallen apart almost as soon as her mother died?

She knew her mother had been the center of their lives. But it was also because Miss Jennie Graves had entered the scene. She sometimes thought of it as a play, her mother exiting tragically, Miss Graves entering from the other side of the stage, she and Abby taking their leave. But plays have endings, Rose thought, and she could see no ending for this. She did not like to think about Miss Graves. The very sight of the woman made her angry, and she wondered if what she felt was hate. She didn't remember hating anyone or anything except parsnips, which she thought were too pale and slimy to be put on a plate.

She's worse than parsnips, Rose thought, as she kept her eyes on the line of trees where the sun would soon pop out of bed. Well, of course she was. You can't compare a person to a parsnip, although Miss Graves was certainly as pale as one, but not as stringy. Rose's anger ebbed, and she almost laughed as she considered Jennie Graves' connection to parsnips. Perhaps, she hoped, as she continued toward her father's house, Miss Graves would make her exit once spring came and went. That was exactly what parsnips did. They never ate them in midsummer or fall. You are getting more and more crazed, Rose told herself, and started concentrating on her morning mission. She was on her way to make a surprise breakfast for Charles, and she reckoned her father would welcome that as well, although she wasn't much interested in his appetites of late. She had Charles' clean shirt folded under her arm and the mended sock in her pocket. That was clean, too, but she wondered about its partner. Her father's stocking had been so grimy that she thought he must have worn it for days. She had better check Charles' room and make certain he at least had clean clothes.

As she arrived at the Hibbard house, she saw her father heading for the barn and knew she had thirty minutes or more to see to things in the kitchen. She immediately noticed that Charles had left no soiled dishes in the sink and that Father had stoked the fire in the wood stove and moved the kettle onto one of the hot lids. At least some things were in their rightful places.

She found the oats and started the oatmeal, stirring rapidly so it would have no lumpy bits at all. As she worked, she thought about how different this kitchen was from Miss Harty's. Same black wood stove, same wide-board wood floor. But the teacher's sink was dark soapstone, quite handsome and easy to clean. Father had pieced together slate for the Hibbard sink. The teacher had elegant kerosene lamps, some with big white globes that seemed to spread the light, while this kitchen was lit by a single lamp with a glass chimney. Rose had never thought about how dark Sarah's kitchen was until today. While she fixed the coffee, her mother's cat rubbed against her left leg, went between her feet and rubbed the outside of her right leg. She took the time to pet the cat and felt herself getting teary when the animal started to purr. She did love the cat. But she straightened up, put two slices of bread on the toaster, and went upstairs with the shirt and the sock. She stepped around some dirty clothes Father seemed to be piling on the floor and left the sock on his unmade bed. Without even glancing at her old room, she went up the attic stairs to see if Charles was stirring.

As she stepped into the room, he sat up, startled. "What in thunderation are you doing here?" he demanded. Then, rubbing his eyes, he added, "Or perhaps you are a nightmare?"

"A vision, Charles, a vision," Rose answered, laughing. "Here's your shirt, get up, the oatmeal is cooking, no lumps. And I am about to disappear into today's sunshine. That's what visions do." She turned to go, but Charles jumped out of bed and threw his arms around her.

"You are real," he said. "I can tell. I know you won't come back to stay, but I would trade my calf for you."

"Cows stand in a much higher place than they should, to my way of thinking," Rose answered. "You and Mr. Chittenden and Newton. All besotted by bovines." And seeing his puzzled look, she added loftily, "Bovine hasn't come to your vocabulary list yet, but it will walk in soon, on four feet with a swishing tail and manure on its legs."

Charles groaned. "Stop it, Rose, just stop it. You know I don't think of you as first or second to a cow."

She relented. "I know that, and I'm leaving anyway. And don't say thunderation. That's for grown men only." And she was gone, running down the two flights of stairs so lightly that he barely heard her feet. She's always talking about her big feet, Charles thought, but they are very quiet on stairs and they float about like butterflies when she's square dancing. She is a wonder, and I will have to just keep praying that she will come back. I can't leave here. Father needs me, even if he doesn't know that. And now there's the calf. Uh-oh—not as important as

Rose. Newton better watch it, Charles thought, grinning to himself as he scrambled for his clothes. He was talking a good deal lately about Jersey cows, and it appeared Rose might be touchy about sharing space with critters. He pulled on his shirt as he hurtled down the stairs, hoping to catch Rose for another second or two.

But he was not quick enough. He heard her leave by the side door just as Father's barn boots thunked onto the floor outside the kitchen door. He was carefully admiring the smooth kettle of oatmeal when Silas Hibbard came in.

"You're up and about right early today," Silas said. Charles stirred the cereal and glanced at the table, which was already neatly set. Rose had been busy down here while he caught a few extra winks, he thought.

"Rose came, Father," he said, deciding that he'd better not take credit for what she had done. Dangerous, letting someone think you had done a good thing. Easy to trip on that later, Charles had learned.

"Did she indeed. Life would be a mite easier if she came every day, Charles, but that's not to be, at least not now. Mebbe not ever," Silas said. "Miss her, I expect?"

"Yes, Father," Charles said, thinking the talk had taken an odd turn. Father was more likely to be silent in the morning than conversational. He decided to proceed with caution, as if an underground wasp nest were in his path. "Rose's oatmeal has no lumps a-tall."

Silas chuckled at that, and Charles turned to look at him, still worrying that he was about to get stung. He noticed with surprise that his father's eyes were clear and his mouth twitching with amusement, two things that had rarely happened since Rose left. Or even before that, come to think of it.

"Are you ready for breakfast, sir?" Charles asked, still apprehensive about this turn of events.

"More than ready, boy," Silas said. "I could eat a horse."

"Not a good idea, sir," Charles said, wondering if he was a fool to take a small risk here. "Especially if you only have one."

That brought a near guffaw from Silas, who reached for the nearly filled bowl of oatmeal and took his place at the table. He poured a little milk on the cereal, added some maple syrup, and extracted a large spoon from the glass holder that always stood on the table.

"Your sense of humor seems to be in good health, young man," he said, shoveling a large spoonful of the steaming oatmeal into his mouth. "Time to tell you I am turning over a new leaf," he said gruffly, no longer looking at Charles. "High time I did. Going to be right here in the evening, seeing to your schoolwork and reading the newspaper. A boy your age bears some watching, I reckon, and I'll be taking that on, too. You've been too much on your own since Rose left."

"I figure I've been doing all right, Father," Charles said, hesitantly.

"Didn't say you weren't. Just meant I am going to be here, not gallivanting about at the hotel."

"It will be good not to be alone," Charles said. Getting a little bolder, he went on, "But you'll have to get another rocking chair for the kitchen. I've become quite accustomed to doing my schoolwork in the one, keeping my feet warm by the open oven door."

He's laughing again, Charles thought, staring at his father in wonder. Twice—well three times if you count the chuckle—since dawn. He's not terrifying today. It's as if Mother is back. But she's not.

"Another rocker will crowd things a bit, but we can't have you getting cold feet, young man," Silas said. Then he went back to his cereal, concentrating in his usual manner on the food, both arms on the table and his face bent toward the bowl. A few orts of oatmeal caught on his bushy moustache and were then washed away when he took a large gulp of coffee and licked his upper lip.

Charles put his napkin in his lap, kept his left hand on it, and raised his spoon to his mouth the way his mother and Rose had insisted he eat. Neither of them, he thought, liked the way Father ate, but they didn't give him any correction. Maybe even Mother hadn't quite dared that.

He finished his breakfast, then decided to take one last risk before grabbing his lunch pail and setting off for school. "You know, sir, I think..." He paused.

"Think what?" Silas prompted.

"Think you... think Rose... think you'd have to get at installing that piping and toilet before she'd take to sleeping here again, sir. To live here, I mean. Sir."

"She's cottoned to that real bathroom at the teacher's house, I guess. Well, hard to blame her. Chamber pots are useful but not elegant, and that privy is a mighty cold place to set yourself in January."

"And it smells bad, Father. Sometimes when you empty a slop jar in there, it roils up a powerful bad smell," Charles said, his nose turning up at the very thought.

Silas guffawed again. "Hold your nose when pouring, boy, hold your nose. And I will think on the toilet. With the running water already in the house, it should be done, and done before we get into planting and haying. Now get along with you. I'll see to the chickens today. Dishes, too, by the look of things."

Charles nodded, put on his jacket and picked up his lunch pail and books. He thought he'd better skedaddle while the going was good. Wait till he told Rose what a couple of cupfuls of oats had done today. He whistled as he walked up to the road and set off for the schoolhouse. Planting and haying would come all too soon, and he wondered if Father would take him out of school early. Some ways he wouldn't mind, but he'd miss seeing Rose, and he was certain he'd need considerable schooling if he was ever going to design buildings for other people. Still, Abby's one-room school was almost across the road, so he could get at least a glimpse of his little sister at recess. He sighed. Life had been a lot simpler before the woodpile fell on Mother.

Silas nodded with some satisfaction after Charles left. Roils, Silas said to himself as he picked up his cereal bowl, the stink roils out of the pit is what the boy said. Sarah must have taught him that word. He guessed he could take a minute to sit in the lone rocker and think about the business of creating a bathroom with a flush toilet.

He had been putting off the toilet project because he hadn't seen his way clear on location. Now he decided the easiest way was to make over the back hall where they came in, just above the milk room. It was already enclosed and wasn't that far from the pipes that came into the kitchen. The unheated privy was at the far end. At one time it had stood alone, and even now, it was only a bridge-like passage that led to it.

He grunted, thinking that the cleaning of that pit would be neither easy nor pleasant. Charles might not last through the first few shovels if he was so delicate about emptying a slop jar. But if Jason was right, Charles might have an idea about how to lay it all out. Architect indeed. Was the boy going to be another education problem like Rose? He supposed he should think more on them being smart and less about their worth as farmers. He reckoned neither would take to farming on a lifelong basis. Still, the way Rose looked at Newton and the way the lad looked at her, she might end up a farmer's wife yet. Not quite old enough to get married, but not far from it, he thought. He hoped that teacher woman was a proper chaperone for those two, but he wasn't about to ask. Ruthann Harty made him feel as if he were seven years old and standing to recite without any answers in his head.

At the schoolhouse, Newton was already in his seat when Rose came in, and she felt her face redden as she walked toward him, but she pulled a small smile from

A New Tutor

somewhere inside her brain and quickly slipped into her seat without speaking. From across the room, Alice was grinning like Lewis Carroll's ridiculous cat, and Rose focused on her inkwell, knowing that her face and neck were now close to the color of beet juice. When she felt the end of Newton's pen pull on her long, single braid, she twitched her shoulders in reply and heard the ever-attentive Peter Granger give a little snort from the back of the room.

"Quiet, please," Miss Harty said, turning away from the blackboard where she was writing the date in her beautiful hand. Unerringly, she looked straight at the older Granger boy. She knew his repertoire of sounds by heart and was about to reprimand him when she remembered her plan to give him more responsibilities and see what that might bring. After all, he was sixteen and apparently cared enough about school to keep coming in the late fall and winter months.

"Mr. Granger," she began, "I would like you to hear the lower level readers today, one by one. You may do this out in the hall where it won't disturb the classroom. Each one should read four or five pages, and they must repeat anything they get wrong. The students are Ethan, Mary, Ida, and John. Take them in any order you wish."

The teacher almost smiled when she heard a small shuffle in Emily's area and saw the astonished look on Peter Granger's face. It took him a couple of seconds to unfold his tall body from his chair and start toward the front of the room, his boots clumping on the oiled wood floor. "I will begin with John," he said gravely, reaching for the text Miss Harty was holding out. "Am I to ask them questions, or just hear them read?"

Surprised in her turn, Miss Harty agreed that questions were in order. "Then you'll know if they understand what they have read. Thank you, Peter."

She turned to the rest of the class as the two boys went out and announced that she had only one copy of a new book by an American author named Mark Twain, so the older readers would take turns reading the story aloud. She explained that the author was using the Twain name but was really Samuel Langhorne Clemens and asked if anyone knew the word that applied to authors who wrote under a name that wasn't their real one.

"Pseudonym," she said, when no hands went up. She wrote it on the board and added "pen name" beneath it. "In this writer's case," she said, "the phrase mark twain is a riverboat term about water depths, and Clemens spent many hours working on the boats that ply the Mississippi River. Who can spell Mississippi?"

Several hands shot up, and Miss Harty called on Emily, who stood by her desk and managed all the esses and pees in the troublesome word. "Please remain standing, Emily," Miss Harty said, "and begin the book for us. You will start with the title page. When you have finished four pages, you may pass the book to Mr. Barnes."

Emily always reads as if she is standing in front of a congregation, Rose thought. Every word is perfect, and she uses so much expression that you just know she understands what she is reading. Rose had seen the new book at Miss Harty's and had riffled through the pages. She had skipped around, reading here and there, and had laughed aloud at some of the things Tom did to torment his aunt. She had some things in common with Tom. His mother was dead, and his mother's sister had taken him in, just as Aunt Nell was letting Abby stay with her. But she and Abby were so well behaved that Tom would probably have disliked them, just the way he disliked the perfect boy in the book. When Emily finished her section and passed the book to Newton, Miss Harty wrote "sagacity" on the blackboard and "get my dander up" and then asked Newton to come to the front of the room to read. Rose could not take her eyes off his face as he read the story of Tom tricking his friends into whitewashing his aunt's fence so he wouldn't have to do it. He is even better than Emily, she thought, as the class laughed when Tom traded time on the fence for yet another horrid treasure.

"Whitewash" went on the board, followed by "philosopher" and "jew's-harp," and Rose realized Miss Harty was creating a whole new vocabulary list from this book. At least the story is fine, she thought, hoping the book would be back in the house for the night so she could read on ahead of the class.

All eyes turned toward the classroom door as John came in, apologized to Miss Harty for interrupting, and said Ida was wanted in the hall. His face was flushed, and the teacher had a moment of wondering if she had created a tyrant teacher. Following Ida out, she asked Peter if everything was all right, and he grinned. "John had some rough spots, but we squared them," he said. "And he understands the story."

Miss Harty retreated, satisfied that the experiment was going well, and an hour later, Peter came back with the fourth pupil and announced that they had all finished to his satisfaction. "Would there be anything else, Ma'am?" he asked.

"You may take your own turn at reading now, Peter, up front here," Miss Harty said. "Alice will show you the place. Before you begin, perhaps Rose could summarize what has happened so far in this book. Take a moment to think, Rose, because you need to be brief."

Quickly, Rose stood and explained the basic plot of *The Adventures of Tom Sawyer* so Peter and his new pupils could pick up the thread. Miss Harty nodded her approval, and Rose sat down again, feeling the tip of Newton's pen once again digging into her braid. She wondered what would happen if she suddenly turned around and kissed him on the mouth, and the very thought made her clap her hand over her own mouth.

"Are you ill, Rose?" Miss Harty asked.

"No, Ma'am," Rose answered quickly, starting to redden again and thinking that this teacher was just like a mother, seeing or hearing absolutely everything. "I thought I was about to cough."

Miss Harty frowned, knowing the answer was not on the mark, but deciding to ignore the matter. She told Peter to read the rest of the chapter that had been started by Alice, and was pleased when he read quite well. As she took the book back from him, she asked the class how they felt about this new story.

Peter turned on his way to his seat and said, "I would have been thrashed several times in just those few pages, so it's a wonderment to me how this boy is going to live till the end of the book, Ma'am."

Miss Harty called on Alice, who said she was taken aback by Tom Sawyer's lies to his aunt, and the way he disappeared from the house at various times and the way he sassed adults. "My parents would have me locked in my room," she said.

"They talk like real folks," Rose said when it was her turn. "It's not unbelievable, like when Alice—not our Alice, but the book one—gets smaller or bigger whenever she wants to and goes down rabbit holes and meets queens. Tom is very naughty, but he seems real, Miss Harty."

Satisfied that the Mark Twain experiment was going to work, Miss Harty moved on to her announcement that at least two, and perhaps more, of the boys in the room would no longer be in class after today. "Some will be taking time off to help with plowing and planting at home. It doesn't look much like spring out there, but it's in the air. I would appreciate it if all those who are not coming to school for the rest of this year would please stand."

With feet scraping around the room, Peter, Newton, and five other boys, including both of Peter's brothers, stood. Miss Harty started to clap her hands, and the rest of the class immediately joined in.

"You may get your lunch pails now, one row at a time," Miss Harty said, "and once we have all finished lunch, we'll call it a day." The entire class applauded that idea, even though each child knew it only meant more time to do chores at home. The first row set off for the cloakroom, making more noise than usual as they chatted about the short day.

"I'm going to Joshua's for the fortnight," Newton whispered to Rose, his voice covered by the noise in the room. "Father gave his permission, and Joshua is coming tomorrow to fetch me because Father couldn't spare a horse for two weeks."

Rose turned in her chair, dismay all over her face. "Two weeks?" she said. "I know Joshua sent an invitation for a fortnight, but you might well learn about Jersey cows faster than that."

Newton started to laugh. "I can't learn it all in a year," he said. "But I aim to try."

They were interrupted by the teacher's voice reminding them that it was their turn to get their lunches. As Peter Granger went past the teacher's desk, he paused, shifting his weight from one foot to the other and waiting for her to look up.

"Yes, Peter?" Miss Harty said.

"I was wondering, Ma'am," he said, not looking at her, "I was wondering... if my pa gives permission, could I come back at the noon hour or thereabouts and hear those four read? Ma'am?"

Miss Harty stood, a wide smile on her face. "I would

be pleased to have you, Peter. It must have gone well."

"Some pleasure in watching them start to get it right," he mumbled, his eyes on the floor. "Not the same as walking behind a plow. Ma'am."

"I expect you like the plowing as well," Miss Harty said. "It's such an orderly thing, putting the weeds under and making the whole field look fresh."

"I hadn't thought of it that way," Peter admitted, finally looking at her. "It's not bad when you're done."

Not bad, the teacher thought. He couldn't say it looked fine. Just not bad. She hoped Joshua Chittenden didn't have that phrase in his lexicon. As she let herself think about Joshua, she had a moment of envy for Newton, who would be with him for two weeks. She wondered if she might join them over a Saturday and Sunday. Was Newton considered acceptable as a chaperone? Probably not. And even if he were, she wasn't certain of her own ability to control her farmer—nor herself, for all that. She was having alternate feelings of relief and anxiety now that she was quite certain he was far more passionate about her than he was about Jersey cows.

Ruthann Harty pushed thoughts of Joshua aside, watched everyone eat, and then dismissed them. She tucked the Twain book under her arm and headed for the door. Outside, she found Newton Barnes and Rose waiting on the steps.

"I was wondering, Miss Harty, if you wanted to send any kind of message to Joshua. I will be off early tomorrow and not back for a fortnight," Newton began.

"You could deliver the letter I wrote him last evening," Miss Harty said. "I was going to post it this afternoon, so that would be a great favor to me. Have you time to fetch it now at my house?"

Newton nodded, and the three started down the road toward the teacher's small house. They were silent at first, enjoying the warming air and the smell of spring. Rose broke the spell as they passed Chandlers' field, where the few remaining patches of snow were surrounded by a huge flock of birds busily pecking away at the grass.

"The robins are back," she exclaimed, clapping her hands together as if she were still a child. She has those moments, Ruthann Harty thought, those precious seconds when she lets the little girl out and stops fretting like a grown woman. She smiled at Rose, who was trying to count robins but failing because they were hopping about so.

"How can you be sure these aren't robins who hid somewhere all winter?" Newton teased.

"Because there are too many," Rose answered quickly. "This is a traveling flock, here from Florida or South Carolina. I wonder where they were yesterday."

The other two did not comment, and they spoke no more until they reached the teacher's house. She invited Newton inside to get her letter and decided it was time to tell these two about her engagement to Joshua Chittenden. He had written her father the official request to marry her and had received a cordial letter in return, so she could make it official with at least these two people she treasured.

How odd it was, she thought, that the people she knew best in Eastborough were these pupils. She hoped they thought of her as friend, too, but she wouldn't ask them that. She retrieved the letter from her desk and took the little ring box from the small drawer inside the desk. She put the ring on, admired it briefly, and turned back to Rose and Newton, handing him the letter with her left hand turned to show the ring.

Rose saw it first. "That's beautiful, Miss Harty," she breathed. "Is it..." She stopped, thinking it would be impudent of her to pursue that thought.

"It is, Rose, it certainly is. Mr. Chittenden and I will be married in the fall, after the second or third crop of hay is in and when the Jerseys are fairly low maintenance," the teacher said. "You two are the first to know, outside of my family and possibly his."

Rose forgot herself completely and threw her arms around the teacher. "I am so happy for you," she said, tears starting to roll down her cheeks. "He is quite wonderful, and I am just so happy."

Newton grinned, took the letter from the teacher, and said he had figured as much from something Joshua had said about bringing the teacher along for the fortnight.

"He said I could be chaperone while he introduced you to Thankful and the other cows," Newton said, starting to laugh. "He's not quite certain you are going to cotton to them the way you do to schoolchildren."

"How I would like to go," the teacher sighed. "But even for overnight, it's quite improper, even though you have already established yourself as a strict chaperone."

"Perhaps I could go, too," Rose said. "Would that make it all right?"

"Likely make it much worse," Newton muttered, thinking how much he would like to spend hours with Rose in a place where Silas Hibbard, Mrs. Munson, Charles, Abby, Uncle Jason, and Aunt Nell were beyond reach. "Much worse," he added, wondering if the very idea made Rose's body react the way his did. Perhaps it does, he thought, glancing up to find that she was looking straight at him, and her face was getting quite pink. Her eyes shifted quickly to the ruby on Miss Harty's finger, and the teacher, watching them both, sighed once more. They are so young, she thought, but they really love each other. Aloud, recovering her teacher-like tone, she said, "You, Rose, will be in school and working at Goodnow's while Newton talks to the cows, and I will be teaching Mark Twain. Now, you'd better get on home, Newton, to help out as much as you can. And I expect neither of you will speak of this until you see the ring on my finger in public."

"Our lips are sealed," Newton said mischievously, glancing at Rose again and delighted to see that she was getting pink all over again. Sealed, indeed, Miss Harty thought, resolving to talk once again with Rose and find out if the girl had spoken with Newton about how they needed to chaperone themselves.

"Have a good journey, Newton," the teacher said as she turned toward the kitchen. "Rose will see you out." And that, she knew, would give them a chance to kiss and hold each other at the door. From the corner of her

A New Tutor

eye, she saw Newton reach for Rose's hand and pull her out of sight. She glanced at the clock, started to get out the dishes they would need for supper and about five minutes later heard the front door open and close, followed by Rose's steps on the stairs.

CHAPTER NINE
The Clock of Grief

Silas Hibbard figured the waste pipes could run from the new bathroom into the privy pit, once that was cleaned out. Henry Goodnow and Ben Chandler both had indoor toilets, and they would know if he needed more drainage than that. It was going to be an expense, but he reckoned Charles might be right about Rose never coming back to a house where a privy was part of the day. Freezing place in winter, he thought, and such a stench in summer, even with the lime he occasionally spared for the pit. Along with her worry about spoiled food, Sarah had often talked about human waste being a bad thing, too. If it wasn't bad, she reasoned, why would a body want to get rid of it almost every day?

She had made him cover the privy pit with lime more often than he'd done in recent days, he realized with a sudden sense of guilt. He'd add lime today, maybe settle Charles' nose a bit. He wanted no part of the boy trying to get out of emptying the chamber pots.

The Clock of Grief

Once chores were done, he'd deliver some eggs to Henry's store and speak with him about supplies for the toilet. He reckoned he'd better inquire about bathtub fixings, too, since he understood the teacher's house had running water for a tub as well. He wondered if the bank would advance him a little money for this venture—certainly he didn't have enough ready cash to buy fixtures and pipe. He could trade off some labor to Ben Chandler—the syrup season had started, so they were shorthanded at Chandler's. Silas was often in charge of boiling the sap and keeping it from boiling over. He always dipped a chunk of salt pork into the pan, which he believed was the reason for his good luck with the boiling. But he and Chandler exchanged time, not coins.

He sighed, knowing that even when it was done, Rose might not come home. He would get at it anyway, so he fetched his rule, paper, and pencil to take some measurements in that hallway space. A few hours later, after tracking Ben Chandler down in the sugar bush to get some advice, Silas had worked out a plan and Henry Goodnow had put in an order for the needed supplies, assuring Silas that he would keep track of the expense and carry it on the books for the time being.

"I expect you want to put these eggs on the good side of the ledger right now?" he asked.

"Indeed," Silas said. "And I want no part of Rose being responsible for any of this—paying for it, I mean. Your arrangements with her need to stand alone."

"Rose is a conscientious worker, and I prize the way

she goes about taking care of my customers," Henry said. "Her pay is not part of this picture."

"Just wanted to be certain," Silas said. "Can't have a daughter footing my bills. Appreciate your faith in me, though I'm not certain I deserve it."

"We all have our times, Silas, and your Sarah helped out more folks in her short life than most do in sixty years, so I reckon we can extend a hand to you now."

"A man can't take credit for what his wife does," Silas said, his voice suddenly hoarse, "but I'm grateful nonetheless." He turned away from the storekeeper abruptly. "I don't know what's come over me," he muttered.

"Grieving sets its own clock, Silas," Henry said. "You can't just swirl the hands around with your index finger."

"Much obliged, Henry," Silas said, moving quickly toward the door so he could escape from this talk. He knew all too well that he wasn't ready to talk about Sarah, had barely been able to say a few things to his children in the months since her death. He thumbed the latch and yanked the door open, then kept his hand behind him to make certain it didn't slam. No need to make Henry Goodnow think he was angry, especially when he'd just gone out of his way be helpful.

Striding along the edge of the road toward his own house, Silas glanced toward the hotel and saw the curtains on Miss Jennie's second-floor window move. Not the wind, he thought, since that window is shut tight. If she doesn't drop in at the noon hour, I'll be a step ahead. If she does come, there may be hell to pay.

Entering his house through the milk room door, Silas paused for a minute by the door to the root cellar. It might be a good day to sort out what was left of the carrots, potatoes, and beets, get rid of the bad ones, he told himself. Couldn't be many beets or carrots left in that barrel of sand, and he and Charles should eat whatever was worth eating. If none of the potatoes had rotted, they'd keep a bit longer. He shook his head, thinking about Charles and the smell of the privy pit. Rotten potatoes were no treat for the nostrils either.

He reached for the latch and then pulled his hand back as if the metal were hot. "You are a fool, Silas Hibbard," he said aloud. "It's not carrots, beets, and potatoes calling you. It's that confounded barrel of hard cider, and by rights, you should get in there and spill it out." But he backed away instead and went up the stairs to the kitchen. Might need a tot of cider for Jason one day, he reasoned. No telling who might come by and need a little hospitality. In the meantime, best that Charles goes after the carrots and beets and let the boy follow his sensitive nose to the potato bin as well.

Without shedding his jacket, Silas opened the icebox and pulled out the remains of a stew he and Charles had eaten the night before. Standing near the stove, he quickly downed the stew, not bothering to heat it up. It wasn't the nicest of noon meals, he thought, remembering how Sarah had always put a good spread on the table in midday, but if Miss Jennie came knocking at the door in another few minutes, he could look her in the eye and say he had already et. Finished, he drank a tumbler of water and decided to spend the afternoon finishing off the walls in the hall where the new bathroom would be.

He could stuff some old newspapers between the studs on the outside wall to make the place less drafty, and he had plenty of odds and ends of boards to make walls. He reckoned he could whitewash the boards and save himself the work and expense of plastering. Ben had suggested he could put a register in the wall to get heat from the kitchen. He'd only seen registers in the floor before, but he figured one ought to work nicely in the wall. Couldn't have a bathroom without heat. Had to keep pipes and people from freezing. Odd, he thought, that frozen pipes were more worrisome than chilled people when the whole thing was for human convenience.

He was gathering up newspapers in the cellar and nearly jumped out of his shirt when Miss Jennie spoke right behind him. "Didn't hear you coming," he said gruffly, straightening up to face her.

"I reckoned you might need a little help with your noon meal, Silas," she said in a tentative voice. "It's that time of day."

"I've had my meal," he answered. Her face fell, and he immediately added, "But you are welcome to whatever you can find in that icebox. I am pretty much moving the heavy meal to suppertime these days so Charles will get a good hot meal at that time."

"Thank you," she said. "Perhaps you'll join me with a glass of your excellent cider?"

"The cider barrel is taking a rest, Jennie," he answered.

"Well, I declare," she answered. "Who would have thought that you'd be answering to the reverend's drummer."

"I promised Rose some time ago that I was about to turn a corner for the better," Silas said solemnly. "That means getting off the drink, building a real bathroom with a toilet and tub, and walking the straight and narrow. The Reverend Lockhead and whatever he's drumming up have nothing to do with me."

"Jason came by this morning," Jennie said, shifting her feet and beginning to wonder if she was already outstaying her welcome here. "And from what he had on his mind—quite rude, he was—I have a feeling I'm in the same pew as the do-gooder reverend. You are considering having nothing to do with me, either. Or your brother-in-law has taken it upon himself to make rules for your personal life."

"Don't want to tangle with you, Miss Jennie," Silas said, turning back to gathering the newspapers and then heading past her for the stairs with a bundle in his arms. "But I can't see my way clear to entertaining you and having Rose back home, so I'm making a choice. Not an easy one. You're a charming woman, and I've indulged my need of a woman. Now I know I need my daughter home more."

Speaking to Silas's back, Jennie said sharply, "That will get you a cleaner house and better meals, Silas Hibbard, but you won't be happy, and neither will she. Mark my words." And with that, she pulled her red shawl closer and whirled away, slamming the door hard as she went out.

"Managed that better than I expected," Silas said half aloud as he stacked the newspapers in the hall, at the same time considering how Jason had stuck his oar in. "But I'll miss her. And there's no guarantee Rose will be back. Nothing like losing both sides of a war. And now I've taken to talking to myself. Well, I expect lots of folks do that. I caught Sarah muttering out loud now and then."

As he folded newspapers and crammed them into the spaces between studs, Silas found himself thinking about the laughing young woman who had made her way into his every waking hour all those years ago and how little she had laughed in the last few years of her life. It wasn't that they didn't still love each other—he knew they did. But like nearly every other woman in the village, he realized, she worked too hard. Before dawn and after sunset, her hands were busy all the time with one thing or another. He worked hard, too, but he was also out and about, delivering eggs and delivering milk and working on projects with other men. She was attached to the house as tightly as a heifer locked in a poke, unable to jump into anything on impulse.

While he thought about Sarah, he worked quickly, making his way across the wall with the newspapers, pushing the edges in with a screwdriver. They did still laugh together, more likely just smiled, like when he brought in the first forget-me-nots in spring, or Charles said something funny at the dinner table, or Sarah herself made one of her quick, amusing remarks. That boy had wit, he thought—still had it—despite having a grouchy father. His mother was gone, but she'd left her sense of humor with the boy, and it was high time he started encouraging it, even if Charles was sometimes a little too sassy.

"Judas Priest," he exploded suddenly, as the screwdriver suddenly slipped on a knot in the wood and jammed his forefinger. In the dim light he could see that a layer of skin had been pushed up, but it wasn't bleeding, so he went on, kneeling down to get in the lower layer.

"Coming right along here, I see," said a voice behind him, and Silas jumped, dropping the screwdriver to the floor. "Need a hand?"

"Nearly ruined one of mine just now," Silas answered, getting to his feet. "And I would take it kindly if people stopped coming up behind me as silent as cats."

"Who else?" Jason asked.

"Miss Jennie came by," Silas said. "She was looking to have a meal, but I was done. And in case your busy mind is wondering, she left in a huff after just a few minutes. Mentioned you had spoken with her today. Said you were rude."

"I expect I was," Jason said. "The reasonable approach wasn't anything she wanted to hear. If you sent her off, then I reckon she may be leaving town soon."

"I'd be a liar if I said I wasn't going to miss her, Jason," Silas said without looking at his brother-in-law. "I know it was sinful, but she's been a comfort."

Jason started to laugh. "The reverend might not admit it, but sinning is often a comfort," he said. "If sins weren't pleasant, we'd all be walking straight to heaven every minute of the day. Have no need of the reverend's reminders."

"You and Goodnow are quite the philosophers," Silas grumbled. "How are you fixed for some spare boards to put on these walls?"

"They might not all match, but I have some fairly wide ones, if that's what you are looking for. Came with the wagon, so we could fetch them now."

Silas nodded. "I'd be obliged," he said. "It's a time when I need to keep my hands occupied."

They set off to get the boards about the time Henry Goodnow was sorting through the day's mailbag and putting the parcels on a shelf behind the counter. He was a little uncertain about whether he should ask Rose to bring a message to her father, but he brought the matter up as soon as she arrived for work after school. Rose shrugged and said hesitantly, "Yes, sir. I could do that."

Mr. Goodnow apologized instantly. "I reckon not, Rose. Sorry. It's just that I've put together part of his order, and he wanted to know right away."

"His order?" Rose said, knowing she hadn't noticed any entries for her father.

"Had the right pipes and faucets in the storage room," Mr. Goodnow said, suddenly realizing that Rose had no way of knowing any of this and worrying that he might have revealed a secret. If that were so, Silas Hibbard could well fly into a rage and he'd be glad of a counter between them.

"It would be best if you wrote a note, sealed it, and I could leave it at the house," Rose said, the whole picture suddenly coming clear for her. He was putting in a bathroom, but Charles hadn't said a word, so it might be a surprise for all.

Henry Goodnow sighed with relief. "You are a smart girl, Rose," he said. "Just as I asked you to carry the word, I realized I was probably supposed to keep my mouth shut. We'll do it your way, and no one will be the wiser." He was startled to see her eyes well up with tears, so he bent to reach under the counter for paper and an envelope, hoping she wasn't going to weep. He never knew what to do when women wept.

Drat, Rose thought. I'm getting all teary over a toilet. But he could have done that for Sarah, too, like getting the icebox. And the running water in the kitchen. And now, I'll wager my buttonhook, he's hoping I'll come home if the chamber pots and slop jars are cleaned and stored. Will I have to? Miss Harty is going to get married, and she will be going to Joshua's farm, and I will be alone again, and Miss Jennie's crumbs will be on the table after the noon meal.

As if he could see inside her mind, Mr. Goodnow looked up from writing his note and said, "No need for you to feel obligated about going back there, Miss Rose. I'm as certain as I am that spring is upon us that Ruthann Harty will keep the latchstring out for you as long as you need it. And if she comes to a place where she can't have you, Mrs. Goodnow and I would be happy to have you at our place."

"Thank you, sir," Rose said somewhat absently. Her attention was on the front of the hotel, where she could see Miss Jennie Graves coming down the steps with a large hatbox in one hand and a satchel in the other. Behind her was the middle Granger boy, who washed dishes and mopped up at the hotel two or three days a week. He had a small trunk hoisted on his shoulder, and the two headed off toward the railroad station.

Realizing that Rose hadn't heard a thing he had said, Henry Goodnow moved toward his front window. "Judas Priest," he said, "she's leaving town. Jason said…" He stopped in mid-sentence, realizing that he was about to spill two secrets in five minutes. "Pardon my language, Rose, but it appears that Miss Graves is moving on."

Rose only nodded. After her father said he intended to turn a corner, she knew he was still seeing Miss Jennie. But Newton had said some people had more than one corner to turn before they found a straight road, and she reckoned Miss Jennie's departure would certainly be one corner navigated. She wondered if her father knew. It hadn't taken Jason Harris long to get Miss Graves out of town, Henry thought. He knew Jason was planning to speak to the woman, but he figured a little paper money might be involved as well. Women like her didn't push easily, and she seemed to have set her cap for Silas Hibbard in a way so forward, so soon after Sarah's death, that the town was talking about it all the time. Tongues would be wagging even faster at supper tables tonight.

Rose turned away from the scene in the street. "I'm sorry, Mr. Goodnow, to be so ungracious. I heard you, and that's a fine offer. I expect you've noticed that Miss Harty has a suitor, and if that comes to anything, it would change her life and mine at the same time."

"Ruthann has already shown me the ring, Rose. That's a secret I intend to keep better than the one about the toilet, but I'm sure it's not news to you."

"No, sir," Rose said, smiling happily. "Newton and I..." She paused. "I am very fond of Mr. Chittenden," she finished. "Where shall I start today, sir?"

Henry Goodnow shook his head in wonder that this fifteen-year-old, who had been through so much, could push it all aside and just be happy for the teacher. He did notice the "Newton and I" phrase and figured the Barnes boy had to be one of the people helping Rose keep her balance. Mother gone, father impossible, two younger children to worry about, everyone living in different places—his wife said Silas Hibbard would have his head in the stocks if he'd lived in Puritan times.

"We need to get the heavy winter clothing put away in the back, Rose," he said aloud. "It's time to get out seeds and fertilizer and garden tools, along with a few straw hats and some of those light quilts you'll find on the top shelves in the back room. I reckon it's time for us to make people think spring."

"With respect, sir, spring mostly makes more work for every housewife in this town. It smells nice, and it's warmer, and the flowers are pretty, but in the house..." Her voice trailed off.

"What makes it so hard, Rose?" Mr. Goodnow asked, hoping spring held no special nightmares for this girl. "Most of us are grateful to have the snow melt and the seeds sprout."

"Spring cleaning," she said with a groan. "Underwear to wash, mattresses to turn, curtains to launder and iron, woodwork to scrub, the stove to black, spiders to chase, windows to clean. My mother said spring was at best a mixed blessing, and it was a good thing the nice parts were very, very nice." She paused for a second and added, "And soap. We'll have to make the soap."

"Never thought of it that way," Mr. Goodnow said, chuckling at her dismay. "Oh, put your mind at rest. I'm not laughing at you. I'm thinking about all those whirling dervishes tearing their houses apart in the next two weeks, and we men aren't really thinking about it a-tall."

"You men just have the manure pile to take care of," Rose said. "Mother said that increases the aroma on the pant legs."

Mr. Goodnow was really laughing now. "And Sarah Hibbard was always a one for telling me about her crocus and violets and her forays through the woods to find the first arbutus."

"Perhaps," Rose said, "but it was mostly work."

"Any idea what those women might want to buy? We've room in the window for more than straw hats and paint pails."

Rose brightened. "Even Miss Harty has a mop she'd

The Clock of Grief

not want the minister's wife to see," she said in a rush. "I could put mops and brooms in a new pail, and we could have a basket of the best clothespins—most everybody's must be soggy with winter by now. And maybe a carpet sweeper?" she finished, almost breathless. "Sir."

"Gather the things, Rose, and we'll do it." He turned away, shaking his head a little. Smart as could be in school, she was, according to Ruthann, along with mothering her siblings, cooking, cleaning, and now turning out to be something of a retailer. He wished he and Edith could have had a child like Rose Hibbard, but the good Lord hadn't seen to that. He frowned, thinking it was hard to figure on the Lord. You'd think He would have had the good sense to keep Sarah and let Silas get killed by the woodpile. Probably take more than a toilet to get Rose back there. Might be she'd go back out of worry for Charles, but he could think of no other reason.

He watched as she trundled several things toward the front of the store and then joined her to lug away some of the winter things and put a new season in place. It took them right up to closing time, with only a few customers interrupting them. Then he sealed his note for Silas in an envelope and gave it to Rose.

"See you day after tomorrow?" he asked.

"I'll be here, Mr. Goodnow, to see how many mops you've sold," she answered. "Good night." She tucked the letter into her pocket, put on her wrap, and went out the door, pausing at the store window to see how their spring ideas looked. She looked up and saw that he was watching. She pointed to the display, nodded, smiled, and was gone.

Rose gave a little skip as she made her way quickly along the road. It really was starting to feel like spring, and even if all that cleaning had to be done, there would be robins making nests, peepers peeping in the swamp, and warm air. Warm enough pretty soon so she and Newton could go to the rock together. The very idea gave her the shivers. But these shivers aren't cold, she thought, and they go right down to my toes.

When she reached the house, she decided not to leave the note on the step where it might blow away. She stood very straight and told herself she could certainly hand an envelope to her father, so she headed toward the barn, where he would surely be milking at this time of day.

He was there, sitting on the little three-legged stool by the third cow in the row, his forehead resting lightly on the cow's flank, the shiny milk pail wedged between his knees. He must have just started this one, she thought, because she could hear the squirts of milk hitting the sides of the empty pail. She scuffed her feet a little, hoping to alert him that she was there. She didn't want to make him jump by suddenly appearing.

"Hello?" he asked gruffly, not turning around.

"Just me," she said. "I have a message from Mr. Goodnow, and I didn't want to leave it on the step, so I brought it here."

"That's right kind of you and him," Silas said. "Set it

The Clock of Grief

on the shelf there, and I'll take it up when I'm done. You want to wet your whistle?"

In spite of herself, Rose started to laugh. For as long as she could remember—until Sarah's death had changed their lives completely—she had gotten drinks here. It had started when she was three and saw her father squirt milk right into a barn cat's expectant mouth. Now she knelt near her father's knee and opened her mouth wide. He aimed the teat perfectly and squeezed, a shot of warm milk going into her mouth. The cow twisted her head around to look at them, and they both laughed.

"I'll be getting along now, Father," Rose said, standing up. "Thanks for the drink."

"Any time," he said, bending to his task again.

That was easy, Rose felt, as she made her way past the house and on to Miss Harty's. He didn't smell of the drink. She was quite certain of that, and he hadn't given her a hard time about not being at home doing for him and Charles. She wondered if he knew Miss Jennie had taken a train. She hoped it was a one-way ticket and decided she might just ask the Granger boy about that.

CHAPTER TEN
Kissing and Telling

Alice was sitting on the steps at Miss Harty's house when Rose arrived, elbows on her knees and her chin resting in her hands. "I'm so glad you're finally here," she said when she saw Rose coming up the walk. "I need to... I think I need... do you have time...?"

Unaccustomed to this stammering Alice, Rose realized something must be terribly wrong, so she merely nodded and invited her friend to come into the teacher's parlor. She hung their wraps on the coat tree in the hall, led Alice into the front room, and closed the door. She lit the kerosene lamp and sat down, hoping it was all right to be in this little-used room. She reckoned whatever was on Alice's mind must be something very private.

"Is that you, Rose?" came a muffled voice from the direction of the kitchen.

Rose opened the door again and called out that she and Alice were talking in the parlor and would join her in a few minutes. "Make yourselves at home," the teacher answered, thinking it was very strange that Alice was here and that the girls had tucked themselves away in the parlor. She hoped nothing was awry.

"Now," said Rose, "what is it that is making you utter incomplete sentences?"

Glum as she had looked on the steps, Alice had to smile at that. "It's Ethan," she said. "I'm uncertain about... I don't know... he seems to think... oh, dear, I'm incomplete again," she finished.

"Begin at the beginning, Alice, so we can get to the middle," Rose counseled. "Did he walk you home from school?"

"He did," her friend answered, with a small sigh of relief at being given a way to start. "And he carried my books, just the way Newton carries yours, and I thought it was so nice, and when we got to my house, he wanted to come in, said he needed to warm his fingers by the stove, but I said my mother wasn't home, and he said that was good, wasn't it." Alice's words were spilling out faster than corn kernels falling from the husker.

Rose frowned, remembering the day Newton had brought her books from school and had practically run out the door when he found out she was alone in the house. No chaperone, no visit, he had said. That seemed so long ago, but he still talked about chaperones now and then.

"Then what happened?" Rose prompted, starting to feel a little anxious.

"I opened the door, turned to say good-bye, and he

just walked right past me into the kitchen," she said, her eyes filling with tears. "He put my books down and took hold of my arms so tight that I couldn't back up, and he kissed me right on the mouth." She stopped talking and looked down at the floor, her hands twisting in her lap.

"And what did you do then?" Rose said, thinking that Father would say this was like trying to get milk from a dry cow.

"Oh, Rose, it felt so good, even though he was hurting my arms, and his lips were warm and soft, and I kissed him back, and then he opened my wrap and put his arms around me and pulled me so close to him that I could hear his heart beating, and his hands were going up and down my back, and I didn't know what to do." Again, she stopped talking and stared at the floor.

Rose waited, but Alice remained silent. "Alice," she said, thinking she sounded the way she did when she was about to scold Abby, "you need to go on with this story." Only maybe she doesn't, Rose told herself, so she quickly added, "Unless you don't want to."

"Of course I want to," Alice said, sounding more like her usual self. "I have to. I have to. That's why I came." She stood up, walked to the window, picked up a small terrarium of winterberries from the table and studied it for a long moment as if it were an important work of art. She put the glass bowl down, turned, and said, "I pushed him away and told him to get out, that my mother would be home in another five minutes and would be angry with me for having a boy in the house, and he put his hands on either side of my face and kissed me again, so hard that time that my mouth was pushed against my teeth. And then he left."

Alice started to sob, but when Rose moved toward her, she held up her hand. "I haven't finished," she said in a shaky voice. "The thing is, I wanted him to stay, I wanted him to kiss me again and again, and I knew we could do that because my mother was at the church getting things ready for Easter and we had time for a dozen kisses. Does that make me a bad girl?"

If her friend's distress had not been so real, Rose would have laughed. Instead, she sat on the floor at Alice's feet, handed her a clean handkerchief and waited while her friend wiped her eyes and blew her nose.

"You're not a bad girl, Alice," Rose said. "Kissing is lovely when it's someone you want to kiss."

"And you kiss Newton, don't you?" Alice asked, still snuffling.

"I do," Rose confessed, thinking this was a private matter she really didn't want to discuss with either Alice or Emily. "But Ethan was wrong to push his way into your house. And wrong not to leave when you told him to get out. And wrong to kiss you again. By the way, did you kiss him back?" she asked as an afterthought. "The second time, I mean?"

"I did, Rose, I did," Alice cried, starting to sob again.

"That's going to make it a little harder the next time you see him," Rose said, thinking about what Miss Harty had said to her. "Alone, I mean."

"What's going to happen next time, Rose? Maybe I just won't ever see him again except in school."

"Don't be silly. If he wanted to kiss you in the afternoon in broad daylight in a kitchen, then he will find a way to see you again," Rose said, thinking she must sound like a gray-haired aunt in a lace cap, but determined to go on anyway. "What you need to understand is that you can't go back—you have already kissed, so you and he will both want to do that again. You can't go back to just looking moony at each other over a box social supper."

That made Alice laugh, even though tears were still running down her face. "Did I really look moony?" she asked. "I was trying so hard to pretend he was my brother or something."

"Better forget the brother thing," Rose answered. "He's not acting like a brother, not a-tall."

"So, what do I do if he walks me home again and my mother isn't there?"

"You stand outside and freeze your toes or get a sunburn, depending on the season, until he decides to go home," Rose said. "And you tell him what the rules are."

"What are the rules? Where did you learn them? All my mother ever said was that I had to be chaperoned at all times if a young man came calling. And this wasn't even calling—it was barging in."

"Miss Harty told me," Rose said. "And as best I can, I will pass on to you what she said." She hesitated, thinking she certainly sounded like a schoolmarm or a preacher now, and added softly, "If you want."

"Oh, please, Rose. You have to tell," Alice said.

"First I had better tell Miss Harty that we are all right in here. She must think the world is coming to an end, what with me taking over her parlor and you howling like a sick cat."

"Do you think she heard me?" Alice said, suddenly quite embarrassed.

"I have a feeling she at least put an ear to the door for a moment or two," Rose said. "Not to eavesdrop but to make sure we weren't about to die or anything." With that, she opened the door and went off to the kitchen to tell the teacher that things weren't perfect, but she and Alice had some talking to do, and then, if Miss Harty didn't mind, they might need a cup of tea at the table.

She was back in two minutes, feeling more than a little nervous about passing on Miss Harty's admonitions. To give herself a minute, she straightened the antimacassar on the chair where Alice was sitting, and then, to her friend's dismay, seemed to be completely absorbed in whether the little squares of lace were precisely in place on the other two chairs. She was about to speculate aloud on why these crocheted things had such a big name when she saw Alice's pleading face. She sat down immediately and crossed her fingers in hopes of being able to do this.

She began with the idea that holding hands led to kissing and kissing led to more kissing, but when she reached the part about kissing with tongues, Alice interrupted. "Yuck," she said, "that's sickening."

"Apparently," Rose said, "you'd be surprised. Apparently playing with tongues makes people really tingle."

"The kissing made me tingle," Alice said. "I never felt anything like that before. And," she added, looking down at the floor again, "I have to say I liked it, and I want to feel like that again."

"Exactly," Rose said. "That's why you can't back up. Because you like it, and what you want is more. The Reverend Lockhead probably calls it the 'human condition,' something he's fond of discussing as if it were a plague. But Miss Harty says we girls are the ones in charge, and we have to say no and back off or we'll be in trouble like that older girl who came to school for a little while last year and then left."

"You mean Mehitabel," Alice said. "She was staying with her aunt, and I heard she had a baby. But I thought it wasn't true because she wasn't married."

"You don't have to be married, it turns out, to have a baby," Rose said. "It can happen to anyone who is old enough to menstruate, and we all do that. Miss Harty said boys sometimes don't know when to stop and we have to tell them so we don't end up like Mehitabel."

"So what did Mehitabel do that she shouldn't have done? Even if you don't have to be married, I don't think kissing makes babies."

Rose started to laugh. "Miss Harty never mentioned babies, but if what goes on in the pasture is any indication, people must have to jump all over each other before they produce the equivalent of a calf."

"You had better ask her," Alice said. "We need to know. She's the only one who might tell, I think. My mother would faint on the kitchen floor if I asked her about people jumping all over each other."

Rose smiled with relief. Alice was starting to sound like herself again, so perhaps the Ethan crisis was over for the moment. But she could see that Alice really liked him, even if he had behaved badly, and she knew the story wasn't over. She had never pushed Newton away, and he had never held her arms until they hurt. But she hadn't talked about rules with him, even though Miss Harty had suggested that such a conversation would be a good idea. She hadn't the least idea what the first words in that conversation could possibly be.

Still, she reckoned Ethan wasn't much like Newton, especially since he was so pleased to find out that no chaperone was present. Just thinking about Newton's anxiety when he found out they were alone made her smile again. And that was before they had kissed. She wished he were delivering books to her now instead of delivering Jersey calves miles and miles away at Joshua's place.

"Rose?" Alice said. "Have you gone off somewhere? Emily thinks your head comes unhitched."

"I'm here, Alice, but my mind did wander for a moment. Sorry."

"Do you want to ask Miss Harty now?" Alice persisted.

"About what?"

Alice sighed heavily. "You did disappear. About people jumping all over each other, or whatever it is they do to have babies."

"We could," Rose said doubtfully. "I think we could."

And perhaps we must, she thought. Whatever happened to Mehitabel was not good. Mother said she was sent here because she behaved improperly at home, and then she stopped coming to school and just stayed home with her aunt and uncle. Rose had seen her working in the garden one day and saw she looked very fat, but she hadn't thought much about it at the time. Did she really have a baby? When she wasn't married? Suddenly Rose thought about Nell and Jason's one child, Clara, who had left home when Rose was Abby's age. Is this what had happened to her, too? This was serious business, Rose realized, so she stood, took Alice's hand, and with her heart pounding, headed for the kitchen. She wasn't certain she knew how to start this conversation either.

Miss Harty was pulling the teakettle onto the hottest part of the stove as they came through the door. She looked at them both carefully, taking note of Alice's red-rimmed eyes and the slight frown of concentration on Rose's face. She saw that Alice was clutching her friend's hand tightly enough to make the ends of Rose's fingers red. Whatever it was, it was no small matter. She fetched cups that had been warming on the upper shelf of the stove, took down the tin of tea leaves and filled a tea strainer.

"Do you take milk in your tea, Alice?" she asked as if that were the only concern of the moment.

"Yes, Ma'am," Alice said in a tiny voice.

"Me, too," Rose said. "I mean, I would like milk also, Miss Harty."

The teacher laughed. "Whatever you two have been up to in my front room, you didn't leave your manners under the rug." She poured hot water over the tea leaves into each cup and asked the girls to sit down. "I'm short on refreshments, but help yourselves to soda crackers," she said. "And if you want to talk about the problem, we might start with each of you giving me one or two words to go on."

"Ethan Tucker," Alice said immediately, and Rose sighed with relief. This would be easier than she had thought.

"And you, Rose?" the teacher prompted.

"Having calves," Rose said and instantly felt very foolish. "I mean…"

"Never mind," Miss Harty said. "I think I see some corner pieces for this puzzle."

"How can you…?" Rose started, then stopped abruptly. She already knew that some things that were pea-soup foggy to her were clear as newly washed windows to the teacher.

"My guess," Miss Harty said, ignoring Rose's half-finished sentences, "is that Alice likes Ethan as more than a friend, Ethan has made advances Alice either welcomes or doesn't welcome, and that you are both worried about what comes next."

"That's about it," Rose said. "Ethan walked Alice home and kissed her in the kitchen, and her mother wasn't there, and he was happy about that instead of loping out the door the way Newton would. And we got to thinking about Mehitabel. And then I wondered about Clara."

The teacher frowned. "Your cousin Clara? She went off, yes, and Nell and Jason don't talk about her, but she was a good girl and wanted to see more of the world. Last I heard she was in California, and I don't know if she is married or still working as a nurse. Now, exactly what do you two know about Mehitabel?"

They looked at each other, both starting to speak, and then Alice backed off. "We think she had a baby," Rose said. "And she appeared to be in hiding, I thought, because she didn't come to school anymore, and she barely went outdoors, or at least we didn't see her outside much, even in decent weather."

"Mehitabel is a very nice girl who didn't know much of anything about kisses or calves," Miss Harty said. "A man several years older than she came calling, and her parents didn't send him away, and she thought he really loved her, so they ended up doing a lot more than kissing. He took advantage of her, she became pregnant, and he ran off."

"What does 'take advantage' mean, Miss Harty? We need to know, and I can't ask my mother because she really would faint, and Rose doesn't have a mother to ask and maybe couldn't ask anyway," Alice said in a rush.

"First you girls have to promise me that you won't go all over the school talking about this conversation," Miss Harty said. "You could put me out of a job before next Sunday."

"Promise," they said together. "Except we'll want to tell Emily," Rose added. "Shouldn't she know, too?"

"Yes, Emily," the teacher said, sighing and thinking she would rather be shoveling manure at Joshua's barn than sitting here with two girls who wanted to do the right thing but didn't know what it was. "Taking advantage," she said, "is when a man has sexual relations with a girl who is not his wife and who doesn't realize that she could get pregnant. He takes advantage of her ignorance because he's a selfish person and it makes him feel good. If it's two married people, they call it making love. Either way, it's when two bodies unite and create another one."

"Whew," Alice said. "So it's not kissing."

Rose's eyebrows were almost meeting over her nose as she considered the teacher's explanation. "You said unite, Miss Harty," she said slowly. "Unite means join. If they join, these two people, then it is like the bull and the cows, and that is disgusting. Running around and jumping on each other. Why would Mehitabel or anyone else want to do that?" The words flooded out and then Rose paused, frowned, and made a face.

"Alice," she moaned. "It must be something about the pee thing."

"Pea thing?" Miss Harty said, puzzled at this odd term. "Where do peas come into this?" Both girls started to giggle and then stopped abruptly.

"Yuck," Alice said, making a face and nodding to Rose. "You must be right. The joining part."

"P-e-e, Miss Harty," Rose said. "Not p-e-a. And did

my father and mother have to do it three times to get three of us?"

The teacher turned quickly toward the stove and made a fuss over moving the teakettle so it would stop bubbling. This was no time to laugh, but she needed a minute to get her face under control. Pee thing, indeed. And three times three. She was in full teacher mode when she looked around at them again and said people didn't talk about these things much, but she reckoned most married couples made love lots of times because it was part of being married. And, yes, the pee thing, as they called it, was involved.

"Do they like it?" Rose wanted to know. "Or is it required?"

Before the teacher could say a word, Alice broke in. "Like it? Getting someone else's pee? What's to like about that?"

It was all Ruthann Harty could do not to laugh out loud, even though she was also alarmed about the things they didn't know and the fact that she had to explain it all to them. But she plunged ahead anyway.

"You remember, Rose, when we talked about the pleasure of kissing and holding someone." She saw Rose nod, so she went on, ignoring the color that was rising on the girl's face and wondering if the same thing was happening to her. She did feel a bit warm in the cheeks.

"And we talked about stages and how kissing led to other things. The ultimate stage would be when the two bodies actually unite. If they are in harmony, they will have a hundred times the pleasure they get from kissing, so it's not necessarily something disgusting."

"But it could be?" Rose asked. "It could be loathsome?"

"With the wrong person, the wrong way and at the wrong time, yes. And since you both apparently have paid close attention to bulls and cows, you know that the bull gets pretty aggressive and just wants to have his way, running around the pasture and jumping on cows, as you so delicately put it. That's why girls have to be the ones who say no, who insist that they go to the altar first and the bed second."

Rose suddenly pushed away from the table, tipping over her teacup and sending a brown stain across the tablecloth. "In bed? That's what they were doing in the bed? In the bed he had shared with Sarah?" She let out a wail and ran back to the parlor, slamming the door behind her.

"Oh, dear," Miss Harty said, "oh, dear, we have opened Pandora's box."

Alice was on her feet, starting toward the parlor, but the teacher grabbed her arm. "We need to think a minute, Alice, and we need to give her a minute, too. We need to think about why she left."

"It's the fornication," Alice said dismally. "I know what it is. It's what sent her to the woodpile and the cemetery," she wailed. "It's the fornication. It's Silas Hibbard and that woman."

"You calm down, Alice," Miss Harty said, gathering her own wits and a bit relieved that she didn't have to explain Rose's flight to her friend. She, too, was certain that Rose had suddenly made the connection between their talk and her father's dalliance with Miss Graves. "You and I must help Rose, which means we don't have time right now to deal with your problem."

"I will be calm," Alice said, choking down a sob. "But it's not fair. She's been so happy, so far away from that awful afternoon."

"And she'll put it away again," Miss Harty said with an assurance she didn't really feel. She thought the day Rose had heard her father and Miss Graves in her parents' bedroom and had seen their clothing on the floor, their bare legs near the foot of the bed, was a lifetime kind of nightmare, improved only in that it might, with time, come around less often. "We'll go see to her now, if you are truly ready."

"I will be calm," Alice repeated woodenly, her eyes wide and dark.

They found Rose curled up tightly on the blue velvet sofa with a pillow over her head. "Go away," she said in a muffled voice that cracked on the second word. "Just go away."

"We can't, Rose," Miss Harty said. "Alice and I are going to sit here and wait for you. We have to talk about this, and we'll be here, right here, even if you don't sit up before morning."

"But Alice's mother will worry," the voice said.

Miss Harty and Alice exchanged glances and the teacher quickly put her finger to her lips for silence. Alice nodded, but now she knew Rose would be all right. She was already worrying about someone else. She is so strong, Alice thought, wondering if she would ever have gotten through all the things that Rose had to contend with. Rose did have Newton, of course, even if she didn't admit it, and that was something big enough to balance off a lot of bad things. Alice watched Miss Harty, moving slightly in her rocking chair, and could not imagine what the teacher was going to say when Rose came out from under the pillow.

The clock struck seven, and Alice knew she had better not wait much longer. Her mother would be beside herself and might even start thinking about organizing a search. But Rose heard the clock, too, and sat up quite suddenly. "You have to go," she said to Alice. "Right now."

"Only when I know you are all right," Alice answered. "What I learned today is that we're not just cows chewing grass and running away from bulls. We're not fenced in. We have choices. Your father made a bad choice when he took up with Miss Jennie, but that has nothing to do with us and Newton and Ethan, even though it hurt you. I want to make good choices, and I need you to help me because you are much stronger than I am."

The relief on Ruthann Harty's face had wiped out every line of worry. She started to speak and then closed her mouth firmly. These were such good friends, Rose and Alice and Emily, and they took such great care of each other. She knew they teased each other and sometimes made fun of each other. But they really cared, and she had said enough for this day.

"I will be all right," Rose said. "Miss Harty has made it quite clear that making love with the right person at the right time is one thing, and the other thing must be the fornication that the reverend is so obsessed with. And now you really must go."

"You'll make sure she's not just trying to get me out of here, Miss Harty?" Alice asked.

"I will," Ruthann said. "And I must say I wish I had a friendship like what you three have."

Alice left, and Miss Harty turned to Rose. "Are you really all right?" she asked. "As all right as a person could be about something like this?"

"She left," Rose answered.

"You told her to go," Miss Harty answered, somewhat bewildered by this announcement.

"Miss Graves, I mean," Rose said, realizing that her mind had taken several jumps without her saying anything. She couldn't believe how many times a day she did that: began a thought and then skipped right over the middle to the end. "She went to the station with her hatbox and a large parcel and her trunk. I saw her."

Miss Harty's jaw actually dropped, and in spite of herself, Rose started to laugh. She had actually taken the teacher completely by surprise, and she wished Alice had stayed long enough for this part.

"You would say she perhaps had all her belongings with her?" the teacher asked.

"She had Simon Granger lugging some of it," Rose said. "Mr. Goodnow said it appeared she was moving on."

"What does Henry Goodnow have to do with this?"

"We were doing the new window displays at the store, getting ready for spring, so we saw her leave the hotel with Simon," Rose answered. "Do you think she really might have moved on? Do you think Father decided not to entertain her at lunch anymore?"

"No doubt we'll get a full report once Mrs. Munson gets her finger in this pie, Rose," Miss Harty said. "But it appears that at the very least she has gone for a long visit somewhere else, which is good news for all of us. And now I think we'd better have our supper before it's right up against bedtime."

CHAPTER ELEVEN
A Different Kind of Tutor

" I reckon you'll want me to be turning the mattresses and scrubbing the woodwork on Saturday, Miss Harty," Rose said as she and the teacher shared a breakfast of oatmeal and toast at the kitchen table.

"Nonsense, Rose," the teacher answered quickly and a little sharply. She was still not accustomed to sharing a breakfast table. "I turn my mattress every two months whatever the season, and you can see to your own. As for the woodwork, does it appear to be soiled? Our time would be better spent sharpening the garden tools and getting ready to plant. The nineteenth of April is near."

"You plant the peas then?" Rose asked, a little hesitant. The teacher seemed to be a little out of sorts this morning.

"Indeed. If we're not still in mud season. Peas and lettuce, at least, don't mind soil as cold as Mr. Manchester's ice blocks. Salmon and peas for the Fourth of July means seeds in the ground by mid-April."

"Too bad we can't plant the salmon," Rose said, relieved that spring cleaning would not be an ordeal in this house. That might give her time to get in some scouring for her father and Charles. She wondered if her father had changed his underwear without Sarah there to give him a nudge. And whether anyone had changed the sheets in a month of Sundays.

"If you are planning to clean at your father's house," Miss Harty began, "you had better enlist Charles' help or it will be too much for you, along with school and the store and the things you do here. One thing we must do, and I consider it a foul process, is make the soap."

Rose nodded, thinking the teacher sometimes lived right inside her head, knowing exactly what was in there. Foul process, indeed. If there was one thing she disliked more than spring cleaning, it was making soap. The smell of the lye stayed in her nose for days afterward.

She finished her toast and started clearing away the breakfast things, working quickly. By the time the teacher had drunk the last of her coffee, the other dishes were clean and in the rack next to the sink. She wanted to get to school a little early to join in the Red Rover game. Everyone was playing now that the snow was gone and the air was warmer.

"Leave them to dry themselves, Rose," Miss Harty said, sensing that the girl wanted to be on her way as soon as possible. Rose knew half the housewives in town would cluck and shake their heads if they saw dishes, even clean ones, left in the sink. She had a sudden picture of Mrs. Munson with a chicken's head and a yellow beak that opened and shut as she squawked. Starting to giggle, she almost ran up the stairs to put on her shoes and brush through her hair. She had brought her prized silver buttonhook with her from home, and with deft fingers, she made quick work of buttoning up her shoes. She laced her hair into a single braid down her back and was ready to leave.

Newton wouldn't be waiting for her today, so unless she came upon Emily or Alice, she'd make her way alone. He would soon be back from his fortnight at the Chittenden farm, but she wondered how she'd get to see him, even then. He would be putting in long days working with his father, starting at first light. Sometimes the dairy farmers, she knew, finished up the milking by lantern, with the cows already starting to doze in their stanchions.

Still, once they had supper, the men's day was done. And she, if she were still at home, would be putting away food, doing dishes, mending socks, ironing, and making sure Abby and Charles did their lessons. She reckoned she'd better find out if Father was leaving room in the day's chores for Charles to get his schoolwork done. At Miss Harty's, her after-supper chores took up an hour or more. The kitchen floor had to be swept every evening and mopped at least twice a week. And the teacher wanted the bathroom cleaned often, although she and Rose tidied up after themselves on a regular basis.

Sleeping in her own bed with her special view out the window would be so nice, Rose thought, and Abby would like to be there with her. But she wasn't like Miss Jennie, who left her dirty dishes on the table and who could get a Granger boy to carry her things to the station. She'd have to do it all herself. She'd done that, and even the idea made her a little tired. She didn't want to start dozing off in school again, especially now when Newton wasn't there to poke her in the back. She smiled, thinking about how, at first, he'd jabbed her with the sharp end of his pencil, which made her jump and sometimes left a tiny spot on her shirtwaist. She had finally ventured to suggest that he turn the pencil around, since the newest pencils at Mr.Goodnow's store came with soft rubber erasers attached.

As she reached the schoolyard, several girls waved, inviting her to join their Red Rover game. Emily and Alice were on opposite sides, and Rose saw that Ethan, on the boys' side of the playground, had stopped playing catch and seemed to be watching Alice. The game went on for several minutes with everyone laughing and shouting, and then Miss Harty rang the bell, and the boys and girls lined up separately to enter the building. When she was Charles' age, Rose had heard her parents talking about having one door at the front of the school instead of building separate entrances for boys and girls. It would save money, they had decided, so Silas voted for the plan at town meeting. Listening to her mother's ideas about the doorway, Rose thought it would have been nice if Sarah could have voted, too.

"Women don't vote," her father had said.

"Why, sir?" Rose wanted to know.

"They tend to things at home," he had answered. Rose didn't think that explained anything, but she could tell from the look on her mother's face that it would be better to keep still. She never did get around to asking her mother about the voting, but it occurred to her now, as the girls' line moved past the waiting boys, that she could ask Miss Harty.

Ahead of her, she saw Ethan turn his head, and when Alice drew near he reached out his foot and touched hers as she went by. Rose didn't think Alice looked at him even sideways, but she saw her friend give a little skip to move ahead faster. When the boys came into the classroom, Rose saw Ethan look right at Alice, but her friend's eyes were already on an open book on her desk.

Uh-oh, Rose said to herself. Alice really does like him. She knows he behaved badly, but she might even be hoping it happens again. Rose knew that feeling, except she also understood now that a girl could be walking on spring ice if she didn't keep her wits about her when that warm tingle ran from her face to her toes. By now, recovered from her initial fear, Alice would be angry if she brought it up again, but it was worrisome. She reckoned she could manage to say it all again if she and Alice decided to pass on the information to Emily. She nodded to herself, knowing that would work.

Miss Harty's voice broke into her thoughts. "Ethan, with most of the boys back at their farms, I would like you to take charge of the water today and for the rest of the week."

"Shall I start now, Ma'am?"

"Please."

Ethan slid out of his seat and fetched the pail at the front of the room. He left, and a few minutes later returned, his body tipped to one side with the weight of the water. He set it down carefully and returned the dipper to the bucket. Turning toward his seat, he looked at Alice again and this time caught her watching him. His back to the teacher, he grinned, and Alice's face turned as red as a fair day sunset. Good thing Emily didn't care for Peter Granger, Rose thought, or we'd be the dizziest three in the school. Two of us is quite enough. She did think she was concentrating on her schoolwork better without the disturbing presence of Newton right behind her.

The morning flew by, once Miss Harty promised more of the Tom Sawyer story if they finished all their other work. They traced row upon row of Ps, Qs and Rs across lined paper, they worked the arithmetic puzzles Miss Harty put on the board, and one after another, they recited the presidents of the United States in order. Alice was first and did them all correctly, which made it easier for everyone else, although several were stuck on Martin Van Buren. But Miss Harty insisted that everyone get it right, even the youngest, so the lesson seemed to take forever.

"Homework," she said, "will be to make a list in best penmanship of the presidents, including their Christian names and their wives' names. The wives," Miss Harty said, "play an important part in keeping the White

House on an even keel every day."

Like a ship, Rose thought, smiling at the idea that getting off an even keel might make everyone in the White House tilt and struggle to keep their footing, the way sailors did. She wondered if President Cleveland ever thanked his wife—she remembered Miss Harty saying the new first lady was quite young—for keeping things in balance. Presidents' wives, she was quite certain, did not have to make biscuits or sweep the kitchen floor. Perhaps she should ask Miss Harty about that, too.

When the noon hour bell rang, Miss Harty said they could take their lunch pails outside if they chose. But she asked Mary, Ida, John, and Ethan to stay in their seats. Peter Granger hadn't arrived, but Miss Harty had a feeling he would show up, ready to help the slower readers.

"Excuse me, Miss Harty," Mary piped up. "Did we do something wrong?"

"We are waiting to see if Peter is coming to help you with reading," the teacher said. "He can only come during the noon hour, so you will have your meal a little later." As if one person, the four sighed, and Ethan slumped in his seat, stretching his feet into the aisle in front of his desk.

"You may talk if you wish," Miss Harty said, sitting down at her desk and taking an apple from her own lunch pail.

"Why can't we start eating, too, Miss Harty," John wanted to know.

"Why not?" Miss Harty conceded. "You can even eat,

I would imagine, while you take turns reading."

They barely had time to unpack their lunches when Peter pushed open the door, a little breathless. "I run all the way," he said. "Sorry I'm late, Miss Harty."

"Ran, Peter. But it's all right. Catch your breath and then perhaps you can manage them as a group today. That way, three can eat while another one reads."

And so the tutoring session began, and even Ethan decided it wasn't such a bad way to spend the lunch recess. He found Peter very amusing, especially when he stopped them in mid-sentence by saying "Whoa there, Nellie, back up" and other un-teacher-like things. Miss Harty had to smile when Mary, who was so precise about everything, corrected him every time, telling him none of them was named "Nellie," and when Peter would go right on, totally ignoring her comments.

By the time the rest of the children returned from the playground, these four were reading along quite smoothly, and Peter was looking at the school clock nervously. "I have to get back," he said. "Ma'am."

"Run along, Peter. You are doing nicely with them, and I hope to see you at least one other day this week."

"Tomorrow," he muttered, and was gone.

Ethan's hand shot up as the door closed and when the teacher called on him, he stood and asked, "Excuse me, Miss Harty, but do we get time out-of-doors now?"

If no one had asked, Ruthann Harty had planned to walk right past that problem. But now she had to reconsider. "You four may put on your wraps and run around the school three times. The boys will go clockwise and the girls counterclockwise, and no collisions, please."

She could see by the expressions on all four faces that each was thinking about clockwise and counterclockwise, and she almost laughed out loud. She reckoned they'd get it figured out by the time they reached the bottom of the steps, and sure enough, she looked out the window to see the boys pelting along as the clock moves and the girls, lifting their skirts a bit, running pretty fast in the other direction. In a few minutes, they all reappeared, rosy-cheeked and panting, to take their seats again. She decided everyone had worked hard enough for this day, so she picked up the Mark Twain book, opened to the marked place and was pleased to hear a little rustle of anticipation as feet, arms, and bodies shifted in their places.

"Shall we take turns reading again?" she asked, and then, not waiting for an answer, beckoned for Alice to begin.

The afternoon flew by with nearly all the children absorbed by the story of this boy who did so many things that any of them would have been afraid to do. Miss Harty wondered if the author would enjoy hearing the children talk about the characters, almost as if they were all real people. She was a little taken aback at the various comments about how such behavior would have resulted in a thrashing, but she asked no questions about that.

When the bell rang, she watched through the window as Rose, Emily, and Alice reached the road together. With Newton away, Rose would be walking with her friends, and Ruthann had complete faith in her. She would get Alice to talk about Ethan, and Emily would ask questions, and the girls would know the things they needed to know.

She sighed, wondering if her confidence in them should go so far as to figure on their good sense not to talk with their mothers. Emily's mother might not consider her an interfering old maid, but she had never talked with Alice's mother before or since the day Rose had disappeared last year. What the girls' fathers might think was beyond imagining. She could only hope the girls would have some notion of what a fragile limb she was sitting on right now. "When the bough breaks," she hummed to herself, "the teacher will fall."

She need not have worried. Alice could not wait to tell Emily about Ethan and Rose and the talk with Miss Harty, but first she made Emily solemnly promise that what she was about to tell was a real secret, never to be repeated except between—"I mean among," she corrected herself—the three of them.

Her eyes wide with anticipation, Emily urged Alice to go on. And so the three, their heads close together, made their way along the road, with Rose and Alice taking turns telling about their afternoon in the teacher's parlor.

"You didn't really ask if people jumped around like cows, did you?" Emily wanted to know.

"We did. And they apparently do, on occasion," Alice said. "But not until they are married. We are allowed to kiss and hold hands. And Rose," she said, unable to resist the chance to tease, "Rose has been carrying on in that very way."

"All very proper, Missy," Rose answered sharply, jabbing her elbow into Alice's side.

"Chaperoned, I'll warrant," Emily said in her most serious voice, and all three burst out laughing and laughed so hard that they stopped walking, bent over and held their sides, not even noticing the attention they were getting from the curious children who overtook and passed them.

"Perhaps," Rose said, "we are the dizziest three in school."

"Meaning what?" Alice asked.

"Meaning that I was thinking when Ethan was making eyes at you in the classroom that it was a good thing Emily didn't like Peter Granger because we would all be in trouble." She glanced at Emily and was startled to see that her face was getting pink.

"You don't like him, do you?" Rose demanded.

"No, no," Emily said quickly. "But he looks quite different when he's teaching the reading, doesn't he?"

She does like him, Rose thought, even though she said he didn't smell good. How simple our lives were when we still thought boys were a nuisance and could just ignore them. Now she didn't seem able to ignore Newton at all, whether he was standing in front of her or far away at Joshua Chittenden's farm. She gave a little shiver as she thought about his kissing her cheek right in front of Miss Harty.

"Are you cold?" Emily wanted to know.

"Too warm, actually," Rose said, smiling.

"Sometimes you are so mysterious that I think you must be crazy," Emily said. "Shivering because you're too warm."

"Thinking about Newton, I'll warrant," Alice said with a wise nod.

"You," Rose answered, "have just reached your turn-off, so be gone!"

Alice nodded again and laughed. "I know a little something about warm shivers," she said, picking up her skirts and running off before Rose could grab her.

When she was gone, Emily put a hand on Rose's arm. "Just a minute," she said. "I need to understand something more. All this kissing and touching and jumping around ends up with babies, right?"

"Right."

"So where does the sin of fornication come in?"

Rose froze, her feet no longer moving.

"Did I do something wrong? What is it, Rose?"

Rose made herself start walking again. "Fornication is when people who are not married do all those things," she said in a voice so low that Emily could barely hear her. "It's like... it's when... it's what..."

Now it was Emily who stopped, her hand curling tightly around Rose's wrist. "Miss Graves," she said. "It's like Miss Graves."

Rose nodded, and Emily's heart started to thump as she saw tears in her friend's eyes.

"Please don't cry, Rose, I'm so sorry," she said. "I'm a dunderhead, a dunce, an idiot."

A tear rolled down Rose's cheek, and Emily added quickly, "You really can't cry, you know. It's still chilly, and the tears will freeze on your cheek and peel your skin off, just like the day that boy we didn't know touched his tongue to the cold hitching post."

"Ooooh," Rose said. "I had put that out of my mind. The very idea makes my tongue twitch." But thinking of tears stripping her face made her smile, even while several more drops rolled out, and she hugged Emily so hard that both girls dropped their books and quickly scrambled to retrieve them before they got wet or muddy.

"We are both dunderheads, I reckon," Rose said. "But we're good dunderheads."

CHAPTER TWELVE
Spring Cleaning

Rose was still trying to find places to store snow shovels, warm hats, and heavy blankets when she heard Mr. Goodnow say, "Good afternoon, Silas. We were pleased to see you at Grange last night."

"Jason said I would be welcome," Silas Hibbard answered in a voice so low that Rose could barely hear him. "I was not so certain."

"But you did feel welcome, did you not?"

"I did. Everyone was quite solicitous. It was strange not to have Sarah at my side or watch her participating in the rituals. She always said Grange was a star in her sky," Silas said, his voice stronger.

Rose moved closer to the storage room door, anxious not to miss any part of this talk. She knew how her mother loved going to Grange meetings. She liked them even better than square dances, Rose thought, and she always came home with new stories to tell about what was going on in town. Charles was always trying to get her to tell them about what they did at Grange, but Sarah had always shushed him and said it was secret. Rose wondered how a meeting could have secrets, but she did know that some of it was like a play with members playing parts. Someday they would be old enough to go and find out for themselves what all the hush-hush was about.

It was her mother's chance to be with adults, Rose suddenly realized. She'd never thought about it before. She herself went to school each day and talked with her friends, but her mother was home, doing the washing, the cooking, and keeping the fire going in the kitchen stove. Sarah spent hours heating water, filling the washtub, scrubbing the clothes, and then heating the heavy flatirons to take care of the ironing once the clothes were dry. Most days she didn't see anyone, except maybe the fish peddler or the iceman. Perhaps Sarah was lonely, really lonely, especially on the days when her father took a lunch pail and was gone for the day, sawing wood or helping Mr. Chandler make syrup. Rose knew about being lonely. Sometimes, even at Miss Harty's house, she felt very alone. Perhaps her mother was so busy getting everything done that she didn't even think about it. But "a star in her sky." That was a big thing. Rose knew her mother loved stars. She hoped she was one of Sarah's stars, too. She must have been. Charles and Abby, too, she reckoned. But now there was no way to know.

The voices in the store caught her attention again. Mr. Goodnow was asking if the plumbing project was coming along, and her father was describing how he had finished the walls and worked with Ben Chandler on installing the new toilet and the piping.

"I reckon we'll make allowance for a sink in there, too," Silas Hibbard said, "but I can't afford to buy one at present. We'll just get the pipes in place."

"Better set it up for hot and cold water," Henry Goodnow advised. "You'll have it for the tub anyway, so you might as well make provisions for the sink while you're at it."

Rose decided it wasn't eavesdropping to listen to talk about plumbing, so she pushed open the storage room door and entered the store, greeting her father with a small smile and moving quickly past him to complete her tasks of the day.

"Hold on there," Silas said. "You're something of a sight for sore eyes, young lady, and I am in need of a better greeting than that."

Henry Goodnow stood very still, thinking Silas was about as subtle as a bull with a springing cow. He wasn't anxious to have a father-daughter row here in the store, but to his relief, Rose turned and smiled again.

"Good afternoon, Father," she said in a very formal way. "I did not think I should interrupt your conversation with Mr. Goodnow, and I do have many things to do before I can get on home."

"Good afternoon yourself," Silas said. "I hope one day getting on home will mean coming back to me and

Charles. In the meantime, as I promised you, I have turned a corner, mebbe more than one corner. Miss Graves is gone, the new flush toilet is nearly ready for use, and Charles is quite set up about the prospect of no longer emptying slop jars. It appears his nose and stomach are nearly as sensitive to privy odors as they were to chickens in their death throes."

Now Rose's face broke into a genuine smile. "You two are getting on then?" she asked.

"We manage, we manage," Silas said a little gruffly. "We don't set a particularly good table, but we manage."

Rose's smile disappeared as if she had swallowed it. She didn't like to think of Charles not having proper meals. He ought to have some chicken and dumplings on a Sunday and even a pot roast now and then. She hoped his oatmeal was smoother these days, but she had a sinking feeling that boy and man were lacking a good deal at the table since she had left.

"Not your concern," Silas said hastily, since he had firmly resolved not to upset this girl again if he could help it. "We are perusing your mother's receipt book, and Charles has proved quite a hand with the pans and skillets, along with raising a thriving calf. He's of no account when it comes to killing and dressing chickens, but he can cook one to a turn."

"I can hardly believe it," Rose said. "He didn't say... he hasn't talked with me about his culinary skills."

"Culinary might be a mite of an overstatement when it comes to the right word," Silas said, coming as close

Spring Cleaning

to a grin as Henry Goodnow had seen on the man's face in months. "'Cooking' will do for description. But he's coming right along."

The three fell silent, all of them picturing Charles at the big wood stove that was the centerpiece of Sarah Hibbard's kitchen, and none of them able to think of anything else to say about it. Henry Goodnow broke the silence by inquiring whether Silas was properly fixed for pipes and connectors for his project.

"And," Rose interrupted with a hint of mischief in her voice, "how is Charles fixed for spring cleaning supplies and tools?"

"Appreciate it if you could take the time to inventory that aspect," Silas said to his daughter. "And we'd empty the sugar bowl into your apron pocket if you spared us a few hours of cleaning time. With Charles at your right hand, of course. We do have," he added, with a trace of amusement in his voice, "a new sugar bowl, and we're storing up nickels and dimes in it as fast as we sell an egg or a jug of milk."

How strange this was, Rose thought. She had smashed that sugar bowl months ago by throwing it against the kitchen wall, and he had never said a word about it. She figured he hadn't even noticed. And now they had a new one, and he was putting the cash money into it. Perhaps he was indeed turning another corner. Miss Graves was gone, and he didn't have that awful stale smell that she reckoned came from having too much of what everyone called the drink. She wondered if she should take pay for helping with their cleaning, or whether she plain owed it to him. Sometimes she went over a list in her head that looked like a ledger book, the things he had done wrong on the one side, the things he had done right on the other. The second list was still much shorter than the first, but she'd have to give him a new line on the yes side for today. Friendly, she could call it. That would do.

"I will see to the inventory," Rose said. "But I am short on time for extra work. Miss Harty and I will be at the soap-making this weekend, I expect."

"You'll need some supplies for that, Rose," Henry Goodnow interrupted, worried that this conversation was unlikely to go on much longer without some kind of confrontation taking place. He never liked confrontations, with customers or with his wife, and he didn't want one now.

But he needn't have worried. Silas Hibbard was touching the brim of his hat, nodding to them both, and heading for the door. "Appreciate it if you'd just add these things to my account," he told Henry, gesturing with the sack of oats he carried. "I'll be getting in some extra egg money soon, now that the hens are laying again."

"Why do hens take time off?" Rose asked Mr. Goodnow as soon as her father was gone. "Do they get holidays?"

"Plain run out of eggs, I reckon," the storekeeper answered, thinking what an odd one this girl sometimes was. She'd just managed a lengthy and civil conversation with her father without turning a hair, but instead

Spring Cleaning

of dwelling on that, her mind was on chicken vacations. He hadn't any idea why a hen stopped laying, but he would ask his wife and get an answer for the ever-curious Rose.

"As for soap supplies," Rose said, "we had better leave that to Miss Harty, sir. I don't take any inventories at her house," she added with a small smile. "Charles, however, will be needing a new mop, and I'd better gather up some rags and find a way to replace what's on the old handle. I don't think the sugar bowl will take care of pipes and spring cleaning goods."

Henry Goodnow shook his head in wonderment and stood still behind the counter for several minutes after Rose had gone back to her tasks. She surprised him almost every day, and he could never quite get over that she was just a child, really, a motherless child with a wise head on her slim shoulders. Sarah Sherman—Sarah Hibbard, he corrected himself—would be downright proud of the way Rose was turning out, even if she would never have said so out loud. Proud of Charles, too, able to stay there with the unpredictable Silas and make a creditable stab at cooking.

"I think that's it for today, sir," Rose said, reappearing at the counter where Mr. Goodnow ruled over the cash register and the little book of accountings. "I'll ask Miss Harty to come by for the soap supplies," she added, her nose turning up at the very memory of the strong-smelling lye that was a key ingredient. "Perhaps she'll put some rose water in hers."

"That's a suggestion I can make," Mr. Goodnow told

her. "Run along now, and I will expect you tomorrow for an hour or two."

Rose started toward Miss Harty's house, then decided she would take the bull by the horns and get right at that inventory of cleaning supplies at her own house. Charles would be home and perhaps she could surprise him at the stove, stirring the stew or frying chicken.

She paused at the door, wondering if she needed to knock. She was family, and her real bedroom was still here. But she didn't live here anymore, so she hesitated, then tapped lightly and turned the knob. And there was Charles, one of Sarah's aprons tied on over his school clothes, stirring something in the big blue enamel kettle. He was too absorbed in his task to hear her, so he jumped when she spoke, and the spoon flew up, sending little spatters of liquid skittering over the hot surface of the wood stove.

"It's a good thing I'm a mere boy, Rose," he said, frowning at her. "If I were an old woman with a weak heart, I would have fainted dead away just now, thinking a beggar or a thief was upon me."

Rose started to laugh. "If you were an old woman with a weak heart, I would be in the wrong house, so that would be really appalling," she said. "I have come to see how you are fixed for mops and dust cloths so you can begin the spring scrubbing, and now I'm flummoxed to find you talking like a textbook."

"Judas Priest," Charles said. "Isn't it enough that I am over a hot stove for several hours of my day? Must I tie a kerchief around my hair and brandish a cloth-covered broom at the spiders who roam our ceilings?"

"You are too young to curse like that," Rose said, trying to stifle her impulse to smile. She wondered how Miss Harty managed to frown at mischievous students when everyone else in the room badly wanted to laugh.

"It is a small swear," Charles said. "And I may be small, but in many ways I am a man. I take care of a growing brood of chickens; I own a calf that must be fed and watered and whose wastes must be shoveled away; I am cook and dishwasher; I have no mother, nor sisters of any account, and I occasionally wash my sheets."

"And you are still talking like a school primer," Rose said, now laughing out loud. "I spend a good deal of time worrying about how you are getting on here, and then I come to find a clown who claims to be put upon but seems to like it."

"Oh, Rose, I am put upon. By Father, by chickens who do not want to share their eggs, by a rambunctious calf who has far more coming out of his back end than he puts in at the front—a miracle of sorts, I suppose—and by a lack of love and devotion," he announced, finishing with an intentional flourish of the spoon.

"I would like to visit you here every day," Rose said, serious again. "You always make me laugh. But I am really here now to see what needs doing in the way of spring cleaning. When did you last put clean linen on your bed?"

Charles turned back to the pot on the stove, stirring with slow concentration. "I always go counterclockwise," he said, holding the spoon up. "It gets the ingredients all riled up, and they surrender all their flavors."

"Linen," Rose said, hiding another smile.

"This is March," Charles said. "I believe it was January. I cannot wash sheets and hang them outside to freeze into great boards that I can barely wrestle off the clothesline. And then they are still not dry. The sheets on my bed are less than clean, but they are dry."

"Errrggg," Rose said, thinking about how Miss Harty insisted that the bottom sheet on their beds be washed at least every two weeks, with the top one then put in its place. It did mean a sheet was used for four weeks in the winter, she realized, but it might not be easy to get Charles' sheets clean ever again. Not wanting to carp at him, she just shook her head and went into the hallway to see about the mop and broom.

"Charles," she called almost as soon as she had disappeared through the door. "Charles?"

"Ah, you have discovered the pipes," he called back. "Next week or the week after I will hurl the slop jar from an upstairs window, and it will splinter on the ground like a raw egg. Or a sugar bowl."

"I trust you are speaking of an empty slop jar," Rose said, coming back into the kitchen and ignoring her brother's eagerness to get a rise out of her. "I knew about the plumbing project, but I had no picture of it in my head. It is quite nice, and it's in an excellent location."

"All that remains, once Father has finished inserting washers and tightening joints, is for us to abandon the privy."

"Bolt the door," Rose suggested.

Charles frowned. "You must live in a hotel," he said. "Once we have a new place for our leavings, we will be down under that two-holer, cleaning out everything that's been put there since the last shoveling. And I don't remember when that might have been. Can your Newton-soaked brain imagine what that will smell like?"

The smell of Newton's winter coat, the sweet soapy smell of his cheek, and then the slightly sweaty smell of his shirt at the end of a square dance went through Rose's mind as if he were standing there. She sighed a sigh as long as most any Charles had ever heard and said, "I wouldn't mind if each of his aromas saturated me as if I were a sponge," and immediately wished she hadn't said a thing.

"Aroma, eh?" Charles teased. "He doesn't smell or have a stench of barn and cow. He has an ah-ro-mah?"

Rose made as if to swat him, but he raised his cooking spoon at her and she backed off. "Sorry, Charles," she said. "But I do miss him, and when he gets back, he'll be so busy with spring planting that I may never see him."

"I'll wager you're dead wrong about that," Charles said. "He's so sweet on you it takes me by surprise the bees aren't all over him."

"They're still keeping warm in their hives," Rose said, recovering quickly from her weak moment. With a hint of sharpness, she added, "And I think I'll be on my way and stop in to see Abby, and perhaps I can amuse her, too, for a moment."

Charles let the spoon drop against the edge of the

kettle and crossed the kitchen in a rush. He threw both arms around Rose, who stumbled in astonishment, and planted a kiss on her cheek. As fast as he had come, he retreated, turned his back on her, and began stirring again.

Touched, and watching the back of his neck grow red, she stepped over and softly kissed the growing redness, whispered good-bye, and left as quietly as she had come. As she hurried along the muddy road, trying to step on the drier ridges, she glanced up at the trees, thinking how like skeletons they were in winter, slim black lines against the sky. And then she noticed that their silhouettes were just a bit less harsh, the winter-hard buds starting to soften. To her chagrin, a tear ran down each cheek, and she had to search inside her brain for the reason. It was Sarah, she realized, her mother; Sarah who had always pointed out the early signs of spring—the tiniest change in a tree's color or the first peep of the peepers—before the rest of the world had stopped thinking about snow and mud. She wiped her eyes and hoped they wouldn't be all red-rimmed and ugly when she reached Aunt Nell's.

Abby, she thought, was like Mother. She saw everything. And even though she was only nine, she understood so many things. She looks through me, Rose thought, as if I were a windowpane. Then she laughed out loud, realizing that Charles had the same kind of penetrating vision on occasion. She had been a fool to blurt out all that stuff about Newton, but it was no news to her brother.

She reached the Harris house and quickly went up the steps to the side door. The knob turned at her touch, and she stuck her head in, calling "Hello, anyone at home?" Abby came flying out of the dining room and threw her arms around Rose, burying her face in Rose's coat. Twice in one day, Rose thought. Not bad, she started to say to herself, and stopped. Very good, she amended.

"Pleased to see you, too," she said, disentangling herself. "I presume you are well?"

"Are you going to give me a calling card, Rose?" Abby demanded. "We have met before, I believe."

Rose sighed. When they were all still living with their father, none of her days was long enough to get everything done. Now, it seemed, none of her weeks was long enough to fit in visits to her brother and sister.

"I didn't mean anything," Abby said quickly. "It's just that I really miss you and you're at the other school, and I don't even see Charles very much."

"I know, Abby, I know," Rose said, shaking her head. "But there's only one of me and so many things to do. I'm here now, so let's milk it for whatever it's worth. Do you need anything, are you all right, and how are Aunt Nell and Uncle Jason?"

"Yes, yes and quite well, thank you, as well as precise, predictable, polite, and practical," Abby said, starting to giggle and then adding, "but you know I am too young to milk."

"Where did that come from?" Rose demanded, a bit mystified.

"The four Ps or the milking?" Abby teased. "Well, Uncle Jason measures everything, and he's terribly polite, treating me as if I were a grown-up lady. Aunt Nell always gives the answer you are expecting, and she's forever telling me something is not practical."

"And I thought it was your new vocabulary list," Rose said, laughing so hard that she could barely get the words out. "I can't see you and Charles more often because you make my stomach hurt. Now what was it that you needed?"

"A new dress?" Abby said hesitantly. "I can't ask Aunt Nell, and she hasn't seemed to notice that I'm getting taller every hour of the night. My underthings don't fit very well either. Is it bad to ask? Mother," Abby said with her voice cracking ever so little, "Mother just seemed to know."

Rose put her arm around Abby's shoulder and looked down at her. "Goodness, I can put my chin on the top of your head without bending. I'll look in the closets at Father's to see what I can come up with, and then I'll talk with Aunt Nell about what we can do. Mr. Goodnow has some ends of bolts at the store, and it's possible we could manage a little money for new fabric. Perhaps you'd like to look them over and choose one?"

Abby was jumping up and down with excitement. "Yes, yes, yes," she said. "When can we do it?"

"Calm down, Abby. I have to talk to Mr. Goodnow first and make sure I'm not overstepping whatever the boundaries are. But we'll do something about your clothes. And now I really have to go—Miss Harty is expecting me to lend a hand with the supper and make a list of what we need for making soap."

"Ugh," Abby said. "I hate the smell of making soap."

"Me, too. But if we put rose water in ours it will have a beautiful aroma when we use it. And now I really must go," Rose said, as she moved quickly toward the door, the word aroma making her think about Newton again.

As it turned out, it took Miss Harty only a week to get her soap-making ingredients together, although Rose kept hoping it would take forever. It was the lye, she knew, that stung the eyes, irritated the skin, and was for some reason, foul though it be, essential to the making of soap. Miss Harty said she had tried a few times to make the lye herself from wood ashes kept high and dry all winter, saved from every stove fire. But that added a whole day to the soap-making process, sometimes more, she explained, because you had to pour water through the ashes and repeat the action until the solution was thick enough.

Rose remembered that Sarah had always put an egg into the lye. If it floated just high enough to suit her, she would pronounce the lye ready. Some people, her mother had said, floated a potato, but Sarah preferred the egg. Miss Harty was brought up in the egg tradition as well, she said.

Miss Harty had closed school at the noon hour because she and Rose would need Friday afternoon to get started on the soap. Then, if all went well, they could finish on Saturday. They certainly didn't want to risk the Reverend Lockhead's accusing eye by boiling soap on Sunday.

When the outdoor fire was ready, Miss Harty produced a great collection of suet she had sliced off the side of beef she had purchased before the winter. Rose didn't even want to ask where that awful looking mess had been stored, but she knew it would all have to be boiled, along with the bones Miss Harty had put aside from her own cooking and the extra ones she had bought at the store.

They were out-of-doors because no one wanted the smell of the boiling fat inside the house. Rose's nose kept wrinkling up as the fats grew hot, and she wondered if the suet wasn't pretty much rotted, since it had been kept for several months. It certainly smelled bad enough to be rotten. Strange that something that smelled so horrid would be used to get a body clean. Miss Harty, however, seemed unperturbed, even though it would take another whole day to finish this process.

Smooth tallow was needed for good soap, and Rose knew the kettle would have to stand overnight so they could skim the fat off the top and leave all the bad parts in the bottom of the pot. Only then could they add the lye and boil everything again. It was enough to make a person give up bathing. But at least at Miss Harty's house, some herbs and rose water would be added to provide a sweet smell to the soap. They would also put in some salt at the very last minute so the soap would be hard.

"Mr. Goodnow sells soap," Rose said rather tentatively. "It has a lovely smell, and he says it is even better than what the village ladies make every year. He has lavender and wintergreen."

"Lovely aroma," Miss Harty said.

"I beg your pardon, Ma'am?" Rose said, puzzled by the teacher's answer.

The teacher laughed. "Smell is for manure, Rose, and aroma is for perfume. And I have sniffed the soap at Mr. Goodnow's and am seriously thinking, as I stand here, of never doing this again. But it's very dear, that store soap."

"Oh, I know all about aroma," Rose said, thinking it was sometimes odd how often a word appeared on a given day. You could go a year without hearing anyone say "aroma" and then it would appear as if it were a new boarder.

"And Mother was very sparing in her use of soap," she went on, "because this is so much work. But we would have to be careful with store soap, too, if it's that costly. She always chipped up the last bits of the hard soap to use for washing clothes."

"I'm sure your mother never wasted anything, Rose. Most of us have to be careful of what we have, whether it's soap or cloth or flour. Now perhaps you could give this kettle a stir for a minute while I wipe my brow."

Rose had tied her hair back from her face, but tendrils kept going off on their own, and she periodically swiped her hand over her face in an attempt to keep her hair under control. Stirring the steaming vat with a sturdy twig, she felt the salt of her sweat run right through her eyebrows and add to the sting the lye was already creating in her eyes. What were eyebrows for anyway, she thought, if they couldn't dam up the sweat and keep it out of the eyes? And speaking of dams, why was it that girls and women with every reason to be angry were not supposed to say the other damn, or damnation, or even Judas Priest. This was hot work, and she just knew she'd feel better if she could say one of those things. She glanced at Miss Harty and realized that the teacher looked as hot as she felt.

Rose wriggled her shoulders, trying to release the back of her dress, which was stuck between her shoulder blades. Beads of water were running down the inside of her long stockings, and she was sure it was only a matter of time before a fly would land on her, relishing the salty sweat as if it were ice cream.

"It's a good thing we love our baths, Miss Harty," she said, "or this would be worse than cleaning fish or skinning a deer."

"Where I grew up, I cleaned plenty of fish," Miss Harty replied, her own face shiny from the steam, and her hair starting to escape from the severe bun where she twisted it into shape every morning.

"My mother refused to do that," Rose said. "She said it was the fisherman's task. And she didn't dress chickens either. Did you ever think about how we pull off all the feathers and take out the guts and call it dressing the chicken when we're really undressing it completely, inside and out?"

Miss Harty began to laugh. "Only you, Rose, would

even think about such a thing. Indeed, we undress the chicken and call it dressed. And the best un-dressers take out all those nasty little pinfeathers. I dislike the pinfeathers. And, by the way, I caught my own fish, lots of times."

"I dislike everything about me right now, Ma'am," Rose said, "and I am wondering if anyone else has thought of making soap with no clothes on a-tall."

"Rose!" Miss Harty said, shock in her voice. "A lady does not appear at the soap kettle without being properly attired." But she could not hold the tone, and her voice crumpled into a wicked giggle.

Rose had never heard anything like that sound from the teacher before. The longer she lived in Miss Harty's house, the more she realized that teachers were just like other people, only better. She knew her mother would call the teacher's giggle very low class, not ladylike. But Rose decided she liked it. She hoped she could make her laugh like that again someday, and she wished—she would wish it on a wishbone next time they had chicken—it would be in front of Emily and Alice. Otherwise, they would never believe it.

Rose wiped her face again, using her long apron, even though it was far from clean at this point. She glanced at Miss Harty and saw a strange look come over her face. The teacher's eyes were on something behind Rose, and she turned quickly, groaning with dismay as she saw Newton striding toward them.

"I look a fright, Miss Harty. Stop him. He can't come here now," Rose said in a panic.

"Oh, but he is coming, Rose. I don't think wild horses could stop him."

Grinning from what Mr. Goodnow would call "ear to ear," Newton had nearly reached the girl and woman standing over the steaming kettle of soap-to-be when he said, "Won't be waiting for the Saturday bath this week, I'll warrant," he said as he reached them.

Rose wanted to slap him. She felt her face turning even redder, but Newton came right up to her, spun her around and planted a quick kiss on her cheek, sweat and all. She stopped wanting to slap him and wished she could kiss him back, right on the mouth. She glanced toward the teacher again, and Miss Harty, muttering something about getting a new utensil, went off toward the kitchen.

"Put that stick down," Newton ordered, and Rose obeyed. He then threw his arms around her, kissed her on the mouth, and with his lips still on hers mumbled, "I cannot believe how much a clean boy like me could miss a messy, sweaty thing like you."

In spite of her dismay, Rose started to laugh. She could not imagine what she looked like, but she knew she didn't want to look in the glass right now and find out. As she started to pull away, Newton let her go and joined in her laughter. "It would be proper to say," he said, "that you are a sight for sore eyes, or that you are a sight to make the eyes sore."

She cuffed him on the arm, but she smiled. "I am so happy to see you, even if I don't want to see you here and now," she answered.

"Give me another here and now, and I'll be there," he said. "I just came back from Chittenden's place last night, sick and tired of the tussock router, and I already have a long list of things that Father says must be done by sundown. But I ran off while they were taking their noon meal, which in fact occurred some time after the noon hour."

"What, pray tell, is a tussock router?"

"A mean device Joshua bought for the very purpose of preparing brand new soil for Miss Harty's potato planting, which is apparently in the offing this year. She read somewhere that potatoes grow best in virgin ground. It's made to bust up the most stubborn sods and make a boy sweat. How about that adjustment to here and now?"

"Are you free at sundown?"

"Or soon after," he said.

"I'll make a picnic and meet you at the rock," Rose said. "And I think I will change my clothes. You might do the same. There's a definite cow smell to what you are wearing at present."

"You win that round, Rose. I will see you at the rock when the sun has disappeared. I will bring a lantern so we can see the food. Then I'm going to snuff it out."

Rose watched Newton's long legs pump up and down as he disappeared around Miss Harty's house, and she shivered with anticipation of dusk at the rock.

CHAPTER THIRTEEN
Filling the Spaces

Rose mechanically wrote the answers to the arithmetic questions and let the other half of her mind drift into a pleasant daydream. Alice and Emily were sometimes annoyed by her two-track brain because they knew she was talking to them with perfect sense and thinking about something else, and they preferred her whole attention. Right now, at her desk in Miss Harty's classroom, she didn't have to worry about what her friends thought. She could work out the problems and think about the empty seat behind her at the same time.

Newton's space certainly hadn't been empty when they met at the rock nigh onto a week ago. And he hadn't left any space between them either. A shiver down across Rose's spine as she thought about how close they had been, arms touching arms, while they ate the supper she had brought. She had promised to be there at dusk, but she reckoned it was more like twilight by the time she had scrubbed all the soap-making smell off her skin and gathered the picnic together and put on a clean dress. Dusk must come before twilight, she thought, and caught herself just in time from raising her hand to ask Miss Harty that question, which clearly had nothing to do with this man and his firkins of butter.

He had bought five firkins, the arithmetic problem said, for seven dollars a firkin. That would be 224 pounds of butter, she thought. But Miss Harty didn't care about that, or about what under heaven a man was going to do with four quarter-barrels of butter. He must own a store, Rose decided, because the important matter was how to price the butter so he would make a ten-dollar profit.

It was so simple, Rose said to herself. It would be nine dollars a firkin. That was much easier than some of the things she had to figure at Mr. Goodnow's store. Mr. Goodnow scooped butter out of firkins and sold it by the pound. So how much would it cost for a pound if the fellow was to get his ten-dollar profit? Stop it, she told herself. He's selling it in barrels. He's what Mr. Goodnow calls a "middle man," and it's Mr. Goodnow who has to price it by the pound. Or sometimes trade for a few eggs or freshly baked bread. She wrote her answer and went on to "How many fifths of an apple make a whole apple?"

She and Newton had shared an apple at their picnic.

She could only find one good one in Miss Harty's cellar, the last of the fall harvest of the teacher's favorite Sheepnose apples, but the teacher had said she could take it. She smiled, remembering how Newton had taken a big bite and held it for her. When she bit the apple on the other side, thinking it really was shaped quite like a sheep's nose, he had leaned forward and bitten his side at the same time. She wrote down: "Five fifths of an apple make a whole apple," and saw in her mind's eye how close his eyes had been, shining a little in the light of the lantern he had brought as promised. And then they had both let go of the apple and kissed. She shivered again, thinking how his tongue had pushed her lips apart and licked away some of her bite of the apple, right off her teeth.

No wonder Eve took the apple, Rose thought. It was probably much prettier than the slightly wrinkled one she had shared with Newton, and it had put the first woman right into Adam's arms, if she and Emily and Alice had rightly interpreted the biblical verses. That wasn't what the Reverend Lockhead said, of course. He went on and on about Eve giving in to temptation and how the apple was a symbol of sin. What Rose knew was that she had wanted to put her tongue right into Newton's mouth as soon as the apple fell, but she remembered what Miss Harty had said and kept her teeth together. Perhaps Eve forgot to do that, she thought.

"Rose?" Miss Harty said from the front of the room, and Rose started. She hoped the teacher hadn't said her name more than that once. Sometimes the second track in her head took over and left the school track way back in second place.

"Have you finished the problems?" the teacher persisted.

"Yes, Ma'am," Rose said, realizing that everyone else had passed their papers forward so the teacher could collect them at the front of the room.

"Perhaps," the teacher said a bit sharply, "you will be good enough to come to the board and put your work there for all of us to see."

"Yes, Ma'am," Rose answered, moving forward quickly and taking the chalk. "Shall I copy from my paper?"

"Perhaps you can do the problems all over again," Miss Harty said, thinking that she was being a little hard on this nice girl just to prove that she didn't play favorites with Rose. She hoped the work was correct, as it usually was. But Rose had seemed quite preoccupied in school this week, and Miss Harty was beginning to wonder what had passed at that picnic in the woods.

Rose put the information on firkins and apples on the board, along with eight other problems, all of them solved perfectly. She did like using the chalk on the slate and lining up the numbers and words on the board, even though there were no lines to guide her. When she finished, Miss Harty said the problems had all been solved correctly, and anyone who had one or more wrong should raise his or her hand. Ethan's hand went up, and Emily's followed.

"You may take your seat, Rose," Miss Harty said. She called Ethan and Emily to her desk, pulled out their papers, and started to review their work with them, telling the rest of the class to continue with their penmanship practice.

Rose was pleased. She had managed the firkins, and now she could dip her pen in the inkwell and carefully make row upon row of letters, each sitting on the line where it was supposed to. She especially liked the S and the Q, but she knew she had better begin at the beginning. And she hadn't lost her place in the daydream about last Saturday, nor would she during the mindless drill of making letters.

She and Newton had both laughed about the apple and then he had suddenly snuffed out the lantern, just as he had threatened to do. With a hand on each of her shoulders, he had pulled her down so they were both lying on the blanket he had brought, looking up at the night sky. As two or three stars appeared, the peepers began to sing, and Newton, holding her hand at her side, chuckled.

"Rubbing their legs together, eh?" he said. "You told me that."

"That's it," Rose had answered. "They're frogs. One of the earliest signs of spring. I first heard them two weeks ago, and then we had more snow, and I wondered if they had gotten up too soon."

"Think they'd be worn to a frazzle by now," Newton had said. Carefully writing a row of capital Es, Rose wondered where that word came from. It was the opposite of dazzle, certainly, and it sounded so harsh and troubled. She didn't think of the peepers as troubled.

She thought they were joyful about spring and singing their hearts out. Well, their legs, actually.

Their talk about frogs and stars was so ordinary that Rose was taken by surprise when Newton rolled toward her and pulled her so close that they were touching from shoulders to toes. For a moment, she had felt, well, dizzy, she reckoned. That was another word filled with Zs. It was an uneasy word. Why, she wondered, wasn't uneasy spelled with a Z?

"I have been dreaming of this moment for days, Rose," Newton had whispered right into her ear. "I would like to hold you forever, and I'm afraid to ask if you want me to because if you say no, if you say you're going off to seek your fortune, I will be quite lost."

"Hold me forever, Newton," Rose had whispered back, wondering what was making her voice crack so oddly. "With intermissions."

He had hooted. "You are the strangest girl," he said. "Forever, with intermissions. And what will you be up to when it's intermission time?"

Instead of answering, she had pulled his head down and kissed him hard, pushing her body even closer to his, and then softening the kiss, feeling a flood of warmth all over. He had buried his face in her neck, running his hands up and down her back. She was writing the S row now and decided she had better put the Newton train on a siding. Her face was starting to feel warm just from the memory.

"Rose?" the teacher's voice said again.

"Yes, Ma'am," Rose answered with alacrity.

"Perhaps you could help Emily, who is still having difficulty with the last two problems, while I finish up with Ethan."

"Yes, Ma'am," Rose said, and smiled at Emily as she came to sit in Newton's empty seat.

"You look a little pink," Emily whispered. "What have you been thinking about back here? That picnic at the rock, I'll wager."

"You mustn't wager, Emily," Rose answered. "It's a sin."

"The question is not about my wagering but about whether you, Miss Rose, are sinning on a rock."

"No sinning," Rose said, and sighed. "Temptation, but no sinning. And we'd better get at these problems or Miss Harty will have us after school."

"I desire to walk home with you," Emily said, "so I can hear all about not sinning on the rock." Then the two settled down, and Rose explained the arithmetic so clearly that Emily understood it immediately.

"You could be a teacher now," she said. "And you ought to be. But I have looked into the crystal ball, and I think you are going to marry a farmer and raise Jersey cows."

"Fortune-telling is also a sin," Rose said, trying not to laugh.

"You must have done something you shouldn't because you're acting like goody two-shoes," Emily retorted, "and I'm going back to my seat."

Rose wished she could skip out and walk home alone so Emily couldn't question her about the picnic. She certainly wasn't going to tell her friends that Newton's hands had traveled right down to her seat and held her so tight that she could feel—she was sure she could feel—his body pushing harder against her skirt. She had seen what happened with horses and bulls, and she thought from what Miss Harty had said that it might just be the same with male humans. She hoped it wasn't wrong to let him hold her like that, because she had liked it. And besides, they'd had all their clothes on, hadn't they?

"I am falling in love with you," Newton had whispered, kissing her face. Then he had sat up quite abruptly, and she followed. He had twirled her around so she was facing away from him, and she could feel his fingers working at her single braid. Then he was separating the three strands and running his fingers through her long hair, which she had washed that day because she was afraid it smelled of lye and boiling suet. Then he turned her around again and reached for the lantern, relighting it.

"I have been wanting to do that almost from the first day I sat behind you in school," he had said. "I want to see you with hair flowing like an angel or a wood nymph or a Greek goddess, not all pulled back and tied in a plait."

Then he had sat and stared at her for so long that she wanted to get up and run away. "You are very beautiful, Rose," he had said. "I think, in fact, I have already fallen."

"Don't get up," Rose had said. "I'm on my way down there, too, and my only wish is that we land softly and in the same place." As the school bell rang, she realized she had no idea where those words had come from. She had so many words in her head, and not one of them before these had seemed romantic. She was filled up with words of worry about Abby and Charles, grief for her mother, fear of her father. Well, she did love spring and flowers and school and living with Miss Harty. But those things weren't romantic, no more so than Tom Sawyer painting a fence.

"I am getting up," Newton had said, "but not from the falling-in-love place. I am getting up because we are on spring ice here, and I must stop touching any part of you before I do something we will both wish hadn't happened and we are suddenly in over our heads."

"I told Miss Harty you would be like that," Rose said without thinking.

"You told Miss Harty what?" Newton had asked, his voice rising. "You talked to her about us and told her what?"

She had answered, "Don't get all in a swivet, Newton. It's something we might have to talk about, actually, so I think I'm glad that popped out of my mouth before my brain knew what it was doing."

"You are confusing as well as strange," Newton had said. "Now, you sit over there, not right next to me, and I'll sit over here, and you will tell what it is that we have to talk about."

So Rose had tried her best to explain what Miss Harty had said about kissing and sometimes mouths opening and not being able to go back to just holding hands and that girls had to take all the responsibility because boys just plowed ahead with these things and that she had said Newton would be responsible.

She had spoken without taking a breath, and by the time she stopped talking, Newton was doubled over with laughter.

"My lips are sealed," he had gasped. "I cannot picture you and the teacher sitting there over tea talking about mouths and tongues and holding hands, but so be it. You had better plait your hair and let me escort you back to a proper chaperone. We seem to be needing one."

Rose had just looked at him, wondering for a second or two if he had lost his senses. She remembered Aunt Nell saying that Father had been so sappy over Sarah that Uncle Jason was afraid to let him near the big saws in the mill. Was Newton sappy? She did think he meant to take some responsibility for the difference between what they wanted to do and what they could and would do. She, for one, was so happy when they just held each other close, as close as possible. And then she had rebraided her hair.

"Rose?" This time it was Emily's voice interrupting her thoughts. Without even thinking, Rose had taken her wrap from the cloakroom and left the school. She was already at the bottom of the steps when Emily called. Realizing that she had been deep in her thoughts, she hoped it was only the first time Emily had spoken. Her friend was very impatient when Rose didn't answer.

"Here I am," she said cheerfully.

"Well, finally," Emily said. "I said your name three

times. And now, sure as toads have warts, I know you have been up to something with Newton. Neither your mother's death nor your father's drinking have dropped your mind plain out of sight like this. Tell."

When Rose just smiled, Emily said, "Please tell, Rose. I won't tell. You know I won't. Not even Alice, if you say so."

"And not Peter Granger?"

To Rose's surprise and delight, Emily's face turned just a little pink, but she did not relent. "Just me, Rose, just me."

So Rose told her a little bit about the picnic and the stars and the peepers and how they had laughed about the frogs and that they had kissed, and that she had liked it. "And I like him, Emily. I like him a lot."

The two walked on in silence for a few minutes, and then Emily said, "We're very young, but I think you are falling in love with him. My mother says sometimes people fall in love when they are very young and stay that way. But you are supposed to be a teacher. How is that going to work?"

"Intermissions," Rose said, laughing. "Intermissions."

"You are in love," Emily said, "because you don't even make sense anymore."

"I am thinking he might wait for me," Rose said. "I really want to be a teacher, and you can't do that if you are married…"

"Married!" Emily exclaimed. "Did he ask you to get married?"

Filling the Spaces

"Don't interrupt, Emily. It's not mannerly. No, he didn't, but he might. I think he might. I'm not old enough to get married anyway. And now I have to hurry to get to Mr. Goodnow's for work."

Emily sighed. She had found out a few things she wanted to know, but it was like prying salt codfish out of the box. You were lucky to get a whole piece now and then, and lots of times it just flaked into bits.

"I'll see you tomorrow," Emily said. "If you wake up in the middle of the night and want to talk about it, just come throw stones at my window. I always answer."

Immediately contrite as she remembered the dark night when she had tossed snowballs at Emily's window, Rose turned and gave her friend a hug. "I want to tell you everything, but not yet, Emily, not yet. Right now it's just for Newton and me, and it's very nice."

Emily hugged her back and said, "I love you, too, you know, and I want you to be very, very happy."

"I am," Rose answered. "And I'm also late," she said over her shoulder as she hurried toward Mr. Goodnow's store. It's like a refuge, she thought, a place without worries. She put her thumb on the brass latch and pushed the door in, glancing quickly at a small wagon and horse that were hitched outside. She wondered if it could be the vanilla man. She knew the supply was gone and that Mr. Goodnow had been hoping spring would bring Mr. Baldwin around again.

Sure enough. He was at the counter, a tall, strapping man with a bushy mustache, writing down an order and chattering away with Mr. Goodnow about setting out on his rounds before all the snow was melted. He had stayed the first night, he was saying, at the Red Lion Inn, about ten miles from his home.

"It's a cut above most of the places where I find a pillow," he said, "and the food beats most boardinghouse fare as well. It's a bit dear, but a fine way to set out. And they usually trade part of my board, sometimes all of it, for a buggy whip or two."

"Have you whips to sell, sir?" Henry Goodnow wanted to know, immediately interested in this extra dimension.

"Indeed. My wife's cousin makes them in a small village near us. If you are out of vanilla, I have a few bottles in the buggy that I could sell you now, Henry."

"Eastborough's housewives would be grateful, Charles," Henry answered. "They pester me regular about that vanilla, which sells here faster than cider or kerosene. Christmas cookies, I think, used up a good deal of it last season. They all swear their sugar cookies have never tasted better."

"Found a way to make a living, I reckon," Mr. Baldwin said. "If my good wife can put up with all the time I'm out peddling, then I've found a way. It's not easy punching a new pillow into shape every night, you know. And some of those straw mattresses are no better than sleeping in a horse stall."

Mr. Baldwin turned then and saw Rose coming up behind him. "Land o' Goshen, but you've turned into a young lady since I was here last," he said. Seeing Rose start to blush, he bobbed his head and added more gently, "Be putting your hair up soon, I reckon, and stepping out with the young fellers."

At that point, Rose felt her face getting really warm and knew she would look like a beet in a minute. But she was trying to face up to the problem, so she didn't turn away. "It's nice to see you again, sir. Our teacher will be overjoyed to learn that we are stocking the vanilla again."

"We?" Mr. Baldwin asked. "Are you part of the store now?"

"I work here after school," Rose said. "Mr. Goodnow was kind enough to take me on when I moved out of my father's house."

Several expressions flitted across Charles Baldwin's face, but he decided he'd better not pursue that last remark. As he turned back to the counter to complete the order form, Henry Goodnow said, "Kindness might have been involved on the first day, but since then, Charles, I've come to depend on Rose's ability to run a store."

"You are fortunate," Mr. Baldwin answered. "Most of our help these days doesn't know a pint from a tablespoon when they start."

Rose began to laugh. "You can't get through third grade here without knowing a thing like that, Mr. Baldwin. Perhaps you'd better move your—is it a factory?—here."

"Not a factory really, Rose. More like a processing place. We get vanilla beans from Madagascar, and we cook 'em up sort of the way you cook hops to make beer, or rye to make whiskey. Lot of alcohol in that vanilla, you know. Our copper percolator runs many hours of the day extracting the goodness from those beans."

"Even Mrs. Munson says your vanilla lasts the best through the baking," Rose said solemnly.

"Even?" Charles Baldwin asked, raising his left eyebrow.

Rose noticed that one eyebrow went up and the other stayed down, and thought that couldn't be common. Most people she knew raised both, creating lines across the forehead and a look of amazement on the face. Then she realized why he had raised an eyebrow. The very way she had mentioned Mrs. Munson put her right at the gossipy woman's level.

"Oh, dear," Rose said aloud. "I didn't mean..." But she couldn't finish, because she realized she had meant exactly what she said. Funny how a single word could create as much damage as a cat's foot in a pie.

But Henry Goodnow was laughing. "Not an easy woman to please, Charles," he put in. "But you can bet your boots she's the best one to pass the word around. Whatever Hattie Munson knows or thinks, the town knows." Then he added, "But may not think it."

Oh, he knows all about her, Rose thought with relief. And apparently Mr. Baldwin, too, since he seems to be chuckling, even though he isn't making a sound. She decided it was time she went to work instead of standing around here gabbing as if she were a customer.

"A pleasure to see you, Rose," Mr. Baldwin called as she moved away. "I'm leaving a sample bottle of vanilla here with the hope that you're learning to bake."

"Learning?" Mr. Goodnow snorted. "That girl," he said, lowering his voice so Rose wouldn't hear, "that girl can bake circles around most women in this town, in addition to cleaning, doing laundry, and getting all her sums right. She hasn't had an easy time of it since her mother died, but she still has a smile for every person who lifts the latch here. Small wonder Newton Barnes has his eye, probably both eyes, on her. But she's aiming to be a teacher, and I am beginning to believe she might manage that, too."

Charles Baldwin put away his order book and watched Rose pick up a feather duster and start flicking it at the shiny doors of the postal boxes.

"Land sakes, Henry, she's a little young for either marrying or teaching, isn't she?"

"Young on the calendar," Mr. Goodnow answered without smiling, "but oh, so much older—for better and for worse—in the head."

Mr. Baldwin shook his head, went out to his buggy, and returned quickly with several small, clear glass bottles of his vanilla. He tested the cork on each and promised Mr. Goodnow that he'd be telegraphing the new orders to his wife within a day or two, as soon as he had several.

"They travel well," Henry said, "packed in all that excelsior. And the stationmaster lets me know as soon as the boxes get here since he knows I'm anxious to replenish. Where do you go from here?"

"Down into Connecticut, then over to the Catskills.

Be crossing the Hudson on the ferry, and I always enjoy that, although the horse always gets a little skittish about it. Then I'll get back home for a spell and brew some more. Take care of yourself, Henry," he said, and he was gone, striding out to his horse and buggy.

CHAPTER FOURTEEN
Intentions

On Friday, Rose knew it was going to rain. All the cows she had seen the previous afternoon were lying down, and Grandmother Emma was fond of saying that was a good way to predict a rainstorm. Rose was only four or five at the time, but she remembered clearly that she had asked why a cow would always lie down a day ahead of a storm.

"To make sure she has a dry place when the rain comes in," Grandmother had said, the little curls around her face bobbing as she nodded her head. "People only think cows are stupid because it's hard to lead 'em and hard to drive 'em. But they know what they need to know just like most people. They show up in the lane near the barn every afternoon for milking time, don't they? Must have clocks in their heads."

Now it was Saturday, so she was setting out for Mr. Goodnow's store. She glanced at the garden she and Miss Harty had planted and saw that the peas were several inches tall, making their way toward the twigs she and the teacher had stuck into the ground. With satisfaction, she saw green spears of newly sprouted onions in a row almost as straight as a ruler. She did like straight rows. Now the rain, she thought, will make everything come along quickly.

In the meantime, she was grateful for the loan of Miss Harty's umbrella. Father and Sarah had never owned one that she knew of, but it was a blessing to know she would arrive at the store without looking like a drowned rat. She'd never actually seen a drowned rat, come to think of it, and she wondered if it happened often. They must swim, she thought—almost every creature seemed to swim if desperate enough. Her mind on the wetness of rats, Rose stepped in a small puddle and felt the water seep into her shoes. This, she said to herself, was another time when it would be nice to say something more than "land sakes." Next to the puddle a couple of earthworms wriggled along the gravel surface of the road. Night crawlers, Father called them, the worms he liked to use when fishing for trout in the Chandlers' brook. She wondered why worms surfaced in the rain when their real home was buried in the earth. Miss Harty said they helped cultivate the soil when they wormed their way along. The teacher also said Chinese worms were the source of silk, something Rose found hard to believe. Squirmy little creatures making silk? Well, now, the teacher couldn't make up anything as outlandish as that.

It was raining so hard that she could see rivulets of water forming in the crannies of bark on the maple trees. Last fall's leaves were moving along in the ditch at the roadside, and water was dripping off every roof. Beside the church, workers were scurrying around the tent where last night's temperance meeting had been held, digging small trenches so the water would bypass the tent area and keep it as dry as possible for the next gathering.

Rose went and heard the Reverend Lockhead rail against John Barleycorn and "the drink." Others spoke as well, telling how they had given up hard cider and whiskey and were the better for it. She had looked around several times to see if Father had come, but she did not see him. She didn't see Charles, either, but she hadn't expected him to show up. He wasn't much for putting on a clean shirt these days. Emily and Alice had come with their parents, but they took the seats she had saved for them.

The minister began with talk about the harm inflicted on mothers and children when the man of the house took to the bottle, and Emily and Alice each reached for one of Rose's hands. For the rest of the evening the three of them sat there, clutching each other and watching the adults around them. Rose stopped hoping to see her father, but she knew Emily and Alice were taking turns hunting for him. She should have known he wouldn't come.

Only two or three people answered the minister's call and went forward to pledge what he called abstinence, which Rose knew meant a promise never to touch another drop. She wondered if people kept those promises forever. She wasn't sure she wanted to promise she would do anything for the rest of her life. That could be a long, long time, unless she was killed by a woodpile, like her mother.

Try as he might, Reverend Lockhead did not persuade any other townspeople to come forward. But he went on to say that outsiders, some of them known throughout the country, would be coming the following night, and it was his devout hope that more sinners would respond to them. Rose decided she would go again and see who these people from away might be and where they might be coming from. She thought a lot about the rest of the country, wishing she could get on a train and go see a big city and a prairie and very high mountains. Someday, she told herself, someday. But Rose knew she would want to come back. Aunt and Uncle's daughter had done that, but she had stayed out west, and they didn't talk about her. Rose wanted to ask Aunt Nell, but she hadn't found the right moment. She hoped she would know the right moment when it came.

When she reached the store the next day, she was surprised to find a shipment of Mr. Baldwin's vanilla and asked Mr. Goodnow how it had come so quickly.

"He was pleased with the size of the order," Henry Goodnow said. "So he telegraphed his wife without waiting for other orders, and she packed up our order right away. It arrived on the train this morning."

"Miss Harty already made cookies with that sample bottle," Rose said. "She was mighty pleased about get ting that. But I reckon the minister wouldn't be liking it much."

"Why's that?" Mr. Goodnow asked.

"He's death on alcohol, and Mr. Baldwin said the vanilla had a high alcohol content," Rose said.

"No one is supposed to drink it, Rose," Mr. Goodnow laughed.

"I reckon they might if they were as desperate as the reverend says," Rose answered, without smiling. "Father wasn't there last night," she added suddenly.

"I'll wager the crowd will swell tonight, Rose," Mr. Goodnow said. "The ladies from the Women's Temperance Union will be there, and they're a feisty bunch, especially if Miss Anthony is with them. Word at the hotel is that they've reserved four rooms for two nights."

"Who is Miss Anthony, Mr. Goodnow?"

"Some say she's a troublemaker who ought to go back to Rochester, New York, and tend to her knitting," Henry Goodnow answered. "Others practically worship at her feet as she goes about the country trying to get everyone riled up about women voting and men giving up the drink."

"Women voting?" Rose asked with a new kind of excitement in her voice. "Sarah, I mean Mother, talked about women voting every now and then. She wanted to but said it likely would never come about."

"Oh, I think it will happen, Rose, but perhaps not in my lifetime. In yours, I reckon. And a good thing it might be, letting the ladies have some say about how things are done. I daresay you might like to put a word in yourself."

Rose laughed. "Alice and Emily think I already have too much to say," she said. "But I would like to vote, and I trust having the vote would also bring the right to run for town office? Or Congress?"

Mr. Goodnow cleared his throat. "Never crossed my mind, Rose, but you could have something there. We'll be hard-pressed to get a noon meal, though, if the womenfolk are off in Washington talking about war, building bridges, and the country's relations with England and France."

"It's too much for me right now," Rose said with a sigh. "I have shelves to dust." And off she went, feather duster in hand, to clean where everything was already neater than most women's pantries.

As she swished the duster around, Rose decided she would wear a Sunday-go-to-meeting outfit to the tent meeting because Newton might be there, along with so many other people she knew. She wondered if that was the kind of vanity the Reverend Lockhead often preached about. He railed against so many things, and it occurred to Rose that most of the time he didn't seem to praise anything except the Lord. Now she was surely getting into blasphemous territory, which had to be worse than vanity. So she went back to considering how she would fix her hair.

She would not put it up as if she were all grown up. That would mean never running down the road again with Emily and Alice, and might even mean not skipping rope or playing Simon Says at school recess. Once your hair was out of plaits and wound into a bun on the back of your head, you were expected to act like a lady. She was not ready for that.

She was so busy with her own thoughts that she started when someone lifted the latch and came into the store. It was Mrs. Munson, a basket over one arm and her purse on the other. Rose hoped Mr. Goodnow would serve her. She had never forgotten the day she overheard Mrs. Munson talking in pitying tones about her and Charles and Abby right in this very store. She knew Hattie Munson was the town's worst gossip, but she hadn't forgiven her. And there she was again, back to the reverend, who was always promising that God would forgive sinners and that every member of the congregation must do likewise. Well, she couldn't and she wouldn't and she wasn't going to forgive Mrs. Munson, Rose told herself, giving the duster such a hard flick that two mousetraps fell off the shelf onto the floor.

"How may I assist you?" she heard Mr. Goodnow say as she bent to retrieve the traps.

"Likely a good thing it wasn't with mousetraps," Mrs. Munson answered. "Those may well be damaged goods."

"I reckon you have no need of mousetraps in any case," Henry Goodnow answered. "Can't imagine a mouse moving into your house."

"I do keep things properly," Hattie Munson answered with a sniff. "You may seriously doubt that a mouse would be in my house, or you may be kidding me. But in any case, I don't have mice. I came here for sugar and buttons, and some of that vanilla you have finally restocked."

"Ah, so Mr. Baldwin's vanilla has met with your approval," Mr. Goodnow said, turning just enough to give Rose a wink that Hattie Munson could not see.

"I had to borrow a bit of vanilla one day, and I must say Effie Chandler was reluctant to part with it. She let me take a scant teaspoon, so I hardly used enough to make a judgment. But I must confess those cookies were about the tastiest I've ever made. I can't fault that vanilla."

While Mr. Goodnow bagged a pound of sugar for Mrs. Munson, Hattie went to one of the glass-front drawers in the big cabinet and poked through the medium-sized buttons with her index finger. She selected several white buttons that were strung together and brought them to the counter just as Rose came with one of the smaller bottles of vanilla.

Over the top of Hattie Munson's head, Mr. Goodnow winked at Rose again as she set the vanilla down. Then he totted up his customer's purchases, and she paid him with a bill she had in her pocket, holding out her gloved hand for the change.

The transaction done, Mrs. Munson nodded to Rose and left the store, muttering something about how precious good vanilla seemed to be. As she unfurled her umbrella on the steps outside, Rose was startled to hear Mr. Goodnow laugh out loud.

"She'll hear you," Rose said quickly. "Sir."

"And if she does?" Mr. Goodnow answered. "Will it matter?"

Rose supposed it wouldn't. And it was nice to have a sense that the storekeeper didn't really like the gossipy Mrs. Munson. Rose had tried not to dislike her because her mother had always said you could find good things in nearly everyone, that a body just had to look carefully sometimes. Rose had been unable to find the good part of Hattie Munson, so she had stopped trying, figuring perhaps Miss Harty was right when she said every rule had an exception. Besides, she knew she and Charles and Abby were a long way from being pitiful. They might not be perfectly happy, but they weren't to be pitied.

Hours later, however, as she dressed for the tent meeting, Rose was still smiling about Mr. Goodnow laughing at his customer. She had never seen him act that way with anyone else, and she realized that his comment about no mouse visiting the Munson house was likely not so much a compliment to Mrs. Munson but more a salute to the good sense of the rodent. Now that, Rose thought, is really funny.

Alice and Emily were joining her for the tent meeting, and she soon heard their knock at the door. Miss Harty had already left on Joshua Chittenden's arm, and Rose wondered if she would be wearing her engagement ring tonight or whether she was keeping that a secret still. She knew the teacher was quite excited about Joshua coming that evening and that he would stay at the hotel for perhaps two nights.

"Alice wants to answer the call tonight," Emily said, the minute Rose opened the door. "We are going to have to hang on tight or possibly even sit on her if you are still of a mind to keep people from pledging lifelong abstinence."

"I am," Rose said, laughing. She hoped Alice wasn't so bent on taking the pledge that they would have to crush her in her seat.

"I am doing it for you," Alice said solemnly. "John Barleycorn would have ruined your life completely, my mother says, if you weren't so spunky."

"Spunky," Rose repeated. "Spunky. No one ever said that about me before. What an odd word."

"It means you have pluck and energy," Emily said.

"I know what it means," Rose said. "But it sounds more like mold and rotted wood than ambition and derring-do."

"That's punky, not spunky," Emily said, realizing even as the words came out that if she knew that then her word-oriented friend certainly did.

"Hmm," Rose answered, not wanting to lord it over Emily. "Glad to know I am not growing a mushroom on my leg. But what's this about blaming me for wanting to show off in front of the tent audience?"

"I'm not showing off," Alice said stubbornly. "I want to do it so other people will do it and so people like you and Abby and Charles won't have the problems you and Abby and Charles have."

Rose felt as if she were choking, and her voice cracked a little as she turned to hug Alice and thank her. When she could speak, she asked anxiously, "But we are doing all right, aren't we?"

"You are the best, Rose, the whipped cream on the shortcake," Alice said quickly, starting to feel a little shy about her resolve to sign a pledge.

"I worry so about Charles," Rose went on, "and I want to be under the same roof as Abby, but we are getting on with our lives as best we can."

"Not bad, I'd say, especially if it's strawberry season," Emily answered with a grin. She ducked as Rose tried to cuff her for using the expression she had come to dislike so much. Ever since she could remember she had seen that tiny shadow cross Sarah's face whenever Father's compliment was "not bad." Someday she would get her courage up—maybe get really spunky—and ask him why he couldn't just say "marvelous" or "beautiful" or "delicious," instead of "not bad." She knew how he meant it, but it was a compliment hidden in what Miss Harty would surely call a negative.

The three girls were quite excited when they approached the tent, linking their arms together so they wouldn't get separated in the large crowd that was gathering. A special hitching place had been set up for those who came by wagon, Rose noticed, and she suddenly realized that she didn't know half the people here. They've come from other villages, she thought, so perhaps it's true that a famous person will be here tonight.

She saw Mr. Chandler's large wagon, the one he sometimes outfitted with seats, and she didn't recognize any of the folks on board. They must have come by train. She smiled, thinking that Mr. Goodnow would say Ben Chandler rarely missed a chance to make a few extra pennies. She was glad she'd worn her Sunday outfit. The women were sitting on one side of the center aisle, the men on the other, and most everyone seemed to be in his best bib and tucker.

She chuckled out loud, and both Emily and Alice stopped walking. "What was that about?" Emily demanded.

"Just thinking about all the best bib and tucker here—you would say that's what everyone's wearing. But what does it mean? No bibs here—those are for babies so they won't spill all over their clothes. And what's a tucker?"

"No doubt you'll find out," Alice grumbled. "You know perfectly well if it's not in your head already, it certainly isn't in ours. I'd like to count all the words you have stored in there."

"Take out one box at a time, Alice," Emily counseled. "She probably has them sorted by color or first letter."

"Stop it," Rose said. "Just stop it. We need to hurry or we won't get three stools in a row." So they dodged around groups of chatting women and made their way down the aisle, quickly moving into a row that had plenty of empty camp stools. As soon as they were settled, Rose started looking for Newton. She felt her face burn when she found him and realized he was looking at her. He gave a small nod and pointed to the back of the tent, hoping she would understand they could meet there after the meeting. She nodded back, thinking how much fun it was to communicate so clearly without any of those stored words at all. In boxes, indeed.

The Reverend Lockhead opened the meeting, as he had the previous evening. He said it warmed his soul to see so many people in the audience and to be able to welcome the Campaign for Temperance to Eastborough. Last night was merely the introduction, he said, but tonight the speakers were all from out of town, a group preaching temperance throughout New York and New England. He stepped off the makeshift platform, gesturing toward the four men seated there.

"So we don't have to listen to him tonight," Emily whispered. Three women in front of the girls turned as one and shushed her, but Emily was undaunted. "We are saved," she said, her grin changing to an audible "oof" when Rose's elbow jabbed her.

One of the women in front of them turned and glared, and Emily focused on the platform again. Three of the men spoke about the evils of drink and how it was time for the Republicans to join in the effort to get intoxicating liquors regulated by the government, that people must be held accountable for their actions, and how laws would provide the way.

Dozens of people stirred in their seats, and Rose knew plenty of her neighbors in Eastborough would object to any laws that told them what they could eat and drink. Then the fourth man stood. He talked faster than an auctioneer, and the audience grew totally still. His keen blue eyes seemed to look at each person under the tent as he thundered through his speech about how John Barleycorn would be the ruin of them all if they continued on the present path, and that it was his fervent wish that every man present would put his future vote where it would count against intoxication.

Rose felt this man, Welford Bailey, had given her a piercing look, and she was afraid he had put a spell on Alice, who was leaning forward, listening to every word. Glancing around once more, Rose saw her father standing near a tent pole on the far side of the gathering. Oh, she thought, oh, he has come, and he's hearing all this, and perhaps we can all go home again. She gave a little shiver, and a tear rolled down her cheek. Drat, she thought, Emily saw that. She sees everything. And indeed, Emily reached over, took Rose's hand, and gave it a squeeze. Alice's rapt face was still riveted on the speaker.

The next thing Rose knew, the speeches were over and dozens of men were lining up to sign their promises to abstain from the drink for the rest of their lives. She felt Alice stir next to her and realized in a flash that they had nothing to worry about. Women were not being invited to sign the testimonials. Come to think of it, she didn't know any women who took whiskey or hard cider, except for Miss Graves.

Reverend Lockhead was back on the platform, thanking everyone for coming and renewing the invitation for men to take the pledge. Alice shrank back in her seat, quite disappointed, and gave only a small smile when Rose patted her hand. Most of the audience was staying in place, Rose noticed, but people were chatting now. They wanted to see who was pledging, she decided. Mrs.

Munson was probably up there in the front row, keeping track of each one.

Then, as the minister started to leave the platform, a group of ladies in black dresses stood up from the front row and moved toward the lectern, obviously intending to speak. Reverend Lockhead tried to head them off, but the two in front were not to be stopped. Emily and Rose started to giggle as the minister began to talk and gesture, his motions getting more and more agitated when the women paid him no mind.

One of them swept up to the lectern, her taffeta skirts rustling, and the audience noise went from a boil to a simmer almost instantly. "We," she said in a voice that could be heard throughout the tent, "represent the Woman's Christian Temperance Union, and we are here without invitation to add the distaff side to this story."

"Oh my God," Emily said. "The reverend just received his comeuppance. There will be hell to pay now."

"Emily!" Rose exclaimed in shock. "Watch your language!" Gratefully, she noticed the women in front of them were among the few who had left, so she was quite certain no one had heard her friend.

"You said yourself that we should be able to use that word now and then," Emily protested.

"But not here," Rose said. Three of the four outsiders who had spoken earlier were dealing with the men signing abstinence pledges, and the fourth had apparently gone on his way. She reckoned the minister would be unable to stop this woman from talking, so she settled back on her stool.

"My name," the lady began, "is Miss Shaw, and I am here to introduce you to a lady who was born not far from here and who has traveled far and wide on behalf of the citizens of this nation: man, woman, and child. We have been denied the right to speak in various forums, including the city of Albany, capital of New York, but we move on to places where we believe freedom of speech still prevails."

"Hear, hear," a man at the back of the tent shouted, and the audience came to life with a combination of clapping, cheering, and catcalls.

Nodding toward the back of the tent, Miss Shaw awed the audience into complete attention when she continued with her introduction of Miss Susan B. Anthony, whose name was already known to many of those present. Miss Anthony moved toward the lectern and announced first, in a firm voice, that she knew how uncomfortable they must be on those camp stools and she would therefore be brief and to the point. Acknowledging that the male speakers before her had sought votes for temperance, she pointed out that it was women who suffered the most when the family coffers were drained into a glass, and that women would be quite likely to vote the way Mr. Bailey and the others desired. The same voice shouted, "Hear, hear," but several other men quietly booed and started to grumble.

Miss Anthony did not stop. "What is this little thing that we are asking for? It seems too little; it is yet everything.... What does your right to vote in this country, men and brethren, say to you? What does that right say to every possible man, native and foreign, black and white, rich and poor, educated and ignorant, drunk and sober, to every possible man outside the State prison, the idiot and the lunatic asylums?... It says, 'your judgment is sound, your opinion is worthy to be counted.'... And now, on the other hand, what does it say to every possible woman, native and foreign, black and white, rich and poor, educated and ignorant, virtuous and vicious, to every possible woman under the shadow of our flag? It says, 'Your judgment is not sound, your opinion is not worthy to be counted.'"

Sarah had wanted to vote, Rose thought. She would have loved hearing Miss Anthony say these things. Right now, she knew, was no time to let her mind wander around, however. She needed to listen.

Miss Anthony was going on. "The poorest ditchdigger's opinion counts for just as much as does the opinion of the proudest millionaire. It is a good thing; I believe in it... but I do want to make you understand the difference in our position. I want to say to you what all of you know, that if there was still left under the shadow of the flag any class of men who are still disfranchised, that class would rise in rebellion against the government... We women cannot rise in open rebellion. Men are our fathers and brothers and husbands and sons. But we shall stand and plead and demand the right to be heard, and not only to be heard, but to have our votes counted and coined into law, until the very crack of doom, if need be."

The women's side of the tent erupted into applause so

loud that Rose was certain Reverend Lockhead would consider it unladylike. She noticed that many of the men across the aisle were clapping also, while others sat as straight and as still as fence posts. Joining in the clapping, Rose was almost overcome with the thrill of the moment. This was a famous lady up there, right in Eastborough, someone they had all read about. And she had made hundreds of people listen to her message. She wasn't pretty, Rose thought, and her hair was very plain. But she had something Rose had never seen before, something almost magic. She had power. Rose wished her mother had had more power, some way to get running water and an icebox before she was killed. But when Father said no and talked about newfangled things, the topic went away as if a bolt of lightning had burnt it to a crisp.

Frustrated and looking red in the face, Reverend Lockhead was starting toward the lectern in a renewed attempt to get rid of the ladies, but Miss Anthony was finished, as brief as she had promised. She and her friends turned their backs on the approaching minister, lifted a side flap of the tent, and disappeared.

With the dramatic moments over, Rose looked around for Newton again and saw him waiting at the back. She could not find her father anywhere, so she and Alice and Emily made their way slowly through the throng to greet Newton.

"Ah," he said, smiling at all of them, "three ladies tonight. Shall I see you home?" The girls nodded, and the four of them set off.

CHAPTER FIFTEEN
Backsliding

Silas Hibbard's left eyebrow went up as he listened to the exhortations of the strangers who had brought their tent to town. In its own way, he thought, it's like a circus. They are all trained, each to outdo the one before him so the audience will keep listening. He had come because he knew Rose would be pleased, and he wanted to please that girl of his, stubborn though she might be. Sarah had that same stubbornness, even if she hadn't said anything or ever stood in his way. When Sarah was worrying a bone, her jaw would set, her lips would thin out, and she could spend a day or two in near silence. But Rose went on from there. She had actually packed up Abby's things and moved her out because she disapproved of his carrying on with Miss Jennie.

Shifting his weight from the right foot to the left, Silas

glanced around the room and saw Rose with her friends on the women's side of the aisle. The fourth speaker was railing now, about Republicans refusing to pass laws about the drink and about the evils of intoxication. Well, he knew all about that, and he was pulling out of it in his own way, wasn't he? If this were truly a circus, lions would abound, but these were sheep, pretty, and pretty useless. Well, he was no sheep. He had no admiration for sheep. If their so-called leader walked off a cliff, he was as sure as he was of sunrise and sunset that every last one of them would go over the edge, too.

Silas sighed and slipped out of the tent, unaware that his brother-in-law, Jason, at first pleased to see him in attendance, had watched him go and breathed a sigh of his own.

Time to take care of the whole business, Silas told himself as he reached his house and entered by the back door. He went straight to the dark root cellar, passing the jelly cupboard and the wrinkled, sprouting remnants of last fall's potato harvest. He reached the barrel of hard cider and tipped it forward, twisting and rolling it toward the door and out into the yard. He would spill it all out, and that would be that. He did not need a law to remove temptation from his path, or a man of the cloth, either. He could do it himself if he was of a mind to.

He reached for the spigot and paused. This was a 'specially fine batch, fermented just right with apples from his own Rhode Island Greening and Snow apple trees, plus some wild ones from the far pasture. He guessed it would do no harm to have a swallow to celebrate the moment. He fetched a dipper from the milk room and returned to the barrel. Just one taste for old time's sake, he thought. Auld lang syne, Robert Burns called it. He opened the spigot and honey-colored liquid ran into the dipper. He shut off the flow and savored the first taste, moving it around in his mouth before letting the warmth slide down his throat. He stretched his tongue out to catch the two or three drops that had stuck in his thick moustache.

First thing Monday, he thought, he would go to the store and let Rose know that he had dumped the hard cider into the rambling roses by the back door. A batch like this would probably make the brambles grow as magically as Jack's beanstalk, even if not as smooth for climbing. He drained the dipper, licked his moustache once again and started to roll the barrel toward the roses, moving quietly so as not to disturb Charles.

While Silas wrestled with the cider barrel, the ladies in black boarded the late train and headed for Boston, and Reverend Lockhead breathed a sigh as he made his way to the parsonage. Those women were too forthright for their own good, he reckoned, and they paid little attention to the Lord as they went about telling everyone what to do. Still, he hoped few of his congregation had seen his failed attempt to block their speaking. It was, at best, a mortifying moment. He determined that his wife, who was nursing a cold, had no need to know about it, and trusted no one would think it proper to tell her. On the other hand, who knew what came out when the ladies gathered around the quilting frame, chattering and stitching. Letting women gather could be a dangerous thing. He'd read his history and knew quite well what had happened when Anne Hutchinson gathered women at her house of a Sunday afternoon to discuss the morning sermon and other aspects of theology. Boston hadn't stood for that, and had sent her away. He wanted no fuss like that in this town.

A short distance away, Newton and the three girls were well on their way to Emily's house when Ethan caught up with them and instantly reached for Alice's hand. Rose noticed that while Alice seemed a little flustered, she did not pull away.

"Take me home first," she whispered to Newton, "then Alice." Newton started to protest and then realized Rose didn't want Alice left alone with Ethan, so he turned at the next corner toward Miss Harty's house.

"We thought you'd save Rose for last," Emily teased.

"Rose needs her beauty sleep," Newton countered, continuing toward the teacher's house and absorbing a sharp jab in the ribs from Rose. When they reached the steps, he gave her a peck on the cheek and whispered, "Be back soon as I'm rid of these children."

Rose didn't dare answer. She just said good night to everyone and went into the dark house. She lit a kerosene lamp and picked out two smallish sticks for the fire in the wood stove, which was just a pile of red-hot coals at this point. If the teacher was back soon enough, perhaps they'd all have a cup of tea. She moved the teakettle forward a bit so it would be on its way to heating. She had no idea where Joshua Chittenden and Miss Harty might have gone from the meeting. They stood at the back the whole time because otherwise they would have been seated separately on those wretched camp stools. So she hadn't seen whether the teacher was wearing her ring or not—it could, of course, be hidden under her glove.

As the clock chimed nine, Rose decided to wait for Newton on the porch. She figured he'd be awhile. Those long legs were getting a heap of exercise that Newton had little need of with all the work he was doing at his father's farm. The now-familiar shiver ran down her spine as she thought about Newton's legs, and then about his arms, and then his whole body. She reckoned she had better banish this line of thinking or she'd be running into the street to greet him.

She took the lamp outside, along with her knitting, and sat down in one of the big porch rockers. The need to concentrate on the needles might keep her mind away from things she was certain the reverend would call forbidden fruit. Despite all of the minister's preaching, she'd never been able to fault Eve for taking the apple. Apples were so good and so pretty to look at. She was quite certain she would have done just what Eve did. Her train of thought chugged on, taking care of the knitting and thinking about apples and about Newton. She had learned to knit when she was recovering from nearly freezing to death, and as her brain jumped about from one thing to the next, she remembered Alice telling her how Newton had burst into Miss Harty's kitchen carrying a silent, half-frozen Rose and how Charles had come first, barely able to talk from running fast in the dreadful cold.

She could recall almost nothing of that event herself, except that she had gone to the cemetery to see if being near her mother's grave would help her sort out the family problems. It was very cold there, and she had slumped down in the snow to stay warm and then had gotten very sleepy. She still couldn't believe several days had passed between that time and when she woke in a bed at Miss Harty's house, where she had been ever since.

It was such a stupid thing to do, she thought, but she hadn't meant it to turn out the way it did. She hadn't meant to upset half the town. On the bright side—and Sarah said the bright side was nearly always there, if you searched hard enough—she had ended up staying with Miss Harty and not going back to see to Father and Charles. But she could not seem to stop thinking about the awfulness of it and the way she had behaved, even though Miss Harty and Newton and Aunt Nell, and even Abby and Charles had told her she had done the right thing. Deep down, she knew that. But it was still a haunting thing.

She had knitted more than an inch when she heard Newton whistling his way along the road, first with "Rock of Ages" and then moving right into "Yankee Doodle," a combination that made her wonder how his mind worked, this boy who thought hers was odd. Determined not to seem too eager, she kept her eyes on the sock and hoped whatever was making her stomach flip-flop wouldn't cause her to drop any stitches. And then he was on the porch, carefully taking the knitting out of her hands and pulling her to her feet. When his arms went around her, she responded with her own, burying her face in his shoulder. For what seemed like several minutes, they held each other, swaying a little and saying nothing.

Then Newton pulled away, eased her back into her chair, put the knitting back in her hands, and perched on the porch railing opposite her. "I believe we are here without the requisite chaperones," he intoned, imitating the cadence of Reverend Lockhead's Sunday morning speaking voice. "We are facing sin, corruption, damnation, fire and brimstone, and public disgrace, and you are there tending to your knitting, Miss Rose." Then, reverting suddenly to his own voice, he asked, "And what is brimstone anyway? It always comes right along with fire as if they were married."

By this time, Rose had dropped the sock and was rocking back and forth, laughing and holding her sides. "You sound too much like him, too much. Brimstone is sulfur. And did you see him tonight, getting his comeuppance from the black dress ladies? If he had not backed off, I think they would have walked right through him." Then she quickly sobered and added, "They were splendid. Mother would have been so pleased to hear them, right here in Eastborough, talking about getting the vote for women. She so wanted to vote, and so do I."

"You want to stay in school, you want to teach, you

want to vote, you want to stop running away from me... you want a lot of things, Miss Rose," Newton said, back to his own voice and suddenly as serious as she was. "When I decide to ask you, will you also want to marry me? Be a farmer's wife? Raise children? Stoke the fire and make the oatmeal?"

"When you decide on that, I reckon you'll get all those answers," Rose said in a saucy manner. "In the meantime, I think the porch is a fine chaperone. We are in plain sight and cannot get into unchaperoned mischief, just a loss of beauty sleep for those who linger. Not much danger of fire and brimstone here."

"A pity, that," Newton muttered. "You could at least blow out the light and tell me more about this sulfur thing. Smelly sulfur?"

"Part of Sodom and Gomorrah," she said. "If you paid more attention in Sunday school, you'd know about the punishments of evil. And they are virtually married—the fire makes the sulfur burn, and it came down like rain because of God's anger, and the two seem doomed to travel together forever in Sunday sermons." Then Rose reached for the small knob on the lamp base and the flaming wick inside the glass chimney disappeared and went dark. "What I want right now," she said, getting up and coming over to stand between his knees, "what I want is to kiss you. You didn't mention that."

"Not worth mentioning to a forward girl like you," Newton said, "a girl so. . ." But Rose had covered his mouth with hers, and when he tried to keep talking, he just sounded like bubbling water. He gave up and kissed her back, so gently that she thought she would pass out from the sweetness of it. Eyes closed and lips together, neither of them moved at all for perhaps a minute, perhaps two. Rose was sure she could never be happier than she was right now, except she did need to ask one thing. She broke away and said, "A girl so what?"

"Ah, I answered that while you were smothering me, so I have no need to say it again," Newton teased. He ran his hands down her back and tightened his knees around her legs. "You are captive now and cannot make demands. And by the way, where are Miss Harty and Joshua?"

"I have no idea," Rose said, "but they did not come back here. I wondered if she would take her glove off tonight at the meeting, but I wasn't close enough to them to see. And they left right when the ladies finished their speeches."

"I reckon he is planning to stay with my folks tonight, engaged or not engaged, so I am going to settle in here until they come, and then make my way home with him. It seems doubtful that beauty sleep is one of your needs, but if you are anxious about it, I can wait alone and think about you upstairs undressing and getting into your night things and sliding into bed."

"Newton!" Rose exclaimed, struggling to move away. "What kind of talk is that?"

"Lovesick talk," Newton said. "Just a boy with a flibbertigibbet girl who wants a lot and gives so little."

"Certainly ailing, you are," Rose answered, "and perhaps in need of Dr. Potter. The flibbertigibbet is feeling quite resentful right now, accused of selfishness and who knows what else."

Newton pulled her even closer with his left arm and tilted her face up toward him with his right hand. Keeping his finger under her chin, he turned her face to kiss her nose, each cheek, her forehead and then each ear. By the time his mouth came back to her lips, Rose was feeling all weak in the knees again and thinking if his legs weren't holding her, she'd sink to the floorboards. Then the touch of his lips revived her, and she responded, suddenly moved to open her mouth and run her tongue over his lips. This is delicious, she thought, raising her arms and circling his neck.

Soon their tongues were touching, flicking out and back as quickly as a snake's. Rose heard Newton moan and felt his tongue move inside her mouth, touching her tongue, running over her teeth, exploring the dark space. Who could imagine, her busy brain asked, that anyone would want to go inside someone else's mouth? Or that anyone would want another tongue in there. She felt tingly all over and tried to remember what Miss Harty had said about hands and tongues and kisses. She leaned back a little, but his face followed hers, and then he released her slightly, holding her under her arms. When the heel of his hands touched the soft edge of her breasts, Rose jumped as if she'd been bitten.

"No," she said. "No."

"I am so sorry, Rose," Newton said, dropping his arms to his sides. "I am so sorry."

"Nothing to apologize for," Rose said breathlessly. "It

was all lovely, and I loved it, and I want—you keep talking about all the things I want—I want to keep right on doing it. But we can't. Or I'll be wanting you sliding between the sheets, too. And we can't do that, either."

"Who needs a chaperone," Newton muttered to himself. "We have Rose. And she's better than most."

"Don't make fun, Newton. I am fifteen years old, and I'm falling in love with you, and you are making fun of me."

"Never," he answered. "I am so serious about you that I could not possibly smile, laugh, or make fun. And I'm not fifteen, which is part of the problem. And now I hear a buggy coming, so we will be saved." Shifting to the minister's voice again, he said solemnly, "We will be saved, we will be saved."

And when Miss Harty and Joshua Chittenden emerged from the buggy, Rose was laughing again and taking note that the teacher had not only taken her gloves off but had let her hair out of its bun so that it fell around her shoulders. How young she looks, Rose thought, deciding that it would be years before she wound her hair into one of those pugs.

CHAPTER SIXTEEN
Barleycorn Wins

Charles hustled into the kitchen, a bit later than usual because it was Sunday, and was surprised to see that no fire burned in the kitchen stove. He quickly took some slivers of kindling from the corner of the woodbox, crisscrossed them in the stove, lit them, and added two slim sticks of wood. To his relief, the fire caught immediately. Sometimes it took him several tries to get a fire going, and the day would not bode well if Father came in from the barn and discovered that breakfast was not under way.

He scurried around, putting water on to boil for coffee, measuring out the oatmeal, slicing bread and doing all the things he had seen his mother and Rose do, morning after morning. He had found he rather liked this routine, all done before he was totally wide awake, pretty much the same every day, and best of all, without anyone around to tell him what to do next. He knew he had become quite adept at the business of breakfast, and he did it in a timely fashion so Father would not be displeased.

As the pots started to bubble, he stirred the oats and thought about how much less grouchy Father had been since Miss Graves left town. He wasn't certain, but he did think Father wasn't into what Rose called "the drink" as much as he had been—if at all, come to think of it. Charles went to the icebox to fetch the butter and stopped, staring at the kerosene lantern on top of the cabinet. When he went to bed, he had left it lit for Father, and now all the kerosene was gone. How long could it have burned to use that up, he wondered. It would have to be hours and hours. He touched the chimney and discovered it was still warm. It was hard to believe that Father would have forgotten to turn the wick down when he went to bed—they tried hard to be thrifty about kerosene, which could only be bought with cash money—but Charles could see the edge of the wick, just barely sticking up into the chimney. He must have been at the cider, Charles decided, to leave the lantern on. His mind was starting to bubble almost as hard as the coffee water, and it dawned on him that if the wood stove fire was out, did that mean Father was still upstairs in bed?

Tiptoeing up the stairs, Charles crept along the hall to his parents' room. The door was open just a crack, and moving without a sound, he put one eye against the sliver of an opening. "Thunderation," he said, shoving the door so hard that it banged against the wall. "The bed has not been slept in, or he was up so early that he pulled it together before he went to do chores. I wonder if Miss Graves bought a round-trip ticket."

Charles knew his father had not come home at all on at least two occasions, but he hadn't mentioned it to Rose, who would just start worrying all over again, or to anyone else. He was only thirteen, but he knew a man like his father might spend much of the evening and early morning with a woman, although he thought it would be quite tiresome to listen to most women chatter for that long. He hated it when the girls at school kept chirping and chirping about nothing. Rose was never like that, or at least not that he knew of.

Perhaps he'd better get on to the barn and see if the cows had been fed and watered and whether Father had started the milking. Sunday often seemed like the longest day of the week, with no fun and no chance to see his friends except when they were all starched up and sitting in hard church pews. This day was quite different. A little excited, Charles hit only a few of the stairs going down, put on his barn boots in the hall outside the kitchen, and headed down the stairs to the back door.

Opening this door brought a surprise so great that Charles was speechless. The hard-cider barrel was on its side near the rose bushes, and Father was on his side right next to it. Neither, Charles noted, was moving. Going closer, he saw that a small pool of cider surrounded Father's head and that a dipper was lying on the grass nearby. Father was wearing the same clothes he had put on for the tent meeting. A black wave of fear swept over Charles as he gingerly moved closer. Was he dead? He would be cold if he were dead, Charles told himself, so he reached toward his father's cheek, drew his hand back, told himself not to act like a chicken, and reached again. This time, his fingers grazed skin, and he exhaled, realizing he had hardly breathed since he opened the door. Father's face was warm. He was alive. But he wasn't moving, except that his chest was rising slightly as he breathed. Leaning close, Charles heard a whistling sound coming from his father's mouth.

Worried now that Father might be furious if he was awakened, Charles clenched his teeth and gave his father's shoulder a shake. Nothing. More boldly, he tried again, saying, "Father, Father, it's time to do the milking." Nothing. Panic swept over him, and he began to yell. Running into the road, he pelted as fast as he could toward the doctor's house, arriving there so out of breath that he could not speak when Dr. Potter answered his knock.

The doctor pulled him inside, gave him a little shake, and said, "You must tell me now, Charles, what the problem is."

"Father. It's Father. He's not dead. He's still warm. He doesn't move."

"And where is he, Charles?"

"By the roses."

"The roses?"

"Outside the house by the roses," Charles gasped, holding his hand against the stitch in his left side.

"On the ground?" Dr. Potter persisted, picking up the black leather bag that he kept right by the door and grabbing Charles with his other hand.

"With the barrel," Charles said.

"The cider barrel, Charles?"

"Yes, sir," Charles said, still breathing hard but finally remembering his manners. "And a dipper."

"I see," Dr. Potter said. "We'd better get back to him as quickly as we can."

"He didn't change, sir," Charles said as they hurried along, his breath coming almost normally again.

"Sometimes changing is next to impossible, young man," the doctor answered.

"His clothes, I mean. He didn't change his clothes."

"From last night?" the doctor asked sharply, turning to look at the boy who was almost skipping to keep up with him.

"Yes, sir," Charles said, thinking this for some reason was an important piece of news. "It's what he wore to the tent meeting."

"Ah," the doctor answered, "I didn't see him there." The bombast of some of those speakers might have deeply offended that part of Silas Hibbard that very few people other than Sarah had ever seen, he thought to himself. "Probably drove him to drink," he muttered, looking at the boy again and wondering how to deal with this child who had already seen and heard too much in his young life.

They reached the Hibbard house, and Charles announced that his father had not moved from the spot where he had found him. The doctor felt for a pulse, nodded once or twice and then startled Charles by picking Silas up and throwing him over his shoulder.

"Lead on to the parlor, young man," Dr. Potter said, breathing hard. "I can't carry this dead weight very far." Charles flew up the stairs, still astonished that anyone could just hoist his father into the air like that, and opened the door to the little-used parlor, which they usually called the "front room."

Coming right along behind him, Dr. Potter heaved Silas Hibbard onto the sofa and told Charles to fetch a sheet and a pillow and then a pail. With considerable effort, the doctor tucked the sheet under Silas, hoping to protect the sofa from the possibility that the man might come to with a spasm of vomiting. When Charles returned the second time, carrying a ten-quart pail, Dr. Potter told him it would do nicely, thank you. He placed it near Silas's head.

"Your mother have any of those oilcloth covers for the table?" he asked, thinking the sheet was small protection for the explosion that might come.

"Yes, sir. Shall I fetch one of those as well?"

"Please."

Once again, the doctor lifted and tucked and fussed until he had done a better job of protecting the furniture. Through all this, the only sound from Silas Hibbard was one small groan and the squeaky breathing.

"I'll take a very cold washrag now," the doctor said, and Charles was back in half a minute with the cloth, which was placed right over Silas's face. He still did not move.

"Now," Dr. Potter said, "you will need to fetch your Uncle Jason. I trust you can be depended upon not to tell Abby about this, and certainly not Rose. Do you understand?"

"Yes, sir," Charles said. He was feeling very strange, almost the way he had felt that day last year when he had to help kill a chicken. He swayed a bit, and the doctor grabbed his shoulder and shook him.

"See here," he said, "you have no call to let me down now. You have been doing exactly the right thing for an hour now, and you need to keep on. Can you do that?" Charles nodded and started for the door, concentrating on putting one foot in front of the other, although both seemed oddly wobbly. In the kitchen, he glanced at the stove and realized he had left pots over the fire. He moved both pots to the back of the stove. He hesitated a moment and then went back to the parlor door and said, rather weakly, "Dr. Potter?"

"Are you still here?" the doctor asked.

"Yes, sir, as you can see, sir, but I have to know. Is he going to die?"

"Someday, no doubt, but not today, Charles," the doctor said in a more kindly tone. "We'll straighten him out. He's not been at that hard cider much of late, I gather?"

"No, sir."

"Well, he went into what I like to call a backslide, drank too much and it did him in for the moment," Dr. Potter said. "He'll come out of it with his head as tight as a newly picked cabbage, and you'll do well to stay out of his path for a bit. He will be worse than cranky. Now, be off. I will see to him here."

Steadied by this news, Charles left at full speed. When he reached the Harris house, out of breath once again, he could see Aunt Nell at the kitchen stove, her back to him. He saw no signs of his uncle or Abby. Without saying a word, he went on to the barn, where he found Jason feeding his prize Chinese chickens.

"Up and about pretty early, I reckon," Jason said when Charles stopped on the step of the chicken house.

"Father's had too much to drink and can't talk or anything," Charles said, and to his dismay, started to cry. "I was to come for you and not tell Abby or Rose," he wailed.

Jason put down the bucket of water he was pouring into a trough for the chickens and squatted in front of Charles. "Where is he?" he asked quietly. "Help me out here, Charles. I need some information."

"In our house on the sofa," Charles said.

"Is that where you found him?"

"No, he was by the roses."

"And how did you get him in the house?"

By this time, Charles had regained control of his sobs. "I went for Dr. Potter and he's with him and said Father's head would be a cabbage when he woke up and I was to fetch you and not tell Abby or Rose. I don't know about Aunt Nell. The doctor picked him up, Uncle, all by himself."

"He's in good hands," Jason said, "so I am going to finish feeding these ravenous clucking creatures, and then we'll take the buggy to your house. You are a little winded, it would appear."

"I have been running around faster than a rabbit," Charles said. "Or maybe even a racehorse."

"Get yourself into the house and your Aunt Nell will fix you a bit of breakfast."

"But I can't tell…" Charles started. Jason didn't let him finish. "Your aunt will ask no questions, and I mistrust that you've made up many a story for Abby, so I will leave that to you. We'll be off in seven minutes."

Charles did as he was told, and to his surprise, Aunt Nell acted as if he came for breakfast every day. Not a bad idea, he thought, digging into the eggs and thick slices of bacon, his appetite back in place now that he had shifted the problem onto Dr. Potter's and Uncle Jason's backs. He smiled to himself, thinking how Rose would love that idea, since the problem had literally—Rose would say literally—been put on the doctor's back. He could not believe the tall, slender Dr. Potter was that strong, but he had seen it with his own eyes.

When Abby appeared, still in her nightdress, Charles greeted her as if he had breakfast at this table every day. Her eyes wide, she just stood in the doorway staring at him until he told her to take a seat. "Nice morning to take a walk," he said, "and have someone else put a plate in front of me." Abby laughed and sat down next to him, still without saying a word.

Minutes later, Jason Harris appeared at the kitchen door, whispered something to Nell, and then took two thick pieces of buttered toast from her and beckoned for Charles to come along. The horse and buggy were ready at the back door, and when Jason flicked the whip and spoke quietly, the horse moved off, quickly getting into a fast trot that brought them to the Hibbard house in next to no time.

"Can you see to watering the horse?" Jason asked Charles. The boy nodded, realizing that his uncle and the doctor would be discussing his father without his ears around. But he hitched the horse to the post near the back door and went off to get a bucket of water. Then he crept up to the parlor window and looked in. Father had not moved, and the other men were talking so low he couldn't hear a thing. He decided the best idea would be to start the milking. It was so late those poor cows must be ready to burst their udders. As he washed the tits on the first cow and sat down on the three-legged stool, he wondered if this pink, swollen bag would actually crack and splatter milk all over the place if too much time went by.

Newton would know, he thought, stretching his short fingers around two of the tits and starting the squeeze and release motion that would bring the milk. He wasn't very good at this, he knew, but he had picked the gentlest cow, and while she turned her head to look at him, she didn't move her feet. She must be wondering what kind of fool I am, Charles thought. She thinks I am supposed to come with a shovel attached, not a pail. He startled the animal by laughing out loud. His head was starting to act like Rose's, going off every which way without warning. He wondered whether her brain had always done that or if it had started when she was thirteen.

The milk was squirting into the pail quite nicely, now that he wasn't paying much attention. He leaned his head against the cow's flank the way he had seen Father do, and let his mind wander wherever it wanted to go.

Up at the house, Jason suggested he and the doctor get a mattress from upstairs and put it in the kitchen where Silas would do less harm if he woke up sick to his stomach. The two men found Abby's old mattress in the attic and wrestled it down the stairs and into the kitchen. Then they picked Silas up and laid him on it with the oilcloth under him.

"He'd best just sleep it off," Dr. Potter said. "Don't reckon we'll be sending him for the Keeley Cure, but mebbe this will be bad enough to prove a cure all by itself."

"Does the Keeley thing really work or is it just snake oil?" Jason wanted to know.

"No idea. There's those who swear by it and others who say it's a passel of organized charlatans," the doctor answered. "But it's costly, staying at one of their places and getting those injections of gold and strychnine, and surprisingly, some alcohol as well. Silas might try the injections, might even foot the bill, but he would never sit down with a Keeley group to talk about his need to drink."

"Ah, how right you are. He runs like a deer from the talking," Jason answered. "Did the same thing when Sarah wanted to talk about something, if Nell has it right. Just clammed up and went off to the barn or the field or the outhouse."

The doctor laughed then. "He's a good man, Jason, but I don't know if he'll ever straighten out. It's tough for those children, who are quite remarkable. Young Charles handled this morning as if he were thirty, not thirteen."

"Barely thirteen," Jason said. "And where is he now?"

After checking Silas's pulse and heartbeat once more, Dr. Potter went out with Jason to find Charles and met him coming toward the milk room with a nearly full pail of milk in each hand.

"More than remarkable, I reckon," the doctor remarked. "Extraordinary."

"Need some help, Charles, or have you milked them all?"

"There's two more, Uncle. I think their udders are about to pop because it's so late."

"You can get that milk into the cooler with no problem?"

"Yes, sir."

"Then I'll see to the other cows," Jason said. He was finishing up the second one when Charles appeared at his elbow and stood there, shifting from one foot to the other without saying anything.

"Speak up," Jason said, not pausing in his task.

"Well, sir," Charles said in a hesitant voice, "I was wondering about Rose. And Abby."

"When I'm finished here, we'll go along to the house and explain how it is to Mrs. Harris. But mebbe not Abby, except to say her father is under the weather. After that, we'll call at the teacher's and speak with Rose."

"Yes, sir," Charles said. "And would we be leaving Father here to shift for himself?"

"Dr. Potter says he won't be doing much shifting of any kind for another hour or two, mebbe more," Jason said. "And you may be better off not being right on hand when he comes to. He's likely to be more bear than pussycat."

"Often is," Charles muttered, turning away. Then, louder, he asked, "Shall I turn out the cows we've milked?"

"Have you done that afore?"

"Yes, Uncle. I often do it," Charles said with a hint of pride in his voice now.

"I reckon it would save time if you got them started, then."

So Charles opened the barn door and started unlatching the stanchions on the cows. As he opened the frames that kept them in their places, each one backed out and headed for the door. Soon they were all in the lane that led to the larger pasture, contentedly eating the lush spring grass. Charles stayed at the door until Jason set his milk pail aside, then released the last cow and sent her toward the door. Then the boy and the man headed back to the house, both of them thinking about how Silas Hibbard's latest mistake would affect Rose.

Arriving at church, Rose was thinking about them, too, mainly because she didn't see them anywhere. Uncle Jason was tall enough to be seen over most of the other townspeople, and she expected to find Charles and her father sitting not far from the Harrises and Abby. The last time this had happened, she reminded herself, Father and Charles were delivering a calf and she had put herself into a state thinking about all kinds of disasters before she found out why they hadn't come to church. She gave herself a little mental slap and resolved that she would try harder not to worry about things that either hadn't happened yet or never would. Aunt Nell said she would have furrows in her face by the time she was twenty if she didn't stop worrying every bone as if she were a stray puppy.

Rose's response was that she and Abby and Charles were all stray puppies in a way, and then Nell had put her arms around her and given her a big hug and said they were the best puppies in the world and not stray at all and Rose had felt better. She told Aunt that the hug was like getting a cure from the doctor, and perhaps Abby would benefit from such as well. On the way home that day, she had patted herself on the back for getting in the plea for Abby hugs, thinking it was smooth and subtle. Subtle, she thought. It should be spelled "suttle," if that's how one should say it. Anyway, however you spelled it, it hadn't been subtle because Abby overheard Aunt telling Uncle that they needed to give Abby a little squeeze now and then so she would know she was loved.

Rose smiled as she rose for the first hymn. Whenever she thought grown folks weren't paying attention, she would find out later that they knew all along what was going on. Miss Harty, for instance, seemed to know all about what Rose was thinking. It was certainly hard to surprise her.

Just then she saw the teacher, arriving a little late, going down the aisle to her regular seat near the front. Mr. Chittenden was with her, his arm across his chest and her hand over his arm. Even from several pews away, Rose could see that Miss Harty had no glove on that left hand—she was carrying it in her right. The ring was there for anyone to see. Now the engagement wouldn't be a secret anymore, and Rose knew it was one of the hardest she had ever had to keep.

Sarah had disapproved of people gawking at church and turning around in their seats, so she did not turn to look for Newton. So she was totally surprised when he slipped into the pew beside her, his big hand covering hers as he reached to share the hymnal. Even through her gloves, his touch sent that familiar shiver down her spine and legs, and she felt her face start to warm, but she glanced up at him anyway, her smile barely creating a pause in her singing.

"Where is everyone?" he whispered, and Rose, taught not to talk in church, shrugged her shoulders. The hymn ended, and everyone sat down except the Reverend Lockhead, who was getting ready to deliver one of his prayers. One of his long prayers, Rose thought.

She almost giggled, thinking about the minister praying away up there for all their souls, acting as if he had all kinds of influence on God when he couldn't even stop those women in black dresses at the tent meeting. She bowed her head, but instead of closing her eyes, she looked at Newton's hands, folded in his lap now, scrubbed clean of all the farm dirt and grease and manure that he'd been working in all week.

She chanced a sideways glance and found he was watching her out of the corner of his eye. She went back to the hands, then closed her eyes and prayed that Charles and Abby and Uncle Jason and Aunt Nell and Newton would all be healthy and nice to be with. And Father, too, she added as an afterthought. And Mother, although the church people had assured her over and over that her mother was with God. Rose wasn't certain of that kind of thing. It all seemed so unlikely, and she couldn't quite figure out where God was exactly. Still, she wouldn't plan on grown-ups being wrong. Except that if Mother was with God, then she could probably take care of her praying directly.

By the time Rose was finished with her private prayer, the minister was at the end of his, and the small choir had risen to sing. At that moment, Aunt Nell and Abby entered the pew and Newton moved closer to Rose to make room. Now they were arm against arm, and Rose thought it quite delicious that they could sit like this in church. She wondered if Newton ever felt the kinds of tingles that seemed to race around her body whenever any part of him touched her.

She heard a rustling at the end of the pew and leaned forward to see that Aunt Nell had seated herself next to Newton as quietly as a lady could when her taffeta skirt was as noisy as a summer breeze. Abby was there, too, so some of her worries could be put on a shelf. But Jason hadn't come. Sometimes he didn't, she reminded herself, and she had never dared ask why. Maybe he wasn't certain about God either. That was a comforting thought. Uncle always seemed so strong and sure of what he was doing, so if he didn't need God every Sunday, perhaps she didn't either. Still, it was nice to put on Sunday clothes and not do ironing or washing or sewing for a whole day, something God had apparently made possible. And what if she had missed today—today when Newton had joined her in the pew. And then they were standing for another hymn, and once again Newton's hand covered hers under the book.

She mechanically joined in the singing, her mind on Newton's hand and then on that day they had gone to the rock together. She knew the first two verses by heart, but for the third, she needed the book and was confronted with, "Just as I am, though tossed about/ With many a conflict, many a doubt/ Fightings and fears within, without/ O Lamb of God, I come, I come." She wasn't the only one, Rose decided, thinking she ought to pay better attention to these songs. Whoever wrote this one could have been inside her own head. Charlotte Elliott, it said at the top. She wondered who Charlotte Elliott might be. Perhaps Miss Harty could tell her.

CHAPTER SEVENTEEN
In Sickness and In Health

Jason snoozed as he sat in the rocker on Miss Harty's front porch. The sun was warm, he'd had a bite to eat from the Sunday dinner table, and it was quiet. It had been a tiring morning, and he had dropped off almost as soon as he sat down and stretched out his legs.

But it was only a catnap. Rose's voice, chattering away, reached him, and he lifted his head to see her and Newton coming round from the back of the house. He stood, thinking what a picture they were, so absorbed in each other, she so like her mother in looks, but much bolder in spirit. If that young man waited for her, he'd have a prize, but not a tame one.

"Uncle Jason!" Rose exclaimed as she reached the porch. "What on earth are you doing on Miss Harty's porch of a Sunday?"

"Waiting for you, Rose," Jason said gruffly. "And wondering where on earth, as you say, you might be."

"Is something wrong?" Rose said, suddenly anxious.

Her uncle never came here, and he ought to be sitting at the head of his table carving the roast chicken. They had chicken nearly every Sunday, Abby said. With stuffing and gravy.

"Everything is all right now," Jason said. "Charles is fine and dandy, and your father is sleeping off a heavy dose of hard cider. I reckon he took offense at the preaching attitude of those tent people last night and had his revenge on them in his own way."

"But he's not been at the drink," Rose protested. "Are you certain he isn't ill? Charles said he didn't think Father had touched a drop in a month or two."

"It was the drink all right, Rose. Charles found him on the grass by the cider barrel and a dipper beside him, so we could pretty much figure what happened. You will be hearing about it around town, I fear, so I wanted to reach you first. Dr. Potter has seen him and got him into the house."

"How could he?" Rose asked. "How could he? And where is Charles?" she wanted to know, starting to collect her thoughts. "And Abby?" She looked at Jason—now believing his story—and then at Newton. "Shall I go there? Shall I go now?"

"I wouldn't," Jason said. "He'll be sleeping a good while, and when he rouses, he is going to be as ornery as a bear with a headache and mebbe a stomachache, too. As for Abby, I figured on telling her that Silas was ailing today and wouldn't be out and about until tomorrow. Charles made it clear this morning that he can handle himself nicely, so I will call there to help him with the evening milking. You've done well with him, Rose. He kept his head delivering that calf awhile back, and he took care of business today without a flutter."

Rose smiled the tiniest smile. "I worry about him every day, but I know he's all right," she said. "He puts a funny cast on things and laughs when I might cry. But are you sure he will be all right with a bear with a headache?"

Newton had stood silently through all this, his eyes on the toes of his Sunday shoes, which had gotten a bit scuffed on the shortcut. "I'll stop in before I leave town, Rose," he said, "just to be sure the bear isn't growling too much. But I agree with Mr. Harris. Charles is quite the fellow for thirteen."

"You called him a thorn the other day, not 'quite the fellow'," Rose said.

"A different time, a different place," Newton answered and went back to studying his toes.

"You two are speaking in tongues as far as I can see," Jason said, "so I'll be off to finish my dinner, see to Abby and then give Charles a hand with his chores and the milking."

He gave Rose a pat on the arm, slapped Newton on the shoulder, and started down the steps. As he reached the flat stones that Miss Harty had used to make a walk, he turned and said, "And since the teacher is not at home, I expect you two will be setting on the porch for a spell until she gets here."

They both nodded, and he strode off. "It's the chaperone thing again," Rose sighed. "It just never goes away."

"Saw no chaperones on the shortcut," Newton reminded her. "And we did not need them, either." He gestured for her to take the rocker, and he turned a straight chair around and straddled it, facing her. "Are you falling into a worry place?"

"No," Rose said, "I am really all right. Mr. Goodnow and Miss Harty told me not to expect Father to suddenly change his ways, no matter what he might promise. He said he was turning a corner, and they said it was not so simple. Even you told me, that night when we saw him with Miss Graves, that some roads have many corners. So I am trying to be like Sarah—like Mother—and figure it will all work out in good time. And I did need a chaperone on the shortcut, but you didn't," she said a little resentfully.

"Rose, Rose, Rose," Newton said, reaching his hand over the chair back and taking hers. "I keep this chair between us so I won't just grab you right here on the porch and kiss you for an hour and never mind what passersby might think. It is probably a really good thing that I'm to be at Joshua's for the summer because you are more tempting than you know."

Rose felt the hot color coming up her neck onto her cheeks. When he talked like this, she felt as if she were a poorly made candle, melting fast. It was so strange, all the prickles that raced through her arms and legs even when it was only words, even when it was just his fingers gently tracing her palm. She never quite knew how to answer these outpourings, and sometimes she felt as if her voice wouldn't work if she asked it to, anyway.

Her eyes met his, then dropped, and she muttered, "Until now, I never really knew what temptation is." Except, she thought to herself, that time she'd never told anyone about. That day when she had pushed against the woodpile and wished it would fall on her. She must have been daft to have done that.

"Which only means you've never been tempted to lie, steal, or cheat," she heard Newton say. "You are so much on the high road that you panic at the first sight of a cliff."

"You, of course, have been a bad person since birth," Rose retorted. "Lying, cheating, stealing at every turn." But the idea made her smile, so Newton relaxed, figuring he had gotten her past her father's slide. He fidgeted in his chair, unable to stop thinking about how, indeed, she was so attractive to him that he wanted to just grab her. To carry her upstairs, if the truth be known. But that was a truth he would step away from, now and for the near future.

He looked up and saw Rose watching him. She looked up the road and down the road and then leaned forward in the rocker, pushed his hair aside and placed a kiss on his forehead.

"You had better get on home," she said. "I have chores to do."

"I had high hopes," Newton answered, "that you'd give me a bite of dinner before I go. They'll be all finished and doing dishes at my house, so where's a fellow to stop the rumbling in his stomach? Never have had a taste for that hotel food."

"If you'll set here by yourself, I'll rustle up something to eat," Rose said, happy to have something real to do, and realizing she was hungry herself. She was on her feet and heading for the door before he could answer.

Once in the kitchen, she settled into the routine dictated by pots, pans, and what was in the icebox. She poked up the fire in the stove, added a couple of small sticks, and without measuring any of the ingredients, combined flour, butter, milk, and salt in a large bowl. Biscuits were so quick, and if she dropped them on the pan, the way Abby and Father liked them, they plumped up in small hillocks, all bumpy and nicely brown on top. She glanced at the temperature gauge on the outside of the big oven door. It wasn't quite hot enough, but biscuits tended to turn out all right anyway. Her mother had always managed with a stove that didn't even have a gauge.

She'd serve Newton a couple of buttered biscuits with a slice or two of cold pot roast, some fresh rhubarb sauce, and a tumbler of the iced tea Miss Harty had made the day before. She hoped it would be enough. The way he sometimes talked about food made it sound as if he could eat a whole pot roast at one sitting. This time, she figured, the sitting would be on the porch, since they still hadn't seen hide nor hair of the teacher and her beau.

That expression bewildered her, like so many of the others. Certainly you could see a person's hair when they were standing in front of you, but it would be quite a shock if the hide was visible. Perhaps that phrase had started during a hunt for a fence-jumping cow, which would have both hide and hair. Except even then, Rose challenged herself, the hide would be on the inside. That's the part they use for shoes. Land sakes, she had taken a long route to nowhere on that one.

She slid the biscuit pan into the oven and glanced at the clock. If the fire was hot enough, these would take only five minutes. She had made them smaller than usual so they would cook faster because Newton had sounded as if he needed nourishment before he could even walk home.

She took the tumblers of cold tea to the porch and set them on the small table by the rocking chair.

"Need chaperoning even while we're eating?" Newton teased.

"Think of it as a picnic," Rose said.

"I like picnics on a big flat rock better," he said, and Rose felt the dratted color rising in her face again.

"The biscuits are about ready," she said, and went back in the house.

Newton stood and leaned over the white railing to scan the road in both directions. He saw no one. He wondered if he had time to slip inside, gather Rose in his arms and kiss her. The very idea warmed him. It was all very well to behave like a perfect gentleman when taking a shortcut, but he was wishing now that he'd taken a different path. He was having mixed feelings about going away for the summer, and was still considering a dash to the kitchen when Rose reappeared at the door with two plates in her hands and flatware sticking

Rose

out of her apron pocket. She had even brought napkins. The moment was lost.

But he had reckoned without Rose. She made space for the plates on the table, walked over to the rail where he stood, and just as he had done, looked up and down the road. Then she turned, pulled his head down toward her, and kissed him on the mouth. Newton knew everyone in town would label a girl as "forward" for doing such a thing. Girls were supposed to be quiet and demure and wait for boys to approach them. He decided he liked this better. She was not only pretty and scary capable, but she was passionate. He kissed her back.

A few seconds later, Rose broke away, peeked around his shoulder and said, "The coast is still clear." She raised her face to his again and when he started to kiss her, he was taken aback all over again. Her tongue was tracing his lips, touching and withdrawing, touching again. He knew this was dangerous ground, but they were on a front porch, after all, so what was the harm? He opened his mouth and touched the tip of her tongue with his and felt Rose's arms tighten around him, drawing him closer.

An ant couldn't walk between them now, Rose thought. She wondered how she could manage almost a whole summer without his arms and his mouth. Forgetting Miss Harty's warnings entirely, she pushed her tongue into Newton's mouth and sent it exploring along his tongue and teeth. She heard him give a little moan, and she jumped back.

"Did I hurt you?" she asked.

"Hell, no," Newton said. "Begging your pardon, Miss Rose." He dropped his arms to his side and backed away. "That was a pleasure sound, and it's not allowed on a porch." He looked down at her, smiled, and turned to the table to take one of the plates.

"I reckon we'd better feed our stomachs now that we've fed our hearts," he said. "You are the loveliest creature in Eastborough, Rose, but you scare me to death with the things you do."

"Remember Miss Harty's warnings," Rose said.

"About what?"

"About the things we do. And don't do. And won't do," she added hastily.

"Mostly won't," Newton muttered, chewing on a piece of pot roast and buttering a hot biscuit. "These biscuits are crumbly, just the way I like them."

"Sometimes your talk jumps about like rabbits, too," Rose said, laughing. "Miss Harty likes the biscuits that way, so I make them a little short."

"Rather tall, I'd say," Newton said, measuring the height of a biscuit with thumb and forefinger. "Tallest biscuit Ah ever saw," he drawled, closing his mouth around the last bite and watching a couple of crumbs roll down his shirt to the floor. For a few minutes they ate without talking.

"I've had enough," Newton said suddenly, starting to get up. "Shall I help wash up?"

"Anything to get out of sight, sir?" Rose asked saucily. "They must be coming back soon. We're way past the noon hour now."

"Probably took a shortcut," Newton said with a quick smile. Rose grinned, too, and wondered how she would ever get a serious word in edgewise. The very idea sent one track of her brain onto a siding, pondering the picture of a word tilted up and trying to make its way into a crack of conversation. Difficult but not impossible, she thought, mentally putting kiss and mouth and watch-your-step on end and watching them disappear in a small slit of a stone wall.

"You've disappeared again," Newton said.

"And you are speaking with your mouth full," Rose said disapprovingly.

"But you are not my mother, so you can't give me instruction," he answered.

"And I don't want to be," Rose answered quickly. "Perhaps today I could walk with you toward your house on the main road where chaperones abound, and we could talk some more about do's and don'ts."

As if she had been summoned by this thought, Ruthann Harty appeared from the backyard, her hair slightly out of place and her face prettily flushed. Joshua Chittenden was right behind her, taking off his hat and making an exaggerated bow in Rose's direction. Rose took one look at them and decided they were also smiling like the Cheshire cat. She did hope their heads wouldn't vanish the way the cat's did, and then chided herself for having more imagination than sense.

Getting back down to earth, she asked, "Have you had any dinner? I have biscuits that might still be slightly warm, and there's cold pot roast. It's not a proper Sunday meal, but…"

"Don't fret about us, Rose," Miss Harty said, pushing stray tendrils of hair back from her face. "We are going to have a drink of cold tea, and then perhaps we'll eat whatever is left from your meal. Sorry we've been so long getting here, but we took a shortcut…"

Newton interrupted with a hoot of laughter. "Sorry, Miss Harty," he said quickly. "Our shortcut turned out to be a long cut. Must be yours was, too."

"Indeed," Miss Harty said, sounding as if she were in the classroom, her eyes so dark they almost willed him to keep still. "Indeed."

"If we may be excused," Rose said, "I am going to walk part of the way with Newton." She would tell Miss Harty about Father on her return. Right now, she didn't want to talk about it.

"And I will collect you at your house, Newton?" Joshua asked.

"Yes, sir," Newton said. "I have my things ready."

"In an hour," Joshua said.

"Just right," Newton answered, "providing we can make a brief stop at the Hibbard house on the way out." He reached for Rose's hand as if she needed help with the porch steps, and they left, walking in the middle of the dirt road toward the Barnes farm.

"We should have been here sooner," Ruthann said anxiously.

"They were eating on the porch," Joshua answered.

Rose

"I'll wager she never let him inside the door."

Ruthann sighed. "I suspect you're right," she said. "But I do worry about them. It's good that Newton is going with you for a spell."

"Do you worry about us, too? Or can we go inside for our dinner?"

"I should worry, but I'm not up to it after that long cut," Ruthann said, picking up Newton and Rose's plates and smiling up at him so warmly that he wondered if he could wait even four clicks of a second hand to get inside the house and pull her close. For him, the long cut had been all too short.

Meanwhile, Rose and Newton walked sedately along the gravel road toward the Barnes farm, her long legs keeping up with his. Even a careful watcher like Mrs. Munson would not have noticed that the back of his sun-browned right hand occasionally brushed the back of her left, nor seen the small smile that played around their lips each time it happened.

Rose wasn't sure she could ever be happier than she was at this very moment, but she remembered having that thought before, so she was considering that perhaps her cup might run over one day.

She suddenly blurted out, "Will you write me this summer from Joshua's? He writes Miss Harty. Will you, Newton?" she asked with a pleading tone that took away any temptation he had to tease her.

"I will, I will. Postcards cost very little and have a fair amount of space. I can buy them at the post office where Joshua lives."

"You'll be cautious about what you write, I hope," Rose said. "Mr. Goodnow reads all the postcards."

"Best I get a tablet and a couple of envelopes for the none-of-your-business things, then," Newton laughed. "Or I'll write in code, and you can spend your days figuring it out."

"I wish I had a postbox," Rose said. "Then I would know the minute I walked in whether I had a letter or not. It would show through the little window."

"And why not?" Newton said, having little or no knowledge of how the post office worked at Mr. Goodnow's.

"It's dear," Rose said. "The people with boxes pay every month, and some of them make a show of coming in with their little keys and sashaying up to the boxes instead of waiting for Mr. Goodnow to get their mail from general delivery."

"Does general delivery take a long time?"

"Not really," Rose said. "He sorts it alphabetically, so he's quick as a wink getting someone's mail. And Eastborough folks don't get a lot of letters. Some people only come in every week or so, and their letters stay and stay. I always worry that birthday wishes arrive at the post office on time but are gathered up when the birthday has gone by."

"Leave it to you to find something to worry about, even in a pile of mail," Newton said, silently considering whether he could ask his father to arrange for a box just for Rose, at least for the first month he was away. One month surely couldn't cost very much. Then she could have one of the keys she apparently prized. And he could write every night and get up early to make sure his letters or penny postcards made the train. Their hands brushed again, and he started thinking about the kiss they had exchanged and how Rose had suddenly thrust her tongue into his mouth. A tremor ran over him, and Rose stopped walking.

"What was that?" she asked.

"Someone walked over my grave," he said, trying to brush off his feelings with a laugh.

"I get those shivers just thinking about you," Rose said softly, her face starting to look like a nearly ripe tomato.

"Now that you mention it, I reckon that was my problem, rather than anyone finding my burial place," Newton confessed. "And since you bring it up, I am making a rule here and now about your tongue. Keep it in your mouth where it is supposed to live.

"You are not Mehitabel," he went on. "I say we can back up if we want, no matter what Miss Harty says. I will tie my tongue to my teeth if need be, or just shove you away if you tempt me. Miss Harty is better at explaining these things, I'll wager, but you are not going to become Mehitabel, even if I am required to jump in the river after each time I come calling on you. Once the summer passes, I'll be calling on you regular and proper."

"You are going to ask Father?" Rose gasped, so stunned that she paid no attention to Newton being tongue-tied or jumping in the river. She couldn't believe

Newton would face her father. "You are going to Father?" she repeated.

"It's what any right-thinking boy must do when he's kissing a daughter," Newton said with a grin as wide as a slice of watermelon. "Probly should have got to it sooner, but he scares the bejesus out of me when he pulls his dark eyebrows together and his eyes nail me to the nearest wall. But it's done, and I have lived to tell the tale."

"You've already spoken to him?"

"Yesterday," Newton said. "Nearly regretted it after I saw you covered with soap and sweat, but I aim to be a man of my word, so the courting has begun. Unless you stamp your size nine foot and say 'Begone!'"

Rose couldn't even laugh at his tomfoolery because she was still in shock about his asking Father for permission to call on her. She knew it was proper, had even thought about how her mother would feel if she knew what Rose and Newton had been up to without Newton announcing his intentions to her father. And he had gone only hours before Father had come to grief with the cider.

"What exactly did he say?" Rose said.

"He said yes," Newton said in a teasing tone.

Rose grabbed his arm and yanked him toward her. "Start with knocking on the door," she said, "and tell me everything that happened. I can't believe you were with me this long and never said a word."

Newton relented and became very serious as they walked on. "I stopped in when I figured he'd be having his noon meal, apologized for the interruption, and he told me to take a seat across the table. He offered me a tumbler of cold tea. I refused. I put both feet on the floor under the table and clasped my hands so he wouldn't see them shaking and..."

"Newton!" Rose interrupted, exasperated.

"You wanted it all," he said, back to teasing.

"Just the meat of it," she said.

"He was having a little cold chicken, not meat," Newton went on, paying no mind when Rose jabbed him in the ribs with her elbow. "I said, 'Sir, I've come to ask your permission to court your daughter.'"

"'Abigail or Rose?' he asked."

"No!" Rose said.

"Yes," Newton answered. "And then we both chuckled, and he said, 'Not many boys are worthy of that girl, but you'll do better than most.' And I said, 'Do I have your blessing, sir?' And he said, 'Never mind the religious things. You may court my daughter if it suits her.' And I thanked him, pushed back my chair, and took my leave."

Rose now knew what it meant in books when someone's jaw dropped. She felt as if her mouth were gaping as it might at a circus freak show. "And you're not making this up? It really happened, cold chicken and all?"

"Did. Does it suit you?"

"Yes. And in the end, you seem to have told the complete story."

"Not the story, Rose. Does it suit you to be courted? He gave permission, but only if it suits you."

Rose's face flamed, and she looked down at the toes of her shoes in hopes he wouldn't see. "Yes," she said, her voice almost whispering. "It suits me fine."

Newton sighed with relief. "Hate to have gone into the lion's den without gain," he said. "And now, suited girl, your suitor is turning you around. You are going back to Miss Harty's, and I am continuing home."

Rose stopped and looked up then, her cheeks still very pink and tears pushing their way into her eyes. "I will miss you," she said. "And I can't send a letter until you write and say where to send it."

"I'll warrant teacher Ruthann has that mailing information at her fingertips," Newton said. "So you can go home and start writing today." He took her hand, bent to give her a peck on the cheek, squeezed her fingers so hard that they nearly stuck together, and then turned away, breaking into a run.

She looked after him and then started back the way they had come. She was being courted. She had a suitor. She could not decide whether to tell Emily and Alice or not, and as she considered that, she suddenly wished she could tell her mother, and a tear spilled from each eye. She had no idea Newton had stopped running and was watching from down the road. He saw her wipe her eyes, and then laughed when she tossed her head, picked up her skirt, and started to run, braids flying behind her.

As Rose's feet flew along the gravelly road, her tears vanished. She would write Newton tonight and take the letter to Mr. Goodnow. As Newton had reminded her, the address would be available from Miss Harty. She wondered how long it took a letter to get to the Chittenden farm. Perhaps Mr. Goodnow would know exactly.

A little out of breath and in sight of a couple of houses, Rose slowed to a walk. Somehow, her thoughts slowed down at the same time, and she started thinking about the report on her father. Uncle had said to leave him be, but she wasn't certain a man really knew what was best. Did anyone know? She felt her eyes getting watery again and spoke aloud, sternly. "Stop that, Rose," she said. "Stop it right now. No need to turn into a faucet."

But when she came to the next corner, she turned toward her father's house instead of continuing on to Miss Harty's. She could see no need to be afraid of facing whatever was there—hadn't she already come up against a few things that Emily and Alice could only hear about? When she reached the house, she went around to the back and up the stairs. Almost silently, she opened the door and peered into the kitchen. It was empty, save for an old mattress on the floor. She walked in, checked the wood stove and saw the fire was dying. As she turned to get three pieces of wood, she wondered why fires died. They should just go out, she thought. Not die. Dying was too final, and a fire could almost always be brought back. Sarah had died and would never come back, and now, it seemed, her father may have been teetering on the edge of death. Thinking back, she decided Uncle had not told all.

She opened the door carefully and put the sticks in. Flames flared immediately, and she moved the teakettle to what would soon be a hot spot. Uncle had said they left Father in the front room, she remembered, so she tiptoed to the closed door and opened it a crack. There he was, sprawled on the sofa on a piece of oilcloth, one leg hanging over the edge. She moved into the room and jumped when he stirred. When his foot hit the floor, his eyes flew open.

"What in thunderation are you doing here?" he growled, trying to sit up and then falling back onto the pillow.

"Seeing to you, Father," Rose said, hoping her voice wouldn't tell him how shaky she felt about all this.

"Don't need seeing to," he grumbled, pulling his leg back onto the sofa and turning over to face the wall. "Didn't sleep well last night."

"Apparently you slept much too well," Rose countered. "Uncle has already told me what happened."

"Child alive, are you going to believe that do-gooder?"

"Yes," Rose said. "Perhaps you'd like a cup of tea, or perhaps you would rather just shout at me?"

Silas Hibbard clutched his forehead and muttered, "Pretty sassy these days, I'd say. Pretty sassy." A little louder, he said, "Tea. I'll try the tea. With milk and a spoon of sugar."

The kettle on the stove was already hissing, and Rose fetched a cup and saucer from the dining room. Rose put tea leaves into the teapot that Sarah had always kept warm on the back shelf of the stove. Not much gained by pouring hot water into a pot that's as cold as a dog's nose, she would say. She filled the pot with boiling water, found the tea strainer in the sink with some unwashed dishes, and placed it on the cup. Suddenly, thinking how he had been unable to sit up for more than a tick of the clock, she switched the strainer to his mustache cup. Less to hold onto, she thought.

"Rose?" Silas called from the front room. "Where in tarnation is that tea? Are you harvesting the leaves?"

Grouchy indeed, Rose thought. Instead of answering him, she poured the tea into the strainer, added milk and a spoonful of sugar, and delivered the tea. He managed to sit up this time, and she saw that his eyes were red and the left side of his face smeared with dirt. He reached for the cup, but his hand was shaking so that she sat down beside him and lifted it to his lips, watching as the little bar across the top protected his mustache from drops of tea.

"Not weak as a kitten," he said gruffly. "Well, as I think on it, perhaps I am." He slurped tea and then shook his head. "Not too much at once, girl. I have not treated my innards well in the past few hours."

"So I heard," Rose said.

"Is the word all around town then?" he asked, a little anxiously.

"Hardly," Rose said. "Dr. Potter tells nothing, and Uncle is not Mrs. Munson."

He nearly smiled at the idea of Jason being Harriet Munson, but she could see that it was an effort. She offered the cup again, and this time, he took it, his hand trembling but getting the drink to his lips nevertheless.

"Need to use the toilet," Silas said. "Reckon you're strong enough to get me from here to there?"

He looked dirty and smelled awful, Rose thought. She hoped he wasn't going to be sick to his stomach. She was still in her Sunday clothes and didn't want them soiled. She sighed, stood, reached out a hand, and hauled him to his feet. Together they lurched through the kitchen and into the back hall where he indicated she should open the newly installed door to the new bathroom.

She pushed it and saw that it was now completely finished, with little brass faucets on the sink, and a shiny wooden seat on the toilet. A matching wooden box high on the wall contained the water that made the toilet flush, she knew, and the chain had a brass knob at the end. It was a wonder, indeed.

"No need to stay while I do my buttons, Rose. I'll holler when I'm ready to walk back."

But his fingers were not steady enough grasp the buttons, so Rose did it quickly and left him, her face reddening at the very thought of helping her father undo his trousers. Outside, with her ear to the door, she considered this addition to the house. It was well done, even to a looking glass over the sink. She wondered if Charles and Father still kept chamber pots under the bed, just in case. But neither was in the habit of peeing in the night, so she'd wager they were clean as a whistle most mornings. What a blessing that would be, she mused, wondering if whistles were actually all that clean. If they were whittled from a piece of wood and passed around, they would be decidedly unclean in a short time, damp from spit and in some cases tobacco juice. Well, then, clean as Sarah's best plates. Those were always spotless.

"You there, Rose?" her father asked loudly.

"Right here," she answered.

"Well, get a move on and open that door," he said. "Couldn't unbutton and can't button either. I've turned into an old fool overnight."

Rose couldn't think of a proper answer to that comment, so she kept her mouth shut. The constantly returning memories of her mother had taught her that quick answers were sometimes a rough route to take, and she was learning, slowly, to think on her words before they popped out of her mouth. This is a sad business, she thought, opening the door, and with her father's hand heavy on her shoulder, taking care of his buttons.

They started through the kitchen where he stumbled on the corner of the mattress. "Doc must have thought I'd be better off in the kitchen," Silas muttered. "Moved almost as soon as I saw his back." Rose nodded and saw him to the sofa.

"I will be going now, Father," she said, settling him on the pillow once again. "I'll leave a tumbler of water here for you. I reckon you're not up to toast yet?"

"Appreciate it," Silas Hibbard mumbled, closing his eyes. "Leave me be. Charles will likely show up soon and mebbe I'll manage toast then."

Rose left him then, moving quickly through the kitchen and then stopping for another closer look at the new bathroom before making her way down the back stairs. Outside, for the first time, she saw the cider keg on its side. She gave it a little push with her foot, and when it rolled easily, realized it had to be empty.

He had dumped it out but took a last taste, or several of them, she realized. And this is where Charles found him.

"Oh, what are we to do now," she moaned aloud. And where was Charles anyway?

She went on her way, knowing she couldn't stay, but her worries about Charles grew with each step away from the house. Perhaps he'd be back there when Newton stopped in. She should have gone to the barn to see if he was holed up with his calf, but she didn't turn back.

In the front room, Silas turned on his side, vomited the tea into the pail Dr. Potter had placed there, and muttered, "She should never have seen me like this. What would Sarah think of me now?" He wiped his mustache with the towel and closed his eyes.

CHAPTER EIGHTEEN
Calf Comfort

When Rose came out of their father's house, Charles ducked around the corner just in time. As was his wont, he had been listening at the parlor window, had missed whatever happened in the new bathroom, and then had caught the last part of Rose's conversation with her father. If I were the kind of boy who blushed, he thought, I'd be beside myself for eavesdropping in this shameless way. But Charles never blushed, and when it came to eavesdropping, he took considerable pride in his expertise. He took great pleasure in knowing things he wasn't supposed to know.

He crouched low and soon saw that Rose was on her way along the road. Father was calling his name, but it wasn't very loud and he was damned—well, darned, anyway—if he was going to spend the day fetching and carrying and being yelled at. He trotted back to the barn to see to his calf. He had named the scrawny creature Ruthann but hadn't told anyone that. He only talked to her by name when he was alone, and he sometimes laughed out loud when he said, "Here's your hay, Ruthann," or "Move over now, Ruthann," or "I wish you made less manure, Ruthann." When he first came up with the manure one, he had laughed until tears ran down his cheeks. It would have been fun to share these laughs, but even Charles didn't have the nerve to let anyone in on his Ruthann jokes.

Once in the barn, he grabbed a shovel and continued to clean the calf's stall. He had built her a small pen so she had room to move around, and he paid close attention to what she was doing these days. She was getting big and frisky, and he knew she was strong enough to tip him right over.

"Move your leg, Ruthann," he said now, trying to get the last of the soiled sawdust out of the pen, and chortling to himself about the unlikely possibility of his telling the teacher to move her leg, even if she put her foot on his head. And she might do just that, it occurred to him, if she knew about her namesake.

With the pen pretty well cleaned up, he shoveled in new sawdust, filled the calf's water pail, and put hay in the manger. As the calf started to eat, Charles put one arm around the animal's neck and laid his face against Ruthann's soft ears. He felt hot tears coming and moved quickly away, heading for the main part of the barn where more piles of manure awaited him. No one, he told himself, cries over cow manure. He was only half done when he heard a scraping sound behind him and turned to find his uncle bent to the task as well.

"Hello there, young fellow," Jason Harris said. "I reckoned you might need a hand. Then I'll see to your father. How is he doing?"

"He was awake awhile back," Charles answered.

"What did he have to say?"

Charles knew what his father had to say all right, but he couldn't answer the question because everything had been said to Rose.

"Dunno," he said, keeping his eyes on his shovel.

"Say what?"

"Rose was here. I heard them talking and skedaddled," Charles said, hoping this was what was called a fib or a white lie and not one of those awful burn-in-hell lies the Reverend Lockhead had on his mind all the time.

"Rose?" Jason said, incredulously. "I told her not to come."

"That's like telling water not to run downhill, Uncle," Charles answered, and then nearly bit his tongue off. He hoped Uncle Jason wouldn't think that was impertinent, but relief came quickly.

Jason's hoot of laughter startled the calf into a loud blat that came so suddenly Charles dropped his shovel.

"Reckon you shot the apple off the boy's head that time, Charles," he said.

It took Charles a minute to remember the story and then he said, "Better to be the shooter than the boy trying to stand still."

"I reckon," Jason said. "But you don't always get a choice."

The two finished cleaning the barn in silence and then opened the door to let the cows in for the night milking. Charles never could get over how they sorted themselves out at the door, the one at the far stanchion nearly always coming in first and the others jostling each other to get in the right order. It didn't always work neatly, but more often than not. They must be smarter than most folks thought they were. As soon as the hoofs quieted, he and Jason clicked the stanchions shut, forked hay into the trough that ran in front of the cows, and then headed for the house.

"I'll stay on to start the milking," Jason told Charles. "Then I'll get on home to my own chores, and Ben Chandler will come by. He has no notion of what went on here last night and today. I just told him Silas was feeling poorly, and you needed a hand."

"It's a secret, is it?" Charles asked.

"Better a secret than town gossip, son," Jason answered. "Your father needs less trouble, not more. And a man has a right, come down to it, to get himself drunk on his own cider in his own yard. Not that you ought ever to do that, you understand."

"If it makes you look the way Father looked when I found him, I'm never going to touch the stuff," Charles answered solemnly. "I could take the pledge at one of Blockhead's meetings."

"Blockhead's meetings?"

"You misheard me, sir. I said 'Lockhead,' sir," Charles

corrected anxiously, hoping he wasn't going to get a thrashing for this mistake.

"Hmmm," Jason said, stopping and turning his back on Charles. The boy stopped, too, wondering what was coming next, but his uncle had tipped his head back and appeared to be examining the sky. His shoulders were shaking a bit. Charles was tempted to cut and run but wasn't sure his feet would move. Not smart to insult the minister. Rose would say he put her at her wit's end. He was just starting to wonder if Rose's wit also had a beginning, when Jason spoke.

"Not going to rain tomorrow," he said, starting to walk again. "Mebbe not the next day neither."

On the stairs to the kitchen, Jason told Charles he would not be staying more than a minute or two, just long enough to make certain that Silas was on the mend. Charles nodded, still a bit worried about making fun of the minister's name, even though he did think the reverend was pretty much a blockhead.

They found Silas at the dining room table, his head on his hands. He looked up as they came in and asked Charles to make him a cup of tea. "I lost the first cup into that pail you mercifully supplied, Jason, but I reckon it's time to start again and see if this cup sets better."

"Take it slow, Silas, without milk," Jason said. "Nell always says milk is the worst thing for stomachs except when she makes the ginger milk during haying season. That's a thought, Silas, the ginger. You might try a piece, if you have it."

Charles came in with a steaming cup of tea and a

small plate with a chunk of sugary ginger on it. "This what you want, Father?" he asked. "We haven't any plain, or if we do, I've no notion where Rose might keep it."

"Appreciate it," Silas said, taking the tiniest possible bite of the ginger. "No need for you two to stand around looking me over as if I were a body in a coffin. I will be helping Charles with the milking within the hour."

"Whoa, there," Jason said quickly. "Ben Chandler's coming by to give a hand with the milking, and you better lie low since I told him you are under the weather today. You can milk tomorrow. Charles has already cleaned up the barn in fine fashion."

"Sounds like I need a nursemaid to keep things straight," Silas muttered. "Appreciate it anyway. Lying low suits me for once." He took another nibble of the ginger and added, "But seems like too many people know about this to keep it quiet. Just when I thought I was on the high road."

"You can step up there again," Jason said. "Told Ben you were under the weather, no more than that. Now I'd better be going. Plenty to do at home, and I don't want Nell to worry." He turned to Charles, who was standing so still the two men had nearly forgotten him. "Offer him a little toast in another hour or so, Charles, and I'll ride over late in the evening to make sure you're all right. You have some supper here?"

Charles nodded, his eyes still on his father, his eyebrows pulled so close together that the creases over his nose were just thin lines. Jason shook his head, thinking it was hardly fair for a boy his age to be frowning over such a trouble. He wanted to give him a hug, but just put out a big hand and squeezed his shoulder instead. Even that brought tears to Charles' eyes, and Jason immediately wished he hadn't done it.

But the boy didn't cry. He just turned away and went to the kitchen. Jason started to follow and heard Silas speak softly.

"What's that?" he asked.

"Put my name in for the deputy sheriff spot," Silas said with effort. "Reckon I've spoilt my chances."

Jason was startled by this news, but he answered evenly. "I told you, Silas, that mum's the word on this. You have the same chances you had two days ago. They might not put you at the top of the list, but you won't move to the bottom on my account."

Silas didn't answer, and Jason moved toward the kitchen where Charles was adding another stick to the wood stove and readying the toaster.

"Let him sleep, Charles, if he can. That's the best thing."

"Yes, sir," Charles answered, looking up, the watery eyes already cleared. "I am all right, sir. We'll be all right, sir."

Jason nodded and went out, closing the door quietly and wishing he could take the boy home with him. He shook his head in wonder, thinking how strong Sarah had made all three of her children. And Silas putting in for deputy sheriff, now that was something. Maybe he had a chance for the high road after all. He figured on keeping that piece of news to himself for the time being.

As the door shut, Charles pulled the pot of soup from the back of the stove to the front, figuring it would heat up enough for his supper once the milking was done. He might have a slice of toast, but he'd need something that would stick to his ribs, as Sarah was apt to say. He was glad Mr. Chandler would be giving a hand. Better be two hands, he muttered to himself, a small smile crossing his face.

"Back soon," he called to his father as he, too, went out the door.

Not far away, Newton Barnes was also helping with the cows, and it crossed his mind that Charles would be tackling that task alone unless his uncle lent a hand. Newton brushed the thought away, knowing he could do nothing himself. As soon as the barn work was finished, he'd be on his way to Joshua Chittenden's farm for the summer. But the question of postboxes remained to be answered first, and he hoped he could do something about that. He was unsure how to approach his father about what might seem a foolish expense.

As they started toward the house with full milk pails, he suddenly blurted, "Can you, would you, get a postbox for Rose?"

"What are you talking about?" his father answered.

"I promised to write Rose, and she likes, she wants, she should have a postbox for the letters, but she can't spare the money, so I thought..." He stopped, thinking he was sounding like an idiot, stammering as if he couldn't speak English properly.

"Bit dear, aren't they?" Samuel Barnes asked.

"Rose sets great store by a box, sir, something about privacy and not being in the general delivery pile. She knows they're dear, so she won't do it. But she would like it, so I…" He stopped, thinking how impossible it was to defend spending hard-earned cash on a box to put letters in.

His father chuckled. "You really fancy that young lady, don't you, son," he said quietly. "I'll advance you whatever it costs, and since you are on your way tonight, I'll arrange it with Henry in the morning. What you won't have time for, and what I can't do for you, is ask Silas Hibbard for permission to court his daughter, if that's what you're of a mind to do."

"I already did, sir," Newton said.

"Talked to Silas?" Samuel Barnes stopped so suddenly that the warm milk sloshed in the pails. "You broached the subject with Mr. Hibbard?"

"And lived to tell about it," Newton answered, grinning. Rose would have a private box for her mail, and he had surprised the daylights out of his father.

"Well, I never," his father said. "You are a brave boy and know your own mind, I do believe. And the girl—did she consent to be courted, or are you planning to ask her in one of these private letters?"

"She did."

"Best of luck, son," Samuel Barnes said. "She appears to be a prize girl with a good head on her shoulders, although I suspect you'll find a mite of stubbornness inside that head. Had to be, to get her through so much. Her mother had moments of digging her heels in, as I recall. Now we'd better get this milk into the cooler, and you best be on your way to Chittenden's place before it's too dark for the horse to see the road."

Newton smiled, thinking this had all gone a bit better than he had expected. He hoped his mother would be just as admiring of Rose, and decided he would let his father take care of telling her he was officially calling on Rose. Well, writing her, since calling on her would be out of the question for the present.

He wondered if Rose would write before going to sleep tonight. As for that mite of stubbornness, he already knew it could be more like a nest of hornets than a mite. He had an idea mites were all but invisible. He would ask Rose in his first letter.

At Miss Harty's little desk, Rose was already trying to write her first letter. She had been staring at the page since the clock struck the half hour, and she knew it was about to ring five times. She had written the month, day, and year at the top, then "Dear Newton," then "How are you? I am well." That was ridiculous. She knew how he was; he knew how she was; they both knew what year it was. She sighed.

"No letter-writing thoughts, Rose?" Miss Harty said, coming up behind her. "I often have that trouble myself. Then I look out the window or take a walk around the garden, and I find something that works. Sometimes the letters are very short, and that's permissible."

Rose stood, smoothed her long skirt, and smiled at

the teacher. "I'll be back soon," she said. "And then I will prepare supper."

Out on the porch she watched a robin with a piece of straw in its beak fly across the yard and land in Miss Harty's lilac bush, which had just finished blooming and was so thick that the bird disappeared completely. Moving toward the end of the porch, Rose tried to find a peephole in the leaves and was leaning close to the bush when the robin suddenly flew out, making her jump. The bird perched on a nearby tree limb and made anxious sounds while Rose brushed a branch aside to see the half-finished nest, a combination of straw and grass, and the mud that would hold it all together. She would write Newton about the robin and hope he didn't think it was a flibbertigibbet thing to do.

Back at the desk, she quickly wrote a single page, signed her name, folded the paper, and tucked it in the envelope Miss Harty had given her. The teacher had written Joshua's address for her, and Rose had quickly memorized it: Chittenden Road, RFD 204, Ripton, Massachusetts.

"Is there room for this?" Miss Harty asked, holding out a folded piece of notepaper with "Joshua" written on the outside.

Rose nodded, surprised that the teacher didn't want her letter to be private. Still, she knew postage was an expense, and this was a way to save. She wouldn't put an open note to Newton in one of Miss Harty's letters, though. She wanted every word she wrote to be private, even if it was about robins.

"Are you all right, Rose?" Miss Harty asked a little anxiously. "Jason told me a little bit about what happened to your father, and I wondered if you would want to go there to see to him tonight. I could go with you."

"I did," Rose said.

"Did what?"

"Went there, made him tea."

"Did he, was he, were you…" Ruthann Harty was ready to scold herself for all this fumbling.

"He was still not feeling well, I was fine," Rose said. She looked up and realized the teacher looked quite worried. "I'm not sure the tea set well on his stomach, but he wanted it. He was pleased I came and not anxious for me to stay and see him in his present condition."

"You are a wonder, Rose," Miss Harty said. "I am mighty glad to call you my friend." She leaned down and gave Rose a quick hug, hoping it wouldn't embarrass her, and left the room.

CHAPTER NINETEEN
Starting Over

"What in tarnation is going on over there?" were Nell's first words to Jason as he stepped into the kitchen.

"No need to cuss at me, wife of mine," Jason said mildly, leaning down to kiss her on the cheek.

"Never mind the sass, Jason," Nell answered tartly. "I want to know what's going on at Silas's house. He seems to jump from ice floe to ice floe faster than Eva, trouble always at his heels."

"Eliza," Jason said.

"Who's Eliza?" Nell demanded. "Have we shed ourselves of Miss Jennie only to move on to Eliza?"

"Calm down, my dear. It was Eliza who crossed the river on the ice floes, not Eva. Silas emptied his hard cider keg in the backyard last night after he went to the tent meeting, but he was moved to taste it before he let it spill. Several dippers of tasting, apparently."

"Where was Charles in all this?"

Jason explained, and Nell sighed. Unsure what to do next, since he rarely saw Nell in such a state, Jason put his big hands on her shoulders and awkwardly drew her toward him, circling her with both arms when, to his surprise, she moved willingly toward him and dropped her head on his chest.

"I beg your pardon for my shrewish greeting," she mumbled into his scratchy wool shirt. "I've been so worried."

"Never think of you as a shrew, Nell. They have sharp, ugly little noses, the better for burrowing. No one has ever accused you of burrowing."

Nell's fist pounded him on the back. "Charles," she said. "What about Charles?"

"Charles is handling things as if he were forty-three, not thirteen." He told her about getting Ben to help with the milking and that he expected Silas to be on his feet by morning, trying to prove he was all of a piece, and sober forever.

"I'll believe it when I see it," Nell said. "Is half the town whispering about this over the supper table?"

"Mum's the word," Jason assured her. "You can't pry information out of Dr. Potter or Ruthann Harty with a spoon, and Charles has been told to keep his mouth shut. Rose, too. As for Newton..."

"That's a lot of folks in the know," Nell interrupted.

"Newton," Jason continued, "is off to Chittenden's place tonight. And he won't breathe a word of any kind that would hurt Rose. He's as sappy about her as Silas was about Sarah."

"I pray it turns out better for her," Nell said, pulling away and looking so downcast that Jason felt a wave of irritation about his brother-in-law rising right into his throat.

"I have faith that it will," was all he said, just as Abby appeared in the doorway, looking a little puzzled by the scene but afraid to ask what was going on.

"You didn't get enough dinner," she said, "and now it's nearly time for supper."

"Time to make up for lost food, I reckon," Jason said. "What are you and your aunt rustling up for this repast?"

"Is repast a new word for Sunday night supper?" Abby asked. "You know we usually have crackers and milk or a bowl of soup and biscuits. What's a repast?"

"Supper, child, or a picnic or Sunday dinner. Probly not breakfast," Jason said, smiling at last. This child was like Rose and not like Rose, much too solemn sometimes, to his way of thinking. "So what do you have hidden in the pantry that will satisfy my hunger better than crackers and milk?"

Abby glanced at her aunt, still wondering why she looked so sad, and said she would take a look in the pantry herself. She scampered off, humming as she went, and both Jason and Nell smiled as they watched her go.

"She'll come up with something," Nell said. "She knows a lot about kitchens and food. You won't starve tonight."

"I thought I wouldn't have the stomach for anything,

Miss Nell, but my appetite is returning," Jason said. "I will wait in the dining room for the repast."

"Can he wait long enough for biscuits?" Abby asked, peering around the corner from the pantry.

"Certain he'll wait for that," Nell laughed.

"Then we can give him some leftover chicken, and I'll make the biscuits," Abby said with satisfaction. She had just learned how to work the butter into the flour until the mixture was grainy but even-textured, and she liked being allowed to use her fingers for the task. When Aunt Nell wasn't looking, she'd lick them, not really liking the taste of flour but loving the buttery part.

She poured in some skimmed milk and added just a little of the top milk for richness, then dropped the sticky dough onto a baking sheet in four sizable clumps. She hoped Uncle Jason wouldn't want all four. She did love these biscuits, and even though she had already eaten, she wasn't quite full yet.

"We'll give him a little honey with those," Nell said as Abby approached the stove. "That will make him really pleased that he waited." She watched as the little girl carefully slid the pan into the hot oven and closed the door. Sarah's youngest had grown up a lot in the past few months, she thought, wondering if Abby still wished she was back home.

"Have you told Rose you make biscuits?" she asked.

"I don't see her long enough to get to talking about biscuits," Abby said. "We have so many other things to talk about."

"We had better get her here for Sunday dinner soon

so we can all have time to talk," Nell said. "And if we can find enough wild strawberries, you can make biscuits for shortcake."

"I know where there are some," Abby said, giving a little skip of excitement. "Mother always took us there, up behind the house, just far enough outside the pasture fence so the cows couldn't reach them. She didn't like it when I mostly ate them instead of putting them in the basket."

"They're a trial to pick," Nell said. "So tiny and so fragile. I used to take whole stems so as not to crush them, but then realized I might be killing off next year's crop."

"Will Father mind if we pick there?" Abby asked, a touch of anxiety creeping into her voice.

"I'm sure he won't," Nell answered, "especially if we leave him a bowlful. I doubt he and Charles have much time for berrying."

Abby took a peek into the oven, fetched a toothpick from the holder on the dining room table and stuck it in the tallest part of one of the biscuits. It came out clean as a whistle and she pronounced them done, thinking that if she were Rose, she'd wonder why whistles were considered clean. Little did she know that Rose had recently thought about that very question. Abby took the pan right to the dining room and invited her uncle to slide one onto his plate. Aunt Nell followed her with the honey, which she had warmed enough to make it runny.

"Worth the wait, I'd venture," Jason said, tucking his napkin into his shirt collar. He split open a biscuit, slathered it with butter and poured on the honey. Abby brought him a small plate of chicken with warm gravy over it and then sat down near him at the table.

"These are light, short, and crumbly, just the way I like them," Jason said, his mouth half full. "Have to eat 'em with a fork. Perhaps you'd like one, too?"

"I would, I would," Abby said, jumping up to get a plate and a biscuit for herself.

Jason watched her and asked, "Are you having butter on a biscuit or a biscuit on butter?"

"I do love the butter, Uncle," Abby said, looking a bit embarrassed. "Rose holds buttercups under my chin, and I'm the yellowest one, so I reckon I'm s'posed to like it."

"Not a problem, child, not a problem. Happy to see you enjoy it," he answered, smiling at her. "Just don't eat the buttercups—they're pretty but they're poisonous."

Abby thought about that for a minute and then asked, "Do the cows know?"

"No idea what a cow knows and what she doesn't. Usually seems like they know next to nothing. But we've never had one keel over in the pasture, so they apparently don't fancy buttercups," Jason said.

Nell cleared their plates as they finished, and she and Abby did up the few dishes. Jason stayed in his chair in the dining room, his thoughts ratcheting back and forth between the picture of Silas on the couch, and Charles sturdily shoveling manure and sitting on a three-legged stool to milk. Then, despite his best efforts, his eyes closed and he dozed.

Knowing how tired he was, Nell pushed the dining room door to and left him to nap. She was tired too, just thinking about how complicated life had become since Sarah died. She knew what her sister would say about Silas's binge last night—Sarah would say he would now turn the corner and be all right—and Nell, often the naysayer, would shake her head and doubt it.

What, she wondered, makes one sister a worrier and the other a smiler. The same blood runs in their veins, they share parents and grandparents, but they don't look much alike nor think alike. Still, it was Sarah who had kept her on an even keel all those years, and she missed her now. She was never sure she was doing just right with Abby, and she rarely saw Rose or Charles. If Nell had been the one who died, what would Sarah have done if she'd had three children? She bent to get a couple of sticks for the wood stove fire, shuddered as she often did at the thought of Sarah being buried under the falling woodpile, and started to cough as she stood up. She didn't seem to be able to shake this cough, but her nose wasn't running, so she reckoned it would go away.

She peeked in at Jason, saw that he was still asleep and sat down in her rocker near the stove to read the newspaper. It had arrived several days ago, and this was her first chance to take a look. The news would be old, but she did love the advertisements, for everything from overalls to pills and potions that would soothe your liver and let you sleep soundly. They ate calves' liver every year when Jason or Silas slaughtered an animal, but she was unsure of what her own liver did. She slipped off her shoes, wiggled a bit to get a perfect fit in the chair cushion, put her stockinged feet on the ledge outside the oven, and opened the Western Journal. It had taken a long time for this day to settle down.

A mile or so away, Ruthann Harty was thinking the day might well have been one of the most unsettled of her life. She had worn her engagement ring in public for the first time, which had caused a fuss among the church ladies who noticed it. So she and Joshua had received the good wishes of many of them after the service that morning. Then they had slipped off for what she thought would be a quick walk through the woods, looking for lady's slippers. The whole hour or so came back into her head as if it were happening anew. She had led him along a path crisscrossed with tree roots, a trail that would circle around and end up behind her house.

Once into the woods, however, Joshua had stopped, taken off his Sunday coat, spread it on the ground under an enormous pine tree, and announced that they should sit and look at the blue sky and white clouds. Ruthann was too happy to think twice about his idea, and dutifully sat down on the coat. She had looked at the sky and started to point out a cloud shaped like a fish and another that could be an elephant.

"See his trunk, just there, and his tail?" she asked.

Joshua had laughed and said he was more interested in the mare's tails that were swishing across the sky, telling him it might rain the next day. She remembered how he sprawled flat on the ground, his head on the sleeve of his coat, and reached over to take her hand. For several minutes, they had been very still, enjoying the silence and the chance to be together.

"It's nice to have everyone know about our engagement," Ruthann had told him. "I've had a hard time not just bursting out with it."

"You were the one who wanted it secret," he had answered. "I'd have shouted from the church steeple the first day; and clanged that old bell, too." He rolled toward her and pulled her down beside him. "Now what we need is a wedding day."

"I can't remember if you had in mind before or after the rowan crop," she had teased, thinking she still wasn't totally happy about playing second fiddle to haying and cows. In hindsight, it occurred to her that third fiddle might be more accurate.

"Once Newton has a few days on the farm, I am yours at any time," Joshua had said. "He's staying the summer, and I'm sure he'll know the ropes in a trice. So you and I can get married and go off by ourselves for three or four days—wherever you'd like within buggy or train distance."

"September first," she had said immediately. "If Newton is staying that long."

"I suspect he'll stay as long as I want him," Joshua had said. "He's in love with my Jerseys."

"Ha! That may be true, but he's also in love with Rose, and she's not in your barn," she told him.

"I'm giving him the use of my horse and buggy to make trips here whenever he wants," Joshua had said. "I haven't told him that yet, but I already know he won't last too long out there if he can't see her now and then. That's a serious thing, young as they may be. Now let's tend to our serious thing."

Ruthann remembered how she shivered at the very idea of their serious thing. Mistakenly thinking she was cold, Joshua took advantage of her trembling and drew her close to him.

She shivered again now, alone in her bedroom, thinking how she had not resisted at all, and how he had kissed her gently on the lips, pulled back to look at her face, then barely brushed her lips, her eyelids, her cheek, and finally, her left ear with his mouth.

When she had shivered again, he realized it had nothing to do with the cool air in the woods. His arms tightened around her, his hands slipping down her back past her waist and his mouth on hers again, now hard and demanding. She knew it had surprised him when she opened her lips. It surprised her to hear herself moan softly as she ran her tongue across his mouth. She was turning into a real hussy, she thought, running her fingers lightly through his hair, over and into his ears, down his cheeks. He muttered that no woman had ever made him feel the way she did and rolled toward her, almost covering her body with his, and she had put her arms around him, pulling away from the kiss.

"Just hold me, Joshua," she had whispered. "It is enough for now. It is everything, for now."

"I know, dear one," he had answered. "But you have to know that you are the bellwether heading for the edge of the ravine, and I will follow you right over."

Ruthann had released him. "So now I'm a sheep," she had told him, grinning. "And I'm smarter than most sheep, so I am thinking it's time to head for the barn." She had tried to straighten her hair, but knew from the way Rose had looked at her on the porch that it was an unsuccessful attempt. As they stood, he wrapped her in his arms once again, kissing her neck softly. Then he picked up his coat, clasped her hand in his, and started along the rough path again.

"You are not a ewe," he had said. She was glad she hadn't laughed before he added, "You are an incredible woman, but you are keeping me to the path."

She had not told him she would prefer to get lost, to find out what it would be like to just stay under that pine tree for hours, to get in his buggy and go back to his farm with him and toss caution and all of Eastborough's good ladies to the wind.

She put on her nightdress and brushed her hair, removing several pine needles from the long strands. She placed them carefully in a small vase on her chest of drawers, knowing they would make her smile every morning.

When Jason Harris walked past Ruthann Harty's house a half hour later, on his way to the Hibbard place, only a small light burned in the teacher's bedroom.

Rose's window was already dark, and before he was past the house, the light went out in Ruthann's room. What a wild ride it is, he thought, the teacher and Rose so happy, Silas so unhappy—morose, really—Charles a little bewildered, Nell still irritated, not only about her brother-in-law's weaknesses but also that God should have seen fit to let her sister be killed. She may never get over that, he knew. She thought it was unfair, and Nell was devoted to fairness.

He knew she was pleased he was going to check once more on Silas and Charles, though. In her eyes, that came under the heading of unnecessary, but the right thing to do. As he reached his brother-in-law's house, he saw light in the kitchen windows. He knocked softly and pushed the door open to find Charles and his father with their feet on the ledge of the wood stove.

"That's how I left Nell," he said, chuckling. "Did you sit up and take nourishment, Silas?"

"Toast and tea," Silas answered. "Prepared by the cook here."

"I can cook other things, Uncle," Charles said, "but he said his stomach wasn't up to anything else."

"Tomorrow, Charles," Jason said. "He'll be a bear for food tomorrow."

"Reckon I'm grateful to you both for even having a tomorrow," Silas grumbled in a not unpleasant way. "I thank you."

"Welcome," they said together.

"And good night," Jason added, slipping out the door again.

CHAPTER TWENTY
By the Sea

A few weeks later, Rose boarded a train with Miss Harty, bound for the teacher's parents' house. Upon arriving, Rose felt very far from Eastborough as she walked along the sand. The beach was just a short distance from the house. The tide was moving out, and it still amazed her that the rise and fall of water here had nothing to do with rain. She had never thought about oceans before, never realized that the very air smelled different on the coast. She was used to the smell of pine needles in the woods, drying hay in the fields, wood smoke from chimneys, and the almost odorless clear air away from the village houses. The air by the ocean was often sharp and salty, and when the tide was out, a muddy, heavy odor came across the sand.

She stooped to pick up a shell, admiring its round

shape, squared-off base, and intricate ribs spreading like the sun's rays. It's enough to make you believe in God, she thought, with or without the Reverend Lockhead. These are more beautiful than even a lady's slipper.

She had written Newton about the shells and about gulls swooping over the water and about the sun creating an orange path on the sea in the morning. Once again, it was Miss Harty who had given her a special chance, and she was grateful for even these few days on the Massachusetts shore. It was the first time in months that she'd had time to think, and the steady sound of water lapping on sand or crashing on rocks seemed to make her mind move even faster than usual. She found she was able to think about her mother alive and her mother dead without getting upset about either. Miss Harty had told her, over and over, that time would heal the bad things that had happened, but until now, Rose had not really believed her. She had always wanted to, but she had not been able to.

She and the teacher had come by train so Miss Harty could make arrangements for her wedding, which would actually take place back in Eastborough. Rose sensed that the teacher's parents were not entirely happy about that, but they seemed to understand that their daughter wanted her pupils at the wedding, and that most of them would be unable to travel across the state to attend.

It was arranged that the Hartys would stay at the hotel, after the teacher assured them that while it was plain, it was clean and respectable. Rose was certain in her own mind that it was more respectable since Miss Graves had moved out, but she did not comment. They would bring the wedding dress with them on the train because it would take some time to get it finished. Rose went for one of the fittings and could barely breathe when she first saw Miss Harty in the wonderful gown.

The fabric was shiny, pulled in tight at the waist and then flowing out in all directions with a small bump at the back that the teacher explained was a bustle. It was longer in the back than in the front, and lace trim in the shape of a V went from the center of the waist toward each shoulder. Horizontal pleats in the shiny fabric filled the bodice, ending with a tiny edge of lace on the high neck. Rose thought she had never seen anything more beautiful. The dressmaker put Miss Harty on a little stand and then sat on the floor, moving around and around the teacher, pins in her mouth and a yardstick in her hand, adjusting the hem here and there, and at the last moment, pulling up a small section and attaching it to the skirt with a tiny blue bow.

"When you have on your petticoats, the lace will show just there," the dressmaker had said with such an accent that it took Rose a moment to realize it really was English. "And it gives you the something blue, " she added. After the fitting, Miss Harty had explained that the dressmaker, a woman named Angela Ferrini, had come from Italy just a few years before and had found her skills as a seamstress most welcome in Gloucester, Ipswich, and Salem.

"What is that cloth?" Rose wanted to know as she

completed her fourth circle of the motionless teacher. "I've never seen anything like it."

"It's satin," Miss Harty had explained. "And we chose the ivory instead of the white because it is softer against the face."

"I've never been to a wedding," Rose had told her. "I didn't know the bride would wear anything like that."

"They don't always," the teacher said, leading Rose out the door of the seamstress's shop. "But my father and mother wanted me to have a traditional gown, and I confess that I do love it. And before we go back to Eastborough, we must get you a dress as well."

"Me?" Rose had said in surprise. "But dresses are very dear, and I can't…"

"Be still, Rose, for once. Just be still and listen. You are my pupil and my friend, and I want you to be part of the wedding, so my father is going to have a special dress made for you."

Rose was silent for so long that Miss Harty looked at her with concern. "What's the trouble?" she asked.

"You said to be still, so I am," Rose had answered, a hint of mischief in her voice.

"You can speak now."

"What does it mean, 'part of the wedding'?"

"You will stand next to me while I marry Joshua, and afterward you will sign the papers as a witness."

As if she were still a little girl, Rose had jumped up and down and clapped her hands, then remembered that she was walking on a town street with the teacher and immediately felt like a fool. Even now, on the beach, her face started to redden with embarrassment, just thinking about it.

But Miss Harty hadn't minded. She commented that Rose seemed pleased, and smiled when Rose, still sounding very girlish, had bubbled, "Yes, yes, yes, and I can't wait to tell Emily and Alice."

They would be going home in two more days, aiming to get to Eastborough before the first of August, and they would take Rose's new dress with them. Angela Ferrini had made that, too, and it was pale blue with long sleeves trimmed at the wrist with lace. It had a tiny high collar, and a skirt so long and full that Rose's shoes were completely hidden under it, once she put on the stiff crinoline that Senora Ferrini said she must wear. She did not tell the dressmaker and Miss Harty that not seeing her big feet was one of the very best things about the gown. She had never gotten over her father ribbing her about her size nine shoes when she had just turned thirteen.

She would have new white gloves, and a tiny bouquet of forget-me-nots if they could find them, or fall asters if all the forget-me-nots were gone by. Rose, however, was quite certain she could find the last of the year's forget-me-nots in a cool spot near the stream that ran below her favorite rock.

She had found she didn't much care for standing on the little platform getting fitted while Miss Harty and Mrs. Harty watched and murmured to each other. She shut her eyes and stood so still that they finally asked if she were asleep.

After the wedding, the seamstress promised, the dress could be fixed to wear to church or tea or a dance, if Miss Rose would like. She was a little puzzled when Rose explained that they only had tea when they were ill, at which time they drank it at the dining room table or in the kitchen by the stove.

"These ladies live way out in the country, Angela," Mrs. Harty explained. "It's a farming town, and the social life is very limited." The seamstress had nodded, but Rose wasn't sure she really understood what it was like to live in Eastborough, where a wife and mother could go a month or two without seeing any outsiders except the iceman and an occasional fish peddler. She certainly understood why her mother had always been so eager to go to Grange meetings and square dances.

It would be nice to get home. But she loved the Hartys' house with its many nooks and crannies, its big front porch and its parlor where the door was always open and where gas fixtures provided light that was so easy to read by. Now that Father had an icebox, running water, and a flush toilet, she wondered if he would consider lights. He'd just say it was another newfangled idea, she knew, but someday she would ask. Sooner or later, electricity would surely come to Eastborough.

It was hot here, just as it was at home, but she liked the way the sea breeze cooled the air, and she quickly discovered that she often needed a light quilt once the sun was down and the breeze was up. But it would still be good to get home—home to Miss Harty's house. She frowned for a minute, wondering where she would go when the teacher married and moved to the Chittenden place. She realized it was the teacher's house that she thought of as home these days. She sighed, knowing that it was wrong to think that way; that her place, like it or not, was still at her father's, cooking and cleaning and sewing and washing. And making sure Charles was all right, that he was doing his schoolwork and minding his manners.

She sat down on a huge rock, bigger than her special rock in Eastborough, but not as flat. She wished it were flatter so she could lie down and just look at the sky. At home, she realized, she only saw part of the sky. Here, on the beach, with no hills or trees, she felt as if she were inside an upside-down blue teacup. The sky just went up and over and down to the horizon again. So much sky. Sarah had always said to think of a clear blue sky, not a flock of jumping sheep, when trying to go to sleep. From now on, she would have this new kind of sky to think about. She took off her shoes and stockings, wriggled her toes in the sand, and then walked to the water's edge, holding up her skirt. Small waves were coming in, foaming as they hit the shore, and she squealed when the cold water hit her bare feet. The water pulled back, and she stayed in place, her feet sinking into the sand. When the next wave came, it was a little bigger, and she yipped like a puppy when she realized it had caught the hem of her petticoat and part of her skirt.

She ran back to the rock, dusted off her feet and shoved them into her shoes. She stuffed a stocking in each pocket and headed back to the Hartys'. It was time to help with dinner, a meal the Hartys served in the evening rather than at the noon hour. So many things here were different from home. She hoped no one would notice that her dress was wet and a little soiled.

As she hurried along, she heard a gull shriek behind her and turned to see the bird diving toward the very rock where she had been sitting. Soaring high, he had dropped a crab to break its shell and now he was landing to eat it. For an instant, she felt sorry for the crab, which had been making its sideways way across the ocean floor only seconds earlier. She reminded herself that she thought nothing of eating a chicken, which a day earlier had been pecking its way through the litter on the henhouse floor, or sitting in a nest on a warm egg.

How they had all chuckled the first Sunday after she and the teacher arrived in Gloucester. At the dinner table, Miss Harty told her parents about the delicious chicken fricassee with dumplings that Rose often made. The teacher's mother asked how Rose prepared the dish, and Rose said it always started with persuading someone else to kill the chicken.

When they began to laugh, she realized that it was impossible for anyone to kill a chicken here, where the area behind the house was filled with carefully kept flower gardens and a small patch of herbs and vegetables. The Hartys had a barn, but nothing clucked in there, nor was there any pungent smell of chickens floating out the windows. For some reason, their laughter didn't bother her, and she went on with the details of the recipe, finishing up by asking who killed chickens for them.

They explained about the butcher shop on the town's main street, where they could select the chicken they wanted and get it dressed. The teacher's mother said she was fond of roasting chickens, as she had done today, if they were big enough so they didn't dry out in the cooking. Rose answered that she, too, sometimes did that, but that even the toughest old bird turned tender when it was done with the dumplings and gravy.

"I can vouch for that," Miss Harty said. And they had shared a smile as the teacher added, "Takes the meanness right out of them."

"Are they mean?" asked the teacher's mother.

"Sometimes," Rose said. "We had one that pecked Abby's fingers something fierce, and she ended up in the pot. The chicken, I mean," she added hastily, as everyone started to laugh again.

"And just how," the teacher's mother asked, hoping to make Rose feel at ease again, "how do you go about this chicken you make?"

"When the chicken, or even an old hen, is ready to cook, I put it in a large kettle with enough water to cover. I add some carrots and a chopped onion, and cook the chicken slowly until the meat starts to fall off the bones." She paused. "Do you really want to know?"

"Certainly do."

"I drain off the liquid and save it," she said. "When the chicken is cool enough to touch, I take every bit of meat off the bones and put it aside. Then I strain the liquid, add some flour, salt, and pepper, and cook that until it's thick and smooth. I make the biscuits, and while they are cooking, I put the chicken in the sauce. Then I arrange the biscuits—they should be dropped, not rolled and cut—on a big platter and pour the chicken into the middle."

Mr. Harty leaned back in his chair and fingered the gold chain on his vest. "That, I reckon, is something I want to have for dinner."

"And you shall," his wife answered.

It was just like home to have everyone dressed up for Sunday dinner, but what Rose couldn't get over was that Mr. Harty dressed every day as if it were Sunday. He went to work every morning in a suit, his vest buttoned, his tie in place, and the gold chain leading across his chest to his pocket watch. The ironing here, she realized, had to be much harder than it was in Eastborough. Those shirts were so white and starched.

He took time off from work to take Rose and the teacher to the train station with his horse and buggy. But once they were settled on the train, she wanted to get there quickly and see everyone again. That Newton would be home was too much to hope for, but she had been several weeks away from Abby and Charles, and she had missed them. Perhaps Father had stayed away from the drink, and things were better. What wouldn't be better would be Miss Harty's small vegetable garden, which was likely to be overgrown with weeds.

She sighed, and the teacher asked, "What's wrong, Rose?"

"I would like to stay and I want to go home, and I can't do both, can I? I really do need to see Charles and Abby—Father, too, I s'pose," Rose said, feeling quite unsure about whether she wanted to see him or not.

"Enjoy the scenery, Rose," Miss Harty said. "All too soon you'll be back at the stove and the store and the weeding."

"It's been a wonderful time, Miss Harty," Rose said. "I never knew water and sand could be that beautiful. And almost as good a place to think as my rock."

They rode on in silence, and Rose listened to the clackety-clack of the train and watched fields and small roads go by. The train stopped often at small stations and at some larger ones, too, and she wrote down the names of the places so she would remember them later on. She glanced at the teacher and saw that she had dozed off, rocked to sleep by the rhythm of the train.

Hours later, they went through the dark tunnel, the engineer sounding the whistle over and over as they went through the mountain. Rose knew workers had died building the tunnel, but it meant the train could get her home that much sooner. She blinked as they emerged into sunshine again, and minutes later, shuddered to a halt at their station. Rose looked out at the platform and could not believe her eyes. Miss Harty had sent word of which train they would take, but it hadn't occurred to Rose that people would actually meet them. There, on the platform, were Abby, Charles, and Uncle Jason. And running toward them from the station was Newton Barnes.

Tugging their valises, Rose and Miss Harty went to the platform between the cars and waited while the conductor opened the door. Four arms were almost immediately around her, as Charles and Abby hugged her and jumped up and down. Newton had turned to Miss Harty to take her bag and then came to get Rose's small case and the large dress box she had set down on the platform.

"Better let me give you a hand, Newton," Jason Harris said. "That's a cumbersome box."

Newton relinquished the box, which contained Rose's new dress for the wedding, and leaned down to plant a quick kiss on the girl's cheek, much to Charles' delight. Rose's reaction was a mix of chagrin and joy because her brother, sister, and uncle were there, but she decided it was idiotic to be perturbed. She was officially being courted now, and they must know all about that by now. It was hard to keep secrets in this small town, even if you tried.

"Charles can carry my bag," she said, and as soon as Newton gave it up, she linked her arm through his free one, smiled up at him, and proceeded down the platform with the rest of the group trailing behind. Jason and Ruthann exchanged amused glances, and Abby looked after the pair, clapped her hands and said, "Oh, my." Then she was off at a run to join them.

Rose certainly hadn't expected her father to meet her train, but she was surprised not to see Aunt Nell or Joshua Chittenden. She turned to Abby and asked, "Where's Aunt today?"

Abby frowned. "She's feeling poorly, Rose, and didn't want to come out because it was a mite damp, and the damp makes her cough."

Rose couldn't imagine Aunt Nell even admitting she didn't feel well, so this was troubling news. But she decided to wait for a chance to speak to her uncle rather than let Abby see that she was a little anxious.

"And Mr. Chittenden?"

"Oh, he's here," Abby said. "He's with the horses."

"Can barely hold his horses, you might say," Jason commented with a grin, "he's so anxious to see Miss Harty."

Sure enough, at the end of the platform, two buggies waited for them, with Joshua Chittenden holding the reins of both horses, just in case they spooked when the noisy train moved, whistled, and belched black smoke. Miss Harty went right over to kiss his cheek, and he dropped the reins to give her a hug, then quickly retrieved them.

"So who's minding Thankful and Prudence and Buttercup and all those other ladies in your life?" Miss Harty asked. "If you and Newton are both here, how can those Jerseys manage?" Everyone laughed at that because they'd all heard the stories of Miss Harty refusing to play second fiddle to a cow, or several cows.

"You might not believe this, but we brought in the new deputy sheriff," Newton said. "He's experienced with cows and was willing. Said he wasn't certain of his welcome here, so he'd best take our place at Joshua's."

"New deputy sheriff?" Rose said. "Who's that?"

"Silas Hibbard himself," Jason said, instantly wishing he had let Charles or Abby be first with this news.

"Father?" Rose said incredulously. "He's a deputy sheriff?"

"Has taken two prisoners on the train to the court in Millerton," Charles said with a touch of pride. "Sober as the judge himself, in case you were wondering," he added.

"No one wrote me any of that," Rose said a little sulkily. She turned her back on them and started to climb into Joshua's buggy, nearly overcome by all that had happened while she was gone. Aunt Nell ill, Father with a badge, Charles looking an inch taller.

"Better ride in mine," Newton said, pointing to the smaller buggy. "Tommy is anxious to meet you and take you wherever you want to go."

"No one wrote me of that either," Rose cried, her annoyance soon banished by her delight. "You have a horse and a buggy of your own now? What else is everyone keeping under his hat?"

"Only my graying hair," Jason said, putting his hand under her elbow to boost her up on the seat of Newton's buggy. "Only my graying hair. Your suitor and your brother and sister have been hounding me for days about your return, and I believe the strain has caused me fifteen or more new gray hairs. And now Newton is cavorting all over town with his new transportation."

Once more, Rose turned her face away so no one would see how this comment struck her. Cavorting. Could you do it alone? Were other girls riding in his buggy? Had she been away so long that he had stopped being her suitor, as Uncle had just put it? Then she was on the seat, Newton had swung up beside her, and he was backing the buggy away from the rail.

"Wait for me," Abby shouted. "I want to come, too."

Newton stopped, and Abby hopped up, seating herself between the two of them. "Can I drive Tommy today?" she asked, as soon as she was settled.

"As soon as we get squared away, put a little distance between us and that smoke-belching train and are moving forward," Newton answered. "Abby has become quite the driver, Rose, and Tommy likes her touch on the reins. I hope you'll learn as well," he added, anxiously taking in the odd expression on Rose's face.

"So we can cavort?" Rose asked, not smiling.

"Call it what you will," Newton answered. "Seemed like it was just me and Abby riding in a buggy, but I don't know cavort from snort, so it's beyond me."

"Are you put out with me for learning, Rose?" Abby demanded. "I've been staying with Newton's parents some of the time while Aunt Nell was under the weather, and…"

"How sick is she?" Rose interrupted.

"Only helping out, Rose, so she wouldn't have to think about Abby on Saturday and Sunday. Mostly, I tried to get home at the end of the week to do chores at my folks' place anyway, and my mother has certainly taken a shine to Abby."

"Please, Newton," Rose said. "How long has Aunt been ailing, and what is the matter with her?"

"Dr. Potter's not sure, but he thinks she'll pull through. She has a bad cough, but it's apparently not consumption. We've all been a little anxious but saw no point in sending word to you. Nothing you could do out there except fret, now was there?"

Rose sighed. "You know me too well. I would have fretted, and as Mother always said, it would be worrying for naught. Except she was a worrier, too."

The two buggies clattered along the gravel road, and Rose was silent, noticing that Mr. Goodnow had changed his window displays, and the hotel had new rocking chairs on the porch. Then they were at the teacher's house, where Newton and Joshua tied the horses and unloaded the baggage. Everyone trooped into Miss Harty's small living room, where she immediately saw that someone had opened the windows to freshen the air.

"I was thinking it would be musty and close in here," she said, "so I thank whoever opened the house today."

"It was Newton," Abby piped up. "He and I came yesterday afternoon, and I dusted while he did the windows."

Jason smiled down at Abby and told her he was going on home to see about Nell. "You come along whenever you're ready, child," he said. Abby nodded, turned back to Rose and pulled her toward the kitchen.

"I made a stew for your supper," the little girl said proudly. "And while you are getting settled, I'll make biscuits to go with it. I already set the table."

"So while I wasn't looking, you've gone and grown up on me," Rose laughed. "Did Newton give you a hand?"

"Only with the sharp knife part," Abby said. "He seemed to think I might cut my fingers off. But I wouldn't, Rose, I wouldn't. That would be stupid. I did use carrots from Miss Harty's garden."

Rose shook her head in amazement. That whole time near the shore she kept picturing everything in Eastborough being just as she left it, and so many things had changed. Not big things, to be sure, unless Aunt Nell was truly ailing, but many things. Abby might be worried about Aunt, but she was blooming, and Charles sounded as if life at home was a whole lot smoother than it had been. And her father a deputy, riding the train to the courthouse. And the buggy and little horse. She could not believe Newton could keep that a secret, but he had, and now they could go out riding whenever they weren't working. She wondered if buggy rides required chaperones. Perhaps the horse could take that on. She giggled, and Abby looked up, surprised.

"What's funny?" she demanded. "Did I get something wrong?"

"No, no, Abby. Just an odd thought that rambled through my head."

"Emily says you have them a-plenty," Abby said, nodding and turning back to stir the stew.

"I must go wash up," Rose said. "My hands feel sooty from the train." She passed the parlor on her way to Miss Harty's bathroom and overheard Miss Harty telling Newton and Joshua how much Rose had loved walking on the beach. As she went into the small bathroom, she started a mental list of all the things she needed to do right away: see Aunt Nell; perhaps see Father; have a chance to talk to Newton alone. Alone was the important word. Alone in the buggy. Or, better yet, alone at her rock. But right now, she had to scrub her hands and face and be in the same room with Newton without touching him. She sighed, looked in the glass above the mirror, and then laughed at the sight of two sooty smudges on her cheek. The train was wonderful, but with the windows open it was terribly dirty, too.

CHAPTER TWENTY-ONE
Smiles and Tears

For the first time since her sister's death, Nell Harris felt a tear roll down her cheek, followed by several more. But these were happy tears, something she knew Sarah Hibbard would have called an oxymoron. Sometimes, she thought, as she watched Rose walk down the aisle of the village church, she wished she knew as many words as her sister and Rose did. How beautiful her niece looked in the blue dress Miss Harty's dressmaker had fashioned for her. Nell wished Rose would smile, and no sooner had the thought flitted through her mind than a wide smile crossed Rose's face. Ah, Nell realized, Newton had just come through the door up front, leading Joshua Chittenden to the minister. And he has eyes only for her, she noted, as more tears spilled down her face.

Beside her, Jason Harris fished out a clean linen

handkerchief and handed it to her. She dabbed at her face, smiled at him, and he immediately covered her gloved hand with his large, sun-browned fist. His touch made several more tears fall, and even as she admitted to herself that she wished it were her daughter going down the aisle, she told herself to stop this nonsense before someone else noticed. But no one did. Everyone was watching Miss Harty walk slowly into the church on her father's arm. Few had ever seen a gown as lovely as this, all shiny and lacy and sweeping very full behind the bride. Few had seen a man as elegant as Miss Harty's father. He would be wearing tails, Rose had informed Mr. Goodnow, who, in his role of village information center, had passed the word to many of the inhabitants prior to the wedding. As Mr. Harty passed, all eyes were on the back of his jacket, which, they could see, certainly had two wide tails falling all the way to his knees. They had surely never seen the like of it in Eastborough before, and several wondered if the teacher's father might be a very wealthy man indeed.

Even the Reverend Lockhead smiled as he looked at the bride, the bridegroom, and the young people attending them. Forewarned, he waited while the bridegroom presented the teacher with a nosegay of tiny pink roses and white baby's breath. Rose had looked everywhere for forget-me-nots, but they had gone to seed weeks earlier. As the minister spoke the familiar words that would marry Ruthann and Joshua, his voice was gentler than usual, and he forgot his objections to Miss Harty's insistence that she would not promise to "obey" anyone. Few in the congregation heard Ruthann Harty's whispered assents to the reverend's questions, but Joshua's voice was confident and clear.

All through the church, middle-aged women suddenly remembered when those words had been directed at them, and with wet eyes, they turned their now weathered, tired faces toward the men they had married. In the last pew, an involuntary shudder shook Silas Hibbard from his shoulders to his ankles, and he froze, hoping no one had taken notice. And then the ceremony was over, the bride and groom left arm in arm, and the townspeople began to chatter their approval as they all moved toward the hotel, where refreshments would be served. The custom was for the ladies of the church to serve their homemade specialties in the parish hall, but the teacher wanted to waltz, and the minister disapproved of couple dances within the church walls. So, Miss Harty had arranged to have tea and sweets served at the hotel, with a musician hired to play whatever music was needed.

Rising slowly from her seat, Nell finally let out the cough she had managed to suppress during the ceremony and wondered if she'd be able to get through at least one dance in the bride's honor. Jason looked at her with concern, worried that she was thinner than usual and that this sometimes hacking cough did not seem to go away. At least he knew it hadn't worsened in the past week or so, and he was sure that was because he had forbidden her to go to the henhouse until she was better. Those chickens raised more dust than a housewife on a spring cleaning binge. He put his big hand under her elbow and shepherded her out of the church. Nell smiled up at him, picked up her skirt just enough to keep the hem out of the dirt road and hoped someone had reminded Rose and the teacher to do the same. She wasn't sure either was thinking with any common sense right now, which was, she decided, just as it should be.

"They were both so beautiful," she said as she and Jason reached the porch of the hotel.

"Sarah would have been very proud of her daughter today," Jason agreed. "Shall we take advantage of our day off and set a minute before we go in?"

A little out of breath, Nell was grateful for the suggestion. Besides, whenever she passed the hotel, she would think about how nice it would be to just ease into one of the big rocking chairs and set it in slow motion for a spell. For once, since the rest of the townspeople were hurrying inside to greet the newly married couple, the chairs were empty. Jason and Nell sat down, he reached for her hand, and then, still holding it, pulled off her white glove with his other hand, finger by finger.

"Can't say as I relish holding a glove," he said, grinning at her. "Not when there's a choice."

"I reckon a wedding has turned you into a sentimental old fool," Nell said, laughing and choking back yet another cough.

"No fool to be sentimental about you, my dear," Jason said. "Best thing I ever did was to get all dressed up in those fancy duds and exchange vows with you. And this wedding is special—the teacher and Mr. Chittenden make a handsome couple, and the other couple is just as handsome and may be headed for the same place. What do you think?"

"I think Rose will hold out for teaching," Nell said. "She loves him, but she's a stubborn one about that dream of hers. I trust she won't lose him."

"Not a chance, I'd wager," Jason said. "He will spend some time getting that Jersey dream of his into a barn, and he'll wait. Ought to. Few are as good a catch as Rose—she is more Sherman than Hibbard, that's certain. And now that the rest of the town is inside the hotel foraging, I think we'd better join them. They'll be chewing their cuds before we've had a first bite."

Inside, Thaddeus Goodell had his mouth organ to his lips and was playing a tune that had everyone's feet tapping, even as they waited in line to speak with Mr. and Mrs. Joshua Chittenden. As the line dwindled, Ruthann and Joshua moved onto the dance floor and Goodell, known through the area for the collection of instruments he had mastered, pulled out his violin and softly played one of the new waltz melodies. As if they had been dancing together since the age of five, the couple moved gracefully around the floor, and the teacher soon beckoned to Rose and Newton to join them.

"Nobody knows how we practiced in the teacher's parlor," Newton said, grinning at Rose, "with the teacher singing the music and Joshua counting. You looked lovely then, even in your apron and plain dress, but now..."

"I can't concentrate if you say nice things to me," Rose

said, frowning. "I'm just trying to keep my feet in all the right places. This is no square dance."

"Miss Harty—I mean Mrs. Chittenden—promised that Thaddeus would do some set dances, too. He knows how to call them. But I insist on telling you how beautiful you look. Like a bride yourself."

Rose knew her cheeks were getting pink, but she didn't care. She didn't even mind that dozens of people were watching as the two couples danced. She was too happy even to worry about what Hattie Munson was saying to the woman next to her, but she was certain it wasn't anything nice. Then, to her astonishment, her father emerged from the circle of watchers and came toward them. He tapped Newton on the shoulder, and to her even greater surprise, Newton dropped his arms and turned away.

"May I have the pleasure?" Silas Hibbard asked, taking her hand and putting his other hand on her waist.

"Certainly, sir," she managed to say, giving a tiny bow. Several townspeople started to clap, and Rose knew her face was really flaming now. But she followed her father's lead and discovered that he, too, knew how to waltz. The Chittendens, as surprised as Rose and hoping to get her out of the limelight, nodded to Thaddeus Goodell, who called out for everyone to dance. And the floor filled with folks who knew how to waltz as well as those who just shuffled their feet, some of them in time to the music.

"Your mother and I waltzed some before we were married," Silas Hibbard told his daughter. "She was good at it. She was good at nearly everything she set her mind to."

"I didn't know you danced," Rose said hesitantly, still keeping her mind on where her feet were going and still a little in shock at the idea of encountering her father here.

"Some say it's easier with a bit of hard cider in the belly," he answered. "But I think that might well lead to stepping on a body's toes."

"More ways than one," Rose said, finally looking him in the eye. They both chuckled, lost the beat for an instant, but were back into proper turns when Henry Goodnow tapped Silas's shoulder. With a slight inclining of his head, Rose's father thanked her and backed away.

"Reckoned you might need rescuing," Mr. Goodnow said. Unlike her previous partners, his feet moved woodenly, flat as paddles on the floor. "Or if you didn't, I'd still get a chance to say you don't look much like a store clerk today, Miss Rose."

"Thank you, sir," Rose answered, adjusting her step to his with some difficulty. "Father was very pleasant. And he's no slouch of a dancer, either."

Then Thaddeus Goodell swung into a polka, and Henry Goodnow shook his head in dismay. "Can't manage this, Miss Rose. May I get you something to drink?"

"I'm going to look for Newton," Rose answered, "if you don't mind."

"Not a-tall, young lady, not a-tall. Quite the nice-looking pair you make, I would say. That boy is quite sweet on you from all appearances." He chuckled and added, "Hattie Munson told me so."

That made Rose laugh. She thanked him for the dance and began to search the room for Newton. Then something told her he was behind her, and she whirled around just as he reached her and asked if she wanted refreshments. They headed for the array of dainty sandwiches, tea, and punch, and found Charles there, heaping a plate with a variety of goodies.

"Hope you have this food when you get married, Rose," Charles said. "It will make wearing the tight collar and silly shirt worthwhile. In case you want me up front there, I mean."

"Don't hold your breath," Rose advised. "You'll have a lot of oatmeal and boiled potatoes between this day and that."

Behind her, she heard Newton sigh, but before he could speak, Emily and Alice appeared and hugged Rose.

"You look scrumptious," Emily said.

"Not bad, Rose, not bad," Alice added, knowing how Rose hated that expression. But it was not a day for Rose to be cross, so she just gave Alice a gentle push and suggested she take a plate and get something to eat. "The fudge or the peanut candy might sweeten your tongue," she advised with a smile.

"You are both looking marvelous yourselves," Newton told Rose's friends. "I can't believe you're not already on the dance floor with a line of boys cutting in."

"We don't know anyone who can do the polka," Emily

Rose

said. "All the old people seem to know how, but our parents never taught us."

But Thaddeus Goodell had noticed all the young people on the sidelines. He finished up the polka with a flourish and called for a Virginia reel, which they all knew. Almost immediately, Rose saw Peter Granger moving quickly toward Emily, and Ethan doing the same with Alice. Peter was wearing heavy boots—clean, but heavy—and Rose wondered how anyone could dance in such. But she knew it was probably all he had. Goodell began to call the moves, and two separate Virginia reels went into motion.

After several dances, Rose told Newton she needed to speak with Aunt Nell and Uncle Jason. She found them sitting together at a small table, drinking tea. Nell immediately told her how proud Sarah would have been to see her at the church that day and how beautiful the new blue dress was.

"Miss Harty has been a godsend for you," Nell said.
Rose nodded, sat down, and took her aunt's hand in hers. It felt quite warm and a little damp, and she saw that Nell's usually pale cheeks were flushed. Perhaps from all the excitement, she thought, knowing how proud her aunt was of her pale, creamy skin. Nell was always one for wearing a huge straw hat in the garden to keep the sun and wind off her face.

"Those who don't wear hats, Rose," she would say, "end up with faces that look like something from the cobbler's bench. When it comes to skin, weather makes leather." Rose wasn't sure about the hat thing. Grandmother Emma always wore hats, and her face had deep lines, especially around the eyes. Crow's-feet, Aunt Nell called them. Rose kept trying to get a good look at the feet of a real crow, but they always flew off when she came near. She did think they were black, though, and that must not be related to face lines. She knew Grandmother often wore a smaller bonnet even in the house, which made Rose suspect it was more a matter of thin hair than worries about the weather.

"How is your cough, Aunt?" Rose asked.

"Better today," her aunt answered. But Rose noticed that Jason had frowned, so she didn't say anything more. Instead, they talked about Miss Harty's dress and how Rose had watched the dressmaker fit it perfectly, talking all the while in her strange English, her teeth clenched on a mouthful of common pins.

"Have to spit quick if those start to go the wrong way," Jason commented. "Never could understand why womenfolk put pins in their mouths."

"Never heard of anyone swallowing so much as a pin, either," Nell answered quickly. "If God had given ladies three hands, life would be easier."

Thinking her aunt sounded like her old self with that comment, Rose started to wonder where the third hand would be attached and decided she didn't want one, even to hold pins. She reminded the pair that Abby was staying with her for a few days, and took her leave.

Hours later, Newton walked Rose and Abby back to Miss Harty's house. While Ruthann and Joshua went away for a few days, Abby would be staying with Rose, and Newton would make his way back to the Chittenden farm to take care of the prized Jerseys. He was sorry not to have more time with Rose, but he was proud to have Joshua's confidence and hoped he could live up to what was expected of him. Joshua's hired man, Caleb, would help him out since the herd was quite large now and included young stock as well as milch cows. He hoped Caleb had been able to manage the day's milking stints without him.

On the porch at Miss Harty's, Abby gave Newton a hug and then announced mischievously that she was leaving them and going inside because Emily and Charles had both told her Rose would want to be alone with her beau. "For billing and cooling, is what Emily said," Abby reported. "Charles just said Newton would want to kiss you. I don't know what kind of game billing and cooling is."

"Cooing, Abby," Rose said, laughing. "I'm sure it's cooing. It has to do with turtledoves and how they cross their beaks and coo at each other."

"You don't have beaks," Abby said solemnly, "so you'll have to manage." And she disappeared into the teacher's house.

Newton was laughing now, but he wasted no time in gathering Rose into his arms and kissing her for such a long time that she thought the moon would come up before he was done. It was still daylight, she thought, and here they were on a front porch billing and cooing. She stopped her mind from wandering and concentrated on kissing him back, her hands joined behind his back and her feet between his. She was as close as she could get, and when Newton slowly, very slowly, pulled his mouth away from hers, she sighed with happiness and rested her head on his chest.

"She's watching," Newton said. "I saw the curtain move."

"Never you mind," Rose answered in a muffled voice. "Now she'll know all about substitutes for beaks. Just part of that birds and bees thing."

"And every day I pray you are not about to sting me," Newton said, tucking his fingers under her chin and raising her face for another long kiss.

"Baking soda will take care of the pain," Rose said, without really taking her lips away from his.

"Flibbertigibbet," Newton answered, closing her mouth with his again. Over her shoulder, he saw that Abby had lighted a lamp, and she was clearly silhouetted behind the curtain, watching them. But he didn't really care. They had little enough time for "billing and cooling."

When Rose ended that kiss, he said he really had to be on his way but would see her again as soon as the Chittendens were settled in.

"I reckon we'll all be coming into town with wagons to cart her belongings to the farm," Newton said. "Not the furniture, I mean, but her personal things. Will you be staying on here? We could just get married and move your things out there at the same time," he added, grinning at her.

"That's not a question, so I don't have to answer it,"

Rose said. "And now you had better be off." Suddenly hearing how abrupt she sounded, Rose reached out her hand for his and gave him a quick kiss on the cheek. "You must go right now before I start to bawl," she said, smiling at him, but knowing she was close to doing just that.

Newton gave her a hug, put his hand on the porch rail and vaulted to the ground. He turned, saluted, and then started down the road at a run. She was surprised when he suddenly stopped, turned, and shouted, "Am I leaving fast enough?"

"Yes," she yelled back. "Not a drop of water yet." And then he was out of sight, on his way to his new buggy and the little horse Tommy. She hoped he would be back right soon. It was hard to be here with Newton and Miss Harty gone. She must start thinking Mrs. Chittenden, she reminded herself. Although the teacher had whispered, as they waited outside the church door, that when she became Mrs. Chittenden she would be just Ruthann to Rose. Friends. Rose wasn't sure she could ever say "Ruthann" to the teacher. Perhaps she should practice when she was alone.

Rose went into the house where Abby greeted her with a hug, confessed that she had watched them through the window, and wanted to know if you had to marry a person after you kissed him like that.

"It was so long, Rose, I thought you would not be able to breathe," Abby said solemnly.

"You breathe through your nose, silly, not your mouth. And since you weren't minding your own business, you can't ask questions. It's like eavesdropping. Mother always said if you eavesdropped, you could never admit to hearing whatever you heard because you weren't supposed to be listening in the first place. I think it's the same with window peeping."

"That's not fair, Rose," Abby wailed. "You are my big sister first and Newton's sweetheart second, and that means you have to answer questions even if I was snooping."

When Rose didn't answer, she added quickly, "It's important to my education."

That made Rose laugh, and she allowed as how kissing a person "like that" might well lead to marriage, but as far as she knew, it wasn't required.

"It's not the kissing, Abby," she explained. "It's the way you care for somebody that leads you to the kissing. You can't just go around kissing anyone and everyone."

"Wouldn't want to," Abby said. "I only like to kiss on cheeks, not mouths."

"Perfect for a nine-year-old," Rose said. "And now I must change into something less fragile than this dress."

As she went upstairs, she started thinking about the opening day of school and wondered what the town fathers were doing about a teacher. Miss Harty—Ruthann—had mentioned some man who might want the position, but he wasn't someone who lived here, and the teacher had no definite news about his coming. School would open after the frost because everyone needed all hands to help with harvesting the potatoes, carrots, onions, beets, and pumpkins that were still in the fields. Rose thought Miss Harty would be back by then, but they wouldn't let her teach because the law said married women couldn't. Now that, Rose thought, was a waste. Sometimes she wondered what lawmakers could be thinking when they voted for these things. Married men were allowed to teach.

Newton was thinking about the same thing as Tommy trotted along the road to the Chittenden place. It would take him some time to get there, but the horse knew the way by now, and even if he snoozed a little, Tommy would get him there. It suddenly came to him that Rose could teach Miss Harty's class, at least temporarily. She was way ahead of everyone else in the books, she was so quick with the numbers, and her penmanship was nearly as good as Ruthann's. Knowing how much she wanted to teach, Newton smiled as he bounced along in the buggy, picturing Rose with her hair pulled back severely, standing in front of the class and demanding everyone's attention.

Little did the two of them know that the school district folks had their minds on the same problem and had already pondered whether Rose could manage Ruthann Harty's class until they found a permanent teacher. They had realized, too late, that they had been lollygagging so long that most teachers had already signed on for the coming school year. They knew Ruthann would be required to leave as of her wedding day—she had even taken the step of notifying them—but they had dawdled. And now they were a little stuck.

A man from Sterling, in central Massachusetts, was interested in the post, but he had a flock of turkeys he was raising for Thanksgiving sale, and he said he couldn't come until after the middle of November. The school's other teacher couldn't take on the whole crew. They decided to have a chat with Jason Harris.

"He has a good head on his shoulders," pointed out Ben Chandler, who was the acknowledged leader of the school hiring committee. "Even though she's his niece, he'll give us a straight answer."

"Henry Goodnow is another one," said Charles Tucker. "Be pleased to ask him before we meet with Jason, if that's your wish."

"She's too young," Calvin Lockhead interjected. "I think she's plain too young."

The other men looked at the minister in surprise.

"Too young in years, mebbe, Reverend, but that girl has seen a sight more of life than most of the other womenfolk in this village," Ben Chandler said, his annoyance barely hidden. "And dealt with every page she was handed."

"I'm sticking to my feeling, Ben," the minister said. "But we can certainly meet with Jason. I reckon he'll come down on my side, not wanting Rose Hibbard to face those Granger boys and their ilk."

"Good of you to talk with Henry, Charles," Chandler said, choosing not to answer the minister this time. "We might well meet at the store tomorrow in the forenoon if that works for Jason. I'll get word to you, one way or another."

Knowing nothing of all these plans being made for her, Rose tucked Abby into Miss Harty's bed, changed into her nightdress, took a last look out the window at the star-filled sky, and climbed into bed to think about her amazing day. When would she ever wear that beautiful dress again? And how soon would Newton be able to come back? As she dropped off, not even needing to count sheep or think about a clear blue sky, her final question was about whether her father had really turned one last, important corner.

CHAPTER TWENTY-TWO
Learning and Letters

"You will need two new skirts and shirtwaists," Aunt Nell said. "A teacher has to dress like a teacher no matter how old she is."

"Or how young," Rose said nervously. "I must be too young. If Peter Granger comes back this year, he will be two years older than I am."

"You have no need to worry about Peter Granger, Rose. He may not be back, unless he decides to continue helping out with the slow readers, which he might well, and he'll be no trouble there. Besides, your uncle and Ben Chandler will be keeping an eye out."

"I still can't believe this is happening, Aunt Nell. I just can't seem to get my head around the idea that I will be in front of those children, and they will be expected to listen to me and do their lessons for me."

"You'll get the hang of it soon enough, I reckon,"

Nell answered, coughing softly. "For now, you best get to Henry Goodnow's place and choose fabric for your new skirts. Figure on black for one, but not shiny, and either a plain cloth in gray or a tiny calico print for the other. If we had time to go to town, you would have more to choose from, but I need to get started on these today. Plain white or ivory or gray for the shirtwaists. You could poke through Sarah's button box and come up with enough buttons, I'll wager."

Rose started to worry about how she was going to pay for all this, even though she knew Mr. Goodnow would be happy to put it on account for her. She hoped Aunt Nell was up to all this sewing, what with the coughing and all, but she knew better than to ask. Aunt didn't take kindly to questions about her health, and she knew her uncle had asked Dr. Potter to see her.

As if she were reading Rose's mind, Nell Harris added quickly, "Your uncle is planning to pay for your teacher clothes, so don't fret about that. You will, however, have to tell Henry that you can't work at the store anymore. It's not a suitable place for a teacher, and you will have plenty of work to do getting ready for your school day."

"I will miss the store," Rose said meekly. "And my pay."

"You'll get paid teacher money at the end of the month," Nell said. "And if you need anything before then, we'll lend you a hand."

Rose stood up, bent to give her aunt a hug, and said she would go to the store immediately. She left, her latest letter to Newton Barnes in her hand. She had stayed up late the night before, writing to tell him about Ben Chandler and Charles Tucker knocking on the door of the teacher's house and asking to speak with her. Her first thought was that something had gone terribly wrong with Charles or her father, but the men were smiling as they came into the parlor, so she quickly pushed her worry aside and asked if they would want tea.

Both refused but said they would like to sit down for a few minutes. So she sat with them in the parlor and heard their proposal that she teach until the turkey farmer could come at Thanksgiving time. She was so astonished that she was sure, when she thought back on it, that her mouth had to be hanging open like some fool, and for a few minutes she was unable to speak.

Ben Chandler, she wrote, had said they knew how young she was, but that her uncle and Henry Goodnow were confident that she could fill the post on this temporary basis. And to make sure she had no problem with obstreperous boys, someone would be on hand every day the first week, and as needed thereafter.

"On hand?" Rose had finally stammered out. "What does that mean?"

Mr. Chandler had explained that he and Mr. Tucker and Uncle Jason would take turns being at the school when the day began and would stay in the building or in her room for the first five days to see how things progressed. They would adjust the schedule later as needed, he said. The other teacher would be in the building, naturally, but she would be tending to her own classroom.

"We foresee no difficulties, Rose," he said. "But we

want to make certain you get off to a proper start. We expect you know what to teach and how to do it, but you have little experience with discipline. You will begin, of course, by telling the children to address you as Miss Hibbard."

"Oh, dear," Rose said, relaxing enough to laugh at that idea. "Miss Hibbard. I shall have to put my hair up."

"Indeed," Ben Chandler agreed. "And Nell Harris is ready to help you with proper attire. We are not prepared to pay you what Ruthann Harty received, but we will try to be fair."

Rose wrote all this, including the dialogue, and covered six pages before she finished with the actual hiring discussion and her excitement after the two men were gone. She finished by noting that she would now find out whether she really wanted to be a teacher or not, and she hoped he would not be in a swivet if it turned out that she liked it.

Rose ended her letter by signing off the way she always did. "Respectfully yours, Rose Hibbard." She could just sign "Rose," she thought. How many Roses did Newton know? And then, feeling a little reckless, she added a postscript in writing as tiny as she could make it. "I love you, and I'm not running."

She had sealed the envelope and set it beside the washbasin in her bedroom. Now, on the way to the store, she thought about that postscript and realized part of the reason she had written it was her guilty feeling about taking the school position. Was she putting teaching ahead of Newton? Was this what Miss Harty—Ruthann—didn't like about playing second fiddle to a herd of cows? She decided she was worrying the bone, as her mother used to say. This was just a temporary job; just a way to help out.

Mr. Goodnow was nowhere in sight when she reached the store and placed her letter on the counter. Then she fished a little key out of her pocket and opened the box Newton had reserved for her. She loved having her mail come in the box. She knew it was an extravagance, but she really loved it. Her letters from him were not mixed in with everyone else's but just resting there in privacy until she took them out. Her heart seemed to give a little thump as she saw that she had a letter on this day. It was from Newton, of course. Once in a great while her grandmother in Vermont would send a postcard, but it was rare. And she would always just tell about the weather, which had been and gone by the time the note arrived, whether she had done a wash that day, and what they had for supper. It was like reading one day, one unexciting day, in a diary.

"Good morning, Rose," Henry Goodnow said behind her. "I reckon you'd like to take a moment to read that missive, and then we'll have ourselves a talk. Congratulations are in order to you, and I expect you'll offer me condolences for my loss."

"Loss?" Rose asked. "I'm sorry, but what loss?"

"Loss of you, my dear, at least until the turkey farmer

gets here to teach, loss of you. Can't think how I'll get on here without your help. Now get on into the storeroom and read your letter."

Rose obeyed, pleased by the compliment but anxious to read Newton's letter. To her surprise, he started out by saying he wished the town would give her a chance to teach for the next couple of months. He wrote that the town fathers probably weren't smart enough to consider that idea, but he knew she could do it. When Ruthann and Joshua returned, he intended to speak up about it.

He went on to tell about his days with the Jerseys and how Joshua was planning to give him the next calf instead of cash pay. That would be the start of his own herd, a small start to be sure, but at least something. Rose finished the letter, folded it carefully, and tucked it into her pocket. He wasn't going to be sad or angry. He had thought of the very thing himself, the very idea Mr. Chandler and Mr. Tucker had come to.

Back in the store, she thanked Mr. Goodnow for his kind words and said she hoped he would take her back when the teaching stint was over. He assured her that he would, that his wife was going to lend a hand while Rose was at the school, so her job would be there when she was ready.

"I can even work more," Rose said eagerly. "Because I likely won't be going back to school myself, not after being the teacher."

"We'll see," was all Henry Goodnow would say. "And are you working today or here on an errand other than your mail?"

"I need fabric for two skirts, one black and one not, and two plain shirtwaists," Rose said in a rush. "Aunt Nell is going to run them up for me so I'll be dressed properly for the classroom. And I need a comb to hold my hair up. And I wondered if you have any of the Smith Brothers cough drops. Perhaps those would soothe Aunt's throat when she gets to coughing."

"Whew," Henry Goodnow said. "You talk so fast when you get going that my mind has to race to keep up. Let's begin with the fabric—will she need thread?—and, yes, the cough drops might give a bit of relief. It would be a fine thing for you to do for her, Rose."

Together they pulled down several bolts of fabric, Rose chose the two she wanted, and Mr. Goodnow measured out the lengths needed. He suggested looking at buttons, but she said she was certain her mother's button box would yield enough for the shirtwaists.

"A bit of lace for your collars, then?" Mr. Goodnow said. And seeing the look of longing as she shook her head, he realized she was worried about the cost. "I would be proud to make a present of it to you, in honor of your new post."

Rose clapped her hands together and then clapped them over her mouth. "Oh, dear," she said, "I am acting like a child at a candy store, and I'm supposed to be the teacher."

"You can still be a child whenever it suits you," Henry Goodnow said, opening the glass door that protected ribbons and lace from dust. He took down several rolls of narrow lace in white and ivory and told Rose, "Choose one, and I'll cut you enough so Nell can use her imagination on your new things."

Rose chose a narrow lace, ivory to go with the fabric she had picked out, and Mr. Goodnow packaged it all for her in brown paper tied with a string. "I gather the cough drops will go on your account, Rose?" he asked.

"Yes, sir," she said, trying to be dignified and failing totally. Instead, she threw her arms around Mr. Goodnow, who was so astonished he nearly fell over backwards, and then, releasing him and feeling her face turn scarlet, she said, "And I will be here to work on Saturday as usual, sir."

As she nearly ran across the store and flung the door open, she found herself face to face with Hattie Munson, who made a noise that sounded like "harrumph," and pushed past Rose into the store. Rose nodded to Mrs. Munson as she went by, but the greeting was not returned. As Rose retrieved the swinging door and started to close it, she heard Mrs. Munson say, "Land sakes, Henry," and knew she wanted to hear no more.

So she missed Mrs. Munson going on to say she could not believe the town fathers were putting that child in the classroom as a teacher, a child with a philandering, alcoholic father and a dead mother, and a brother and sister who needed caring for.

"She should get herself back to the kitchen and see to things is what I say," Mrs. Munson finished. "And I hope you've told her that and not been encouraging any more of this outrageous behavior."

"Calm yourself," Henry Goodnow said, struggling a

little to keep his tone even, and still warmed by Rose's sudden hug. "Rose Hibbard will be fine as the temporary teacher at the school. She'll have some adult supervision there, her father is doing well these days, she can't help having a dead mother, and both Charles and Abby seem to be thriving. So it's hard to know what you are all worked up about."

"All worked up? All worked up? Everyone in this town should be all worked up about Silas Hibbard and what he's done to his family. And Rose staying with the teacher and being courted without proper chaperoning. It's hard to believe that nice Barnes family wants to be mixed up in all this. A fifteen-year-old, just think of it."

"That nice Barnes family has embraced Rose and made her feel right at home there, so you're paddling upstream with that idea. Now, is there something I can help you with here?"

"What was she buying, I'd like to know, and with whose money?"

"Now that would not be any of your business, if you'll pardon my saying it so bluntly. I don't tell anyone what you buy, nor do I tell you what they buy."

The "harrumph" sound came again, but Mrs. Munson stopped talking and began poking about in the fabric section, where the bolts from Rose's purchases were still on the table.

"I expect she bought these," she said, fingering the fabrics. But Henry Goodnow merely rolled up the cloth and put the bolts back on the shelf.

"Is there something I can help you with, Mrs. Munson?" he asked again, determined to keep his temper. She really was the most irritating woman in town, he thought, and couldn't hold a candle to Rose in any way he could think of. Henry sighed, thinking how he had offered Rose a place in the Goodnow home if she needed it, and wishing, not for the first time in his life, that he and Edith had been able to have children. Sarah Hibbard had always known what a blessing they were. He sighed again, wondering how Silas Hibbard could not have seen that more clearly, clearly enough to stay on the straight and narrow, as the reverend was fond of saying.

"Are you daydreaming?" Hattie Munson demanded, her slightly whining voice edging into his thoughts. "I said I'd be wanting a bag of sugar and about a quarter-pound of your best tea."

"Sorry. Lot on my mind, what with losing Rose as a helper here, at least for the next little while."

"I have to admit, Henry, that she has spruced up this store some since she came," Hattie said.

"Good of you to notice," he answered. "Shall I add these things to your account?"

She nodded and stood close to the counter, trying to see the most recent entry in his book, but he placed his left hand in the way as he wrote down her purchases. At the end of the day, he would transfer each sale into the book where nearly everybody in Eastborough had a page of his or her own. Most of them paid it all down on a monthly basis, but he had a few who always wanted to carry over part of the bill. Henry obliged them because in the long run, few people had ever cheated him. Even Jennie Graves had come in to pay up before she left town, although he was quite certain it was Jason Harris' money she had at hand.

He handed Mrs. Munson her purchases and muttered something about getting back to sorting the mail, so she said good-bye and went on her way. She'll be looking for something new to talk about, he knew, but he had the satisfaction of knowing she'd found no tidbits in his place.

On her part, Hattie Munson gave a little slap of the reins to her horse and decided Henry had become a little sour, spending so much time in that store, much of it alone. He had practically accused her of prying into Rose Hibbard's business, and then of all things, had defended her getting the teaching position. Hard to know what the world was coming to, a child teaching children. Nell Harris must be making up new clothes for the new teacher, she decided. Perhaps her cough was better after all, although Hattie had noticed she looked quite flushed at the wedding. She gave the horse another little slap with the reins and whirled up the road with a small cloud of dust behind her.

At the Harris house, Rose was telling Aunt Nell about Mr. Goodnow wanting her back at the store as soon as the teaching stint was over. She spread out both lengths of skirt fabric. Nell nodded her approval and then admired the fine cotton Rose had chosen for the shirtwaists. She especially liked the lace and said it was good of Henry to recognize what a diligent worker Rose had been there.

"His windows weren't worth looking at until you came along," she said. "Now I must take some measurements and get right at this while my cough is taking a rest."

"Oh, Aunt," Rose cried. "I brought you a present, too. Some of the Smith Brothers cough drops. You just place them in your mouth and let them melt on their own, and it soothes the throat."

"Now that's right thoughtful, Rose," Nell said. "I'll keep them here at the sewing machine. Now you run along and let me get at these skirts."

Rose knew she should get back to the teacher's house and see to Abby, but she decided to go to her rock instead. Just for a minute or two, she told herself. Every now and then, she really needed to be alone, and there had been little time for that lately. So she walked quickly up the road and into the woods, and in just a few minutes, she was at the big flat rock she considered her own. She sat down, pulled her knees up to her chin and made certain her skirt covered her legs and ankles. She had never understood why a lady's legs—limbs was the proper word—were such a delicate matter. They were just two posts that held up the rest of a person, but they had some kind of appeal. She had noticed at the last square dance that the young men on the sidelines weren't even looking at girls' faces, just at their legs, swathed in stockings, of course, when someone swung a girl hard enough so her skirt flew out around her. She would have to ask Newton what was so special about legs.

Breasts, now that was something else. She had wrapped a cloth tight around her chest when hers started to get rounder and rounder so no one would notice. She knew neither girl nor lady ever showed anyone their breasts unless they were hussies. She loved that word. Hussy. It just sounded like someone up to no good. Still, some of the magazines she had seen at Miss Harty's parents showed ladies in elegant gowns, certainly not hussies, with very low necklines that showed the crevice between their breasts. Cleavage, Miss Harty had explained to her, at the same time telling her it wasn't mannerly to stare at cleavage. Crevices were spaces between rocks, not breasts. If anyone showed cleavage in Eastborough, she thought, that would certainly take attention off legs. She might not look, but she'd wager her new length of lace that the Granger boys would.

Rose suddenly grinned. Her mind was certainly taking strange journeys here on her rock. She released her knees, stretched her legs out and lay flat, hands behind her head. The rock was warm, small cloud puffs were chasing each other across the sun, and she could hear a woodpecker drumming on a tree. She closed her eyes against the brightness of the sky and let her mind wander backwards through the year since her mother's death. In a few minutes, she dozed off.

The sun was low in the sky when she woke, feeling quite chilly. She couldn't believe she had slept that long on a hard, bumpy rock. She wasn't nearly as tired these days as she had been when she was taking care of Abby, Charles, her father, the chickens, and her schoolwork. Sometimes she wondered how she had done all that. And then, as now, she would think she ought to be back there, paying attention to the family and enjoying life less. The minister certainly didn't think life was to be enjoyed. He talked all the time about burdens, and one thing Rose knew was that she didn't like burdens at all. She could take them on, but she saw no reason to like them. At least Abby and Charles had always been good, and they made her laugh, whatever her day of burdens. Now Abby was sort of farmed out, mostly with Aunt Nell, but sometimes, these days, with the Barneses. She did hope Aunt would get better soon.

She sat up, wondering why a lovely dreamless sleep should make your mouth feel so awful and your eyes so gritty, as if the sands of Cape Ann had just blown right into them. Perhaps the story of the sandman was really true; maybe some kind of elf actually did sprinkle sand over your eyelashes when you were asleep. Rose laughed aloud. She'd be believing in Saint Nicholas next. She had better get back to the teacher's house and see what Abby was up to.

CHAPTER TWENTY-THREE
A Fine Seam

Nell spent nearly all of Saturday at her sewing machine or cutting fabric on the dining room table. In his cellar workshop, Jason could hear her walking back and forth, and then he would hear the rhythm of the machine as her feet tilted the treadle up and down. If he wasn't sawing or pounding himself, he could even hear the steady thrum of the needle. He always marveled at how evenly Nell ran the machine, never faltering with her feet. He'd mentioned it to her once, and all she said was that it was the same as when he drove a nail. The beats of the hammer were as steady as her needle punching the cloth.

Once in a while he heard her cough, but he did think those Smith Brothers lozenges had done her some good. Rose was another one who didn't miss a beat, he thought, and lucky for all of them. His stomach growled, and he wondered if Nell would have time to put something together for the noon meal or if he should lend a hand. Silas, he knew, had never lifted a finger in the kitchen when Sarah was alive, and he reckoned Sarah probably preferred it that way. He had an idea much of the cooking was now in Charles' hands, but he himself had always liked scrambling an egg or seeing to the toast. He wasn't up to making butter or Dutch cheese, but he could take a turn with the churn. Now the sewing machine stopped, and Nell wasn't walking around, so he decided to get upstairs and see what was up. She might be resting, he knew, unfamiliar as that was. But since the cough came, he frequently caught her sitting in the rocker in the kitchen, even at mid-morning.

Jason was worried about Nell's cough and the way she sometimes felt all damp in the night. Once he had offered to fetch her a different nightdress, but she had shrugged him off. Said it was her age. Nothing to bother about. If he bumped into Dr. Potter at the store, he reckoned he'd better ask him. Nell would scoff at seeing the doctor, but forewarned, the doctor might just stop by, friendly like, and see what he could see without getting her dander up.

When he reached the kitchen, Nell was dozing in the Lincoln rocker. She started as he came in and it made him laugh. The look on her face was the same as a boy caught taking a trout out of season.

"I set down just for a second to adjust my stocking," she said, and then realizing how foolish that was, added, "and to rest my eyes a bit from all that stitching. But Rose will look a proper teacher on Monday, even if I have to hem the skirts on Sunday."

"What about taking Sunday stitches out with your nose when you get to heaven?" Jason teased, knowing that Nell was too practical to put much stock in those grandmother tales.

"Not worrying a bit about that," Nell said. A shadow crossed her face, but she said no more.

"What do you worry about these days?" Jason asked, stooping down in front of her. "What puts those two sharp lines between your eyebrows lately?"

Nell thought about telling him she hadn't a care in the world other than finishing up these garments on time, but she saw the concern on his face and relented. "I fret over what will happen to Rose with Ruthann gone, and what is happening to Charles and what will happen to Abby if I'm gone."

"It's my devout hope that you're not going anywhere, Nell," Jason said, "although I would feel better if you took that cough of yours to Dr. Potter for a look-see. It's my feeling Rose may find her way home again if Silas sticks to his knitting, and then we'll lose Abby." He paused and took her hand in his. "And I'll miss her," he said. "She's added something here, taking Clara's place in a way."

Nell nodded. "The cough is probably just one of those things, Mr. Harris, but I've no objection to seeing Dr. Potter if it will ease your mind. And you're right about Abby. One of these days, one way or 'tuther, she'll be back with Rose. We've only had the loan of her for a while. And the pleasure. And I trust you don't fret over Clara much, now do you? She wanted to see the world, or at least this country's part of it, and she is."

"You strong-minded Sherman girls are bound to grab the reins when you have your heart set on something," Jason answered, but he smiled as he said it.

They both stood, and Nell said, "I'll take a strong-minded look at the noon meal now. I expect Abby will stay on with Rose, so it will be just the two of us." She smiled up at him and patted his arm. "The way it's been most all these years, Mr. Harris, and that's been a pleasure too. Seems like we've shared the reins a good deal of the time." She chuckled, coughed, and added, "Now where did I set down those lozenges Rose brought?"

To help out, Jason poked up the fire in the big wood stove and put two dinner plates on the small shelf at the back of the stove. He pulled the blue enamel teakettle onto the hottest part of the stove and added two cups to the warm shelf. In a short time, the two were sitting across from each other in the dining room having their noon meal. They had barely finished when they heard a tap on the door and both Rose and Abby appeared.

"Not here to eat, I trust," Jason said. "I've cleaned up just about everything in sight already."

"Hello, Uncle. Hello, Aunt," Abby said saucily.

"Humph," Jason said. "Are you a young whippersnapper trying to correct my manners?"

"Yes, sir," Abby said. "I do like to be greeted properly upon entering a room."

To Rose's relief, Nell and Jason both started to laugh. She could not imagine Abby having the audacity to be so sassy with her elders. But she had always managed to get away with things that Rose never could. Come to think of it, Rose remembered, Charles often did the same. It must be because they were funny when they were being fresh. She reckoned she was much too solemn to march onto what she considered thin ice. She sighed softly. Sometimes she wished she couldn't see past the end of her nose, didn't see so clearly what might come next.

Rose wanted to ask how the sewing was coming along, but she was afraid even that might be rude. But, like Ruthann Harty, Aunt Nell could see inside her head, or read her face, or something. She nodded toward the little alcove she called her sewing room and told Rose to take a look.

"Oh, it's lovely," Rose said, carefully picking up the shirtwaist.

"I'm making a plain collar and a stand-up collar with a lace edging, and you'll be able to change them. They'll button on and look as if they are attached," Nell said, a hint of pride in her voice. "The first skirt is over a chair in the parlor, and since you've come by, we'd better see to the length of it."

Rose hurried to change into the new skirt and twirled around twice to watch it flare out. Then she stood very still so Nell could measure the length. This was a scene worth watching, Jason thought. The three women he liked most in the world, excepting Clara of course, all fussing around over a skirt. Nell already had common pins in her mouth, and Rose was holding the skirt in place while Abby danced around babbling about how exciting it would be for Rose to have her own classroom.

"Just for a little while," Rose cautioned. "I'm not a real teacher."

"But you will be, Rose, you will be. And Father won't stop you now, will he?" she asked, stopping in mid-hop, suddenly anxious.

"Certainly not," Nell said, forgetting that she needed to keep her lips closed. Pins fell to the floor, and Abby quickly rounded them up. "That argument is over and done with. Now stand still, please, and don't bend your head."

It had better be over, Jason thought, or he and Silas would be having another session in the henhouse. This tidbit of teaching might well make Rose want a full course of it, and it would be shameful to take it away again, no matter how young she was. But Silas was no longer at the center of the picture as far as Rose was concerned. It seemed Newton Barnes had taken that place, at least for now. He wondered if the boy had the patience to wait for Rose. Mebbe those Jerseys would keep him busy for a while, but he knew, how well he knew, how impatient a young man could be when his head was cottony with love, and his body longing to gather up a pretty young thing and carry her off. That was a long time ago for him, but he had not forgotten. He stacked Nell's plate on his, used two fingers to carry their mugs, and took all the soiled dishes to the kitchen where he set them in the soapstone sink and ran a little water over them. No sooner had he put them down when Abby joined him and said, "Just leave them, Uncle. I'll do them up."

"Wasn't planning on washing 'em, child. I wouldn't want to deprive you of all that entertainment."

Abby had come to love this kitchen, where the sun came in the windows for much of the day. She liked the rough table where Aunt Nell rolled piecrusts and stirred cookies and peeled potatoes. And the icebox was so much bigger than Father's. It had big brass latches as if valuable things were inside. She sometimes wondered if her mother would have liked prettier things in her kitchen. She knew Sarah Hibbard had wanted running water and an icebox and that Rose was very upset when her father installed both after their mother was dead.

"I really don't mind," Abby told Jason. "It gets my hands very clean."

He chuckled and went back to the cellar to work on a table he was making for Hattie Munson. She was the worst of gossips, he knew, but she was also one of the most educated of the village womenfolk, although he doubted most of the others knew it. She had come to him with a small but clear sketch of a drop-leaf table she wanted for her house. She wanted it done in cherry, and while the drawing was of a very plain table, he thought it might be quite beautiful if done right. It was quite long and slender with plain legs.

"The finish, Jason," she said in her firm way, "must be such that my gloved hand glides over it as if it were clean glass. The leaves must go up and down without squeaking, and the wood must not warp after a year or two in our summer humidity."

"Where did you see this?" he had asked her. "You must have seen one like it."

"Can you do it?" she demanded.

"Yes."

"I saw it over at Hancock where those Shaker people live. They are as crazy as bedbugs when they dance in their meeting house. It's enough to make Mr. Lockhead shiver in his boots, what with the way he makes all of us sit like graven images in church. Plus their ideas about celibacy and adoptions and what-all. But they make furniture that takes your breath away."

Jason had allowed as how he'd heard about Shaker woodworking, something he'd like to see for himself. In the meantime, he'd be on the lookout for some fine cherry boards, and if she wasn't in a hurry, he would make her a table that would earn approval even from the Shakers.

"And it won't warp?" she said anxiously.

"Not in your lifetime, Hattie," he'd answered. "But it will be dear."

"I just want it perfect," she said.

"Something you ought to remember, Hattie," he'd gone on to say.

"What's that?"

"Bedbugs aren't crazy. They find the warmest places to live, and they make everyone else crazy trying to find them." That made her laugh.

"Don't tell anyone who it's for, Jason," she had said as she turned to leave. "I don't want the whole town talking about my costly table."

"If you're not telling, Hattie, how would anyone find out?" he asked. She had scowled and slammed the door as she left. But he assumed the table deal was still on, so he'd found cherry boards, planed them smooth, and begun shaping the table legs and making hinges that would work in silence. One day he would go see the Shakers. But right now, with the chickens, and Nell being poorly, and the table, he didn't have time.

Using a wood-handled chisel his grandfather had given him, he shaped one of the table legs and sanded it. Minutes later, he heard the girls leave and then the rhythmic sound of the treadle sewing machine started up again. He did hope this project wasn't too much for Nell, but he wouldn't say so. He reckoned he wouldn't wait to run into the doctor but would take a minute today to stop in at his house.

CHAPTER TWENTY-FOUR
Lonely and Not So

Rose was feeling a little sorry for herself when she joined Emily and Alice at the square dance that night. It was the first time in months that she would be standing with all the girls on the sidelines, hoping someone would ask her to dance.

"Don't go all gloomy on us," Emily chided her. "You look as if a buggy had just run over the cat."

"Nothing like a barn full of Jerseys to take a man's mind off everything else," Alice teased.

"He is in charge while they're gone," Rose said more sternly than she intended. "It is a great responsibility."

"No greater than your new position, Miss Hibbard," Emily said. "Am I to call you Miss Hibbard on Monday? My mother said I would be doing just that."

"You and everyone else," Rose said, a smile finally crossing her face. "Charles, too, if he's moved into that classroom."

"Oh, that would be too funny," Emily said. "But we are very proud of you, you know, and we'll behave perfectly at all times."

"Most times," Alice said. "I can't promise all times."

Rose suddenly felt much better. Emily and Alice knew

how to deal with her moods, and she had thought many times that she should have talked to them before she went off to the cemetery to speak to her dead mother and nearly got herself killed. They would have told her not to go or insisted on going along. She treasured them. They were funny and saucy, but she knew she could depend on them for anything she needed, anything at all. And she would do the same for them. It was selfish to be thinking about dancing when she knew how much Emily and Alice wanted certain people to ask them. People who were right there in the room.

As if he had heard her thought, Ethan appeared in front of Alice and held out his hand. She took it and he led her to a square that was forming on the far side of the room. A second or two later, Peter Granger asked Emily to dance, and Rose was standing alone, the very thing she had dreaded about this evening. But Charles was watching, and he bounced up almost immediately.

"Wouldst deign to dance with me, lonely lady?" he asked.

That ended Rose's sulk, if it really was a sulk. She went off with Charles and discovered that he had really learned the dances. He was a little short to swing her, but he managed, and he followed the calls perfectly. She began to enjoy herself, and quickly discovered that the whole town knew she was going to teach at the school. When her corner swung her and when they did a grand right and left around the square, she received congratulations from one dancer after another.

The evening was more than half over, and she had

gone to the refreshment table to get a drink when she felt a hand on her waist. She whirled to snap at whoever it was but was left standing there with her mouth open and her eyes tearing up. Newton. He had come. He shouldn't have, but he had come. She wanted to kiss him on the spot, and she didn't want to cry so she curtseyed with her head bent, and when she straightened, she was smiling and in control again.

"Tommy thought it a good night for a run," he said, grinning at her. "Is Miss Hibbard dancing or have you put away such childish things?"

"Charles has danced my feet off," Rose said. "And I'm ready for more, Mr. Barnes. And where is Tommy? Has he had water and a rubdown? And who will do the morning milking?"

"Now hear the lady who turns up her nose at beautiful Jerseys. Didn't ask if I needed water and a rubdown, just asked about the horse."

Rose started to giggle and offered him her tumbler of punch. To her surprise, he tipped his head back and drank it all. When he returned the glass, she refilled it at the refreshment table and picked up two small sandwiches for him.

"I wouldn't think of giving you a rubdown here, sir," she said, her face as solemn as she could manage.

"Thank heavens," Newton said, quickly eating the sandwiches and emptying the second glass. "Now let's dance."

They did two squares, deftly executing one move after another. Newton swung Rose faster and faster until she finally squealed and told him her feet weren't even touching the floor. She whispered as they promenaded around the square, "I'm certain my petticoats are in full view." Not proper for a teacher, she was certain.

Newton just laughed and said he hoped Thaddeus would slow down soon and play a waltz on his violin. They had waltzed at the teacher's wedding and at the very idea of being that close to Newton, Rose felt the familiar shiver run down her spine. It was like a herd of ants in a hurry, she thought, and then giggled at the idea of ants being in a herd. But they weren't a flock. So what would they be? She did not know.

"You've gone off somewhere," Newton said, as the four couples joined hands and circled left, then right, stopping when they were back in place.

"Just thinking about ants," Rose said.

"And uncles?" Newton asked.

"Other kind of ants," she said. "And I don't say ant when I mean Aunt anyway."

"A highfalutin flibbertigibbet," he tossed over his shoulder as they neatly executed a do-si-do with their corners. "Next thing I know you'll be putting your hair on top of your head," he added when she was back at his side.

Then the caller abruptly changed his rhythm and announced that he hoped all were ready for one of the new waltzes. "The fiddle takes to them like ducks to water," he said, bending his head and starting to play.

"Or farmers to young girls," Newton said, breathing a sigh of relief and putting his arm around Rose's waist.

Newton and Rose led the way on the dance floor, soon joined by others who made up for stumbles with enthusiasm. Knowing how the minister had frowned on this dance where two people touched in a way far different from reels and squares, Rose glanced around the room. And there he was, Reverend Lockhead, his brows furrowed. Now that, she thought, is a word that makes sense. He has indeed turned his face into furrows, just as the plow does in the field. She started to laugh and nearly missed a step.

"What now?" Newton asked, as he continued to circle around the floor.

"It's the minister," she said. "He doesn't like this."

"I like it," Newton answered. "I like it much better than grand rights and lefts where you hold hands with all those other people."

Ooh, Rose thought, maybe he's a little bit jealous. Emily says that's a good thing, means he really cares. Now maybe I can talk to him about the teaching and how his idea came true without him doing anything about it.

But before she could say a word, Newton bent his head and whispered that his mother said the town fathers were smarter than he had given them credit for. "Your hair will be going up, flibbertigibbet," he said softly. "But I'll take it down every chance I get."

Rose tightened the fingers of her right hand around his left and whispered back, "I wrote you all about it. What they all said and how I would be supervised and everyone would have to call me Miss Hibbard." She tilted her head back to look at him. "Including you, I expect," she added.

"Except I'm not going back to school," Newton said. "Remember?"

"Not even when the turkey man comes, and I'm back in my seat?" Rose asked.

"I reckon you won't be back in that seat, my daisy. One way or another, you'll be at the school, but not in your old seat."

Rose was silent then, concentrating on the singing fiddle and the waltz steps. She wondered how close waltzers could get to each other before it became improper. It would be nice to just close up the space that separated them. She hadn't hugged Newton for such a long time. Or it seemed like a long time. As if he once again read her thoughts, Newton tightened his arm around her, and their bodies almost touched as he swooped her about, passing all the other, less practiced dancers.

Rose was suddenly aware that almost everyone else had left the floor and were watching her and Newton. She felt her face burn, but she kept her feet moving, following his lead. The fiddler stepped up the tempo, and they swirled faster than the usual waltz, finally coming to a breathless stop when the caller finished the tune. The circle of townspeople burst into applause, and Rose knew she must be scarlet by now, with all those eyes on her. But Newton was unfazed. He stepped back, his hand outstretched to hers, and bowed. She curtseyed back, relaxing into a laugh, and he pulled her toward him so the two could bow to the applauding group.

When Abby ran onto the floor to hug Rose, everyone started talking again, and the moment was over, to Rose's relief. Still, part of her had loved it, loved that she and Newton were so in tune with each other, even loved the attention, which was quite different from some of the attention she had been subjected to in the past year. Over everyone's heads, she saw Mr. Goodnow's face smiling at her, and beside him, her father, who looked quite proud. Now that was something, she thought. And he seems also to be quite sober.

"Let's take a walk outside where it's cooler," Newton said, offering his arm.

She took it, her stomach doing its usual flip at the idea of finally, maybe, being alone with him. But outside the Town Hall a cluster of older boys, including Peter Granger, were shoving each other around and talking. Newton nodded to them and kept walking until they were a few rods away and could put a large maple tree between them and the other people.

"Sometimes I cannot wait for this," Newton said, kissing Rose so gently on the mouth that she thought her knees might buckle. "And then I have to wait through "Red River Valley" and one-two-three, one-two-three until I am nearly crazy," he added when the kiss ended. He turned her so her back was against the tree, leaned against her and kissed her again, harder and longer.

Returning the kiss, Rose briefly touched Newton's lips with her tongue and knew she loved him to pieces. The second track in her head, taken up for days with her worries and plans for the first day of teaching, had suddenly turned to considering whether she really wanted to be Miss Hibbard even for a few weeks or would just like to become Mrs. Barnes as quickly as possible. It was so hard to be away from him.

Newton buried his face in her neck, and Rose lifted both arms around his neck. She knew they didn't have long here because the older people would start leaving Town Hall, and they were only a short distance away.

"Can we go to your rock?" Newton asked, once again seeming to read her mind.

"Will we be chaperoned?" Rose countered, a little worried about how much she longed to say yes.

"I will take care of you," was his only answer, so she took his hand and they started along the dirt road toward the little path that led to her rock. His fingers were hard with calluses and very warm. She quickened her step and felt him look down at her, but she did not turn her head. She just wanted to get out of sight and reach the rock where, he had promised, he would take care of her. She wasn't sure what that meant exactly, but she aimed to find out.

It didn't take long. It seemed Newton had gone to the rock before he appeared at the dance, because his lantern was there, along with a bundled-up blanket and a small basket.

"What if I had said no?" Rose asked, looking at the preparations.

"I would have walked you home, pecked your cheek for Abby's benefit, picked up these things, and gone back to Chittenden's place with Tommy," he answered. "But you didn't, although I must point out that you didn't say yes, either. Why was that, Rose?"

"Should I tell you? Do girls tell boys things like that?"

"How would I know? You are the only girl I've ever looked at twice and the only one I've ever kissed twice and the only one whose life I've saved and…"

"Stop!" Rose cried. "I am being serious, and you are making fun."

"Saving your life wasn't fun, Rose. Kissing might be called fun, but it's a lot more than that. Looking at you is a great pleasure, not twice but a thousand times, although most of the time it has been your back."

"You are still being funny," Rose said, starting to feel a little sulky.

"Sit down," he said. "And tell me why you didn't just say yes. I won't poke fun at you."

Rose sat, very straight, with her knees pulled up to her chin and her skirt pulled down over her feet. "I am afraid to be alone with you," she said in a muffled voice.

"Afraid of me?" Newton said, incredulous. "I am as harmless as a newborn kitten."

"No, afraid of me," Rose said, looking up. "When we're alone…" She stopped, then started again after Newton picked up her hand and held it tight. "When we're alone, I don't want to teach or cook or clean or weed or read. I just want to stay with you, be as close to you as I can get without breaking Miss Harty's rules."

She stopped again, and he squeezed her hand but said nothing.

"And sometimes," she said suddenly, "I want to break all her rules, even though I don't know exactly what that means. I just know it's more, lots more, and I want more."

"Someday, my love, someday," Newton answered softly. "But when I said I would take care of you, I meant with the rules. I love you, and I won't let you break those damnable rules."

"Oh, Newton," she said, turning and almost flinging herself at him. "You are so good."

"Perhaps not as good as you think," Newton said. "What I am is a hungry boy, not filled by those tidbits they gave out at the dance." He reached into the basket and pulled out a small parcel and unwrapped a chicken leg. Another reach produced a heel of oatmeal bread and a ripe peach.

"A picnic at night?" Rose said. "You really are funny."

"Actually I was thinking about a swim in the river, being so hot and sweaty from all that dancing, so I brought a towel along."

"Swimming?" Rose said in shock. "With a boy? Without a bathing costume? I haven't been in the river that way since I was six!"

"Figured you'd say that. So let's eat."

"Miss Harty gave me a hand-me-down bathing costume when we were at the shore, but I didn't happen to bring it along," Rose said, still trying to recover from the very idea of swimming at night with a boy.

"Not in the nude, foolish girl," Newton laughed. "Just swimming. You shed only your outer clothes and leave on whatever contraptions you wear underneath those petticoats, and I shed my shirt and pants."

Rose admitted to herself that this was a really exciting idea, but she wasn't going anywhere near the river tonight. "No," she said. "No, thank you. But I can wait right here while you cool off if you like."

"That wouldn't be fun a-tall," Newton drawled, thinking that the cooling off part might be a good idea. He took a bite of the chicken leg and then offered it to her. Rose took a nibble and handed it back.

"You're not going silent on me, are you?" he asked. "I didn't spoil everything, did I?"

"Of course not," Rose said, and then laughed when she realized how stuffy she sounded. "Next time I'll bring my bathing costume."

"Do you still have your dancing feet?" he asked.

Puzzled by the sudden change of subject, she nodded. "They stick around for at least a day after the square dance is over," she said.

Newton stood up and pulled her to her feet, then drew her close. When she tried to move away, he whispered, "Let's us have a private dance here, by the rock, and then Tommy and I must be on our way. Morning comes early."

The minister would be speechless, Rose thought, if he could see them now, almost pasted together and waltzing in the woods while they hummed one of the fiddler's tunes. As the song ended, Rose leaned away from him and said, "You are an adventure, Newton Barnes."

Newton answered by pulling at her ribbons until he had set her hair free. He ran his hands through it, combing with his fingers from her scalp down to the ends that nearly reached her waist. She stood still inside the circle of his arms, so overwhelmed with new sensations that fear rushed over her again. He seemed to know, she realized, because he stopped, pulled her close, waited for her to look up, and kissed her.

They swayed together for several minutes, looking at each other, then kissed again. Just as Rose started to think her knees were going to give way entirely—they felt as wobbly as a newborn calf's—Newton let her go, hunted around for the bare chicken bone, which he tossed into the basket, and picked up the blanket.

"I reckon Miss Abby has been alone quite long enough," Newton said, sounding as if he were forty years old. Rose nodded. Then, hand in hand, they walked out to the road and on to the teacher's house where, it turned out, Newton had stabled his horse before he came to the dance. Abby was watching from the parlor window and ran to open the door, so Newton gave Rose a quick kiss on the cheek, said good night to both of them, and disappeared around the corner of the house.

Together, Rose and Abby waved as he and Tommy rolled past a few minutes later.

"He's very nice, Rose," Abby said.

"M-m-m-m," she answered.

CHAPTER TWENTY-FIVE
First Day of School

Rose was standing behind Miss Harty's desk when the children filed in from the cloakroom and took their seats. Even though they'd known each other all their lives, Emily and Alice barely recognized their friend. They looked at her, looked at each other in amazement, and took their seats. Emily saw that Rose's hair, usually in a braid or two down her back, was pulled back tightly from her face and wound into a neat bun, fastened in place with several large tortoiseshell hairpins. She was wearing a white shirtwaist with a high neck edged in lace—well, it was really not quite white, Emily thought, sort of ivory color like the handle of her buttonhook—and a long dark skirt full enough so it completely covered her shoes. She glanced over at Alice and mouthed "Miss Hibbard," which made Alice smile.

Rose didn't look at either of them. She was as nervous as a cow crossing a plank bridge and hoped it didn't show. She had come an hour early, had written her name on the blackboard and had stacked the books she would need in the order she would need them. She had dusted the room, which was already clean, and she had been both relieved and anxious about the fact that no supervising adult had appeared. She didn't know what she would do if the older boys acted up, but now she saw that not all of them had come. Some would wait until the rowan was in before they would have time for school.

When everyone was seated, she pointed to her name on the board and said, "Good morning, class," and they dutifully answered, "Good morning, Miss Hibbard."

"We seem to have no new pupils today, and I see that you are all in your customary seats," she said. "We will begin today by changing all of those places."

Facing them, she saw how startled they were by this idea. She wasn't sure she would survive having all those eyes looking at her. But she went on. "I would like each of you to take a slip of paper from this basket and hold onto it. It bears a number."

The children passed the basket around the room, each taking a piece of paper, each wondering what Rose was up to and each reminding himself or herself that they must remember to call her Miss Hibbard. Once in a while, Rose would take a number out and set it aside, mindful that she didn't want all the absent older boys clustered together.

Rose pointed to the seat at the front of the room nearest the door. "That is seat number one," she said. "Perhaps you should all stand and make a ring around the room so we can do this in an orderly way." As the children started to spread out, she saw that Mr. Chandler had made his way almost unnoticed to the back of the room. "Who has number one?" she asked.

It was Ethan, and she beckoned him to his new place in the room. She moved to the next place and asked for number two. And so it went, with the children jostling each other and starting to chat amongst themselves as they found their new places. In less than ten minutes, they were all settled again.

"We all seem," Miss Hibbard began, "to get stuck in the places where we sit. We have one view of the dining room because we always take the same place at the table. We have one view of church because we sit each Sunday in the same pew. The same is true here. My view of this room has changed considerably since the last time I was here…" She paused when several of the girls giggled, then went on, "and I thought that perhaps yours might benefit from change as well."

And she's broken up the older boys, who always sat at the back together, Emily thought to herself. What a clever thing to do. If they decide to snort or stomp, they'll stand out like a pig in the cow pasture. She looked at the board, glanced out the window, saw new heads in front of her and decided she liked the change. She noticed that Alice was fidgeting. Alice, she knew, liked things to stay the same, so she would fret over her new place at first. But she was only one person away from Emily now, which was nice.

"I know you'll remember where your new seats are," Miss Hibbard was saying. "But I would like you also to remember your numbers. We will be using them in various ways each day." She sent the basket around the room again to collect all the little slips of paper, and placed the refilled basket on her desk.

While all this shifting about had been going on, Ben Chandler remained standing at the back of the room, his face completely expressionless. He didn't quite understand what this very young teacher was doing, but he saw no harm in it. When Rose looked up and nodded in his direction, he nodded back but said nothing. He had taken his jacket and cap off and was leaning against a windowsill, trying to be as still as a deer hunter, something he knew well how to do.

"We will begin today with a new book," Miss Hibbard said. "Mr. Clemens, who introduced us last school year to Tom Sawyer, has also written a book that is more about Tom's friend, Huckleberry Finn. It is different from the first book in some ways, but similar in its adventurous bent. And we will learn grammar from it by doing the opposite of what Huckleberry Finn does. His grammar is terrible, as you will see."

She produced the book, opened it to show them a drawing of Huck Finn, and then said that the reading would begin with the person who had drawn number one. Ethan stood up, already worried because he wasn't one of the best readers in the class, and Rose handed him the book, open to the first page.

"Read carefully, Ethan," she cautioned. "As I said, Huck's grammar is poor."

"You don't know about me without you have read a book by the name of *The Adventures of Tom Sawyer*; but that ain't no matter," and Rose was instantly pleased to hear a gasp from more than one corner of the room. Ethan looked up to see if he had mispronounced something, but Rose nodded that he should go on, so he did.

By the time he had finished the first two pages, Rose had written that opening line on the board. With all eyes on her, she asked if number seven could correct the sentence into proper English. Startled, Emily realized she was number seven. She stood and went to the board.

"Cross out what's wrong and write the correct wording above it," Rose said.

With a hint of mischief in her voice, Emily said, "Yes, Miss Hibbard." When Rose didn't smile, she turned quickly to the board, crossed out "ain't no" and wrote "doesn't" above the two excised words. Serious now, she turned toward Rose and waited.

"Anything else?" Rose prompted. Emily looked at the board again and shook her head. "If there is, Miss Hibbard," she said, all respect now, "I cannot find it."

Rose turned to the class. "Can anyone help Emily?" she asked. "How about number twelve?"

That was Ida. She hesitated for a second and then said she thought the word "without" sounded bad, but she didn't know how to fix it. Emily immediately reread the sentence, crossed out "without" and wrote "unless" above it. Ida clapped her hands in approval.

Rose wasn't certain clapping should be allowed, but she made no comment. She then told Emily to take her seat and called on number two, John, to read the next two pages. When he was finished, she explained, as best she could, how Mark Twain was trying to make people talk the way they really did, instead of perfectly.

"We tend to write English more properly than we speak it," Rose said, "and Mr. Twain wants his characters to sound like real people. He also uses words that we wouldn't use in polite society, but that's because those words actually are used when certain kinds of people talk. So you will be surprised at some of the language in this book. We're not going to correct every line because that would spoil the pleasure of the reading, but now and then we'll stop to talk about it again."

They are all interested in this, Rose thought, looking down at the faces that were upturned to hers. They like it. They like having people make mistakes when they talk.

The next subject was arithmetic. Rose drew three numbers from the basket, had the designated children stand and asked the class to add them up as quickly as they could. Once they had caught on to number ten, number twelve, and number eight turning into thirty, she tried subtractions. And then she had them multiply. A few minutes into the exercise, they were laughing but paying close attention at the same time. They like this idea, too, she thought, and the numbering had been a practical way to break up that older group at the back of the room. It was the noon hour in what seemed like no time, and she dismissed them, then sat at her desk and opened her lunch pail. Just as she took a good-sized bite of a chicken leg, Ben Chandler approached the desk, greeted her, and said he thought the morning had gone well.

"I'll be going along now, if you're comfortable," he said. "Have to pick up some things at the store and get them to Mrs. Chandler. It might be two o'clock before I can get back here if that isn't a problem for you."

"Not at all, sir," Rose said. "I appreciate your taking the time this morning."

He smiled, left the room, and walked quickly to Goodnow's. "You cannot imagine what that mere girl is doing in that class over there, Henry," he said as he came in the door.

"Well, no way I can know exactly what she's up to, Ben, but I'll wager it has plenty of imagination involved. She's got every housewife in this town wishing she had a new mop, and I haven't sold three mops a year for a decade."

Ben laughed and told the storekeeper about the numbering system and how he figured she had done it to break up the older boys. "What she told them," he said, "was that she was giving them a new view of the world, that things looked different when you sat in a new place."

"Certain amount of philosophy in that," Henry said. "Are you on duty this afternoon as well?"

"I'm s'posed to be, but Mrs. Chandler needs a sack of flour as soon as possible, so I thought I'd gather up a few things here, scoot home and get a bite to eat, and then get back there by two or so. If you see smoke coming out

First Day of School

the windows, you can rush over there, I reckon."

Henry laughed. "Won't be any smoke. She'll keep everything together, just the way she's been doing ever since her mother died. How much flour you want?"

"I'll take twenty pounds," Ben said. "And I need a dozen tenpenny nails and four of Jason Harris' eggs, if you've got 'em."

Henry Goodnow wrote down the nails, flour, and eggs on the Chandler page in his book. When he was finished, Ben said, "I will plan to go to the class tomorrow."

"But you needn't go two days in a row," Henry said. "We have several people at the ready."

"Don't mind telling you that I'm pretty intrigued by the new Mark Twain book those young uns are reading," Ben said. "Reckon I'd like to hear the next chapter."

Minutes later, Ben was on his way home, and Henry Goodnow went back to sorting the mail, smiling to himself and nodding now and then as he considered what might be happening over at the school. Imagine Ben getting roped into a book the youngsters were reading. As he worked, he noticed a letter for Rose and a postcard as well, so he put both in her box. She would have been surprised to know that he didn't even glance at the message on the card. He knew both missives were from Newton, and he wasn't going to pry. If Hattie Munson had a card, now that was a different matter. His thoughts returned to the Mark Twain book, and it occurred to him that he might stock two or three of Mr.

Twain's volumes. Ben Chandler might like one of his own to read. He made a note to ask Rose about that next time she was in. Next time? He could hardly believe she was not going to be at his right hand for the next few weeks.

Across the street, as soon as the children returned from their noon hour, Rose put her number plan to work again. This time it was penmanship. "If you are number one," she said, "you will write the word one on the first line of your paper, then a line of Os, a line of Ns, and a line of Es. Then do each letter in capitals. And repeat until you reach the bottom of the page."

"Miss Hibbard," Simon Granger said, "I'm eleven. So I have more letters to write than Ethan does. Ma'am."

"Quite true, and you will have plenty of practice with the Es," Rose answered. "If you feel you haven't had sufficient practice with the other letters, you may stay after school and do another page."

"I'm sure it will be enough, Miss Hibbard," Simon said hastily. If he had to stay after school his father would get out the willow switch, and he would never be able to explain this numbers thing to his father anyway. He dipped his pen carefully in the inkwell, inspected the tip to make sure it wasn't going to blot, and started to write "eleven" across the page.

With some effort, Rose kept her face expressionless and started moving around the room to observe how everyone's letters looked. Her own handwriting was nearly perfect, and she had written all of the numbers on the board, plus all the capital letters. She saw that several of the children were looking at the board as they struggled to imitate her hand.

And then it was three o'clock and time for everyone to go home. They all trooped out, starting to chatter as they reached the cloakroom, and she sat down at the desk, giving a great sigh of relief. Ben Chandler had returned as he had promised, and he came forward to tell her he thought the day had gone very well.

"You have a way with them," he said, as he took his leave. "I will see you first thing tomorrow."

Rose erased the blackboard, except for her name, wrote tomorrow's date and started a spelling and vocabulary list from *The Adventures of Huckleberry Finn*. She listed shrivel, tolerable, dismal, limber, dandy, stile, raspy, genie, and magicians. That was enough for a start, she decided, thinking it was quite unlike any list she had been given in the past. She then pulled two numbers from the basket. Number ten would take care of the water supply tomorrow, and number eight would ring the bell. She wrote that on the board, too, thinking she rather liked this system. It could be used in many ways. And it was funny to add the children together. Tomorrow she'd see how they did at dividing themselves.

Once she had neatened her desk, she headed for the door and nearly ran into Peter Granger, who was making his way in. "Why, Peter," she said, "whatever brings you here at this time of day?"

"Sorry, Rose, I mean Miss Hibbard, but Father had me out straight at the farm with his late crop of hay, and I come as soon as I could," the tall boy said breathlessly. Past his elbow, Rose saw that Charles, who was in the room across the hall, was waiting for her, but she focused her attention on Peter.

"Came," Rose said without thinking.

"What?"

"You said 'come' when you should have said 'came,'" she said, feeling a little foolish. "But tell me what brings you."

"I have been hankering to teach those young ones to read better, Rose—Miss Hibbard," he said, acting almost shy. "But I had no way of knowing if you'd want me to go on with them."

"It would be a great help, Peter," Rose said slowly. "Since your father is riding you hard these days, why don't you come when you can. The noon hour is perhaps the best, but we'll make space for your tutoring. We do have one problem."

"And that would be what?" he asked anxiously.

"It will take practice at home," she cautioned.

"I could do that in the evening if I'm allowed an extra candle," he said.

"It doesn't require a light, Peter. You have to practice calling me Miss Hibbard, and I expect I could call you Mr. Granger if you require it." Past Peter Granger's elbow, Rose saw Charles double over in silent laughter. He was such a scamp.

Peter's shoulders relaxed then, and he grinned. "Certainly, Miss Hibbard. I shall try to remember. But you can just go on calling me Peter. I thank you, Miss Hibbard." And he was gone.

"How was it, Miss Hibbard?" Charles asked with a gleam in his eye. "Did you whack anyone with the pointer, Miss Hibbard?"

Rose began to laugh. "Too bad you're not in my room," she said. "Your knuckles would be raw by the noon hour."

"Was it all right?" Charles asked, now sounding a little anxious. "Was Mr. Chandler a bother?"

"He didn't say a word until he left," Rose answered. "And my day was, I think, quite wonderful. Will you stop by Aunt Nell's with me now, or are you in a tearing hurry as usual, you who have hearing as good as a whale's?"

"The calf will wait, Father doesn't pay any attention to when I get home as long as my chores are done and the meal is ready. Lead on, Macduff."

"Are you reading Shakespeare?" Rose asked, a little incredulous.

"Not in school. But I found this Macbeth book in Mother's bookcase, and I've been dabbling in it. It's fierce and bloody," Charles said. "I like it."

"Never underestimate a boy you think you know," Rose muttered as they walked along the road to the Harris house. Apparently blood was just fine in Scotland, even for a brother who couldn't kill a chicken without getting the vapors. She had so much to write to Newton tonight, and she had to plan tomorrow's school day as well. She knew Abby would go straight to Aunt Nell's and wait for her, but she hoped the nine-year-old had some ideas for supper at the teacher's house.

"Rose? Have you gone off somewhere?" Charles' slightly whining voice cut into her thoughts, and she realized he had asked some question or other. She tried to think back and hear it, but it didn't work, so she had to ask him to repeat it.

"Whales," he said. "What do you know about whales' hearing?"

"When I was on the coast with Miss Harty, they were talking one day about how whales could hear sounds from far, far away, probably heard the whalers' boats long before they were anywhere near. And you, young man, you certainly hear a great deal from a great distance."

"And proud of it," Charles said jauntily. "It's how I keep track of things I'm not supposed to know a-tall." She laughed, and beside her, Charles gave a little skip and grinned. It was good to see Rose like this. She's shedding happiness all over the place, he thought. He hoped some of it would land on his shoulders.

CHAPTER TWENTY-SIX
A Sneaky Killer

Abby was staying with Rose at the teacher's house most of the time because Aunt Nell had suffered a bad spell right after Thanksgiving and had taken to her bed for nearly a week. Even now, she was moving at what Jason told Rose was "a snail's pace," so Abby had stayed on. Just as well, Jason said, because it wasn't right for a girl of Rose's age to be alone in a house.

Rose didn't argue with him because she could see how worried he was about Aunt Nell, but it crossed her mind that she was a sight happier alone in the teacher's house than she had been with a group at her father's place, even though she still felt guilty about Charles. She had also been very busy. Her classroom days had flown by, and the new teacher had arrived right after the holiday to take over. His name was Clyde Hawkes, and he was boarding with the Goodnows for the present. He had complimented her on what the class had learned in the six weeks when she was the teacher, and he asked if she would return as a pupil and lend him a hand now and then.

Rose was happy to be back in a regular seat and to be helping the teacher as well. She had been surprised at what mixed feelings she had about giving up her place at the front of the room. She had loved it. It was her dream come true, and she plain loved it. It delighted her that the man she referred to as the "real" teacher had kept her number system and was inventing new ways to use it. But it was also a relief not to face all those eyes every morning and not to be responsible for stuffing all those heads with knowledge that she had barely mastered herself. When the stint was over, she realized Aunt Nell was quite right when she said Rose was getting too worked up about this new job.

"You need to flow into it," Nell said. "You are as tight as a newly strung length of barbed wire. Watch that you don't get just as prickly."

Thinking how many times she had nearly caught her skirts trying to crawl through a barbed wire fence, Rose had watched out for the prickly part. She caught herself now and then being impatient with Abby for no reason at all other than her tiredness at the end of the school week. And she had to admit she had been a little jumpy at the end of October when the older boys returned to school, the potato, pumpkin, and squash crops safely stored in root cellars. She had worked hard that month, too, harvesting the last of Miss Harty's garden. She had pulled a basketful of beets and stored them in sand in the cellar, and picked close to a bushel of red kidney beans that she had spread to dry in the teacher's attic.

And then, because Aunt Nell had seemed so worn out, Rose had offered to finish up Abby's new dress, hemming the skirt and sewing on the buttons. She hadn't minded that task at all. The hard part had been figuring out how to persuade Aunt and Uncle that Abby really needed something brand new, not clever adjustments to her old clothes. Hand-me-downs and fixed-up clothes were all right—even necessary—Rose knew, but Abby was growing fast, and it had been a long time since she had made the square dance skirt for her. She was certain that was Abby's newest garment.

The other grand part was how excited Abby had been when she saw the dress for the first time. It was a dark blue and white print that Rose found at Mr. Goodnow's store, the very last of the bolt, so it wasn't costly. Nell had added a plain white collar, and Rose found enough white buttons in her mother's button box, shirt-sized buttons but in the shape of a four-leafed clover, to take care of the opening in the front. Perhaps the little clovers would make the dress a lucky garment. She was grateful to Aunt Nell for taking care of the buttonholes. She knew how to make them, but she had a terrible time getting one started properly and sometimes had to start over more than once. Even after she watched Nell several times, she couldn't quickly get that second stitch neatly parallel to the first. She would have to keep working at it, she decided. Buttonholes properly done were quite handsome, regular as the tines in a fork.

Now she was here on a Saturday, knowing that Joshua and Ruthann might appear at any moment. She went quickly through the house with the feather duster. She checked on the bathtub, toilet, and sink, and made certain that no spoiled food was hiding in the icebox. The couple came to town frequently, each time reassuring Rose that she was quite welcome to stay on a bit longer, especially now that the ground was starting to harden and someone had to stoke the fires and make sure the pipes didn't freeze. Rose had asked about paying rent, but the teacher shrugged off the suggestion, saying it was important to her to have the house cared for.

What she didn't tell Rose was that she was afraid Joshua would never take time off from his beloved cows if the house wasn't available. In her heart, of course, she knew that sooner or later she would have to rent the place, probably to the new teacher, once his wife and youngsters joined him. She understood from Charles Tucker that the young man was on temporary hire until after New Year's. And she had no idea how she would tell Rose or what Rose would do. Some of her talks with her young friend made her feel very uneasy about the whole picture.

With each visit, Ruthann made time to sit with Rose at the kitchen table and talk about what was going on in their lives, and each time Rose realized how much she had missed having a cup of tea and chatting with the teacher. She told Ruthann how worried she was about Aunt Nell, whose cough didn't go away, and how Uncle

Jason sort of looked off in another direction whenever she had the courage to ask him what Dr. Potter said about her.

"He just won't answer," Rose said. "And he really doesn't want Abby there, and he doesn't want me to come help out, either. He's doing it on his own."

Consumption, Ruthann thought, after Rose told about the cough and how weak Nell Harris seemed to be and how Jason had isolated her from the girls. She had wondered at the wedding when she saw Nell's flushed face and noticed her lack of energy. Perhaps she could ask Del Potter herself, although he was so close-mouthed about patients that he might not share an iota of information. She smiled, thinking that the village had Delbert Potter at one end of the seesaw and Hattie Munson at the other. Fortunate that in between there were the rest of the townspeople, who pretty much kept their own counsel and only occasionally passed on juicy tidbits of gossip.

"I suspect Jason may think Nell's sickness can be passed on to others," was all she said aloud. "He's not shutting you out because he doesn't want you. He's trying to take care of her and you girls, too. Perhaps you could bake a pie or make a floating island pudding and ask Henry Goodnow to take it in for you."

"I can do that," Rose answered quickly, pleased with the idea. She knew very well how much Charles appreciated her occasional stops at her father's house to leave a batch of biscuits or a pie. Charles was growing faster than weeds in the garden these days, and it startled her to find she was no longer looking down at him, at least not very far. She had gone through his chest of drawers when he wasn't there and found his clothes stacked far more neatly than she would have expected. But when she saw him at school, she noticed his trousers were too short. She had put two new pairs on account at Mr. Goodnow's and tucked them into the chest. At school two days later, Charles had done a little dance in the hall for her benefit, kicking out his newly clothed legs and then taking a bow. No other boy, Rose thought at the time, laughing out loud, would do that in front of everyone else.

As for her father, she had hardly seen him since Thanksgiving. That had been a hard day for her, and she decided to talk to Ruthann about that, too.

"But Aunt Nell is not my only problem, Ruthann," she said.

"It would be amazing if any human had only one dilemma at a time," the teacher answered. "What's next?"

"Father came to the store and pleaded with me to come home for Thanksgiving, make the dinner, bring Abby, and be a family again. He was very calm and serious, and he kept saying it would mean a lot to all of us and that he knew Sarah would think it the right thing to do. That was the part of the argument I couldn't counter, so I told him Abby and I would come, and we went, and..." She stopped in mid-sentence when her voice cracked. Ruthann Chittenden watched as Rose's finger traced the knot in the tabletop, the way she always did when she was troubled and didn't know what to say next.

"And it was dreadful, wasn't it?" the teacher asked.

"Yes, Ma'am," Rose said in a small, tight voice.

"What was the worst part?"

"When we all sat at the table, and Mother's place was empty, and Father didn't say more than three words until Abby fetched the dessert from the kitchen," Rose said, her eyes and her finger still on the table knot.

"And what broke the silence?" the teacher asked.

Rose looked up then and nearly smiled. "Charles watched Father take his first bite of the pie and muttered just loud enough for everyone to hear, 'Not bad, Rose, not bad at all.' And then I had to say that Abby actually made the whole pie this time, and Father looked up and said, 'Not bad, Abby,' as if he hadn't heard Charles a-tall, and we three burst out laughing."

"What did your father do then?" Ruthann asked, feeling as if she were pulling a rope through the eye of a needle but determined to make Rose talk.

"He looked around the table, first at Abby, then Charles, and then me. And he said, 'I am grateful to hear your laughter again, and I hope it won't be the last time. We must needs try this again to see if we can get the hang of it once more. If you young uns are willing, that is.'"

"Did anyone answer that?"

"I'm afraid not, Ruthann," Rose said. "I never asked Abby and Charles, but the thought of another dinner like that one…" Her voice trailed off, but at least she had stopped tracing the knot in the table. "I know the commandments say to honor your father and mother, but there's nothing that says you have to love them. And I don't know if I'm ever going to honor him again, although he seems to have turned that corner he's always talking about. Oh, why don't I honor him, Ruthann?" Rose said, speaking much louder. "He's sober, he's a deputy sheriff, he's my father, he gave up Miss Graves, he seems to want what's best for us. He even put in a bathroom. So what is the matter with me?"

"You have it in your head, no doubt implanted by your wonderful mother, that you are supposed to forgive and forget when people do bad things. It's easy enough, Rose, as a teaching, but it's powerful hard to do as a practical matter. And even if you speak of forgiveness, you cannot forget. What happened with your mother, your father, Miss Graves, and all the rest is a memory you will have for life. The hope is that time will dull the edges and fade the pictures."

Rose nodded, knowing that the teacher was quite right. She had many things she could never forget, and it was only in the past few weeks that she had stopped having nightmares about them. She could still remember the bad dreams of last year when her mother's grave had opened, and she and Emily and Alice were jumping over the stones. Once she recovered from nearly freezing to death, that dream had never come back at night. But it still made its way into her head in the daytime.

"The Reverend Lockhead would say I have to forgive

and put it all behind me," she said slowly. "You don't think that's true."

"I think you can't, Rose. And more importantly, perhaps you shouldn't. You learned a great deal from all of your father's missteps, and it made you grow into the person you are now. A young girl who is also a competent woman, housewife, teacher, and substitute mother. What happened was terrible, but what came out of it is almost a miracle."

"It's the silver lining thing," Rose answered, nodding her head. "Mother talked about that a lot. Especially when Father had just refused to get one of the things he called newfangled. Her mouth would thin into a tiny line, and she would tell us to look inside the clouds and not fret."

"Good advice, Rose. Your mother may not always have been happy, but she was always wise, it seems."

"The good news was that Aunt Nell was well enough to make Abby a new dress, and they were both so pleased. Abby had asked me if she could have just one, and I realized she's been going about in hand-me-downs and stretchers for a year or more."

"What on earth are stretchers?" Ruthann asked. "I only know them as a thing they use to carry a sick or injured person, and Abby's neither."

"It's when you cut a skirt just above the knee where it starts to get a little straight, and you set in a piece of fabric that looks nice with the old fabric, and then the dress that was too short is long enough. Aunt Nell usually puts a ruffle of the new fabric on the hem or at the wrist so it will look like a plan instead of a stretch. Abby is getting tall so fast that she has two or three of those now."

"I have a lot to learn about fixing and saving and redoing," Ruthann said with a sigh. "I'm almost ashamed to say that whenever I grew fast, my mother took me to the dressmaker to have something new made. And I didn't have an older sister for hand-me-downs, so that never happened."

"Not a problem Charles has, either," Rose said. "Although I can't imagine how Aunt Nell would go about stretching his pants with a complementary fabric."

They both started to laugh, thinking about Charles with a stripe of a different color around each leg. "A piece of lace, perhaps," Ruthann said, still chuckling.

"Or red silk," Rose said, "if any of us had any." At least she had taken a stab at Charles' wardrobe. And the teacher was pondering how she could provide Abby with a ready-made perfect outfit for a nine-year-old without insulting everybody. She knew her mother would be very taken with the idea, but presenting it here might be a different story. She would think on it.

"Would it be foolishness to take Abby into Ripton in her new dress and have her likeness taken?" Rose asked.

"It would please her mightily," Ruthann answered. "And you no doubt saved some of that teacher pay, so you would have the twenty-five cents. Keep in mind that you need to take an early train because that photographer often has a line waiting outside his studio. I hear the girls from the hat factory often treat themselves to a new tintype."

"I saved it all," Rose said. "They paid me three dollars a week and apologized for giving me so little, but I was grateful for whatever they decided."

Half as much as they were paying me, Ruthann thought, but kept the knowledge to herself. Those men saved themselves a little money at Rose's expense and then felt guilty because they knew she did a superb job, what with Ben Chandler taking every shift of supervising the first week so he could hear the children read *The Adventures of Huckleberry Finn*. She heard he had actually ordered a copy at Henry Goodnow's and announced he would give it to the library when he was finished.

Rose knew little about Mr. Chandler's interest in Mark Twain, but as she made her way through the house, she hoped the teacher would have time for another of those kitchen talks. Emily and Alice were great listeners, but they had no idea how hard it was to grow up without a mother, never mind trying to replace one for a brother and sister. When she was in front of the classroom for those few short weeks, she had put all other things out of her mind. But now the old worries were cropping up again, making her wonder if she was doing all the things she ought to do.

She was finishing up when she heard a rap on the kitchen door and saw through the window that a buggy was standing in the worn path that led to the teacher's small barn. It looked like the Barnes' buggy, and she hurried to the door. Sure enough, Newton's father was on the step, removing his hat and nodding to her.

"Come in," Rose said, her first dismay dissolving when she realized he was smiling.

"Don't mind if I do," Samuel Barnes said, scraping his boots on the mat and stepping inside. "The wind is up, and it gets a man right in the face when the horse is trotting along." He shed his jacket and put it over the back of a kitchen chair.

"Will you sit?" Rose asked. "Would you like a cup of tea?"

"Ayuh and ayuh," he said, chuckling. "Nice of you to offer."

Rose pulled the teakettle to the front of the wood stove. She could not imagine what errand Mr. Barnes could have here, but she knew she couldn't hurry him. Newton said his father never spoke quickly, even if he had something important to say. The kettle began its boiling song, and she poured the steaming water over the tea into a mug. She watched as he pushed his chaw aside with his tongue, making his right cheek bulge a bit, and then took a sip of tea, added a little milk, took a longer drink, and let out a sigh of satisfaction.

"Hits the spot," he said. "I thank you. Now, you are on tenterhooks wondering why I have showed up at your door. No, no, don't shake your head. You are at the very least curious. Fact of the matter is that Mrs. Barnes and I would like the pleasure of your company—and that of Miss Abby—for our Saturday night supper today."

"Why," Rose exclaimed in delight, "that would be

perfectly lovely. I will accept for her, too, since she's not here right now." She saw that Mr. Barnes had resumed chewing on his plug of tobacco and hoped none of the vile liquid created would ooze out of his mouth. She was glad Newton didn't chew tobacco. Cleaning the cuspidor on the steps of Mr. Goodnow's store was her worst chore there and always made her stomach churn a little.

"We'll consider it settled," Samuel Barnes said. "Mrs. Barnes is puzzling out how to seat seven at the table, but she'll have that squared away, I'll wager, before I get back home."

"Seven?" Rose asked, mentally counting Newton's two brothers, the parents, Abby, and herself.

"Seven," he said. "We had a postcard from Newton yesterday saying he'd be along about suppertime if we held off until six-thirty or so. I'm surprised Henry Goodnow didn't tell you already since everyone knows he reads all the postcards."

"Newton's coming? Tonight?" Rose couldn't believe it. She hadn't dared to even think about when he would be able to get away from the Chittenden place again.

"Yep. And Mrs. Barnes was all in a dither about you receiving him over here, so we decided to invite you and Abby for the meal and the evening."

Rose was trying hard not to look as if she wanted to dance around the room, and she knew her face was getting very pink. But suddenly she didn't care. She would be so glad to see Newton, and maybe he'd figure a way for them to take a walk by themselves for at least a few minutes after supper, unless his mother was set against that, too. She smoothed her apron with both hands and asked, as calmly as she could, whether he would like more tea.

"Appreciate it, but no," he said. "Mrs. Barnes needs a few things at the store, so I'd better get on with that. She's baking a cake and says she must have some of Mr. Baldwin's vanilla that all the ladies are talking about. It's costly, but she shall have it. I'll be busy with chores right up to supper hour, so I expect you and Abby can walk to our place? We'll get you back home all right."

Rose thanked him, handed him his jacket, and saw him out the door. As she expected, he spat on the grass before getting back on the buggy seat. He wasn't even out of sight when she let out a whoop and pranced around the kitchen table. After a few minutes, she flopped in the kitchen rocker and sat there, breathless and smiling. Maybe all her straightening up here had not been needed. She couldn't imagine Ruthann, Joshua, and Newton leaving the farm all at the same time.

"I mustn't lollygag in any case," she told herself. "I must iron one of my teaching skirts to wear to supper. And Abby can wear her new dress. The roads are dry, so we won't soil our good clothes on the walk there."

With that, she set two flatirons on the stove and added a couple of sticks to the fire. Miss Harty had taken the old ironing board with her, so Rose placed a thick pad and part of an old sheet on the table so she could iron there. By the time she fetched her skirt, the irons would be hot.

CHAPTER TWENTY-SEVEN
Ups and Downs

Rose and Newton perched on the top rail of the pasture gate behind his parents' house, with Abby on the lowest crossbar below them. All three were staring east, where a patch of sky was getting brighter by the minute. It was very late and very cold, but the three were determined to see the full moon appear behind the dark fingers of leafless trees and then float into the sky. They had enjoyed a lively time at the Barnes' supper table, eating an entire pot of baked beans, two loaves of brown bread, and half of Eliva Barnes' delicious baked ham, followed by slabs of warmed apple pie. Then they had played euchre, which was still one of Rose's favorite games, at least partly because she nearly always won. To Newton's dismay, she had topped everyone again that night with her clever maneuvering of her right and left bowers.

Rose had spent very little time at Newton's home, but it didn't take long for her to like being there. They were what Sarah would have called "warm folks," she decided, not because they were hot to the touch but because they teased and laughed as if they liked each other. Newton ribbed his younger brothers, and Mr. Barnes told more than one funny story about his own childhood in Eastborough. Their table was not surrounded by the gray clouds she always saw at the Hibbard house, caused by her ever-present fear that her father's temper might explode. She still wasn't sure whether his outbursts were connected to John Barleycorn or not, so she worried that the anger was still simmering. At the Barnes' table, such matters did not cross her mind.

"It's very cold," Abby piped up from below them. "I want to sit up there with you."

Newton and Rose, who were happily snuggled as close together as fence-sitting allowed, exchanged a glance, and Newton removed Rose's hand from his jacket pocket, reached down, pulled Abby up, and set her between them.

"How's that?" he asked.

"Much better," she said. "But my feet still feel as if they were on a cake of ice."

"Do you want to go in?" Rose asked.

"No!" Abby said emphatically. "I want to see the moon when it's as round as a silver dollar, no little slices off the side."

"It's always round, you know," Newton said.

"Is not," Abby retorted. "It goes from nothing to a sliver of silver—hey, did you ever notice that silver and sliver are exactly alike except for where the 'l' lives—to a crescent and then to a kind of dumpy shape and then to round."

"It's parenthetical," Rose said.

"What on earth does that mean?" Newton wanted to know.

"It waxes with a little curve; it wanes with the opposing curve," Rose said. "And the two slim moons have the needed material between them."

Newton groaned, then grinned at her. "Parenthetical or not, it's always round."

"Is not," Abby repeated.

"Newton's right, Abby," Rose interjected. "The moon is always round, but we can't always see the whole thing."

"I don't believe it," Abby said firmly.

"It's like," Rose went on, "when you hide in the pantry and stick your head around the corner. All I can see is your head, but I know the rest of you is still there."

"Hmmm," Abby answered, not wanting to give in, but getting the idea. "So where's the moon's pantry?"

"The earth," Newton said quickly. "It's because the moon goes around the earth and the earth goes around the sun and sometimes the earth hides part of the moon from the sun. The moon doesn't have a light of its own. It just reflects the sun."

"Dear heaven," Abby said. "Well, I like him anyway, even if he's been fooling me all these years."

Rose and Newton both started to laugh, and Newton reached behind Abby to pat Rose on the back. She dropped her mittened hand behind her sister, grabbed his, and swung it. They smiled at each other over Abby's head, and she turned quickly and saw that they were holding hands.

Abby turned to Newton and said, "I think you are like the moon."

"How's that?" he asked.

"Part of you is hiding. You are sweet on my sister, and when I'm around, you don't show it. But I saw you kiss her, and it wasn't the way Uncle Jason gives me a peck on the cheek."

"And you, Abby, are a snooping imp, and if the moon weren't arriving right now, I would take you straight home to bed," Rose said.

"He is sweet on you, Rose," Abby insisted. "He really is, and I think you are sweet on him. I heard Aunt Nell say so."

"And now you're an eavesdropper like your brother," Rose said, a little exasperated about the direction this talk was taking. "You know perfectly well that if you overhear something you weren't supposed to hear, you have to pretend your whole life that you never heard it at all."

"I," Abby began, "think that's silly and…" But just then the moon appeared behind the dark, bare branches of the willow trees that overhung the pasture brook, and she finished with a soft, "Ooooh, look at that." And they all watched in silence as the moon rose high enough to make a patch of gold on the brook, and then, reflecting off the snow, make the whole place almost as bright as day.

"Now that," Newton said with satisfaction, "that is a moon. And it will light me all the way back to Joshua's place."

Rose's heart sank just a trifle as she realized that the evening was nearly over. Being with Newton's family had turned out to be very entertaining, and she hadn't been nervous at all. Now she and Abby would go back to the teacher's house, and she was quite certain she and Newton would have no time alone at all. But she had reckoned without his ingenuity. As they all jumped off the gate and turned toward the house, Newton told Abby to run along ahead and ask his mother to make him a cup of tea before he started out.

"I trust you can help me harness Tommy," he said to Rose in a very businesslike way. "Sometimes he gets a little restless when he sees the bridle coming."

"I'll try to soothe him," Rose said, straight-faced but pleased that neither Newton nor Abby could see that her face was warm and red now, not merely pink from the cold air.

Abby just nodded and ran off toward the house to carry the message. She glanced over her shoulder once, wondering if Newton really thought she was fooled by these two requests. He was probably already kissing her sister, she thought, but she did not see them. They were in the barn and out of sight.

As they went over the well-worn boulder that served as a step into the horse barn, Rose started to giggle. Newton smiled at her but said nothing. He pulled her into the warm barn, unbuttoned her cloak, pushed her scarf aside, and slid his arms around her, drawing her close and burying his face in her neck.

"You weren't giving me enough credit, were you?" he murmured in her ear. "I might freeze to death if I failed to get a little private warmth from you and had to make that long journey tonight alone."

"I can't believe you managed this moment," Rose answered, lifting his head and kissing him on the mouth. "I can't even believe you came all this way just to eat and watch the moon come up. You'll barely be at Chittendens' in time for milking."

Newton turned her so the moonlight coming through the small window lighted her face. "Believe," he said. "Believe. I intend to make it a habit." He kissed her again, softly at first and then so hard she wondered if her teeth would get pushed in. That would bring false teeth, her capricious mind told her. She shoved the thought aside and kissed him back, then impulsively ran her tongue over his lips, still cool from their moon watching. He pulled back immediately and went to get Tommy's harness off the big hook at the end of his stall.

"Get along with the soothing," he said, smiling at her, and Rose moved in beside the little horse, stroking his face and running her fingers through his mane while Newton harnessed him from the other side. As he backed Tommy out of the stall, he paused, one hand holding the ring by Tommy's mouth and the other buttoning her cloak. Then he leaned over the horse's head, kissed her once more, and said, "I'll bet a bowl of popcorn Abby didn't believe a word of my maneuvering."

Ups and Downs

"Doesn't matter," Rose said, starting to laugh and thinking he was probably exactly right. "I'm not a betting girl, and it turned out nicely." She was so full of happiness at the moment that she didn't care what Abby thought.

Minutes later, they were on their way, Abby perched on Rose's lap, her mittened hands wrapped around the jar of tea Newton was taking with him. When they reached the teacher's house, Rose reminded him that Ruthann hoped he could bring back one of the boxes she had packed during her most recent visit to Eastborough. She and Joshua had taken back as much as they could fit in their buggy, and now they were working on moving the rest out.

"Do you know which box she wants?" Newton asked. "I don't have a great deal of room."

"You can choose from the four or five in the front hall," Rose said. "It likely doesn't matter which." She didn't like watching the pile of boxes get smaller, even though she knew time was running out for her in this house. Newton pushed a couple of boxes aside and chose one of the smaller ones, which was marked fragile. He took it out and carefully placed it near his feet in the buggy. Then he came back to the porch, gave Abby a hug, and said, "Run along, little girl. I'm sweet on your sister."

Abby giggled and went in the house as told. Newton drew Rose close, kissed her once more, and whispered, "I don't know how many days I can last without seeing you. But it will have to be at least seven. Please write. I read your letters twelve, fifteen, twenty times."

"I'll begin tonight," Rose said. She put her hands on both sides of his face and said, "These are parentheses holding the important part in their grasp. You are my moon, coming and going, waxing and waning."

"Poetry, Rose? I like it. Will you be my star?" He did not wait for an answer but looked up at a dark sky bright with millions of stars. "I'm picking one out. I choose the left star in Orion's belt, and I leave it to you to figure out why."

"It was an astronomical evening," Rose said, liking this word game. "And now I wish you a safe journey."

She turned up her face, he gave her a quick kiss on the cheek, and she quickly ran into the house without looking back. He watched the door close and heard the latch slide into place. The parlor curtain did not move, so little Miss Abby had apparently decided to mind her own business. She was nine going on nineteen, he decided, but she surely loved her Rose. As do I, he thought fervently, as do I. And he climbed into the buggy seat and spoke softly to Tommy, who immediately headed out.

Newton knew the horse would make his way back to Joshua's with little or no direction, but he also knew he wouldn't be taking any naps. He was all keyed up about Rose, his whole body tense from the brief contact with hers. Each time they kissed and held each other, it was harder to hold back than the time before. He was determined to act the way Rose wanted him to act, but he had a feeling that restraint was easier for girls than for boys. He had no older brother to talk to, no one to ask about all these things his body was doing to him. And while he loved Rose too much to let himself make a mistake, he was sometimes in real pain after holding her and kissing her. He wondered if that was normal. He hoped so, but it sure wasn't comfortable.

His hold on the reins had loosened, and Tommy slowed, trying to look over his shoulder. Newton smiled, tightened his grip, and saw that the path ahead was well lit by the full moon. He looked up at the moon, considered the likelihood that Rose was looking at it also, and then fixed his gaze on the left-hand star in Orion's belt. While he stared at the star he had labeled as Rose's, it suddenly came to him that he could talk to Joshua about all this. He stretched his legs out as far as he could, pulled the horse blanket over his knees, and took five deep breaths, blowing air out slowly, forcing his body to relax as he exhaled. A dip in the river might help, he thought, except he'd be chilled to the bone. Then, because he figured Tommy could see the road just as clearly as he could, he gave the reins a small snap, the little horse picked up the pace, and Newton leaned his head on the seat back. It was a good thing he hadn't settled for a wooden stool for this buggy. His eyes focused on the Rose star once more. He'd likely see Orion move across the sky, watch the moon set, and see the sun rise before this night was over. But he'd be in time for the morning milking.

Back at the teacher's house, Rose was also looking at that particular star in Orion's belt. She wondered why Newton had chosen that one. Perhaps because it was so easy to find. She knew different groups of stars had special names; names they had been given centuries ago, and she wanted to be introduced. Perhaps Miss Harty—Ruthann—could find her a book. Or possibly Mrs. Goodnow at the library. She would ask on Monday after school.

She turned away from the window and sat down at her desk to begin the promised letter. But before she had filled a page, her head fell forward, snapped up and fell forward again. She roused herself regretfully and told herself she could finish the letter either before or after church the next day. Actually, this is already church day, she thought, smiling as she blew out the candle.

"We stayed up for the moon," she said aloud. Her mother, she thought, might have done that, but her father would think it a strange notion. She went back to the window for a last look at the perfectly round orb, knowing that Newton and Tommy were trotting along in its light.

CHAPTER TWENTY-EIGHT
Heart to Heart

Despite her uncle's protests, Rose went to see Aunt Nell on St. Valentine's Day. Aside from Christmas and Thanksgiving, Valentine's was a day Sarah Hibbard had cherished, although Rose wasn't certain why it came ahead of other days. Still, Sarah had always cut out heart shapes for her three children, painted them red, and trimmed them with lace bits from the old trunk where she kept leftover fabric. Rose was starting to fear for Aunt Nell's very life, so she decided a little extravagance was appropriate. She had tucked part of her teacher pay in the pocket of her woolen skirt and stopped at Mr. Goodnow's store to purchase a fancy, ready-made valentine. At first, Henry Goodnow smiled knowingly, figuring Rose was going to send a special missive to Newton. Then he realized she wasn't looking at the most romantic cards, so he asked if he could help.

"It's for Aunt Nell," Rose said. "She is still feeling poorly, and I reckon if Sarah—I mean Mother—loved Valentine's Day, then perhaps the idea came to both sisters from Grandmother Emma. I want to take her a fancy valentine today."

Together, the clerk and store owner pored over the small assortment of cards that hadn't sold and came up with one that expressed friendship and admiration rather than undying love. "Some of these," Rose commented, "are as gooey as soft taffy."

"So they are," Mr. Goodnow said, not revealing that Hattie Munson had purchased one such but had carried it off rather than mailing it from his post office. He made it a practice not to gossip about the incoming and outgoing mail, but he sometimes admitted to himself that he relished knowing a few things no one else knew about the people of Eastborough. It occurred to him that Hattie might be delivering her card in person, but he suspected it was more likely she would go to Ripton to mail it, just to keep him in the dark. For a woman so willing to talk about everyone else, she was remarkably private about her own doings.

He and Rose settled on a card with a little blonde girl on the outside, surrounded by a garland of pink roses and simulated lace. Rose ran her fingers over the slightly raised roses and lace, then opened the card and read, "True friendship is golden, and yours is a treasure." That would be just right, she thought, since Aunt Nell meant more to her than any other aunt. Or anyone else, actually, other than Abby, Charles, or Ruthann Harty.

"I think we are friends," she said to Mr. Goodnow rather tentatively.

"Indeed you are," he reassured her.

She fingered the outside of the valentine again and just as she opened her mouth to ask about the strange texture of it, Mr. Goodnow said, "That's an embossed card, very special. They put it under pressure to create the look of lace even though it's just paper."

Rose reached in her pocket for her money, and Henry Goodnow was on the verge of saying he wouldn't charge her for the card when he realized that would offend her.

"That will be a dollar fifty," he said. "It's a beauty."

Rose gave him two dollars and waited while he made change in the cash drawer he kept behind the counter. Then she borrowed his pen, dipped it in the ink bottle, and signed her name inside the card. She blotted the ink carefully, waved it a few times, and then, satisfied that it wouldn't smudge, slipped it into the envelope.

"Thank you, sir," Rose said.

"You are most welcome, Rose. I hope you find Nell doing as well as can be expected. Please give her my regards."

Rose nodded, wondering if she could manage this visit like an adult. It was time to "hold up," she knew, much as she had come to dislike that term. Aunt Nell wouldn't be pleased by a teary Rose. It would make her fret, which was the last thing Rose wanted. So she smiled at Mr. Goodnow and set off. He watched her until she was out of sight, hoping she understood how it was with Nell Harris and wishing at the same time that she had no idea how ill her aunt was.

But Rose did know. She had finally asked Ruthann

outright, and the teacher had told her she was quite certain Nell Harris had consumption. Most people, Ruthann told her, believed consumption wasn't contagious, but she had read articles in old issues of *Atlantic Monthly* magazines with opinions to the contrary.

"I thought when Mother said I was contrary it meant I was being difficult," Rose had commented.

"That's right," the teacher had said. "But it also means an opinion on the opposite side of yours."

"So it's possible a person can catch consumption from another person," Rose had mused, "and that's why Uncle Jason won't let Abby live there anymore."

"Your uncle may or may not have read up on consumption, Rose, but he's a naturally cautious man," the teacher had said.

None of this made Rose feel better about Aunt Nell, and she certainly didn't want to catch consumption, but she felt obligated to visit her aunt. When she reached the house, she lifted the latch and went right in, hoping to see Aunt Nell bustling about in the kitchen, but she was nowhere in sight. Rose glanced into the empty dining room where dishes from the noon meal were still on the table, and then stepped into the front room, which Nell always called the parlor.

There she was, eyes closed, in the Morris chair, which was tilted back so she was nearly lying down. The antimacassar behind her head was crumpled, and her stockinged feet stuck out past the crocheted afghan that she had pulled up to her chin. Rose moved almost soundlessly, but Nell's eyes snapped open, and she gestured for Rose to go away.

"I've brought you a valentine, Aunt Nell," Rose said, standing her ground. "Ruthann says what you have might be contagious, so I won't come any nearer, but I needed to see you."

"Thank you for coming," Nell said in a near whisper. "Jason took me outside before noon for the fresh air, and now I seem to be all tuckered out. But the air cleared my head and seemed to make me feel a little better. Perhaps you could pull in a dining room chair and set there just outside the door so we can visit."

Rose fetched a straight chair from the dining room immediately and sat where she was told to sit. Even with this wispy voice, Aunt Nell was in command, she thought. Everyone always did what she said almost instantly. She wished she had that kind of power with Abby and Charles, but she doubted it would ever happen.

"I need to tell you some things," Nell began. "I am not getting better and it may well be that I will join your mother and my beloved sister in heaven before the first hay is in."

Rose felt tears forming, despite her best efforts. She looked away, took a deep breath, told her eyes to behave, and said in a voice that cracked at first and then steadied, "I pray that isn't so, Aunt Nell. We need you here, and while I have little idea of what heaven is like, I reckon no one there has needs, including Mother."

"You are too funny, Rose," Nell answered with a sudden smile. "I mustn't laugh because it makes me cough, but you are funny. Now let me go on before I run out of steam. You uncle won't have Abby here because he thinks my ailment is contagious, and he may be right. You and Abby cannot stay at the teacher's house much longer because the new teacher is working out just fine, and he'll be wanting to bring his family to Eastborough and I hear he was promised rental of Mrs. Chittenden's house for the rest of the school year at least. So the question is, if you can't stay here and you can't stay there, where will you go? I'm certain as I am that the sun gets up even on a cloudy day that you are mostly trying not to think about that. And I'm saying you must think about it."

Rose squirmed a little on her seat, her fingers tightening on the card, and said, "Shall I give you the valentine, Aunt, or leave it in the dining room?"

This time Nell could not help herself. She chuckled and then coughed, quickly covering her mouth with a linen handkerchief that, Rose noticed, had not been ironed. When the spasm ended, Rose could see little beads of perspiration on her aunt's forehead, but Nell just reached for the small box of lozenges and put one in her mouth.

"Changing the subject will get you nowhere, Rose. You may not want to talk about this, but when you are out there on your rock in the woods, you need to puzzle it out."

"You know about my rock?"

"Everyone in town knows about your rock, Rose. It's one of the places your friend Alice knew to look when you disappeared after your mother died. You may be there for quite a spell since you have other questions to answer, too."

"Like what?" Rose was intrigued now, although the idea of moving out of the teacher's house was very troubling, not to mention everyone in town knowing where she was when she thought she was hiding.

"Are you going to be a teacher?"

"Yes."

"Are you thinking on marrying Newton Barnes?"

A hot blush spread over Rose's face, turning even her ears red. Forgetting the card she had brought, she covered her face with her hands, and the card fell to the floor. She retrieved it and summoned the courage to look across the room at Aunt Nell, who was looking directly at her. *Her eyes are so bright*, Rose thought. *Why are they so bright?*

"Rose?" Nell prompted.

"I... you... we... yes."

"Yes, you are planning to marry Newton?"

"Yes."

"Well then," Nell said, speaking in a voice almost like her usual practical tone, "you haven't as many things to consider as I thought. You just have to decide what order they belong in."

Rose laughed a little shakily. "I have to teach first," she said. "Married girls aren't allowed to teach."

"It's rubbish," Nell said, with a hint of her old tartness. "But it's true. Maybe someday we women will make enough of a fuss so we can vote, and then we'll see about what married ladies can and can't do."

Rose laughed again, a little more sure of herself. Aunt Nell couldn't be at death's door and be thinking all these things. Could she? And if she was, where was cousin Clara? Did they know? Should she ask? Inwardly, she shook her head and heard Nell saying, "That young man of yours, Rose, is a treasure, and I pray he'll put up with your desire to teach and not run off with some more willing young thing. It may not be seemly, but you'd better ask him right out."

"Oh, Aunt, we've talked about my teaching and his Jersey cows, and we agreed on time to follow our dreams before…" Rose stopped, not knowing how to finish the sentence. This was a most unusual conversation to have with Aunt Nell.

"Before you settle down together?"

"Yes, Aunt."

"It seems you both have good heads on your shoulders. I may not last long enough to see you making a home for Newton Barnes, but I want you to know right now that you have my approval. And Jason's too, I reckon. What your father thinks will be up to you to find out."

"I'm not certain I'll ask," Rose said. "But Newton did, you know."

"What are you saying, child?"

"Newton went to Father and asked if he could court

me," Rose said. "And then he told me about it."

"Sakes alive," Aunt Nell exclaimed, starting to sit up. "He's even better than I thought."

"Now," Rose said, "You are to lie down again, and I am going to give you your valentine, and then I'll be on my way before Uncle comes in to say I shouldn't be here a-tall." She stood, saw Nell cover her mouth and nose with the handkerchief, and brought her the card.

"Imagine I'm giving you a hug, Rose," Nell whispered. "Jason and I think of you as we would one of our own." Seeing Rose's eyes fill, she added quickly, "And no tears, please, no tears. Remember you are supposed to hold up."

Rose nodded, trying to smile and failing. She turned quickly, returned her chair to the dining room, and closed the parlor door so Aunt Nell wouldn't hear her washing up the noon meal dishes. She finished them quickly and was putting on her coat when the front room door creaked open.

"Not quiet enough," Aunt Nell said, slowly coming into the room, her mouth still partly covered. "Thank you for washing up and for the card. Sarah put great store by valentines, and I've quite missed getting one each year." The familiar stern look came over Nell's face and she added, "I trust Henry gave you a decent price on such a pretty thing, what with all you do for him."

Rose nodded and turned to go, but Nell's pale hand on her sleeve stopped her. "Never you mind telling Mr. Harris about our visit today, young lady. I wouldn't take it kindly if you passed on what I said and caused him to give up hope. Hope is what keeps him going these days."

Rose nodded again, unable to speak, and headed for the door, nearly choking on a sob that threatened to break through like thunder in midsummer. Shutting the door carefully, she picked up her skirt and ran to the road, where a scream of grief and frustration tore from her throat, just far enough away so she was sure Aunt Nell would not hear her.

"It isn't fair," she shouted into the cold February air. "It's not fair," she said again in a more ordinary voice. "It's not fair," she muttered over and over as she made her way toward her rock. She would decide nothing today, she knew, but she could not face anyone just yet. The rock was icy and cold, but she sat anyway, listening as the wind came up and the leaf-bare branches scraped together over her head. Her sighs echoed the whisper of the pines, but except for the sounds stirred up by the wind, it was quiet. After a few minutes, she raised her head from her knees and saw that the sky was pewter gray, a sure sign that snow was coming again. She must be on her way or they'd be sending a search party for her.

Despite Rose's hope that no one had heard her outcry, Nell Harris had watched her sister's daughter run for the road, heard the scream, and then allowed herself to shed the tears she had held back during the visit with Rose. She stood at the window a long time, then went back to her chair where she opened the pretty valentine and reread the printed message inside. She did consider Rose a friend. Blood was thick, but friendship could be even thicker, Nell thought, and it was friends who had stood by Rose through times when relatives had proved not enough. Nell still brooded about how long it took her and Jason to realize that Rose was in over her head and Silas was out of control. Well, she told herself, he'd always been steady as a rock. What she and Jason hadn't taken into account was how much her sister had contributed to that steadiness.

Rose should not have come today, but Nell treasured every part of the visit. A wracking cough pushed up through her throat, and she grabbed the back of a chair to steady herself, holding her handkerchief to her mouth. When the attack subsided, she started to tuck the handkerchief back in her pocket and saw that she had coughed up several spots of blood.

This cussed disease, she thought. Del Potter warned me it would come to this. She stretched out and pulled up the afghan, curling her legs so her feet were covered. Perhaps she could catch a little rest before Jason came in for supper. Just as she started to doze off, she wondered if he had thought about finding Clara to let her know her mother was dying.

CHAPTER TWENTY-NINE
Of Cakes and Stars

Abby was making a cake when Rose came into the teacher's kitchen. There was flour on her nose and all over the kitchen table. But Rose saw that she was at least wearing an apron and had apparently stoked up the fire to heat the oven. She watched Abby crack a brown egg into Ruthann's enamel bowl and was puzzled when the little girl then ran her finger around the inside of each half of the shell and carefully wiped it on the edge of the bowl.

"What's that about?" Rose asked.

"What?" Abby said.

"Wiping out the inside of the egg like that. I never saw anyone do that."

"Aunt Nell does," Abby answered a little smugly,

secretly pleased that Rose apparently didn't know everything. "She says it's wasteful not to get all the white out of the shell." She looked up as she started to crack the second egg and added, "You get quite a lot of extra, you know."

"I'll be doing it your way from now on," Rose said, laughing. "Wouldn't want any of that egg to get away."

Abby was busy fishing bits of shell out of the bowl because the second egg had not cracked neatly. After she removed several small pieces, she added the mound of flour she had sifted onto waxed paper and began to stir. Rose saw that the large cake pan was already greased and lightly floured, so she sat down to watch the rest of the process. She smiled a little at the way Abby gripped the handle of the spoon as if she were churning butter, but the ingredients were blending nicely, so she said nothing.

Suddenly the stirring stopped and Abby looked up. To Rose's surprise, her eyes were all teary, and as soon as she looked at Rose, she started to cry.

"What is it, Abby?" Rose asked, getting up quickly.

"I'm making the cake for Uncle Jason, but I don't think he wants cake or needs cake, but I couldn't think of anything else to do," Abby said, choking out the words as if a piece of biscuit were caught in her throat.

"Uncle? A cake?" Rose persisted, her heart sinking. She didn't want to have this conversation; she was certain as she was standing there that she didn't want to have it.

"I stopped by to see his chickens. You know how I

like to hold them because they are really soft, and they're friendly, too. And I couldn't go see Aunt Nell because you said not to, but I figured the chickens were all right for a visit."

"Indeed," Rose said, dreading what was coming next.

"And Uncle was there, in the chicken house, sitting on the step." She started stirring again, and Rose feared salty tears might soon fall into the cake batter, but she didn't say a word.

"He had his head in his hands, Rose, and chickens were all around his feet, pecking at his barn boots, and he wasn't looking at the birds or talking to them. He always talks to them, Rose," the little girl said, looking up. "He didn't even hear me behind him. I waited long enough to make sure he was breathing, and I left without saying anything." She stopped stirring and gave Rose a determined look. "I'm not a baby, Rose, and you need to tell me what's going on."

"You had better finish up that cake first, young lady, or its ability to rise properly will be all stirred out," Rose said, thinking she sounded more like Aunt Nell than herself and hoping Abby would decide the cake was more important than whatever was going on with Jason. At least she hadn't encountered Abby at the Harris house, although they must have missed each other by mere minutes.

Without speaking, Abby poured the batter into the pan, scraped every last bit off the sides of the bowl, and then picked up the pan and gently dropped it on the table. "That," she told Rose, "takes out the holes."

"It brings the bubbles to the top," Rose said, "so you are right. Then the cake should not be holey."

Once the cake was in the oven, Rose took Abby to the parlor, sat next to her on the sofa, and told her Uncle was upset because Aunt Nell was quite poorly and not getting better.

"Is she going to die?" Abby asked. "Is it going to be like Mother?"

Rose felt as if she were juggling raw eggs as she tried to quickly balance telling the whole truth against putting off the worst parts. But when she looked at her little sister's face, the face that had always trusted her, she knew only one way to go.

"She may die, Abby," she said quietly, and gathered Abby into her arms. Abby's small body shook as she cried on Rose's shoulder, and in a few minutes, when she was still and silent, they separated and looked at each other, each seeing fear in the other's face.

"I can't give him a cake, Rose," Abby said. "He won't want a cake."

"Oh, I think a cake would be just the thing," Rose answered. "He doesn't even know you can make one, and he will be pleased. People who are sad or worried need new things to think about, and he can talk about the cake with Aunt. We'll take it there this evening."

"But we can't go in," Abby said.

"No," Rose answered quickly, deciding she wasn't going to let on that she had already been in and had a long, troubling visit with her aunt, and that even sitting on her rock she had not made a single decision about the questions Nell had posed. "And now we are going to pull together some supper, frost and deliver the cake, and darn some socks before we put out the lamps."

Reassured by Rose's matter-of-fact tone, Abby checked the clock and said the cake needed at least another fifteen minutes. Rose sliced the last of the oatmeal bread, put butter on the table, and set a cast iron pot of leftover corn chowder on the stove. She pulled the teakettle onto the hottest part of the stove and sent Abby to the cellar to get a pickle from Ruthann's crock. They would have a simple meal, with very little cleanup, and then she would take the cake to Uncle. She reckoned it would be better if Abby didn't go along, so she'd set her to mending stockings and tending the fire.

The sisters were quiet as they ate their supper, each lost in her own thoughts about the turn the day had taken. But Rose came out of her reverie when she heard Abby slurp her soup rather loudly. "That's not good manners," she said, watching as Abby took the next spoonful more carefully.

"It's very hot, Rose," Abby said. "When I suck it in, I make sure I don't burn the roof of my mouth. And you already told me I can't blow on it, so it's hard to know what to do."

"Such overwhelming difficulties, Abby," Rose said. "No slurping, no blowing. That's it. You'll never be able to dine with the queen if you slurp and blow. And when we finish, you can do the washing up and start the socks while I deliver the cake."

"I don't even know the queen," Abby grumbled, "and I reckon she never has to wash up." But she smiled a little and ate the rest of her soup with what she now thought of as royal manners.

An hour or so later, her cheeks rosy from the cold, Rose returned to report that Uncle had been surprised and pleased to get the cake, and had called back to Aunt Nell that dessert had arrived on the doorstep. They were still at the table, Rose told her sister, and she could hear the teakettle talking on the stove, so she knew it really was perfect timing.

"I always listen to the kettle now that you told me it talks to you," Abby said, smiling at the news about the cake. "But it only speaks French or Portuguese to me. I never get the message."

"It only says that it's ready," Rose said, smiling herself and wondering what Abby knew about France and Portugal. Two mended socks were on the table beside Abby, and the little girl had Ruthann's darning egg shoved firmly into the toe of yet another one of Charles' socks and was earnestly trying to mend a rather large hole. It wasn't quite smooth, Rose noticed, but she didn't say anything. If Charles couldn't manage his own mending, he would have to take whatever he got. And his feet must be growing because holes in his toes were coming more and more often. With her teacher pay, she best get him a new pair at Mr. Goodnow's.

"I like the egg better than the mushroom," Abby said. "I can get a good hold on the sock with the egg in there, and the mushroom slides around."

Relieved that conversation was now centering on teakettles and darning tools, Rose said she much preferred the mushroom. "But if I had my druthers, I'd never darn another sock in my life," she said.

"What would you do with the holey ones, Rose?"

"I would burn them in the stove so no one would know I had thrown them away," Rose answered firmly.

Abby was shocked by this admission. No one ever threw anything away that she knew of. Mother had saved every bit of string that came into the house, Aunt Nell saved even the smallest nits of leftovers from meals, Uncle Jason saved eggshells and plowed them into the garden, and when underwear was in tatters, everyone cut up the pieces and used them as cleaning cloths.

"You couldn't, Rose," she said. "You really couldn't."

"Could, would, and already did. Just one time."

Abby was silenced by this new piece of information. But in a few minutes, fishing the darning egg out of the sock, she held it up and pronounced it wearable again. "You mustn't ever burn this one," she said. "Promise?"

Rose looked at the sock, figured the heel section would be the next part to go, and nodded. If need be, she'd just stuff it in a drawer when the time came to get rid of it. She knew one ought to save everything, but sometimes she just wanted to see the last of a dress, an apron, a hat, or even a basket that seemed to have served its time and more.

With the darning done, Abby's mind was back on Aunt Nell. "Why can't Dr. Potter fix her up as good as new?" she asked. "He made you well again when everyone was so worried that they kept talking to me about chickens and arithmetic problems and the color of my eyes and never about you. That's how I knew it was bad, Rose, what you had. They all kept talking about other things. When you almost froze to death, you slept for, I think it was three days. And nights. I knew no one who was all right could sleep that long."

Rose shook her head in wonder. She could never get over how much this little girl could see and how foolishly adults underestimated her. The color of her eyes, indeed. She wasn't sure of her ground on this subject and didn't want to talk about it anymore, so she grabbed the sock from Abby and said, "If you pester me anymore about Aunt Nell, I'll burn this sock right now."

Abby shrieked and tugged at the sock. "I won't ask anything more," she said. "But I think you think she's going to die. It's not that she may die. It's that she can't live because no one knows how to fix what she has."

Rose's face started to crumple, and Abby quickly added, "I'm sorry, Rose. I'm really sorry."

"It's all right, Abby. You and I must not talk to anyone else about this. Do you understand?"

Abby nodded and said she was about ready for bed. "I think I'll go outside first and wish on a star," she said.

So the sisters put on their wraps and went out to the yard. Bright stars filled the sky, and they stood quietly for a few minutes, holding hands and staring upward.

"They're so bright," Abby whispered, as if she might disturb them.

"Because the moon is still asleep," Rose answered.

She pointed out Orion's belt and told Abby about Newton naming the left star as hers.

"I will be the middle one," Abby said, still whispering. "Can I be the middle one?"

"Why not? And we'll take the one at the end of the Big Dipper handle for Charles if you think he'd like that."

"Oh, yes," Abby said, giving a little hop. "I'll wish on my star because we're too late to wish on the first one," she said with a giggle. "Much too late. If we stayed out all night, we couldn't count them all, could we?"

"Doubt it," Rose said, glad to have yet another diversion from the Aunt Nell story. And then, with Abby squeezing her hand so tight that she thought the blood had stopped moving, each wished on their chosen star.

"You mustn't tell your wish," Abby cautioned as they turned back toward the house. But each knew what the other had wished for.

CHAPTER THIRTY
Looking for Answers

Henry Goodnow found himself in a quandary when Rose arrived for work after school. He wanted to ask about the visit to Nell Harris, but he was put off by the solemn look on Rose's face. She had been in the store for nearly thirty minutes now, not looking at him once, although she had greeted him when she first came in. As he pondered what his next move should be, he realized he wasn't even sure what a quandary was. Did it have a shape? Short? Wide? Metal or wood? He felt it had jagged edges at the very least. He was certainly feeling as if his edges were a bit raw. A tiny smile flickered across his face as he realized he was thinking like Rose. The shape of a quandary, indeed.

Time to take the bull by the horns, he reckoned,

pushing away the temptation to think about that in a real way. He walked over to where she was dusting the glass-front cabinets that held buttons and lace, and spoke her name as quietly as he could. Even so, Rose jumped as if someone had shot a cap pistol behind her.

"Sorry, Rose," Mr. Goodnow said.

"It's quite all right, sir," she answered, so formally that he wished he had stayed behind the counter. "Oh, Mr. Goodnow," she suddenly went on, "I'm sorry, too. I don't mean to be rude and silent as a church choir between hymns, but I have a baker's dozen of things running around in my head."

"You must be in a quandary, too," Henry Goodnow said, and instantly wished he hadn't.

"Quandary?" Rose asked. "Why are you in a quandary?" To her surprise, Mr. Goodnow made a sound that she thought would be spelled "harrumph," and flushed all red around the neck and cheeks.

"Couldn't figure whether to speak to you today or not, Rose, to be truthful with you," he blurted. "You have an aura of 'Don't bother me' floating around you."

"Sorry, sir," Rose said once again. "You are always welcome to bother." Then, before he could answer, she burst out, "I am in a swivet about Aunt Nell and where to live and what to do with Abby and Charles and Ruthann and . . . and . . . and Newton."

"Start with Nell," he said, "that is, if you want to be bothered. Sometimes a little sorting out helps get the thinking cap on straight."

"She's going to die, Mr. Goodnow," Rose said in a flat

voice. "That's what she all but told me yesterday. She's going to die, and it isn't fair."

"We'll deal with fairness later," Henry Goodnow said. "What about somewhere to live?"

"The new teacher is staying on and wants to rent Ruthann's house," Rose said. "Aunt Nell says I can't expect to go on living there by myself, nor being there alone with Abby, and Abby can't stay with Aunt and Uncle because whatever she has could be contagious. And I am sure everyone from Hattie Munson on down is saying it isn't proper for me to live there by myself."

"From Hattie Munson on up, you mean," Mr. Goodnow said, hoping to coax a smile onto Rose's gloomy face but not succeeding.

"Yes, on up, I reckon," she answered, still unsmiling. "And I haven't talked to Ruthann in a long while, and I can't seem to think my way out of this tangle without her. She never tells me what to do, but she is so good at putting the choices in a kind of list," Rose said. A small smile did come then, to Henry Goodnow's relief, and she added, "I do like lists."

"Then we ought to get you one," he said, trying to think quickly enough so he wouldn't promise anything he couldn't manage.

"How?" Rose said, looking directly at him. "Just how?"

He paused for a long minute, stroking his beard with one hand and tapping his finger on the counter with the other. He knew he should make no promises he couldn't keep, but he could not have Rose looking this way any longer. He cleared his throat and stopped tapping his fingers.

"Mrs. Goodnow and I," he said firmly, "will set out for the Chittenden place with you early tomorrow," he said. "We can take Abby along if that suits you, and you can do the rest of your sorting with Ruthann right across the table. Give you a chance to see that young man of yours, too."

Rose thought her ears must have stopped hearing properly. He would take her to Ruthann? Tomorrow? She could not believe it. No one just set off in a buggy without an invitation to visit someone. And it was a fair piece out there to Joshua's place. She knew it took Newton hours to get there, and while he wouldn't admit it, she was certain he usually saw the sun coming up and was just about in time to start milking Jerseys. And Mr. Goodnow had the store to keep.

As if he were inside her head, Henry Goodnow said, "I can close the store for a day. It's my store. I will send a wire from the railroad station. It's costly, but it would give Ruthann time to make up a bed for you, and another for Edith and me."

They would be staying overnight. She would have time for Ruthann and Newton, and she would see his Jerseys and Joshua's place. Rose lunged toward Mr. Goodnow and gave him a giant hug, letting go suddenly when she realized she was being unseemly. But he hugged her back, and when she backed away, struggling to regain her balance, she saw that his face was redder than hers felt.

"Can we really do that?" she said, sounding as eager as a child. Henry Goodnow nodded, reminding himself that she was little more than a child, and ought to have had at least a couple of extra years before she was forced to be so adult. He wondered if he could leave the store in Rose's hands for a bit while he took himself to the library to place this plan in Edith's lap. It wasn't that she would be against going—she loved a visit and had said more than once that she'd like to see Ruthann's house and those cows Joshua Chittenden was so fond of. But she didn't take to surprises, and this was surely going to surprise her.

"You mind the store while I go speak to Mrs. Goodnow," he said aloud. "If she's willing, I'll send the wire before I come back. Get cash from all the customers."

They both smiled at that. Almost everyone in town had a page in Henry Goodnow's book, and they paid up as much as they could when they could. He carried them all the year-round, and most were grateful enough to pay up as soon as they were able. Rose said she could manage nicely, although the very idea of being alone in the store made her stomach feel a little queasy.

Before she could think about it, he was gone, and she was alone. The first thing she did was get her little key from her pocket and unlock her postal box. She had forgotten it entirely the day before when she was choosing Aunt Nell's valentine, so she was surprised to see two envelopes inside. One, a day late because she wasn't paying attention, was a valentine from Newton, all hearts and flowers. The second was his regular letter, telling her that indeed he had seen the sun and moon rise on the day of his most recent visit, then saw both set and saw the sun come up again.

> I hear some folks walk in their sleep, Rose. I think I milked in my sleep that morning. The cows didn't seem to mind. These Jerseys give more milk than any other animal I've seen. Tommy says I slept on the way here, too. Who knows? I only know it was worth it, seeing all those risings and settings and seeing you.
>
> Your respectful suitor,
> Newton Barnes

For the first time that day, Rose laughed aloud. Sun, moon, and cows. She was right in there with the sun, the moon, and the cows. She had been a little worried that he might fall asleep in the buggy on the way back to Chittendens', but now she realized that Tommy knew the way and would get him there safely, awake or asleep. She heard the bell jingle on the door and went to stand behind the counter, hoping whoever it was would figure Mr. Goodnow was right there in the back room.

It was Peter Granger, wearing dirty coveralls and a jacket with ragged edges on the sleeves. His hands were black with grease, and he must have wiped his face without thinking, because a long black streak crossed his left cheek. Her hope of pretending Henry Goodnow was in the back flew out the window.

"Mr. G. in?" he asked.

"Not right now," Rose said. "If you want to wait a few minutes, he'll be right back."

"Can't wait. Got a busted wheel and need to fix it before Pa has a hemorrhage right there by the barn."

"Broken," Rose said.

"That's what I said," Peter answered.

"You said busted."

"Still teaching, aren't you? Well, you had a good run at it, and everyone says that, and working with those young uns makes me understand why you like it so much. Now, can we see what we can find to fix the wheel? I pretty much know what we need, and Pa is not a patient man. I know Mr. G. sometimes has some used pieces that aren't so dear."

Rose pointed to the door leading to the back room and said he should look in there for wheel parts. Peter disappeared, leaving Rose to wonder whether she should be watching him or watching the store. The answer came when the bell jangled again and Hattie Munson sailed in, the feather on her hat bobbing up and down as she walked. Rose's heart sank. How many minutes had it been, anyway? Not enough, she knew.

"Where's Henry?" Mrs. Munson demanded, looking Rose up and down.

"He stepped out for a few minutes, Mrs. Munson," Rose said in a small voice. "Is there something I might find for you?"

"I should hope so," Hattie answered. "Give you a chance to earn your keep in this establishment."

Rose

"I earn my keep in any case," Rose answered, deciding not to take another mite of abuse from this woman. Now that she knew how Mr. Goodnow felt about her, she could take a stand, even though it made her very nervous. She hoped that didn't show.

Mrs. Munson looked surprised and then said in a softer voice that she needed four pewter buttons, half-inch size. "I don't want cheap metal," she said. "I want the pewter."

"We have them in several designs," Rose said, pulling out one of the drawers in the big wall cabinet that stood next to a rack holding bolts of fabric. She loved the buttons and was particularly fond of the pewter ones, so this was an easy task. She spread several designs in the half-inch size on the counter for Mrs. Munson's approval.

"I reckon you've learned a good deal here, young lady," Mrs. Munson said. She poked at the buttons, lining them up vertically to see how they would look on a garment. "I will take these four and a spool of the J.P. Coats' white thread as well. You can put it all on my account. On second thought, if you can manage the cash box, I'll just pay for them."

Rose smothered a grin and said she understood the cash box. Peter would be putting his wheel parts on account, but Mrs. Munson could be the cash customer. Rose counted out the change, wrapped the buttons and thread in a piece of paper, and tied it with a string.

"Thank you," Hattie Munson said, tucking the small parcel into the large tapestry bag she always carried. "I find you quite helpful."

"Yes, Ma'am," Rose said, struggling to keep a straight face until her first paying customer was out the door. She was still watching Mrs. Munson drive away in her buggy when Peter emerged from the back room looking as if he'd found a gold mine.

"All kinds of things back there," he said. "These are the pieces I need. Any idea how much they'll set us back?"

"Not really," Rose admitted. "Perhaps you could show me where you found those two things and then give me a name for them. I'll ask Mr. Goodnow when he gets back."

"Pa's account isn't in very good shape," Peter said. "But we can't go without the wagon, so I'll hope for the best on the price." The two of them went to the storeroom and Peter showed Rose exactly where he'd found the secondhand pieces. Then he described them as best he could while Rose made a note for Mr. Goodnow.

"One other thing," Peter said as Rose finished writing. She looked up, but he was staring out the window. "Do you think..." he began and then stopped. He shuffled his feet and studied the floorboards while Rose waited. Then he looked up and said in a rush, "Would you know if Emily might go to the dance tomorrow night with me? If I asked?"

"I reckon she would, Peter," Rose said. "Once you get that grease streak off your face."

"I figured on cleaning up some," he started to say, and then looked at her and saw that she was laughing at him. "Came right from the broken wagon, Miss Hib-

417

bard," he said, and laughed with her. "I'd like to meet her there and see her home," he added, all serious again.

"I have a notion she would like that," Rose said, hoping she was right. Peter nodded and hurried out of the store. Rose wasn't quite as certain as she'd indicated to Peter, but Emily had certainly seemed a bit interested. And he hadn't taken offense when she'd all but told him to get cleaned up before speaking with Emily.

By the time Henry Goodnow returned with the news that Edith was quite set up about the idea of going to the Chittenden place and that his wire had been sent to Joshua, Rose had taken care of two more customers, one of whom had paid cash money for a small bag of flour and three eggs. He was startled but pleased that she'd had so much business to see to and amused by her retelling of the encounter with Mrs. Munson.

"I hope I wasn't too rude," Rose said, wondering if he would think she had sassed the widow.

"Hattie dishes out plenty, Rose," Mr. Goodnow said. "Every now and then it's just as well if somebody steps on her toes. Now explain again, slowly, what the Granger problem was?"

Rose went through it again, Mr. Goodnow figured on a cost for the parts, put it in his book, and commended her for getting instant payment from two customers.

"Sometimes I get to thinking I'd like one of those newfangled cash registers that ring up the sales and provide a nice cash box drawer," he said. "And then I remember that my box in the drawer rarely has a great deal of cash in it anyway."

"What time will we leave tomorrow, sir?" Rose asked, unable to wait another minute.

"Edith says we should be on our way by eight in the morning," he answered. "We will come by for you and Abby. You'll need nightdresses, warm outerwear, and something for church on Sunday if they're of a mind to go. You might cook up a little something to take as a gift to Ruthann."

It would be a busy evening, Rose thought, what with gathering the various clothing needs and hairbrushes, taking their Saturday baths on Friday, and cooking something as well. But she just smiled and nodded. In another hour she'd be on her way home and could get at her preparations. Tomorrow she would talk to Ruthann, and best of all, she would see Newton on a day when she hadn't expected any such windfall.

Rose still had Nell very much on her mind as she worked around the store, but she was settled enough to hum a hymn tune as she worked. Hearing the faint sound, Henry Goodnow nodded and told himself that on some occasions he and Edith could move quite smartly. He had to admit he was anxious to see that Chittenden place anyway. He thought it quite amazing that a young man should graduate from Dartmouth, study law, and then choose to set himself up with a farm and some deer-colored cows that traveled the Atlantic to get there.

CHAPTER THIRTY-ONE
Cows and Conversation

"They're here, Rose, they're here!" Abby shouted from the living room window where she had been fiddling with the curtain for the past twenty minutes.

"No need to tell them, Abby," Rose cautioned, coming up behind her. "They are well aware of where they are."

"That's not what I meant," Abby said, frowning. "You know that's not what I meant."

"Just don't raise your voice so much that it flies through the window," Rose said. "Now you take the satchel with our clothes, and I'll bring the squash pie and lock the door behind us."

She was just as excited as Abby and kept trying not to show it. It was confusing to be so eager to take this trip and at the very same time be on the verge of tears because Aunt Nell was so ill. No one ought to be sad and glad at the same time, she thought. It mixed up everything inside your head. She'd try to think of the trip as the silver lining that Mother said was somewhere inside every cloud. It was actually true, Rose told herself, because on the other side of the darkest of clouds, the sun was still shining. Still, she had a hard time believing that, just as Abby couldn't believe the whole moon was always there. But she knew both things were true. Funny to think that when she couldn't see the sun, someone her age in China was looking at it. It just never went away.

Mrs. Goodnow sat in the front seat of the buggy, wrapped in a buffalo robe, and Mr. Goodnow was standing ready to stow the satchel. Abby skipped her way to him and then, with Rose, climbed into the second seat where they found another buffalo robe, and to Rose's surprise, a foot warmer.

"Put your feet right on that little box," Rose told Abby, who was delighted to find that the simple tin box was quite warm. "It has hot coals inside, and if we keep our skirts over it, they'll last a long time."

"The heat won't last all the way to Chittenden's place," Mr. Goodnow said, "but it'll keep your feet from turning into icicles for most of the way. Do you have all your things?"

"We're ready, Mr. Goodnow," Rose said, pulling the buffalo robe up to her chin and moving Abby closer. He gave the reins a little slap, the horses moved off, and both girls immediately lowered their heads so they wouldn't get the wind in their faces.

"It's good we have them in front of us," Abby whispered. "They're blocking some of the cold."

"But we're going to be pretty chilly by the time we get there," Rose said.

As they neared the railroad station, Mr. Goodnow guided the horses to the left and stopped the buggy. "Better see if an answer to my wire came," he said, climbing down. He was back quickly, waving a yellow sheet of paper and announcing that their beds would be ready at Ruthann's new home.

"We'll be most welcome, she says." He handed the paper back to Rose and Abby, who had never seen a wire before.

"It's not in good English," Abby said. "And it keeps saying STOP."

"That's because they write as few words as possible," Rose explained. "You have to pay for each word. Stop is used instead of a period."

Abby nodded and gave a little bounce. "This is a very exciting day, Rose," she said.

Rose nodded, still thinking about the goodness of the day and the badness of it and unable to accept the fact that it was just the way things are. She snuggled closer to Abby and put one of her sister's hands in her pocket, the way Newton always kept one of her hands warm in the winter. She smiled at the thought of seeing him soon and eventually relaxed into the rhythm of the slightly swaying buggy and the sound of the wheels crackling against the frosty road.

After the first hour of oohing and aahing at trees, cows,

snow, and an occasional house, the girls dozed off. They woke when Edith Goodnow asked them if they were ready for something to eat. She had brought a hamper of food, something that hadn't occurred to Rose, but it seemed it held enough to go around. Soon she and Abby were devouring cold drumsticks and slices of bread that Mrs. Goodnow had buttered at home. They shared a cup of lukewarm tea that Mrs. Goodnow poured from a jar she had wrapped in newspaper to keep it as warm as possible.

"It's a buggy picnic," Abby crowed, forgetting that her fingers were getting quite cold.

"Mr. Goodnow can't travel far without sustenance," Mrs. Goodnow said.

"It's all delicious, Ma'am," Rose said. "I never thought…"

"You didn't have to think, dear," Edith Goodnow interrupted. "That was on my list of things to do. But I see you've brought something for Ruthann."

"A squash pie," Rose said, relieved that she hadn't failed some test she didn't know about. "She's fond of squash pie, and we still had two winter squashes in the root cellar."

"Now that's what I see as right thoughtful, Rose," Mrs. Goodnow said. "I have heard that you make a fine pie, and that Miss Abby, in fact, turns out a beautiful pie shell."

"Thank you, Ma'am," both girls said in unison, which made them laugh. Edith Goodnow marveled at that. As the town librarian, she heard many things in the course of a week's work, and Henry could always fill in with some extra news he had from the store. She knew a fair amount about what these girls had been through, and she also knew they were unfailingly cheerful and polite when they came to the library. She wished they stopped by more often, but she realized neither had much time for pleasure reading. She was also aware that Rose, all by herself, had set the town to reading Mark Twain's books about two bad boys in Mississippi.

"We are nearly there," Mr. Goodnow announced. "Joshua said it was only a few minutes past the cemetery, which is coming up on your right, and then we turn left. I reckon we'll know his place by the color of his cows."

"What color are they?" Abby wanted to know.

"Some are the color of deer in the fall," he answered. "And some will have a nice mix of brown and black on their faces. Makes them look intelligent somehow, but they're not. They're just cows."

Rose wondered how Mr. Goodnow's low opinion of cows would go over with Newton and Joshua. They were besotted about cows, she thought, and she knew Ruthann sometimes joked that the cows were more loved than she was. Rose hoped no cow was going to come out higher on the love ladder than she did. She giggled, and three people turned to look at her.

"What's funny?" Abby asked.

"Nothing," Rose said. "I was just testing to see if my mouth was frozen." But she smiled to herself at the thought of cows on a ladder. Then she saw the cemetery, the thin marble stones in straight rows, white against the white snow. She peeked around Mr. Goodnow and saw a small road on the left, and sure enough, he was turning the horses. She felt something leap inside her in anticipation of seeing Newton and wondered what might be in there, making such a jump that she could feel it.

"I see cows the color of deer," Abby shouted, leaning far to the right in the buggy. Rose grabbed her arm and pulled her upright, then leaned behind her as far as she could. And there were the Jerseys, pushing snow aside with their horns to get at the brown grass beneath. And there was the house—a beautiful house—two stories with shutters on the front, and she could see, on at least one side. It was the color of butter with white trim, and the big barn was red like nearly every other barn in the county, except for the ones that had never been painted at all. The rambunctious frog inside her jumped again, even though she couldn't see Newton anywhere.

As they rolled into the yard, Ruthann ran out of the house, pulling a shawl around her as she came. A dog came from the barn, so Mr. Goodnow pulled up on the horses, speaking to them quietly so they wouldn't react to the barking. Rose jumped down and helped Abby, then flew into Ruthann's open arms. She wasn't much used to hugging, but she knew it was all right this time, and the teacher held her tightly before greeting Abby and the Goodnows.

"You have shutters on the side," Rose said, instantly realizing that no one here would understand the importance of that. "We don't, you know," she started to explain. "It was one of the newfangled things that Father thought was just wasteful. Mother always wanted them." She stopped abruptly, thinking she was rambling on and not letting anyone else talk.

"Welcome," Ruthann said, laughing a little at Rose's opening speech. "Welcome to the land of Jersey cows and few neighbors. And come in where it's warm. You must all be as cold as Mr. Manchester's cakes of ice by now."

Abby and Mr. Goodnow fetched the satchels, Rose took the pie, and Edith Goodnow brought the picnic hamper with what was left of its contents. The Chittenden kitchen was warm and cozy, with a delicious aroma coming from the oven. They all lined up at the black wood stove, holding their hands over the heat. After a few minutes, everyone except Henry Goodnow shed a layer of clothing, and Ruthann invited them into her parlor where a small stove was also providing heat. Henry announced that he would be going off to the barn, if the menfolk were there, and Ruthann assured him that they were probably just finishing the milking.

Rose wanted to go, too, but she went into the parlor instead, and marveled at what she saw. The bookcase was large and had glass doors and lots of books. The clock was black and gold like her mother's, and Ruthann had kerosene lamps on three different little tables, all of them lighted. Rose noticed a silver sugar bowl and creamer on a tray on the largest table, along with pretty teacups and a plate of what looked like filled cookies.

Would they have tea before dinner? And sweets? Apparently that was precisely what was going to happen. Ruthann was coming in with a silver teapot in her hand, and she quickly poured a cup for each of them, including Abby.

"I don't usually take tea, Ma'am," Abby said.

"You need to at least warm your hands on the cup, Abby," the teacher answered. "I'll put milk in yours and extra sugar, and you may like it."

Abby sipped and decided tea tasted like a dessert, it was so sweet. And the little cup did feel warm in her hands, which were starting to feel normal. The plate of pastries was passed around, and Rose was surprised to find that they weren't sweet at all.

"Savories, Rose," Ruthann said, seeing Rose's face. "The pastry isn't very sweet, and the filling is just a tad of mincemeat. I didn't know," she said, nodding in Mrs. Goodnow's direction, "you would have a winter picnic en route."

"It was delicious," Abby piped up. "Ab-so-lute-ly de-li-cious."

That made everyone laugh, relax, and all start talking at once. But they stopped when Ruthann held up her hand and announced that she hoped they would save the travel story for the dinner table, where they would be as soon as Joshua and Newton came through the door.

So they drank their tea and asked about the house and how Ruthann spent her days now that she didn't have a classroom occupying her. She said the farm was keeping her so busy she barely had time to think, and she also had one pupil who came every Wednesday afternoon after school to work on all of his subjects. He had come from a state way down south, she said, and he was lagging behind the children in his age group.

"Are the schools different there?" Rose wanted to know.

"For some children, yes," Ruthann answered. "Some of the schools are just as good as ours, but some others are nowhere near as good, and some don't even have books."

"I reckon those are the schools where the Negro children go," Edith Goodnow said.

Ruthann had been trying not to get into that, but she allowed as how her pupil was a Negro and had come from one of the schools where the few books they had were very old and had to be shared by twenty or thirty children. Everyone looked a little shocked at the idea that a town didn't take care of its school, no matter who went there.

"But I want to know what's going on in Eastborough," Ruthann said, trying again to change the subject. "I haven't been there in so long, and I'm way behind on everything." She looked at Rose with concern and added, "You all look well, so I trust the sudden nature of this visit doesn't bring bad news."

Rose started to speak, but stopped with her mouth halfway open. So Henry Goodnow, who had returned from the barn ahead of the other men, gave a small smile and allowed as how they had mostly been pining to see the farm, and that they would indeed have some things to discuss later on. "But for now," he said, "we'll just give you the gossip of the day."

So they each told a couple of stories about the way things were in Eastborough, and an hour went by before they heard the kitchen door open and the other men arrive. Abby jumped off the small stool where she was sitting and ran to greet Newton, but Rose suddenly felt shy and hoped her face wasn't going to turn as red as a cooked beet.

But Newton, once he had given Abby a hug, didn't even look her way. He moved toward the sink, rolled up his sleeves, and scrubbed his hands and arms. He dried them on the roller towel that hung from the wall and then came straight to her, leaning over the back of her chair and kissing her on the cheek. His hands were on her shoulders, pressing just enough to bring the familiar warmth to her face. She saw Abby wriggle a little in her seat, smiling with sheer delight, but the others went right on with their greetings and carefully paid no attention. She relaxed, looked up at him with a smile, and decided she should enjoy his welcome. After all, they all knew he was officially courting her.

"You men find a place at the table," Ruthann said, "and we'll bring in the food." Rose saw that tumblers had already been filled with water at the table and guessed Ruthann must have put in an extra leaf to seat all these people. Newton and Joshua led the way, pointing out a place for Henry Goodnow, and Ruthann took in the platter of chicken and dumplings, placing it in front of

Joshua. Abby brought the stack of plates that had been warming on the high shelf at the back of the Mansfield stove, and Rose carried the buttery parsnips and a basket of white bread. Newton pushed the butter dish and pickles aside to make room for the food, and patted the seat beside him, pulling the chair out a bit for her. So she sat and quickly discovered that his knee pressing against hers was going to be a considerable distraction during the meal.

"It's Rose's recipe," Ruthann announced, while Joshua served the chicken and dumplings. "And we didn't really need the bread with the dumplings, but you may want to sop up the sauce with it. It's such a good sauce."

"It's my favorite," Abby said, stopping abruptly when she realized she was very young to be talking at this table.

"And mine," Joshua added, handing her a plateful. "I could eat it once a week if my wife deigned to make it that often."

Rose looked around with wonder. Every face at this table was a happy face, and she could not remember being at a table with this many people when they were all pleased with the day. Picturing her father's house, where everyone was likely to keep his or her eyes on their plates, she sighed and immediately wished that sound had stayed inside her body. They all heard it and looked at her, then quickly looked away when Newton asked in a whisper, "Is everything all right?"

"I'm fine," she smiled, "just fine."

Everyone went back to chattering. Rose knew the

Goodnows were good friends of Ruthann's, but they didn't know Joshua well, so they were asking him one question after another about his family, the Jerseys, and how he happened to come to these parts. After a few minutes, silence fell over the table while everyone ate and then reached for chunks of bread, as Ruthann had foreseen, to sop up the thick sauce from the fricassee.

"This is mighty good," Henry Goodnow remarked as he passed his plate for seconds. "If I'd had any idea under the sun that Rose could produce such a dish, I would have put a kitchen in the back of the store months ago. Been wasting her talents with all the dusting and dressing up of those front windows."

"I reckon the windows were good for business, Henry," Edith chimed in. "You never sold as many mops in a year as you did in the two weeks after Rose did up that spring cleaning display last year."

"Ayuh," Henry replied. "But I'm thinking we could sell a few helps of chicken, too, for folks like Hattie Munson who aren't partial to doing much cooking themselves."

Abby still wasn't certain about speaking up. She was told to keep still at her own home, but Aunt and Uncle always included her. But she couldn't let this pass and burst out, "Rose is going to teach school, not cook chicken."

"So she is," Ruthann said, nodding her approval. "She can cook for us, Abby, but not for the world." Abby sat back, satisfied that this group wasn't trying to derail Rose the way Father had tried. She silently passed her plate for seconds.

Rose

When the meal was over, Newton asked Ruthann if Rose could be excused so he could show her his Jerseys. The teacher raised an eyebrow and asked, "In the dark?"

"Yes, Ma'am," he said, keeping a perfectly straight face. "I've waited months to introduce them."

"Get along, then, and take a lantern so she'll remember their faces in the morning," Ruthann laughed. "I reckon you'll be back in twenty minutes or so?"

"Yes, Ma'am," Newton said, and to Rose's disappointment, turned to Abby and asked if she'd like to go along.

"I want to see them in daylight," Abby said, her eyes dancing. "Besides, I will be taking Rose's place with the cleaning up here." As Newton and Rose went out the kitchen door, Joshua called after them, "Mind where you set that lantern down, young man. That barn is full of sawdust." That brought a deep chuckle from Henry Goodnow.

"I had to see you alone," Newton said, as they walked toward the barn. "I just had to."

"I'm happy that you had to," she answered. "And didn't Abby, Little Miss Mischief, know that? Did you see her, talking about joining the dishwashing?" She stopped walking, took the lantern from his hand, set it down in the snow, and said, "I think it can't start a fire there." And she turned up her face to kiss him, putting her arms around his back and holding on as if she would fall down if she let go.

"I love you, Rose," he said, placing several soft kisses

on her face, her eyes, and then, at last, on her mouth. They kissed gently at first, then with so much passion that Rose broke away and buried her face on his chest.

"Are you all right?" he asked anxiously.

"H-m-m-m-m," was all she could say, her head against his shoulder. He bent down and kissed her ear, exploring it with his tongue, and she moaned, thinking that if she died at this very minute, she would die happy. But it wasn't right, was it, she thought, and she pulled away.

"Let's meet the ladies," she said, and handed him the lantern.

Newton nodded, and they went on to the barn where he shone the light in the face of three startled cows, and introduced them as Flora, Moppet, and Louisa. Rose petted each one before they moved on to the iron bars that enclosed the bull's pen at the end of the barn. When the bull snorted at the sight of the swaying lantern, Rose jumped back and refused to go closer.

"He can't get out," Newton said. "But you are quite right to be wary. His disposition is not sweet."

"Quite formidable, I'd say," Rose commented. "And you and I better get back to the house before they send a search party to find out if we've been gored and stomped."

Newton laughed, but he took her hand and led the way out of the barn and back to the house, where they found Abby absorbed with a stereopticon that had several pictures of Niagara Falls, and the Goodnows deep in a game of euchre with Joshua and Ruthann, all of them still at the dining room table. Henry Goodnow played a card and then yawned such a yawn that Rose thought his tonsils must be showing. Then, one by one, everyone else started to yawn.

"It's catching," Abby said from her chair. "Yawning is just as catching as measles, but it doesn't hurt you."

"Yawning," Ruthann said, "means it's time to turn in," and she tossed her cards into the center of the table.

"Aw," Henry said, "just when I was winning."

"I was afraid of that," Ruthann said, smiling and pushing her chair back. Henry scooped up the deck of cards and stacked them neatly on the sideboard. It had been a long day, and he was more than ready for bed.

CHAPTER THIRTY-TWO
Joining the Links

Joshua showed Henry and Edith Goodnow to a small bedroom on the second floor of the house when they announced they needed to turn in. Ruthann and Rose followed with Abby, who would share a bed with Rose in the attic.

"It's cold up here," Ruthann said, "but there are lots of blankets on the bed, and I've taken the chill off the sheets with the bed warmer. You can snuggle in and make it even warmer for when Rose comes up. But she and I must talk awhile first. Will you be all right in the dark?"

"Oh, yes," Abby said, searching in their satchel for her nightdress. "And I used the bathroom."

"There's a chamber pot under the bed anyway, Abby," Ruthann said. "Just in case."

Abby wrinkled her nose and said she wanted no "in case." They waited while she undressed, put on her flannel nightgown, and clambered onto the bed. It was a four-poster, Rose saw, marveling at such a fine bed even in the attic, and the spool posts were shiny in the lamplight. She kissed her sister's forehead and whispered, "Thank you for not meeting the cows," which made Abby grin. Then she tucked her sister in and promised to be along a little later.

Downstairs, everyone had gone, so Rose and Ruthann settled themselves in front of the stove, and Ruthann said, "Henry tells me you have many decisions to make. I'm happy your questions brought you here, but I hope they're not too troubling."

"Oh, they're troubling," Rose said. "Life and death troubling."

"Oh, dear," Ruthann said. "If we're going to be here half the night, we'll have to crack some butternuts while we talk." She fetched two flatirons, two hammers, and three bowls, one of them full of butternuts.

"Nut meats in here," she said, pointing to one of the bowls. "Shells in the other empty bowl. And try not to send pieces all over the kitchen." She handed a hammer and flatiron to Rose, secured her iron upside down between her knees, and whacked a nut. Rose thought this was a strange way to have a visit, but she did as she was told.

"Now," Ruthann said, "let's get those troubling things out in the air and see what we can do to civilize them."

"I don't guess they're exactly wild," Rose said, smiling a little. "But troubling." And then, in a flood, she said, "It's Aunt Nell dying and me teaching and the teacher wanting the house and Newton wanting to get married and me and Abby at loose ends without a bed to sleep in."

"Life and death to be sure," Ruthann said. "I had no idea all those things were coming to a head at one time. Shall we start with Aunt Nell?"

So Rose recounted her whole talk with her aunt and the questions Nell Harris had posed and the answers she had tried to give. She tried to hold up, but she kept getting teary, and once her voice cracked completely when she said she didn't think her aunt would last through the summer. Ruthann went on cracking nuts and listening without interruption until she finished.

"Now you crack, and I'll talk," she said when Rose finally fell silent. "The troublesome thing is that every one of your questions is tied to the others, but it's a chain where the links can be arranged in several different ways. Perhaps we should look at how you might put the links together?"

Rose nodded, and Ruthann went on, "You are thinking that Nell's death is the biggest part of this problem, but perhaps it isn't. You are already quite certain that she cannot get better, and Dr. Potter has already told me that. It is very sad, and you will miss her, but you can't change that. One of the things you will learn about worrying is that it's a waste of time unless you can do something about it."

Rose frowned, then nodded again but said nothing.

"Now we'll go on to something you can change," she said, sounding so much like a teacher that Rose nearly smiled. "Marrying Newton. You could, you might, you don't have to."

"Oh," Rose said, leaning forward, "oh, yes, I do have to. He is the most important link of all." She sighed. "But I can't hook them properly."

"The only question, then, is when will you marry him?"

"After I teach a spell," Rose said right away. "I loved my days in the classroom, and I want to do it again. And once we are married, it's against the law."

"A foolish law, indeed," Ruthann said, "since it tosses a good deal of talent into the rubbish. But it is the law." Rose began to relax. The kitchen was warm. It was wonderful to have Ruthann listening and talking and sorting things out, even though she knew, in the end, that her friend would make her do the sorting herself. But right now, despite Nell's illness and the problem of where to live, she felt comfortable. She began to crack butternuts in earnest.

"Where to live," Ruthann said gently, knowing this would be the hardest part. Rose stiffened, her feeling of well-being dissolving in a cloud of fear. "Nell is quite right that you will be required to move soon. I would like nothing better than to keep you and Abby in my house, but it can't go on. I think you know that, Rose."

"I do," she answered, twisting her hands and keeping her eyes on her feet, which were sticking out from under her long skirt. "But where will we go?"

"You need to think about where you can't go, first. Not my house, not the Harris house. Henry and Edith would take you in for a short time—he's very partial to you, Rose—but they aren't up to having Abby as well. If you're teaching first, you can't move in with Newton."

That last made Rose laugh, but her smile quickly turned to a frown. "You left one out, Ruthann. You didn't say we couldn't live at Father's house." She hit a nut very hard, and chunks of shell flew onto the floor.

"That's true, Rose," Ruthann said, nodding and not smiling. "I didn't say that."

"I knew it would be one of those links," Rose said, her face as sorrowful as a hound dog's and her sigh so long that Ruthann wanted to put her arms around this wonderful girl and tell her to stay right where she was. But she couldn't. Newton was courting her, it would be dreadful if the town began to talk, and the two girls needed to get settled. Besides, before she could even imagine all these problems, the house had been promised to the new teacher.

Rose finally looked up, a tear on her cheek. She asked, "What would Sarah say?"

"You tell me," Ruthann answered.

"She would say," Rose said, speaking so slowly that the teacher thought it might be dawn before she finished, "that you have to make the best of it, whatever it might be. I reckon that might include moving back with Father. I 'spose because I walked out on Charles and Father that I must now make up for that." She had gone right on pounding butternuts while she spoke.

Ruthann took the iron away from Rose and took the girl's hands in hers, thinking how young she was to have such calluses on her palms. "You have nothing to make up, Rose, and Sarah Hibbard would never say that. She would say that you did right by Abby and the best you could on everything else." She shook Rose's hands a little, and the girl looked up. Ruthann went on, "I am not just saying that, Rose. I believe it. And I hope I haven't done this backwards, and made you feel terrible, but I did save one of the best parts until now because I wanted you to see these links clearly. And maybe," she said, her face softening, "maybe you'll see it as a solid silver lining."

"Sarah always talked about silver linings. But I see nothing silver in all this. I just see my mother's face at the end of her day in that house, her mouth a thin line, her eyes so tired. I don't want that."

"Certainly Newton is part of a silver lining, Rose," Ruthann chided. "Don't lose sight of that. But the big news is that Henry Goodnow has it on good authority that Miss Temple is taking a position in New York City, so the one-room schoolhouse will need a new teacher, and Ben Chandler is bound and determined that you be given the post."

Rose jumped out of her chair, and the "Yes" that came out of her mouth was so close to a scream that Ruthann feared everyone would be leaping out of their beds to see what was the matter.

"Hush, hush," she said. "You'll wake everyone, and we don't need them right now. And it's a good thing I took that iron away, or you would have broken your foot."

Rose sat down again, rocking back and forth, a real smile splitting her face for the first time that day. "If Mr. Chandler wants me there, will that make it happen?" she asked.

"I reckon it will," Ruthann said, delighted that her news had overshadowed everything else. "And perhaps you could then manage to live across the road? Only," she added quickly, "if you can reach a solid agreement with your father."

Rose thought a minute and said, so seriously that Ruthann felt a little teary herself, "He would have to promise to talk to us at table, treat us like adults, and never take to the drink again."

Except for the drinking part, Ruthann had not expected that answer. She was more concerned that Rose would find herself working her fingers to the bone and her mind to distraction once again. "I would also ask," she said gently, "that he get in a hired girl, and you, in turn, could promise a small bit of your pay toward the household."

"Oh, Ruthann," Rose said, sighing a happier kind of sigh, "that would make life easier, wouldn't it? But dare I ask for such a thing?"

It was Ruthann's turn to sigh. "You should dare to ask for just about anything, Rose, with what you've been through in the past. You can't go back there unless you have sorted out all kinds of things. It will, however, be precisely what Charles needs."

"I have worried about Charles," Rose admitted. "But he's managed nicely, I do believe. And then," she added eagerly, trying not to think too much about the impending discussion with her father, "I could teach awhile and then marry Newton and move out again."

"Indeed," Ruthann said, knowing that Newton's plan was to move his Jerseys to the Barnes place within the month. But she had told enough secrets for now, and that was Newton's to tell anyway. For some reason, and she couldn't put her finger on the why, she wanted Rose to decide on moving home before she found out that Newton would be just down the road seven days a week. She had been so reluctant to give up her teaching post, despite her feelings for Joshua, and now she wouldn't trade her new life for that desk, beloved though it had been.

Rose sat very still, thinking about the links. Even if Aunt could get better, she realized, they would still have to find another place for her and Abby to live. And she would be very happy to be under the same roof as Charles. She wished she had a father like Mr. Barnes, or Mr. Chandler, or Emily's pa. But she didn't. Sarah had loved him, she told herself. She had truly loved him.

"I must look for what Sarah saw," she said aloud.

"What does that mean?" Ruthann asked, puzzled. "I've lost your train of thought."

Rose laughed. "My thought train, Emily and Alice say, is forever heading for a siding, then returning, then going off again. It is not much like a train that's going somewhere."

"Oh, I think it's always going somewhere," Ruthann said, chuckling a little herself. "But it doesn't go from A to B with any regularity. It's not a train anyone should put on a timetable. So, what did you mean?"

"She loved Father," Rose said simply. "I need to look for the things that made her love him, because I don't."

Ruthann had no answer for that. She couldn't say Silas Hibbard was a fool for driving his daughters out of his house. The man had never seemed lovable to her, but she knew Rose was right. Something had to be in there, something that had made him stop drinking, build a bathroom, and put in a water system. Sarah Sherman Hibbard certainly had loved him and he had loved her. At least he was smart enough to do that. She stood, squeezed Rose's shoulders, and said if they didn't get themselves to bed, the menfolk would be getting up when they went in.

"Have we settled anything?" Ruthann asked anxiously as the two went toward the stairs.

"We've cracked enough nuts for a pie," Rose answered, "and the chain is put together. I just have to decide whether I want to be chained to it." But she smiled as she said it, and Ruthann knew they had made progress. "I feel better," Rose added. "It always feels better to talk to you."

CHAPTER THIRTY-THREE
Good Things in Threes

For the first time in several days, Rose slept so soundly that she hardly moved. About four in the morning, her snoring woke Abby, who remembered her mother saying she had to make Father move to stop what she called his "night noise." So she poked at her sister until Rose rolled over, and the noise stopped. It took Abby a few seconds to remember where she was, and she thought she heard a door close somewhere in the house, but she soon went back to sleep. Several hours later, both girls woke at the same time and saw daylight and blue sky through the tiny attic window. The attic was very cold, and while they lay there, snuggling under the covers, a mouse ran across the rafters over their heads and vanished at the edge of the roof.

"I hope that mouse wasn't in bed with us," Rose said solemnly, watching the space where the creature had disappeared.

"Rose!" Abby cried out. "If I sleep here another night, I'll feel its tail running over my leg!"

"And its little feet scuttling across your hair," Rose teased.

"Rose!" Abby said again. "You are being mean. A mouse doesn't sleep in a bed."

"You must admit it's quite cozy in here," Rose said. "But I do think you are right. He's probably more worried about us than we are about him. We invaded his territory last night."

"You are cheerful today," Abby commented. "But you snored and woke me up."

"I never did!" Rose said with alarm, thinking how dreadful it would be to get married and snore.

"Uh-huh," Abby said. "Loud. I poked you, and you stopped. Then I heard a door shut downstairs, and I went back to sleep."

"That was probably the men going to the barn, and we'd better get a move on, little sister, because it must be very late by now."

They scrambled out of bed and dressed quickly because the attic was indeed nearly as cold as it had been on the buggy ride. Rose pulled out the chamber pot, glanced at Abby, shook her head, and pushed it back under the bed. "We'll see if there's heat in the bathroom," she said.

They pulled the big quilts up on the bed, plumped up the lumpy pillows, and headed for the stairs. The second floor hall was empty, and all the doors were open, so Rose was starting to feel a little embarrassed about sleeping so long. Except, she remembered, it really wasn't. It was past what Newton called the witching hour when they went to bed, and the house was so quiet that she had heard the parlor clock strike one. She didn't think she had ever been up so late, except for that night when she went to see Emily and threw snowballs at her window.

In the kitchen, the station clock on the wall was chiming seven and Ruthann was washing dishes. She stopped as soon as she heard them. "Sleepyheads," she teased. "I reckon the sandman took extra pains with you two last night."

"We were the only ones in the attic, Miss Harty," Abby said. "I mean Mrs. Chittenden."

Rose and Ruthann laughed and quickly reassured Abby that the sandman was imaginary, but supposedly came and sprinkled sand on sleepers' eyelids, weighing them down so people stayed asleep.

Abby frowned. "I hate it when sand gets in my eyes." The other two merely laughed again, and Ruthann asked if they would like baked beans and fried ham for breakfast.

Abby frowned again. "I am not talking anymore. You people just laugh at me."

"With you," Rose said immediately. "Never at you, Abby. We just like your young view of the world. It's better than ours, really."

"Beans and ham, then," Abby said. "I never have that for breakfast, and it sounds like Saturday night dinner all over again. Except not last night."

"It's Joshua's favorite," Ruthann said, pushing the spider onto the hot part of the stove. Two thick slices of ham started to sizzle, giving off a tempting aroma. She pulled the bean pot out of the oven and took two warm plates down from the upper shelf at the back of the stove. She toasted two slices of bread, put them on the plates, and covered each with steaming beans. She added a slice of ham to each and gave the girls the plates.

"You'll find forks and knives at the table," she said. "As you may have figured already, the rest have eaten, and they are all at the barn visiting Jersey cows, even Edith."

"I'm anxious to see them in daylight," Rose said with her mouth half full. Staying up late apparently made a body very hungry. She couldn't remember when she had relished breakfast this much. Maybe it was because she hadn't prepared it. She wondered if men minded milking the cows every morning and every evening of their lives. She had never liked doing the same thing over and over, whether it was arithmetic or cooking breakfast. Except, she thought, for penmanship. She did like making those rows and rows of cursive letters, each one as identical as possible to the last. If she truly was going to be the teacher at the little school, she must try not to bore the children to death with drills. She hated drills, even though she knew they were part of learning.

"Rose?" Ruthann was saying. "Rose?" And Rose realized that the teacher had been trying to get her attention while her brain was wandering off.

"I beg your pardon," she said. "I didn't hear you."

"As usual," Abby muttered.

"Good news comes along with bad news," Ruthann

said. "I told you one piece of good news last night, and the next piece is also good, and for me very exciting. Joshua and I are expecting."

"Expecting what?" Abby said, and instantly realized she had made another mistake, but this time neither of the others laughed. Rose was on her feet and giving the teacher a big hug, saying over her shoulder to Abby, "Expecting a baby, Abby, a baby!"

Ruthann held Rose close, then stepped away, saying, "I can't tell you how pleased I am that you didn't think it was a new calf coming. We are quite excited about having a child, but sometimes I fear Joshua thinks it's going to be just like having another calf."

"Calves don't wear diapers, and they don't drink from bottles," Abby said, her self-confidence still a little shaky, but not wobbly enough to keep her from talking. The two women laughed again, but this time she didn't mind. A baby was much better than a calf any day. She reckoned Charles would prefer his calf, but she was glad no one had given her one.

"When?" Rose wanted to know.

"About the time the last apples are picked," Ruthann said ruefully. "But it's hard to find a good time at a farm, and at least we won't be snowbound."

"Does Newton know? Do the Goodnows know?" Rose asked.

"They all know, including the hired man," Ruthann said. "Now you two had better get yourselves to the barn to see the Jerseys because the Goodnows will be itching to get on the road again soon. I'm packing Edith's basket with some food to keep you going on the journey. And never mind the dishes," she added, as Rose and Abby both started to clear the table.

The sisters put on their warm wraps and headed out the door for the barn. Ruthann watched them go, arm in arm, and once again wondered at the way Rose handled one thing after another. It had occurred to the teacher that her mother always said a new person arrived in good time to replace a dying one, but she wouldn't spoil Rose's day by saying that aloud.

Once at the barn, Rose and Abby went along the stanchions, looking at one Jersey after another, all of them chewing hay that had been scattered in front of them. Behind the cows, Rose noticed two flat-tined manure forks hanging on hooks, along with some odd chains she didn't recognize. Over each cow's head was a hand-lettered sign with a name and a painted flower—different for each cow. Rose couldn't believe it. A yellow buttercup for Buttercup; a blue forget-me-not for Remembrance; a pink lady's slipper for Lady Jane. And so it went, through the herd of twenty-one.

Newton caught up with them as they reached a sign with small red berries and the name Wintergreen.

"Who made the signs?" Abby asked before even saying hello.

"Good morning, Abby. Good morning, Rose. Ruthann," Newton answered. "They're stenciled, same as she did on the parlor walls."

"Sorry, Newton. I didn't mean to be rude."

Newton gave her a pat on the head and kissed Rose

on the cheek, to Abby's delight. "Run along and find Joshua, Abby," he said. "I need to talk to Rose in private."

"I am certain of that," Abby said saucily. But she left them there at the end of the barn.

"Ruthann just told us about the baby," Rose said excitedly. "Isn't that the best news ever?"

"Mebbe," Newton said, "mebbe not. Best is what she told me about that teaching position at the little school, I figure. And you might warm up to one other piece of news as well."

"What's that?" Rose demanded, thinking this overnight trip had been rather overwhelming so far.

"I'm bringing my Jerseys to Eastborough in May and will be at home for the summer and into early fall. Then we'll bring them back here to breed, and I'll be working with Joshua again."

"Home? You're coming home?"

"I reckon," he answered, taking her hand in his. "You'll be in that schoolhouse some of the time, and I'll be in the barn and field some of the time, and some of the time we'll be sitting on a big rock I know about."

"And I'll bring you switchel in the hayfield so you won't pass out from the heat, and we'll have picnics at the rock—or even in the hayfield if you wanted lunch brought there," Rose said. "Oh, Newton, it will be the best spring and summer ever." But then her face clouded over. "Except Aunt Nell is going to die, Newton, she's going to die!" And despite all the good things that seemed to be falling into her lap, she started to cry and turned away from him, embarrassed by her own inability to hold up.

From behind her, Newton encircled her with his arms, despite the fact that he smelled like a cow barn. Rose didn't notice that. She just leaned back against him while he pressed his face into her hair and whispered, "You have to make peace with that, Rose. You have to accept it and help Abby and your uncle and, I reckon, even your father, as they try to deal with their loss. Please, Rose, don't cry. The cows will give sour milk, and Joshua will have my head on a pole."

"You are impossible," Rose said, turning toward him. But she had stifled her sobs at the very thought of the milk going bad. "They don't really think that way, do they?"

"Who?" Newton said, mystified.

"The cows," Rose said. "They don't get upset and curdle the milk, do they?"

"You are a most curious young lady," Newton said, throwing back his head and laughing so loudly that Abby reappeared to see what was happening.

"Just trying to learn about these precious cows," Rose retorted. "You seem to think they're quite thoughtful, so I reckoned they might be sensitive as well."

"Especially when they kick the bucket over," Newton said, still chuckling. "Very sensitive. And by the by, did you two sleep forever or eat the county's longest breakfast?"

"Both," Abby said promptly. "It was so cold in the attic that we couldn't get out of bed, and breakfast was so good we couldn't stop eating."

As they walked along, Newton kept pushing stray clumps of hay back into the trough in front of the animals, and pretty soon Abby was doing the same. At the end of the barn, Newton asked if she wanted to see the bull.

"Oh, yes," the little girl said, jumping up and down. "Is he ferocious?"

"First," Rose said, "I want to know what those chain things are in there with the manure forks."

"Tail holders," Newton said, grinning and waiting for Abby's next question.

"Whose tail?" she demanded.

"Cows' tails. So they don't swish in your face when you're milking. Some of them don't, but others make a habit of it."

"Yuck," Abby said. "That would feel terrible. And some of their tails aren't clean." Newton nodded and asked again about the bull. Rose and Abby said they were ready.

"You have to be very quiet near him," Newton said seriously. "He is not sweet-tempered, he startles easily, and Joshua will be in a swivet if we get him going. No hands inside the fence, Abby, and no talking or giggling."

"I rarely giggle," she answered loftily. "What's his name?"

"Lord Coopersmith," Newton said. "It's the name he

came with from England. They have roomfuls of royalty there: lords and earls and counts and duchesses, and of course, a queen."

"And a king?" Abby ventured.

"Actually," Rose said, "he's the Prince Consort rather than a king. His name is Albert, and he's married to Queen Victoria, who is very old and has been queen nearly forever."

They reached the bull's pen, and Abby peered between the iron bars that surrounded the bull. Inside that first fence was a second one, and behind that, the Jersey bull stood looking at them.

"He looks like cow royalty," Abby whispered. "He looks very proud of himself. Does he have a ring in his nose because he's royalty?" Newton choked down a laugh and said he'd explain later.

"Hush," Rose whispered. She could not wait to move on. She thought the bull quite formidable and the fences indicated that he needed something close to a prison to keep him from breaking out. Lord Coopersmith pawed the sawdust under his feet with one hoof, and both girls jumped, then quickly stepped back, afraid they might have bothered him. Newton took a large pumpkin from a pile by the bull's pen, quickly split it into pieces with a hatchet, and tossed the chunks into the pen. The bull moved slowly toward the food and started to eat.

"He's not a bad sort," Newton said softly. "He just leads an unhappy life except when he's with the cows."

"Why does that make him happy?" Abby wanted to know.

"Same reason it makes boys and girls happy," Newton answered quickly, noticing from the corner of his eye that Rose was still searching for an answer and starting to blush. He sighed, wishing it was easier for him and his girl to be happy. They were rarely alone for more than a few minutes anymore. It was as if Abby and the grown-ups were in a conspiracy to keep them from being by themselves.

"We should get back to the house, Abby," Rose said. "Will you come, Newton?"

"Best I do. You and the Goodnows will be heading off soon. Mr. Goodnow doesn't want to be on the road in the dark, and the sun goes to bed terrible early these days. Also, it's time for my third breakfast."

Abby looked from one to the other, eyes dancing, and said, "I'll run ahead and tell them you're coming. Will you want tea, Newton?"

"That would be just right, Abby," he answered, thinking she was a piece of mischief this one, but he might have been a little hard on her when he was wishing she'd vanish.

Off she went, and Newton immediately pulled Rose close and gave her a sweet kiss that quickly lengthened into a long kiss. "Sorry if I smell like a barn," he said. "You smell like lavender."

"It was in the sheets, I do believe," Rose said. "How long can we stay here, hiding in the barn?"

He kissed her again, then took her face in his hands and kissed her eyelids, her cheeks, and her neck. His hands moved to her back, and he pulled her very close.

She felt his hands move down to her bottom, and she gave a little shiver. Who knew that would be a sensitive spot? She had always considered sitting the only reason to even have a bottom. Now, despite all the winter clothing, she felt as close to him as she'd ever been. His body was so strong. She wriggled her hand up his back inside his jacket and then around to the front where she could feel his heart beating through his shirt. It was as fast as a puppy's, and she wondered if hers was doing the same. She unbuttoned the shirt and slid her hand inside, feeling his skin and chest hair. She felt him shudder, and he pulled away.

"Sorry," she said. "It's so warm in there."

"And you are a wicked, wicked girl," Newton said. "And I have come to like wickedness. But no more now. The herald has already announced our arrival."

Rose backed away, patted her hair, and rearranged her wrap. Newton buttoned his shirt, thinking she was a wonder, this girl of his, finding new ways to drive him a little crazy. Joshua had assured him his reactions to Rose were all to be expected, and had laughed when Newton said he sometimes wanted to jump in a cold river. "Might help," Joshua had said. "But only until the next time. You have some waiting to do, my friend."

Newton reached for Rose's hand and swung it back and forth as they walked to the house where Henry Goodnow already had the horse harnessed and the buggy ready to go. For this girl, he'd wait.

CHAPTER THIRTY-FOUR
Making a New List

Rose was so quiet on the ride back to Eastborough that Edith Goodnow craned her neck to see if all was well behind her. She saw that Abby had already fallen asleep, lulled by the rocking rhythm of the buggy, and Rose was staring straight ahead, her face expressionless. Edith reached as far as she could and patted Rose on the knee, giving her a reassuring smile and getting a small smile in return. Then she left the girl to her thoughts.

They were complicated thoughts. Rose always had lists in her head. Lists of things to do right away and things to do the next day or the next week. She had vocabulary lists stored in her head from school, and lists of the things on Mr. Goodnow's shelves so she could answer customers' questions quickly. Emily and Alice laughed at her lists, but Emily had confessed, just once, that she envied Rose the ability to have so much order in her brain. She said hers was more like a pudding, where each new ingredient was slowly absorbed until it was out of sight. She saw Rose's with all kinds of shelves and a desk with dozens of adorable drawers.

They had both laughed, but Rose went on keeping

those lists. And now, because of Aunt Nell and Ruthann, she was drawing up a list of the things she would want in place before she moved back home. She might well have to go, she realized, but she wasn't going on any terms except hers. She knew her father wanted her back—he had made that clear—but she feared he had no idea how much water had gone over the dam since the day she left. She was not the same girl, and she wasn't certain he knew that—or would accept that. But if he wasn't willing, she would find another way for her and Abby. She had done that before, at a time when she knew much less than she knew now, and she could do it again.

That much decided, Rose also succumbed to the pleasant movement of the buggy and the steady sound of the horse's hoofs on the frozen road, and dozed off. She woke when the buggy clattered through a covered bridge, and Henry Goodnow announced that they would stop a few rods along here and find out what the picnic basket had in store for them.

"I could eat a horse," he announced, "but that would not be practical at this time. So I'll settle for whatever Edith and Ruthann put together."

Minutes later, they reached a tiny hamlet, and he pulled into the driveway of a small church. Rose didn't remember seeing this village on the way to Chittenden farm, so she figured she must have been asleep at the time. Mr. Goodnow stepped down, threw the reins over the posts of the cemetery gate, and they all joined him. Edith produced chicken legs and buttered bread, and they ate hungrily. Mr. Goodnow stamped his feet while he ate and told the girls to follow his example or their feet would freeze up. So all four chewed and stamped. It was indeed chilly, but Rose had noticed that she couldn't see her breath, so she thought it couldn't be actually freezing weather.

The food took only a few minutes, and then they were on their way again, this time with Abby up front and Mrs. Goodnow next to Rose. "That way," Edith confided to Rose, "Henry can answer all her questions, and it will keep him awake. As for us, if you don't want to converse, that's fine. If you'd like to talk, go right ahead. I'm agreeable to either."

Rose laughed at the idea of Mrs. Goodnow putting Abby's perpetual questions to work and said she would be happy to talk if she could stay awake herself. So the two women conversed quietly, now and then hearing another of Abby's comments on the passing scene. Hours after leaving the Chittenden farm, they pulled into Eastborough and went directly to Ruthann's house, where Mr. Goodnow insisted on going in with the girls and making certain everything was in order. He lit a lamp in the kitchen, filled the wood stove and started the fire, and asked if they wanted a fire in the parlor stove as well. Rose thanked him and said that wasn't necessary. As he turned to go, she ran toward him, grabbing his sleeve and saying, "Mr. Goodnow, I can't ever thank you enough for taking us to Ruthann's. I didn't get much sleep, but I see the way now, the way to find answers for me and Abby. And Charles, too."

Henry looked down at her. "It was my pleasure, Rose, to help out in any way possible. You are a remarkable young lady, and Edith and I want your path to be smooth from now on. You are most welcome. Now, I assume you will get rested enough to be back in the store following school tomorrow?"

"Yes, sir," Rose said. "I'll be there. I will be leaving school a mite early because I have a visit to make, but I will come in only a few minutes late for my store work."

"Fine," Henry said, wondering if she was going to see Nell Harris again, but he wouldn't ask. She was such a private person, this Rose, so much in her head that no one really knew about until she decided to let something out. "Get a good night's sleep," he said, and then he was gone.

The girls did sleep well and went off to school the next morning as usual. But Rose asked her teacher if she could be dismissed early so she could visit her grandmother. Mr. Hawkes immediately granted her request and to her relief didn't ask any questions. She couldn't tell him Grandmother Jane was ill, because she wasn't. Nor explain why she needed to go there so suddenly of a Monday. But despite the fact that she didn't see Grandmother Jane often, she felt a need to do so now. She set off soon after lunch, and after walking for nearly a half hour, began the steep climb to the farm where her father had been born. When she reached the small house, she rapped on the door and without waiting for an answer, lifted the latch and went in.

Rose

"Now here's a sight for sore eyes," Grandmother Jane said from her chair by the window in the kitchen. "It's been a month of Sundays since you were here, Rose, and I am pleased as punch to see you."

Rose could never get over how many expressions her grandmother could tuck in to her ordinary conversation, all of them what Ruthann would call clichés—common and thus to be avoided. But she just smiled and said, "You are looking very well, Grandmother, and how is Grandfather?"

"Fit as a fiddle," the elderly woman said. "What brings you here?"

"Abby and I are living at the former teacher's house..."

"I know, I know," Jane Hibbard interrupted. "We're up here near heaven, but we get the news."

"Well, we have to move," Rose continued, "because the house is promised to the new teacher, and he's working out, so he wants to move his family to Eastborough."

"Aha! So the question is where do you girls go now, is that it?"

"In a word, Grandmother, yes."

"I like your style, young lady. You have grown up a good deal since you left Silas, and it becomes you. I suspect you may have a plan in mind?"

"Yes," Rose said, and then hesitated. "I am thinking about going back to Father's house."

"Dear God in heaven, why would you do that?" the old lady asked.

Making a New List

"We do not have a multitude of choices," Rose said. "Aunt Nell is too ill to take us, and I haven't enough money to rent rooms for us."

"I know something about what sent you away from that house, Rose, and I wonder at your thinking now. Has that son of mine tightened his bolts at last, enough so you'd now feel easy about taking Abigail there?"

The idea of her father tightening his bolts made Rose grin suddenly. She hadn't realized that her grandmother had such a clear picture of the story. "I think he's holding together now, Grandmother," she answered. "He's sober, he's a deputy sheriff, Miss Graves has moved on, and he put in a toilet, sink, and bathtub with hot and cold running water."

Jane Hibbard started to chuckle, which set her little white curls to dancing. "That's quite a list, young lady. But the real question is how he's going to treat you. A little bird told me you might be teaching by the fall term, and you can't do that along with the washing, the cleaning, and the cooking, the way you were doing before."

Almost speechless that her grandmother knew even that, Rose said very softly, "I thought I'd draw up a list of conditions." She had always been a little in awe of this grandparent, who spoke her mind quickly on every subject, and she was quite unsure of how her idea would be received.

"An end-of-the-war treaty as it were?"

"A truce, at least," Rose said, laughing with relief. "Pardon me, Grandmother, I know this isn't an amusing matter, but you put it in such an interesting way."

"I know him, Rose, better than you do, I expect. He's a good man, but he has blind spots, and you will need to shine a light on those before you agree to go back. He'll want you there, that's certain. But he can't expect you to be Sarah, the way he did before."

"And I don't want to be Sarah. I tried to do that, and it was a poor plan on my part," Rose said. She started to get up and added, "Thank you, Grandmother, especially for the parts about bolts and blind spots. I will be looking out for both. Now I must get to the store and help Mr. Goodnow. I did need to see you."

"Testing the waters, eh?" Jane Hibbard asked. "You have my approval for whatever you can work out. Just work it out before you move under that roof again. Don't make the move because you feel guilty about Charles. He's quite all right. As for Silas, he will take you on almost any terms, I reckon, but he has to know what they are. No point in jumping from the frying pan into the fire."

Another one of those clichés, Rose thought, as she bent to kiss her grandmother's wrinkled cheek, which was as soft as rose petals, but she was right. Jane Hibbard reached out both hands, taking Rose's in hers. "You pike right back here if you run into any trouble," she said. "We haven't room to house you, nor means, but we could put all three of you up somehow for a fortnight, if your truce talks drag on."

That made Rose laugh again. She squeezed her grandmother's gnarled fingers gently, not knowing if they were painful and wondering how she went on knitting with them, and said she would let herself out. She skipped most of the way down the hill and along to the store, where she arrived so out of breath that Mr. Goodnow ordered her to sit on one of the barrels by the stove.

"I had to see Grandmother Jane," Rose explained, gasping a little. "Sorry I'm late."

"You'll make up for it before you go, little doubt about that," he answered. "Not thinking of moving up to Hibbards' Hill are you? Or am I prying by asking?"

"You can ask anything you want, sir," Rose said. "She was pleased as punch to see me, said it had been a month of Sundays, and she'd take us for a few days if it came to that."

"Put a few of her favorite phrases on you, did she," Henry said. "She sounds like an old book sometimes, but she's as levelheaded as they come."

"Yes, sir," Rose said, getting up and starting to attend to her store duties. She didn't want to talk about this anymore, not even to the storekeeper. She was sorting things out in her head, and it wasn't coming easy.

Just before the store closed, she came back to the counter and asked Mr. Goodnow if he would be willing to get her father to the store so she could talk to him day after next.

"I reckon I could," Henry said. "But what would be the purpose of that?"

"I need to speak to him privately but not alone," Rose said, feeling a little sheepish. "If you are nearby, he'll be calm, and if he's calm, I think he will listen. He does have such an awful temper when it blows up."

"Certainly could ruin a decent conversation," he said, nodding. "I'll figure out something. You'll be ready for this encounter by midweek?"

"I have to be," Rose said, her mouth suddenly in a thin line and her eyes dark. "I must be."

Henry Goodnow knew when to end a conversation, so he announced that it was time for him to sort the day's mail, and he disappeared into the corner where he kept the mailbag. He heard a small crash as several objects fell to the floor in the main part of the store, but he didn't come out to look. He knew Rose would take care of whatever she had disturbed. Probably not paying as close attention as usual, he thought.

That was exactly it. When Rose's feather duster sent several tins of biscuits and a few seed packets to the floor, she stopped thinking about meeting her father and started watching what she was doing. But she still had a knot in her stomach, a twist of worry that she couldn't get rid of. So in a few minutes, she carefully let part of her mind wander to the list of things she would present to Silas Hibbard.

By the time she went home to the teacher's house, she knew what she wanted from her father, and once she and Abby had their supper, she sat down at Ruthann's desk and wrote them out. Not long after sunset, she told Abby she was really tuckered out, and the two sisters went up to bed, snuffing out their lantern much earlier than they usually did.

Ordinarily, if they went to bed at the same time, they chatted before falling asleep. But Abby, who knew her sister as well as Emily and Alice did, had a feeling this wasn't the time. So she said her nighttime prayer to herself, said good night to Rose, and rolled over. In a few minutes, she heard Rose breathing softly and evenly and knew she was asleep. She slipped out of bed and went to the window to see if any stars had appeared, and when she finally found one, she wished she and Rose and Newton and Charles would live happily ever after. That was how her favorite fairy tale books always ended, and she reckoned she could deserved the same, even if she wasn't a princess.

The next morning, Abby was relieved to see Rose looking her usual self, making the breakfast and getting the two of them ready for school. But when she came home from school in the late afternoon, Rose was already there and didn't even look up from the sheet of paper she was studying.

"Rose?" Abby said softly. "Rose?"

"Sorry, Abby. I was reading."

"Noticed that," Abby said. "Is everything all right?"

"I am hoping it will be soon, Abby. I am trying to take care of our future."

"Does our future include supper?" Abby asked.

Rose smiled at that and put the paper aside. "Of course it does," she said. "Let's see what's in the icebox."

When they sat down at the table an hour or so later, Rose told Abby she had high hopes they would be moving back to their father's house so the new teacher could take his place in Ruthann's house. She saw a look of near fright cross the little girl's face, and she quickly added, "But we will have new rules, and everything will be all right. Father has turned a corner in his life, and it's time for us to do the same."

"I think I like straight roads better," Abby answered. "I can't see around corners."

Rose had to admit that this was true. No one could see around corners until they went around them. But life, she told Abby, has lots of turns. "We have to take some of them, like it or not, and we look for others," she said. "You said you wanted to be under the same roof with me and Charles, and I think this is the turn we need to take. I have a plan that will make it work with all of us, including Father."

"I wished on a star last night," Abby said. "And if this is the answer to my wish, then I will just do whatever you say."

"You mustn't tell your wish, Abby," Rose cautioned. "It only comes true when you keep it a secret. And what were you doing out of bed, anyway?"

Abby laughed. "You were asleep. I knew I could find the first star, so I went to look."

Rose shook her head. Every time she thought she knew all about Abby she had another surprise. But she was glad she had talked to her about the stars. They were one of the hand-me-downs from Sarah, and she had to remember all of those so Abby would never forget their mother.

CHAPTER THIRTY-FIVE
Confronting Demons

Rose fidgeted in her seat at school. In her skirt pocket was what she thought of as her personal declaration of independence. She wasn't sure it would bring life, liberty, and the pursuit of happiness, but she had her hopes. Aunt Nell, Ruthann, and Grandmother Jane had made it clear that she needed to do something dramatic, not just pack her things and walk back into the house. But none of them would be there this afternoon when she came face to face with her father and presented her plan.

Maybe the waiting was the worst part, she tried to tell herself. It certainly wasn't good. What had started out as a barely noticeable tweak in her stomach had turned into a dreadful tight feeling. She'd been unable to swallow a bite of her lunch. Why, she wondered, does talking to a blood relative turn one's whole system upside down. What if aunt, friend, and grandmother were wrong? Perhaps she should have bought train tickets for herself and Abby and Charles and disappeared into the west the way Clara Harris had.

Well, at least she had stopped at the Harris' house the day before, found Uncle in his workshop, and asked about Clara. Her question had taken him by surprise, but he answered her. It turned out that they heard from their daughter several times a year but didn't speak of it because it was so hard being separated from her. A letter had come a fortnight ago, and Uncle had written back to tell Clara of her mother's illness. He didn't seem to think she would come all the way from California, but he expected she'd write Nell direct. Rose had taken his hand and squeezed it as hard as she could, unable to speak. Then he had turned back to the table he was making, and she had left.

She should have asked him to tell Aunt that she was about to have the talk with her father, but the idea had flown out of her mind when he started talking about Clara. She'd go there after it was over and report the results, she decided, whether it came out right or not. If he lost his temper and told her she wasn't to set foot in his house ever again, she would tell Aunt Nell. Rose didn't think her aunt, sick or well, was ever shaken by anything.

When the bell rang for dismissal, Rose realized that the teacher had mostly ignored her from the lunch recess on. It was just as well. She had mechanically done her written work, but she had paid almost no attention to what he was saying. Now she hurried to the cloakroom and found her wrap, hoping she could get out the door

Confronting Demons

and down the steps before Emily and Alice caught up with her. She couldn't tell them what she was about to do, and she needed time to get her thoughts in perfect order. As she almost ran down the road, she heard Emily call her name, but she didn't turn around.

As she neared the store, she slowed down to catch her breath, thinking that she wouldn't be able to speak a word in the event that Father was already there. She had no idea how Mr. Goodnow would get him to come, but she was sure he would not fail her. She lifted the latch, already feeling as apprehensive as someone about to recite for the first time in school, and was relieved to see that the store was apparently empty.

Henry Goodnow emerged from his post office corner to greet her and said, "He'll be along in an hour or less, Rose. He's coming in to have a look at the looking glass we brought in for bathrooms."

Rose smiled her thanks and went to put her wrap away. She fingered the paper in her pocket but decided not to look at it again. Instead, she picked up her duster and started making her usual rounds of the various shelves, straightening items as she went.

"Shall I disappear when he comes, Rose? Or stay within sight but not hearing? What is it you need?"

Rose sighed. "I honestly am not certain, sir," she said. "In sight, at least, I think. And you'll have to show him the looking glass."

"Whatever suits you," he answered, hoping that whatever this was it would turn out all right for Rose.

When the latch clicked a few minutes later, Rose

jumped but did not turn around. She heard her father speak to Mr. Goodnow, who immediately started telling Silas Hibbard about the need for a good mirror in a bathroom. The two moved off to have a look at the two different styles Henry Goodnow had purchased, and Rose pulled out her piece of paper and unfolded it.

She had titled the page "Rose's Declaration of Independence." Under that, she had listed the conditions of her return to the Hibbard house and the role she was prepared to assume there.

When the two men came back toward the counter where Mr. Goodnow kept his cash box, she was waiting for them.

"Hello, Rose," Silas said. "I trust you are well?"

"I am very well, Father," Rose answered. "And I need to speak with you if you have a few moments."

Somewhat puzzled, since his daughter had rarely sought contact for months now, Silas Hibbard told her he had a world of time, as long as he wasn't late for milking. "Chickens can always wait, Rose, but cows can't."

She nodded, and her voice was almost steady when she said, "Father, I would like to move back to your house with Abby, but some things need to be settled…"

"Move back?" Silas interrupted, his voice almost booming. "That would be a godsend, indeed!"

"As I started to say, Father, some things need to be settled before that happens," Rose persisted.

"Such as?" he asked, a note of suspicion entering his voice.

"Such as what I will do and what you will do," Rose

said, her voice firmer. Ten feet away, Henry Goodnow's eyes widened as he listened. This girl never ceased to amaze him. Just when he decided she had reached the top of the haystack, she made the stack higher and scaled it. She was going to tell Silas Hibbard what to do, and Henry couldn't think of anyone else in town with the gumption to do that. Well, maybe Del Potter. He had a feeling the doctor had given Silas what for somewhere along the way. Rumor had it that Silas's illness after the tent meeting was connected to drink, not disease, but there had been no talk since then, and everyone knew asking the doc about it was as useless as asking a live clam.

"Get on with it," Silas said gruffly, concentrating on keeping his tone even. He had no desire to make a mistake now, not after all these months. If Sarah were here, she would listen, he told himself, and he must do it her way.

"I've written it all out, so you can take it and think on it," Rose said. "But I would like to say it, too, while we are face to face. If we come back, I will not be the hired—actually, unhired," she said with a hint of a smile—"girl in the house. I will do my share of household work, as will Abby, but you will need a hired girl. I suggest Mehitabel, who needs the work, and is, if I hear right, dependable and pleasant."

Silas cleared his throat and started to speak, but Rose shook her head, so he said nothing.

She went on. "You will need her at least three days a week to clean, do laundry, help with cooking and preserving, make soap, et cetera. In the fall, you may need her for four or five days because I will be the new teacher at the one-room school."

"Four or five days?" Silas almost gasped the words. "That will cost a pretty penny." And then, suddenly digesting the rest of what she had said, he added, "And you'll be a full-time teacher? Right across the road? Now that, Rose, that is splendid news, and I'm proud to hear it." He started to move toward her but stopped, realizing she was not finished.

"Pretty or not, the pennies will be needed," Rose said. "And for my part, I will contribute part of my teacher pay toward her wages. In addition, we will have no alcohol of any kind in the house, nor will anyone imbibe elsewhere."

"Agreed, Rose," Silas interrupted again. "Never again, Rose."

"I want to believe you, Father, but you have let us down in the past, so I am uncertain about your resolve."

Her eyes never wavered from his face as she spoke. It was Silas who broke the connection and looked over her head and out the store windows into the street. On the other side of the store, Henry Goodnow was thinking he would probably faint about now if he were a fainting sort. He stood stock still, not wanting to make a floorboard creak for fear he would interrupt this drama.

When her father looked back at her, Rose went on to say that she would be in charge of bringing up both Abby and Charles in the way that she felt Sarah would have done, and that she expected him to give his opinions on that but not make rules for them. She said she expected that all cash money that came into the house would be put in her care, and that she would keep the accounts for what came in and what was owed at the store and elsewhere.

"In addition," she said, "you gave your consent for Newton Barnes to court me, and I expect that will continue until such time as I give up my teaching position and marry him."

"Has he asked you?" Silas demanded, his voice strong again.

"Not exactly," Rose answered. "But it is part of the plan. And when that time comes and I move on, you must agree to renegotiate all of this so I will not worry about my brother and sister."

Silas' chin dropped almost to his chest, and Henry nearly stopped breathing, wondering if the fireworks were about to begin. Rose's father stood perfectly still for what seemed like several minutes but was actually only a few seconds. Then he looked at her. He held out both hands, and she hesitated, then took them in hers, still watching him intently.

"Whatever you want or need, Rose," he said softly. "Your mother must have turned in her grave when I was all at sixes and sevens after she passed, and I cannot tell you how I feel about your willingness to forgive me and create a new path for us. We will welcome you back as soon as you are ready. And if Henry here thinks as highly of Mehitabel as you do, I will set out to see her in the morning and make arrangements, if she is willing."

"I don't know that I've really forgiven anything, Father," Rose said. "That might have to wait a spell. But I believe it's time to move on, and I want you to read what I've written before you give a final answer. And one other thing, which I didn't put in here, is that I hope we will find our way to smile and talk at table." Then she handed him the paper, and his eyebrows nearly met his hairline when he saw "Rose's Declaration of Independence" across the top of the page.

"Anyone else read this?" he asked. "The teacher? Nell?"

"Not a soul," Rose answered.

"Well, I'll be damned," he said. And without another word, he strode to the door and pushed down so hard on the latch that Rose was waiting for him to slam the door. But he went out, closing it so softly behind him that only the final click made a sound.

Rose watched him go and let out a long breath. "Thank you, Mr. Goodnow," she said. Turning away, she took her little key from her pocket and went to her postbox to see if she had any mail.

CHAPTER THIRTY-SIX
Ever After

On a beautiful June day, Mehitabel was in the yard hanging up an enormous load of washing, and Rose was in the Hibbard kitchen assembling a small picnic. It was the third sunny day in two weeks, so the men were raking hay as if their lives depended on it, and every woman in town was scrubbing clothes and getting them outside to dry. Rose was surprised at how quickly Mehitabel had created a place for herself in the house, quietly working at whatever needed to be done and always cheerful. And it had turned out to be quite easy for her and Abby to move back. The first night in her old room was a little strange, but then she had settled into the space as if she had never left it. Her quilt had followed her to Miss Harty's and back again, a familiar blanket to snuggle in.

Father had taken her Declaration of Independence to heart and followed everything in it to the letter, beyond her greatest hopes. And even after nearly two months, Charles was still wriggling in his seat at the table because he was so pleased not to be cooking and to have people to talk to. She had known all along that it had made life hard for him when she and Abby left, but he had managed. She supposed his relief at not keeping his end up alone was why he caused the one problem they'd faced. Or maybe he was merely a boy being a boy.

He had gone to school and then went off fishing without thoroughly mucking out his calf's pen and without giving the animal fresh water. Rose shivered a little just thinking about how furious Father had been when he heard the calf blatting and found the messy stall and the empty water trough.

"Deserves a good thrashing," Silas told Rose, pounding his fist on the kitchen table. "I expect your declaration document doesn't allow for that, but no one in my family is going to abuse an animal while I'm still breathing. He's even late for feeding that young un, so I took care of that, too. Where in tarnation is he?"

"No thrashing, Father," Rose answered, her chin jutting out just a bit. She had hoped never to have one of these encounters, but she realized Charles wasn't ready for sainthood yet, despite the easy relationship he seemed to have with their father. Until today. He'd regain his place, she knew that, but right now she needed to remind her father that she was in charge of the children.

"He went off fishing with one of the other boys, but I never dreamt he hadn't taken care of his chores this morning or after school. I will find a serious punishment for him, Father," she went on, more calmly than she felt. "None of us approves of anyone neglecting or hurting an animal, whether it's horse, calf, or cat." She wondered if her father even remembered the day he had kicked Sarah's cat. She reckoned the memory was long gone.

"You do that," Silas Hibbard said. "And I would appreciate knowing the details of the punishment. If he's to be thrashed, I'll take care of it, not with any pleasure, but to spare you. In the meanwhile, I have cleaned that pen and given the calf water and feed. Most of the time Charles is besotted with the animal, so I can't fathom his going off scatterbrained like this."

That was the very minute the door had opened and Charles bounced in, holding up two beautiful trout. Before he could speak, Silas' hand shot out and grabbed him by the collar. As he lifted him off the floor, Rose took hold of her father's arm and shouted, "Leave him be!"

Silas took one look at her face, dropped the boy, and headed for the door, slamming it hard as he went out. Charles had sunk into one of the kitchen rockers, a bewildered look on his face. But it cleared immediately when Rose explained what had happened. He jumped up and said, "I clean forgot, Rose, I just forgot. How could I forget? And this morning I was late, so..."

"You've broken a trust, Charles," Rose had said in her most schoolmarmish voice. "The calf has been properly seen to by your father, and I'm to see to you. While I think on your punishment, you clean your fish and then go to your room and write down what you think a suitable penalty might be. Thrashing has been suggested, but thrashing is not going to happen."

She was stunned by the proposal he brought back to her. He said he would apologize to Father and to the calf, and then the calf must be sold because he no longer deserved to have her. Rose accepted the apology idea but vetoed the sale on the basis that it would punish the calf as much as Charles. Knowing very well how Charles felt about killing chickens, she said he would have to assist with killing two chickens here and two at Uncle Jason's whenever the next four chickens were to be dispatched.

Charles had looked at her in horror but said nothing. The one time he had helped Father kill a chicken he had been sick to his stomach. But he had left a calf hungry and thirsty, and he knew what a bad thing that was. So he had gone out to find his father and make his first apology. When Rose told her father about the punishment, he had nodded his approval and said the apology had taken place and he had overheard the boy telling the calf how sorry he was, half sobbing the words.

"He called her Ruthann, Rose," Silas had reported. "He named that calf after the teacher. It took me a few minutes of listening before I got it through my head that he had actually named a calf after Ruthann Harty. At first I thought he was pleading to the teacher for help or some such. Judas Priest, what will that boy think of next?"

It had all been settled quickly, but Rose knew it was a close one, that Father had nearly forgotten his promise to let her rear the children. A few days later he came into Mr. Goodnow's one afternoon to purchase one of the small American flags that were always in stock. He presented it to her and told her to hang it in the kitchen.

"If I am about to violate that Declaration of Independence, you wave that flag at me. Or if I have already violated it, take it down so I'll know when I come in," he said. "I may lose my temper, but I don't plan to lose it with you. I never raised my voice to your mother, even though I didn't always do right by her." He turned to go out, looked back at her over his shoulder and muttered, "And I'm sorry about the cat."

So he had remembered, and she had received an apology of her own. But she knew her mother wouldn't have liked the way she had dropped the cat into the conversation. It was a little mean, and Sarah Hibbard hadn't approved of meanness. She did think the whole idea of the flag was both sound and quite funny.

Rose finished filling the basket, took the jar of ginger milk out of the icebox and wrapped it in newspaper to keep it as cold as possible. She headed down the stairs to the backyard, where Mehitabel had just hung up several pieces of Rose's underwear on an outside line. Rose hurried over to have a word with her.

"We hang all of the unmentionables on the inside lines, Mehitabel, and sheets or work pants or men's shirts on the outside."

Mehitabel laughed as she unpinned Rose's drawers and a petticoat, and disappeared behind some larger items to hang them where no passersby could see them.

"Everyone knows what we wear, Rose," she called over her shoulder. "But I'm glad to hide your things if that's what you want."

"Thank you, Mehitabel. Father will be in for the noon meal, I believe, but I am taking a picnic basket for me and Newton. You'll take care of his food?"

"I had it in mind, Rose. He'll want bread and tea, and mebbe some of that cold roast beef with the fresh horse-radish?"

"And a piece of pie, Mehitabel, don't forget the pie."

As she walked quickly to the hayfield, swinging the basket and humming, she realized she was having a particularly pleasant day and that her life had smoothed out a fair amount in the past couple of months. Except for Aunt Nell's illness, things were going well. She would stop to see her aunt on the way home, even though she had to talk through a window now that the whole town knew she had consumption. Dr. Potter had said some folks doubted it was contagious, but he felt it could be and he wanted no visitors. So Jason fixed up a comfortable place by the window, and that's where Nell entertained. He had put a little hook on the outside frame so the visitor could lift the window, as Nell was often too weak to manage that these days.

When Rose reported the decisions she had made after the Chittenden farm visit, Nell had been so pleased that she had figured things out, apparently without giving an inch to Silas, although Rose had provided no details. It was Henry Goodnow who came by, swore Nell to secrecy and then told her, nearly word for word, about the father and daughter meeting at his store. Unless Rose said something, Nell would never let on that she knew the whole story, but she could not have been prouder of her sister's daughter.

The sight of Newton on the tedder interrupted Rose's thoughts. She liked the way the little forks on the rake flicked the green grass as the horse moved along the swaths. If the sun lasted another day or two, Newton would be on the dump rake, dragging the grass and then releasing it in piles that could be pitched into the wagon and taken to the barn. He made a turn, saw her coming across the newly mowed field, and pointed to two large trees in the hedgerow. That must be the picnic spot, she thought.

"I'm nearly as messy as you were the day you made soap with Ruthann," Newton said, climbing down from the tedder and tossing the reins over a fence post. His arms and hands were covered with hayseeds, but when he tried to brush them off, he found sweat had glued them in place.

"I brought a damp dishcloth in case you wanted to wipe your hands," Rose offered.

"That was brilliant," he answered, taking the cool cloth and rubbing his face and hands with it. "Much better," he said. "I'm nearly ready for a square dance."

"The cicadas don't make the right kind of music," she answered. "Best you eat instead." So they sat in the shade under the two trees and shared what she had brought. Newton took no time at all to empty his first mug of ginger milk, which they both knew would protect him against the heat and humidity. With a mustache of milk around his mouth, he smiled at her and said, "That's not a drink I want at any other time, but it's just right for haying."

"Mother made it by the gallon every year," Rose said. "But why did I see your father leaving with his horse and mowing machine?" Rose said.

"They're so organized, Rose, it's almost scary. They have this thing set up better than a firemen's bucket brigade. We just move along farm to farm and get everyone's haying done, something they figured out over the winter. This way the equipment gets used with efficiency, and if the weather holds, everyone's hay will be in the right barn on time. This is a good town for a farmer, and I hope to be one of them soon."

"What's soon?" Rose asked.

"Soon as I own ten Jerseys and you say yes with no intermissions," he answered without missing a beat.

"I'll say yes before you have ten Jerseys if that means you'll get them faster," Rose countered.

"And the teaching job?"

"I'll be teaching this year," Rose said. "But I'm sixteen

now, and Charles is fourteen, and he and Abby don't need me as much. So when I'm seventeen…"

"When you're seventeen, what?" Newton asked in a voice so serious that Rose paused for a long minute.

"I'll say yes."

"You could say it now."

"Yes."

"Yes, what?"

"Yes, I could say it now. And this is such a wonderful day that I will. Yes."

Newton stared at her. She saw his mouth move, but no words came out. She saw his eyes get all watery and still he said nothing. Then he hitched toward her without getting up, knocked off her large straw hat, and dropped his head on her shoulder. Trying not to overturn the tin plate in her lap, she put her arms around him and held him; sweaty, hayseed-filled shirt and all. Then he lifted his head, stroked her cheek with his hand and said, "Yes. All those words you know, and I reckon yes is the greatest one you ever spoke." He sat up, looked around at the sharp stubble on the field, the horses and the sweat-soaked men some distance off, and added, "And in such a romantic place. I had thought to propose on your rock with leaves rustling, chickadees calling to each other, and the river rippling off in the distance."

"You can ask me again there," Rose said, smiling at this rare outburst of poetic talk and so happy she was barely able to sit still.

"Never," Newton said. "You might change your mind."

"Never," Rose said. "No matter how many times you ask. Now I think you'd better take a handful of those strawberries and get back to the tedding or the men will think you're shirking."

"Little do they know how long and hard I've worked at prying out that small word," Newton said. But he stood, took some berries, and strode off toward the waiting horse and tedder. A few rods away he looked back and said, "The rock? About dusk?"

"Yes," Rose said, and surprised herself by giggling. She was sixteen, and she was engaged to be married, and her answer had made Newton all teary. She'd ask him tonight about telling Aunt Nell. Feeling a little light-headed by all that had happened, she retrieved her hat, gathered up the remains of the lunch and headed back to the house. Sixteen and engaged. It went through her head over and over, like some lesson she was trying to learn. She couldn't stop to see Aunt Nell now. She had to tell Charles and Abby first, and she knew it would be impossible to keep this secret from her aunt if they were sitting there on opposite sides of the open window.

So many secrets and so many people she'd like to tell. She'd never told anyone about the Declaration of Independence. She and Father had never told Charles they knew about the calf's name, but they had laughed together over the idea of the teacher having a bovine namesake, and Rose wondered if it would betray Charles if she wrote Ruthann about it. He was funny, but he was thoughtful, too. Rose was certain Charles was the one who had planned for her birthday. He and Father and

Abby had put their heads together and refused to talk with her about it. They asked Mehitabel to make the dinner, and they invited not only Newton but his parents. It was out of the question for Ruthann and Joshua to come since it was planting time, and in addition, Ruthann was expecting and not feeling well some of the time.

So she had turned sixteen, and that very day she had reckoned she was now old enough to be engaged. She had sometimes considered herself engaged before, but this was different. It was real. She hadn't kissed him out there in the hayfield, and she felt certain that people usually kissed when they became engaged. But she couldn't manage it in bright sunshine with any or all of those men possibly looking their way. She would wait until they met at her rock that night. It wasn't Saturday, but she hoped Newton would be moved to take a bath before then.

At home, she did up the few dishes from her lunch basket, poked up the fire even though it was hot, and set three flatirons on the stove. She set up the ironing board, telling herself that many of those clean clothes on the line would need to be ironed. Besides, she had to press a skirt to wear to the rock that night. She feared the afternoon might last forever if she didn't put her hand to something practical, something where she had to pay attention to what she was doing.

So she ironed. She couldn't help humming as she worked, and occasionally she sang out loud. It didn't matter. The house was empty, and she could dance if

Rose

she wanted to, just dance from the joy of saying yes to Newton and seeing the look on his tanned face. Instead, she carefully ironed the ruffles on Abby's new dress, the collar and cuffs on Charles' Sunday shirt and her father's work clothes, but her mind was on Newton and the evening ahead.

"Will Miss Harty's rules change for engaged people?" she asked herself. She thought not, and she had no way to find out, at least not quickly. "Will Newton think he must ask Father for my hand?" And if he intended to do that, she wondered if she would have to tell him about the Declaration of Independence. She was not, it seemed to her, one of Father's possessions, so he need not be asked to "give her away," as they apparently said at every wedding.

She had freshly ironed clothes hanging on every chair in the kitchen and the front room by the time Charles and Abby came in from taking care of the calf and the chickens. Charles had also been helping with haying, and to Rose's dismay, his first words were, "What were you and Newton up to over there lolling under the tree?"

"What's lolling?" Abby asked.

"Lying about," Charles said. "Certainly not sitting up straight and eating lunch. I saw you. I even think he might have kissed you there, in broad daylight and in front of people."

"So, Charles," Rose answered quickly, "is it worse to kiss in the dark when alone? Does it matter whether there's a crowd about or whether the sun is up?"

"Aha," Charles said. "So he did kiss you. I hope Father didn't see that, or you'll be the one getting the thrashing."

"Maybe suitors are allowed to do that," Abby said. "Are they, Rose?"

"Day or night," Rose answered, "but not in church, not in school, and never in front of grandmothers."

"That would set Old Blockhead off, now wouldn't it?" Charles asked. That made all three laugh. They could not imagine boys kissing girls in any of those places.

"I for one, Rose, not being a suitor, don't want to kiss anybody, especially one of the soft, wrinkly cheeks grandparents have."

They laughed again, but Rose cautioned, "One day, Charles, one day. You'll find someone to kiss, and you'll like it. It's not the same as hugging a calf."

"I don't hug calves," Charles said instantly. "She's getting too big for that."

"So you did hug her," Abby crowed. "I knew it. I knew it."

Charles glared at her and seemed ready to chase her around the room, so Rose interrupted to tell them they should set themselves at the table for supper and try not to knock over the salt or the spoon holder. Father, she said, was taking a prisoner on the train to Ripton and would be back late. They could see to cleaning up because she was going out.

"Are you going to be a suitor?" Abby wanted to know.

"Newton's the suitor," Charles told her in a superior

tone, still miffed that these girls apparently had seen him hugging Ruthann the calf. "Girls are never suitors. She must be going to see the suitor, I'll wager. Ah, see? She's turning pink."

At that, Rose's predictable face flamed, and she reached out to grab Charles, but he slipped away, taunting, "It's going to get a little dark, and if you're not going to church or school…"

"Charles," Rose said, exasperated now. "Behave yourself, if that's possible. And the two of you can put away all these ironed clothes as soon as the dishes are done. They were a little damp when I finished, but they should be fine now."

"Pile it on, Rose. We're happy to serve," Charles teased. "Suit yourself with the suitable suitor out there at the rock."

Rose threw up her hands, took her shawl, and went out the door, saying over her shoulder, "Don't wait up for me," and saw Charles raise his eyebrows as high as he could. It is amazing, she thought to herself as she hurried up the road, how he knows everything, and he knows exactly how to get a rise out of anyone, while the rest laugh. She wished she could snap out answers the way he did. Perhaps she and Abby should take to watching him with the calf. Ruthann, the calf. Now that would be something to tease him about, but she knew she wouldn't.

As her feet crunched on the gravel road, she calmed down and went back to thinking about the hayfield picnic. Deep down inside, she must have been wishing

Newton would ask her again because the answer had come out with no hesitation. She hadn't even thought about it. She just said yes. And meant it. She would wake Charles when she was home again and tell him he did see a kiss and what it meant, and apologize for being so stiff-backed about his riding her so unmercifully. Newton was right, though. Charles could be a thorn.

She turned off on a small path that led into the woods and reached the flat rock where she had spent so many hours of her life. No one was there, but she could see the sun setting through the trees, and the whole sky was lit up with pink and purple clouds. It would be a good haying day tomorrow, she thought, and she'd make the ginger milk again. They'd be needing Charles as soon as they started loading the wagons. He'd be on top, pulling the forkfuls of hay into place and stomping them down. And he'd come home with scratched arms, bits of hay stuck all over him, and a proud look in his eye because of his day with the men and older boys.

She heard a stick crack on the path, then another, and hoped it was Newton or a deer, not a bear. Dear or deer would be fine, she thought, and laughed at herself for feeling silly and giddy. It was Newton. Even in the fading light she could see he looked fresh and clean and wonderful. When he reached her, he dropped to his knees, took her hands in his, and said, "I am terrified but brave, so I ask again, will you marry me?"

"Yes," Rose whispered. "Oh, yes."

He looked at her for a long minute, then dropped her hands and pulled a tiny box out of his trouser pocket.

"I've been putting this in and out of my pocket so many times it's a marvel it hasn't made a hole in my pants," he said. "Will you try it on?"

She saw a glint of gold as the sun fell out of sight, and gave him her left hand. He slipped the ring on her third finger and leaned forward to kiss her very gently. Then he sat back on his heels and looked at her. "You aren't saying a word," he said.

"I can't even breathe," Rose said. "I'm not sure my voice will work. I never thought about a ring, and I don't know what to say."

He reached for the lantern he had set on the ground and lit it so she could see the ring. "It's lovely," she said, "absolutely lovely. What is that stone with all the fiery colors?"

"An opal," he said. "Surrounded by the tiniest diamonds a fellow could find. Does it suit you?"

She started to laugh, thinking of Charles with the suit and the suitor and the suitable and stopped quickly to explain so Newton wouldn't think she was laughing at the ring. "It's wonderful," she ended. "Even Charles will probably find it suitable."

Newton moved to sit beside her, holding the hand with the ring. "You decide when you want to wear it where people will see it," he said. "I remember Ruthann kept her engagement a secret for some time."

"I love you, Newton Barnes, and I want to wear it starting tomorrow at suppertime."

"Why then?"

"I want to tell Aunt Nell first," she said. "Then Charles, Abby, and Father."

"I should ask your father before you wear it, Rose. You know that."

"He can't give me to you, Newton, because I'm no longer his. You may tell him we are engaged, but please don't ask him for my hand. It's not his to give, and he knows that."

"Someday you'll tell me what all that means," Newton said, a bit puzzled, since his father had already told him he should speak to Silas before he spoke to Rose. "In the meantime, I'll do it your way because I love you and trust you." He stood, pulled her to her feet, drew her close and kissed her long and sweetly. Then he dropped his arms and whispered, "And now we're going to leave this rock or I will want to stay all night. You are more tempting than wild strawberry shortcake."

"I'm suitable but not edible," Rose laughed. "I feel as if I'm floating on air, feet not even touching the ground, and I want to stay here and lie close to you and swim in the river, and, and... but I love you and trust you, so I'll do it your way."

That made Newton laugh. "You are always going to win the word wars," he said. "I'd better get that under my hat from the start."

They strolled slowly back to the road and then to the Hibbard house. No shortcuts tonight, Rose thought, wishing there were. But Newton seemed determined to take her home, so she would go. And everyone would still be up, she realized. "No one will be in bed yet, Newton," she said, pulling on his arm.

"Better yet. Then we can tell Charles and Abby right now, and if your father is there, I will tell him."

Rose quickly accepted that Aunt Nell would not be the first to hear the news. She sighed, hoping this wonderful day wasn't going to end with her having to wave the little American flag that hung above the kitchen sink. So far, she'd never used it, and she didn't want to do it tonight. Perhaps Father wasn't coming until the very late train.

"It will be fine, Rose, just fine. If they're all awake, would you walk on to the farm and tell my parents, too?"

"Oh, yes," Rose said, anxious to add any minutes possible to the evening.

Silas was sitting on the front steps when they came along, arm in arm. "You two are looking quite cozy," he remarked. "Charles and Abby said you were out, and I didn't expect your return this early."

Rose extended her left hand, the ring just visible in the quickly fading light. Silas jumped to his feet, hugged Rose, and turned to shake Newton's hand. "You will be most welcome in this family, young man," he said. "You're pretty much a part of it already."

Rose breathed a sigh of relief and heard Newton say in his most formal tone, "Thank you, sir," just as Charles appeared from around the corner of the house. "I'll wager he has been eavesdropping," she said, but Charles approached with a totally innocent face and asked, "Why are you back so soon?" And then, to Newton, "If you are dumping Rose like so much dried hay, I shall challenge you to a duel, your choice of weapons."

Silas hooted with laughter, a sound so unfamiliar in the past few years that Rose started. But she soon joined him, as did Newton. Knowing they knew him too well, Charles dropped his pretense and grabbed Rose's hand to look at the ring. Then he hugged her and said, "I hope you'll drop in now and then to make the oatmeal." And they all laughed again.

"You have more than a year to put up with me, Charles," Rose said. "But where's Abby?" She immediately appeared from the spot where Charles had been hiding and hugged Rose and Newton.

"We'd go in for a celebratory swig of hard cider," Silas Hibbard said, "but we haven't any." He chuckled, which made Rose hope he no longer cared about "the drink," and went on, "And then I have a notion you'd like to tell Nell the news."

"Isn't it too late?" Rose asked.

"She doesn't sleep much these days, Rose, and time is running out for her, as you know. So take yourselves over there and see her and Jason. And don't get all teary, girl," he said gruffly. "This really is a time to hold up, like it or not."

"Thank you, Father. I will be all right when we get there." But she brushed away a tear that had already escaped from her left eye. Why, she wondered, does one tear leave and the others stay? She shook off the thought, wanting to keep her foolish head from wandering off right now. She focused on the little circle again and heard Newton say again, "Thank you, sir. I believe we'll stop in to tell my father and mother before I see Rose home."

"Get along then," Silas Hibbard said. "You haven't asked for my daughter's hand, but I reckon Rose would say it's not mine to give away. So I will wish you, instead, many good years together."

Rose didn't touch her face, hoping it was dark enough so no one would see the new tears tipping over the edge. She took a deep breath and in an almost normal voice said, "Thank you, Father."

In a few minutes, she and Newton came to the Harris house, where lamps were still lit, and he stepped up to rap on the door. When Jason opened the door, he immediately said, "Is everything all right?"

Newton nodded, and Rose came closer to show him her left hand. To her surprise, he stepped outside, picked her up, and whirled her around. "You have given me a moment of real joy," he said. "And they're few and far between these days. Step over to the window I fixed, and I'll fetch Nell."

"You won't be waking her, Uncle?" Rose asked anxiously.

"Never you mind, Rose. She sleeps in fits and starts, and this will be the best news she's had in some time."

They sat on the bench Jason had placed outside the window and watched as he carried Nell to her chair there. She was in her nightdress, and he covered her with a soft quilt after he set her down.

"So, Rose, Newton," she said in her whispery voice, "what brings you here in the dead of night?"

"Only the beginning of night, Aunt," Rose said, her tears gone. She could hold up, she would hold up. "Newton and I are to be married next year, and we wanted you to be the first to know."

Nell clapped her hands, a wide smile crossing her thin face. "The best news, the very best," she said. "But Jason knew first, didn't he? So I'm second."

"Actually fifth, Mrs. Harris, with all due respect," Newton said. "Rose wanted to tell you before anyone else, but we told Mr. Hibbard, Charles, and Abby first."

"Rightly so, rightly so. Now, let's see... next year means you'll be teaching at the little school in September, Rose?"

"Yes, Aunt. I think I'm having my cake and eating it, too."

"Best way to do," Nell said, her voice catching on the start of a cough. "Now you, Newton Barnes, you are to be congratulated on having the good sense to propose to this fine young lady."

"I know, Mrs. Harris, I do know."

"You start right in now calling me Aunt Nell, young man," she answered, sounding more like her old self than Rose had heard in a long time. "And run along with Jason and have a tot of his cider in celebration. I trust you did no toasting at the Hibbard house?"

"No, Ma'am. Uh, Aunt Nell." And Newton turned to find that Jason was waiting for him.

"The ladies will have things to talk about without

us," he told Newton. "Have a good batch of cider in the root cellar."

As soon as they left, Nell reached her hand toward the windowsill, and Rose answered with her left one. "Oh, what a beautiful ring," Nell said softly. "He is a splendid boy, your Newton, and Jason said he'd wait for you so you could teach, at least for a bit of time. You've answered all those impossible questions now, haven't you? Don't bother to answer. My voice doesn't hold out well these days, and I have things to say to you." Rose nodded and said nothing, leaving her hand in Nell's.

"Something old, something new, something borrowed, you know, and I've been hunting up things for you in hopes you meant it when you said you would be marrying Newton Barnes one day." She let Rose's hand go and reached for a small box on the table by the window and handed it to Rose. "Wear this cameo on your wedding day. Jason bought it for me from a man who came to this country from Italy and sold some of his treasures so he could build a house for his family. You will kindly return it after the ceremony. That's for the borrowed."

Rose took the brooch and tilted it toward the lamplight. She had seen Aunt Nell wear it many times to church and knew how much her aunt treasured it. But she didn't speak, since she'd been told in no uncertain terms not to.

"Something old and something blue? I took a handkerchief from Sarah's drawer after she was gone. She was just a girl when she made the blue tatting, and I can see her now, sewing the lacy edging onto the linen. Carry it on your wedding day. I think you know I can't promise to be in my proper pew that day, but believe you me, my spirit and Sarah's will both be there, and you'll sense that."

Rose was so determined to hold up that she had bitten right through her lip, but this last about her mother's spirit was too much. Her head dropped to the windowsill, and she started to cry, at the same time choking out, "I wanted to hold up. I promised myself I would."

"Nothing wrong with tears, Rose," Nell said firmly, patting her head with her free hand. "When I go, I expect you'll shed some more. In fact, I must say, if you don't, I shall come back to haunt you. Tears are a sign of love and respect, except for the killjoys who are all dried up. Never you mind about them. You'll remember all the good things, like that day when you played with the hats in Ripton and when we darned socks together and my going into a bit of a fit over Miss Jennie Graves, and you'll smile. You will. Out there on that rock of yours."

That made Rose smile now. "He proposed there, Aunt, with the ring. But he really proposed at the hayfield when I brought food and the ginger milk at the noon hour today. Imagine that? Getting engaged at the hayfield?"

"Jason asked me one morning at the sawmill," Nell answered. "Said he couldn't wait for another minute, so we became engaged between making boards out of a maple tree and sawing up a pine. So you will teach and then be a good wife to a farmer, Rose. And have children and teach them. I know it. And if there's a heaven—sometimes I think so, sometimes I don't—I'll be there with Sarah keeping track of you."

Rose nodded again, unable to speak. She squeezed Nell's hand, then let go and blew her a kiss. "I love him, Aunt," she said, "and I love you, too." Then she turned away and found Newton waiting for her. Without a word, he took her hand, waved to Nell, and they walked away. They did not speak until they reached the Barnes house, where Newton stopped, kissed Rose on the cheek, and asked, "Are you all right?"

"I am," she said. "I have something borrowed, something old, and something blue in my pocket, I am grieving for Nell, but I am all right."

"So we'll go in."

Samuel Barnes had caught the scene at the hayfield as he drove away with his horse and mowing machine, so he reckoned Newton had taken the big step this day. He and Eliva could not have been more pleased, and they both hugged Rose and wished the couple well. Mrs. Barnes brought out a pitcher of fresh lemonade, and they all sat around the kitchen table while Newton and Rose laid out their plans.

"Ben Chandler will be mighty glad to hear you will be at the little school for at least a year," Mr. Barnes said. "He admires your way with the young ones."

"Just a year, sir," Rose said. "I've promised. Just a year." A few minutes later, she and Newton left and started back toward Rose's place. They walked a short way and then she hesitated, and Newton said, "One more stop?"

"Yes," Rose answered. "Do you really already know where?"

"I think so," he said. They were at a crossroads, and he turned left, then left again at the small white gate of the cemetery. Even in the dark, Rose could find the stone that marked her mother's grave, and she went straight there, Newton close behind her, worried that this might not be a good thing to do at all.

But Rose had been through the hardest part of the evening, the visit to Aunt Nell. She touched her mother's gravestone with her left hand, bowed her head for a long minute, and then turned back to Newton. "I'll not cry here tonight," she said, kissing him softly. "I won't be a flibbertigibbet, either, but I won't cry. Sarah would like this night, and I know that. I thought I lost her all those months ago, but now I know you cannot lose your mother. For good or not, she stays with you, and mine is good."

Newton held her face in his hands and said, "I think now I'll stop having nightmares about this place."

"I stopped a long time ago," Rose answered. "From now on, it's dreams, your dreams and mine."

ACKNOWLEDGMENTS

So many people gather when you write a book. The story of Rose began with my grandmother, to whom I am still grateful for many things, including the fact that the drama of her teen years provided me with a story. As a grandmother, she never let on, but my father's memoir about his childhood revealed that Rosa Adelaide Warner Haskins had to take over her New England farm household when she was fourteen, deal with raising her younger siblings, and try to coexist with her increasingly alcoholic father. It was a kernel of reality that cried for fiction, a way to fill in years that were never talked about. And so *Sarah's Daughter* came about.

Closer to the present, many people contributed to this book, the sequel to Rose's original story. Margery Atherton, Debbi Welch, and Charlotte Finn read many chapters and pushed me toward the finish line. Granddaughter Summer Wojtas, now twelve, begged to read manuscript pages and delighted me by always wanting a few more. But the best reader, as always, was my husband, who said I needed to continue; that I had a gift. I am never sure of that, but I try to believe him, always, and without his support, neither of these books would have emerged.

Other gifts have come from lots of places. My aunts and uncles in the Allen family told stories of their early twentieth century life on a New England farm, which provided some of the information for this book. Billings Farm Museum in Woodstock, Vermont introduced me to all sorts of nineteenth century tools, including the marvelous tussock router; and Charles H. Baldwin & Sons of West Stockbridge, Massachusetts, creators of delicious vanilla since 1888, helped me make the original Charles Baldwin a real person in the book. In addition, Lynn Sherr's book *Failure is Impossible*, along with an intensive tour of Susan B. Anthony sites in Rochester, New York, allowed the famous feminist her place in the story, and the speech quoted was actually delivered by Miss Anthony in Boston.

While the portrayals of Rose and her family are almost entirely fictional, Welford Bailey was a historical figure in the temperance movement, and the Keeley cure was an early version of group therapy for various kinds of substance abuse.

I am grateful to Miss Harty, who appears as a fictional character but who bears the name of my first grade teacher, a blessing to me when I was only six. Pharmacist Art Nichols of Pittsfield, Massachusetts, provided historical information on soda fountains, and Dr. Charles Hall of Middletown, Rhode Island, was the medical consultant for treatment of alcoholism in the nineteenth century. Lynne Daley Nilan and her seventh and eighth graders asked so many questions about what happened after the last page of *Sarah's Daughter* that this sequel seemed almost mandatory.

Thanks go also to Daniel Greengold, aka The Nephew, and Wanda Potter, who have convinced hundreds of Gatlinburg, Tennessee, visitors that they needed my first book and should look forward to this one. I am, of course, delighted with any kind of feedback from our three adult children, Michael, Elissa, and Amy, each of them writers in their own right.

Lastly, very special mention must be made of Gadd & Company Publishers of Great Barrington. Larry Gadd, Rachel Kaufman, and Cia Elkin were essential players in getting Rose Hibbard out into the world, and Cia's belief in the possibility of a second book was essential to my commitment to the computer chair. She encouraged me along the way and then did her customary superb, meticulous editing of the final version, paying close attention to the gremlins who are the problems of a sequel.